"The interplay of ... ith the strong central ... try in the fantasy adv ... *nal*

"Seamlessly woven into a multilayered world written with subtlety and purpose, *Queen's Hunt* is an engrossing tale of political machinations played out over a foundation of old wrongs and fresh crises."
—Kate Elliott, author of *Cold Fire*

—PRAISE FOR—
PASSION PLAY, WINNER OF THE 2010 *RT BOOK REVIEWS* REVIEWERS' CHOICE AWARD FOR BEST EPIC FANTASY NOVEL

"*Passion Play* immediately plunges you into a deep world of past lives and magic. You can't put the book down!"
—L. A. Banks,
New York Times bestselling author

"*Passion Play* is, in my estimation, a brilliant debut novel, a poignant love story. Please write a sequel to this one, Beth Bernobich!"
—Anne McCaffrey

"Readers will be impatient for a sequel."
—*Publishers Weekly*

"Bernobich's debut is a rich, compulsively readable fantasy."
—*Booklist*

"One of the most intriguing of today's new writers, Beth Bernobich has a lush imagination, a vivid sense of atmosphere and setting, and an evocative prose style."
—Gardner Dozois

TOR BOOKS BY BETH BERNOBICH

Passion Play
Queen's Hunt
Allegiance (forthcoming)

QUEEN'S HUNT

BETH BERNOBICH

TOR®
fantasy

A TOM DOHERTY ASSOCIATES BOOK
NEW YORK

This is a work of fiction. All of the characters, organizations, and events portrayed in this novel are either products of the author's imagination or are used fictitiously.

QUEEN'S HUNT

Copyright © 2012 by Beth Bernobich

Maps by Jennifer Hanover

A Tor Book
Published by Tom Doherty Associates, LLC
175 Fifth Avenue
New York, NY 10010

www.tor-forge.com

Tor® is a registered trademark of Tom Doherty Associates, LLC.

ISBN 978-0-7653-6199-8

Tor books may be purchased for educational, business, or promotional use. For information on bulk purchases, please contact Macmillan Corporate and Premium Sales Deportment at 1-800-221-7945 extension 5442 or write specialmarkets@macmillan.com.

First Edition: July 2012
First Mass Market Edition: June 2013

Printed in the United States of America

0 9 8 7 6 5 4 3 2 1

TO ROB, FOR EVERYTHING

ACKNOWLEDGMENTS

Many years ago, I wrote a wildly different version of this book. Different characters, with different past lives, and almost a different story line. Eventually I realized my mistake (with some help), threw out the original version, and started over. Still, the bones of that first novel remain, however much I've transformed them.

And for that transformation, I have a number of people to thank. First among these is my splendid editor, Claire Eddy, who pointed out the true focus of the story. Next, my very kind and patient readers, Delia Sherman, Jennifer Ford, Celina Summers, Fran Wolber, and Sherwood Smith. Thank you all! I am grateful for your critiques, comments, and suggestions.

And finally, I thank my husband and son for giving me the space to write, dinner when I forgot, and hugs when I badly needed them.

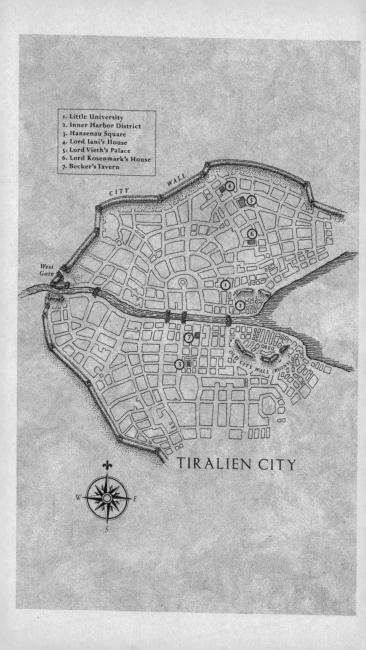

1. Little University
2. Inner Harbor District
3. Hansenau Square
4. Lord Iani's House
5. Lord Vieth's Palace
6. Lord Kosenmark's House
7. Becker's Tavern

CITY WALL

West Gate

OLD CITY WALL (RUIN)

TIRALIEN CITY

W E

S

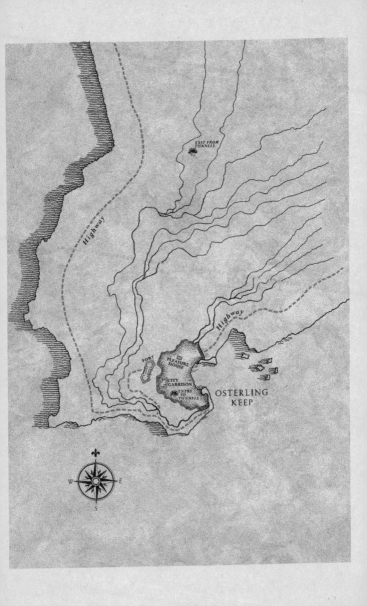

QUEEN'S
HUNT

CHAPTER ONE

ONCE, WHEN HE was a young child, six years old, Gerek Hessler had asked his great-grandmother about her life dreams, those vivid imaginings of past lives that came like nightmares upon a person in their sleep. Though she no longer saw anything but shadows, she swung her head around and stared at him, her milky eyes like pale moons in her dark face. *Nothing,* she whispered. *I dreamed of nothing, little man.*

But when he asked again, she sucked in her lower lip. For a moment, her eyes brightened, her gaze turned inward, as if recalling those dreams. Then her mouth twitched in an unhappy smile, and she touched his cheek far more gently than she used to. *Live blind and you die blind,* she said in swift soft tones. *One day, Blind Toc himself makes sure you see the truth about yourself.*

She had not answered his question, not directly, but he had not dared to say more. Three weeks later, between midnight and dawn, she died in her sleep. One life ended, her soul winging through the void to its next. Later, after he had studied the old philosophers, Gerek always wondered about his great-grandmother's words. Had she lived blindly, life upon life, absorbed in the daily dull minutiae? Or had she at last faced the truth with eyes open, unflinchingly?

Gerek passed a hand over his face. Strange, unsettling memories. They had come upon him unexpectedly as he passed through Tiralien's northern gates. Was it the sight of that aged fresco of Lir and her brother Toc over the gate itself? Or did the memories revive because of Tiralien itself, because of his cousin Dedrick, whose death had brought him so many miles?

Dedrick. Years ago, as children, he and Dedrick had spent a month here, along with their families. A second visit came about when Gerek's parents decided he might study with an old scholar in the Little University. Now, riding in a freight wagon along a boulevard crowded with morning traffic, Gerek stared around, trying to see if the present city matched anything from his vague recollections. He remembered that bell tower, built of dark red brick and topped with an elaborate openwork crown for the bell itself, which flashed in the thin sunlight. That bridge led over the Gallenz River to the southern highway. And there, on the rising hills above, was the regional governor's palace—Lord Vieth was the man's name. He could not see the coast from here, but he could smell its heavy salt tang. He closed his eyes and tried to recall the hushing sound of water against the shore. A foreign sound to someone from the inland hill country.

From the nearby tower came the creak of ropes, the dull thump of the clapper. A pause, like the silence between each breath, then bell and bell and bell rang out over the morning.

The driver shouted to his team of horses. Abruptly the wagon jerked to the left. Gerek, used to this maneuver, braced himself against the nearest crate. His bones ached from sitting too long, his teeth rattled in time with the wheels as they jounced and bounced over the stone-paved streets. Soon they left behind the chaos of mules and carts, fishermen selling their catch, farmers arriving from the surrounding countryside to trade for supplies; it dropped away like an old cloak as they entered a quieter neighborhood where the merchants and richer tradesmen lived.

After the merchant houses came a district of fine shops, then a bleak expanse of counting houses and storage buildings. Just as he wondered how much longer until they arrived, the driver flicked his whip and barked out a command. Once more the wagon lurched, and they turned onto a broad avenue. Oh yes. Here were houses such as Gerek had imagined. Here was a neighborhood where a duke's son might live. Even without his cousin's description, Gerek recognized his destination.

The driver reined his horses to a stop. Gerek climbed awkwardly from the wagon. His legs, cramped from the long ride, buckled. He grabbed the wagon to keep from falling. His shin banged against the wheel. He yelped, in spite of himself.

The driver coughed. It sounded suspiciously like a laugh. "Would you like me to unload your trunks here, sir?" he asked.

"N-n-no." Gerek swallowed and started over. "No. Thank you. Please leave them at the warehouse. I will send for them later."

"As you wish, sir." The man spoke politely enough. He clearly regretted that ill-timed laugh. Perhaps he knew of Gerek's connection to House Maszuryn, itself elevated by the queen's friendship with Gerek's cousin Alia. More likely, he simply hoped for a few extra denier from his passenger.

Gerek paid the driver the final installment for his passage, then added five more silver coins. "For the safe delivery of my belongings. And for your kindness during the journey." The words came out steadily, if not elegantly. It was more than he often hoped for.

The wagon lumbered off, its wheels rattling over the paving stones. Gerek stood alone on the broad and quiet avenue. He sniffed, smelled the scent of freshly turned dirt in the cool, clean morning air. This was one of the richest quarters in the city. A handful of stone mansions were visible through the trees, which were still winter-bare on this early spring day. The one that interested him—Lord Raul Kosenmark's—stood directly opposite, behind a tall iron gate. In the center of the gate, an artisan-smith had twisted the iron bars into the likeness of a sinuous leopard. The insignia of House Valentain.

Memories, thirteen years old, came to life.

Gerek remembered his cousin Dedrick riding from his father's estates, breathless with the news. A letter had arrived from Tiralien, delivered by a special courier. Their great-grandfather was to receive an award for his service to the Crown, and from the regional governor's own hand.

"We shall all attend," his great-grandfather had declared.

Standing here in Tiralien once more, Gerek recalled distinctly the shimmering summer heat in the governor's palace. The pervasive stink of ocean tang, overlaid by sweat and too many bodies crushed close together, which even the sweetest herbs could not overcome. He could see clearly with his mind's eye their great-grandfather kneeling before Lord Vieth to receive an astonishingly ugly chain, worked of silver and gold and studded with jewels of all sorts. His cousins whispering jokes to each other. Dedrick's handsome face bending close to his, then retreating just as quickly, but not before he'd made some deliciously sarcastic comment. (Directed at the king? That vulgar chain? At Gerek himself, fat and stuttering and so misplaced among his cousins of all degrees?)

No, Dedrick had never mocked him, not like the others. Dedrick had saved his bitterest comments for his own father and the family's ambitions. Especially his sister's.

More recent memories overwhelmed the rest. The terrible news from Duenne—a riding accident, according to the official letter, but everyone knew better. Knew that Dedrick had died by order of the king and the King's Mage. Then, months later, Gerek's decision to come here, to the house of the man responsible for leading Dedrick to his death.

Voices chattered inside his brain. Relatives dismissing him, consigning him to a useless life, a romantic with few qualities beyond an attention to history, philosophy, and clever handwriting.

Ignoring the voices, he crossed the avenue. That grand central gate was not for him, but for visitors of quality. And, of course, those clients who frequented the other side of Lord Kosenmark's business—the pleasure house and its many courtesans. But Dedrick had faithfully described the house to Gerek many times, so Gerek knew to look to one side, to a lane leading between the house and a wall demarcating the property from that of the next elegant mansion.

Guards observed his entrance. He knew that, even if he could not see them. They would, however, view him as no threat; simply a large clumsy man ambling toward a service entrance. Gerek tried not to mind.

The lane brought him past a long blank section of wall, then a bare courtyard with a few equally bare trees and a lonely stone bench. Here windows broke up the expanse of golden stonework, but they were all dark, like eyes without the illumination of the soul. Gerek continued on to the side door his cousin had mentioned. The door itself was ordinary, but the story his cousin had told was not—about a young woman beaten and raped and close to death. She had knocked on the door and Raul Kosenmark had taken her in.

Gerek knocked at the door. His large hand thumped against the painted wooden panels, sending echoes down the lane. He stepped back and waited.

It was quiet here—even quieter than the main avenue. From far away, he heard a horse whickering. Flies buzzed past, fat and hopeful. A breeze tickled his bare neck, lifting away the sweat from his fur-lined collar, reminding him of how he must appear. After six days riding in a wagon, spending the nights in the cheapest hostelries, or camped beside the road, he looked more like a tramp than a scholar. Hurriedly he shook the dust from his clothes and swiped a hand through his stiff, tousled hair. His boots were filthy. He bent to rub them with his sleeve.

The lock rattled. He straightened up.

A young woman stood in the doorway. She wore a plain black skirt and a blue smock with the sleeves rolled up. The pale sunlight cast a shadow across her dusky brown face. Gerek blinked, unexpectedly surprised by her ordinary appearance.

"Yes?" she said at last.

He immediately dug out the letter from inside his coat and offered it to her.

She took it, glanced from the paper back to Gerek's face. He thought she was smiling, but he couldn't be sure.

"For the duke's son," he said. "My n-n-name is-is Gerek Hessler."

"Ah. They told me that you would arrive today. You are here to apply for the position of Lord Kosenmark's secretary."

He released a breath in relief. "Yes. That."

If the young woman noticed his stuttering, she gave no hint of it. She stood to one side and politely motioned for him to enter.

HER NAME WAS Kathe, she told him. Normally she did not attend to admitting visitors—she worked in the kitchens—but so many of the maids were taken sick with colds, and Lord Kosenmark had not wanted to increase the size of his household, even temporarily. Not to worry, she said, they would soon have him settled. He would want to see Mistress Denk, the steward, and after that Lord Kosenmark, but surely he would appreciate a few moments in a private room to recover from his long journey.

Listening to the flow of her chatter, Gerek took away only one detail. She *had* noticed the dust and dirt and sweat. He rubbed in vain at his face and wished he had taken his brother's advice to stop first at an inn to bathe and dress in fresh clothing. But inns required money, and he had none to spare. Not if today did not produce the position he hoped for.

"I'm sorry," Kathe said. "I chatter too much, Lord Kosenmark tells me."

She'd stopped in the middle of a wide corridor. Rooms opened to either side—bright rooms filled with silk-covered couches and chairs, their tiled floors gleaming in the sunlight. The scent of beeswax and fresh herbs hung in the air. There was also the unmistakable scent of expensive perfume, but no other sign of the courtesans Dedrick talked about, nor of Kosenmark himself. Merely the elegant and richly furnished spaces one might expect to find in the household of a wealthy man, the elder son of an influential duke.

"I-I— My apologies," Gerek said. "What did you s—say?"

She smiled. (A kindly smile, he noticed.) "I can see that you're tired from your long journey. Would you like a private room where you might bathe your face? You look as though you aren't used to our southern seasons."

"N-no," he said, then felt his cheeks heat. "Yes. Very tired. Could I-I—"

"Right this way," she said.

Kathe left him in a small sunny room, comfortably furnished with a padded chair and several wooden benches. A high table stood by the single window, which overlooked a lawn and trees beyond. An antique tapestry of Lir and Toc hung from one wall — this one depicting their season of love—and a silk carpet covered the red-tiled floor. There was no fireplace in the room, but the air was pleasantly mild. A brass mirror hung from the opposite wall. Gerek ducked his head to avoid seeing his reflection.

Before he had time to wonder what came next, several maids, some of them red-eyed and sniffling, appeared with towels and robes. He would find the baths in the first basement, they told him, down the stairs located at the end of the hallway.

Gerek muttered something about not keeping the steward waiting, but the girls had already disappeared. Through the half-closed door, he heard them giggling.

Damn them. I'm not a dumb beast. I'm—

Nothing but the second son of a minor branch of an unimportant family. (Never mind the queen's recognition of Dedrick's sister, Lady Alia.) Not even that, because to these people, he was a mediocre scholar seeking employment. They were right to laugh at him. Everyone else did.

Everyone except his brother and Dedrick.

Gerek closed and locked the door. Still furious with himself and the maids, he undressed doggedly and put on the robe. The fabric was thick worsted cotton, soft against his skin and warmed by a fire. The warmth and softness irritated him further. He stomped from the room to the stairs, down to the baths. Those, too, drove him to an unreasonable fury. He scrubbed himself clean—hair, nails, and body—from all the grime accumulated in six days of travel. He'd scraped his hands raw from catching the wagon, and bruised his shin against the iron-plated wheels. Good. That felt more believable than this impossibly huge pool, the scented soaps, the surrounding luxury, which, no doubt, he would have to leave behind when Lord Kosenmark refused his service.

Scrubbed and annoyed, he returned to the room to discover the maids had removed all his clothes, even down to his loincloth.

He was about to curse out loud when he remembered Dedrick's warning: *He listens. To friends, to enemies. There is no one he absolutely trusts. Oh, perhaps Maester Hax, or his new love, but no one else.*

Hax was dead, however. And Ilse Zhalina had left Kosenmark five months before.

Gerek scanned the ceiling and spotted a vent placed where none would normally be found. It was true, then, what Dedrick had claimed. The man had rebuilt the house to install listening vents and pipes, closets with secret panels, all manner of means to overhear conversations between the courtesans and their clients, between friends and enemies. And strangers most of all.

"Are you well?"

Kathe stood in the doorway, a tray balanced against one hip.

"Why do you s-say that?" Gerek demanded.

"You were staring so. I knocked," she added. "And you had left the door unlocked."

"I-I—" Gerek forced himself to speak deliberately. "I am weary from the road. But I do not wish to keep Lord Kosenmark waiting."

"You will see Mistress Denk first," Kathe said. "She knows you've arrived. But you have time to refresh yourself. I brought you coffee and tea, and some biscuits and cold meats. Would you prefer wine?"

"No wine," he said shortly. Wine made his tongue even more uncertain.

Kathe said nothing to his abrupt speech. She slipped past him and set to work, laying out the dishes and cups onto the table by the window. In the room's diffuse light, he could see her features clearly for the first time. Her face was round and pleasant, her eyes a dark and brilliant brown. Her hands, he noticed, were deft, her fingers slender, and the nails clipped short.

When she finished, she glanced up and met his gaze directly, in a way he found both disconcerting and refreshing. "For your comfort and refreshment," she said. "And please, do not be anxious. Lord Kosenmark told me himself you were not to hurry on his account."

Over her shoulder, Gerek caught his reflection in the mirror. Plain round face, the chin blurring into folds of skin. Broad shoulders and chest. A study in brown, even to the robe he wore. His mother affectionately called him her favorite ox.

He jerked his glance away. "Thank you," he said stiffly.

She paused, as though she expected him to say more. Her eyes narrowed. Assessing.

"You are right to be careful here," she said, and was gone.

THE MAIDS BROUGHT his clothes—brushed and pressed—before he finished his coffee and biscuits. Luckily, none of them offered to help him dress. When he had resumed his clothing, a runner took him through a labyrinth of hallways and galleries, up two flights of stairs, to a wing populated entirely with offices. They were all beautiful and yet utterly businesslike, very unlike the frothy silk-strewn chambers he'd glimpsed below.

Mistress Eva Denk received him with a perfunctory smile. Her office, he noted as he took his seat, was spacious and neat. There were no windows here, but two lamps hung from the ceiling, and a branch of candles sputtered on the table next to her desk. She was exactly like her letters—forthright and competent. He knew her history from his own investigations. She was born in Duenne, had risen from apprentice to senior clerk for one of the leading merchants of the city. After twenty long years with that same merchant, she had given up her position to work for Kosenmark. It spoke of the man's persuasion.

She offered him wine. He politely refused. That brought another smile. Was she testing him?

"You have an interesting history," she said.

Gerek shrugged.

Denk frowned slightly and let her gaze fall to the papers on her desk. Among them, Gerek recognized his own résumé, plus several letters that ostensibly came from his previous employers, including the letter of introduction from Maester Aereson, a merchant in Ournes Province. Denk would find no fault with any of them. Gerek had written them himself, modeling his career on that of an old tutor. Informal studies at the

University at Duenne, regrettably incomplete. Several years at various posts as tutor, scribe, or general factotum. His latest posting had come to an end when Maester Aereson's sons grew older, and Gerek thought a warmer climate might suit him. An acquaintance had mentioned that Lord Kosenmark needed a new secretary.

"You understand the terms?" Denk asked.

"I do." Short sentences were best. He could manage those.

"Your pay? Your duties?"

Again he nodded. He was to handle all correspondence and to keep Lord Kosenmark's schedule. For that he would receive a monthly sum of ten gold denier, plus his room and board. If his duties required finer clothes, say for a meeting with nobles such as Lord Vieth, Lord Kosenmark would provide them. He would have one rest day every week, plus an afternoon to himself twice a month.

It was all very easy and pleasant. Too easy. Denk asked him fewer questions than he expected, and her apparent lack of interest in his credentials puzzled Gerek. He once tried to expand on his supposed employment with Maester Aereson. Mistress Denk had waved aside his speech with the comment, "Lord Kosenmark will want to know surely. The decision is his, not mine, to make."

It would be, Gerek thought. If everything Dedrick had hinted at were true, this man wanted more than a secretary, he wanted an accomplice.

An accomplice for treason, Gerek thought. *But first I need to find the proof, before I go to the king or any of his people.*

And he would find it here—he knew it—in this house.

* * *

"MAESTER HESSLER."

Lord Kosenmark studied Gerek over the tips of his fingers.

"My lord." Gerek bowed.

"Sit," Kosenmark said. "And let us discuss the possibility of your employment here."

Gerek sat down, unsettled and nervous and trying not to show it. None of Kosenmark's letters had promised employment outright, but after his interview with Eva Denk, he had begun to relax. He wondered now if he'd given himself away to her, or to Kathe.

I am Maester Gerek Hessler. Second-rate scholar. Nothing more.

The repetition failed to counteract his anxiety. He had taken several great chances in this endeavor. He had used a name nearly like his own, thinking he would remember it better, and trusting that Dedrick would never have mentioned a poor second cousin to this man. He had involved his brother and old tutor to handle any untoward inquiries. At the time, these had seemed like reasonable risks.

The voices chattered at him, more insistent than before. *Fool. Idiot. Useless.*

Kosenmark continued to study him in return. He was as handsome as all the reports claimed—golden-eyed and fair, his pale brown skin almost luminescent against his blue-black hair. Sculptors who followed the classicist school might use him as a model for Toc, the brother-god and consort of Lir, except that Toc was blind, and this man's eyes were whole, unnervingly bright and direct. The one element, which everyone knew about, but which Gerek still found unexpected, was his voice.

He speaks like a woman. A woman with a husky voice, but nevertheless not a man, not even a tenor.

In his latter years, when his mind ran feverishly upon conspiracies, Baerne of Angersee had insisted on a peculiar sacrifice by his nearest councillors. They would be gelded, or they would lose their place, and therefore their influence. Later, when he took the throne, Baerne's grandson had dismissed these men from Duenne's Court. Some said it was a way for Armand to establish his own rule, to declare that his famous grandfather would not overshadow his reign. Others said Lord Markus Khandarr had influenced the new king to ensure his own preeminence.

Most of those unwanted councillors hid themselves away. They had sacrificed their manhood and could not bear it when Armand dismissed them. But this man—he lived. More than that. He had fashioned a network of advisers and colleagues and agents throughout Veraene—a shadow court, through which Kosenmark continued to influence Veraene's politics from afar.

Clever, handsome, determined. And only a year or two older than Gerek himself.

Everything I am not.

"Do I meet with your approval, Maester Hessler?" Kosenmark said drily.

Gerek shook himself into attention. "My apologies, my lord. I-I was merely—"

"Wondering about my sexual habits and how I might satisfy them, in spite of my shortcomings. You need not stutter. The entire world knows."

Gerek's cheeks burned with humiliation. For once, anger kept his tongue under control. "What the world knows is not my concern, my lord. My thoughts are my own. Whether or not you've guessed their shape correctly, I will not discuss their finer details."

Kosenmark blinked. Then his lips curved into a slow smile. "Harlaef the Younger. Of the late empire, in his letter to the emperor answering certain unfounded charges. So you are a scholar."

"Did you doubt me, my lord?"

"Not exactly. But there are degrees of truth, just as there are degrees of scholarship."

He likes to play with words and double meanings. He likes to provoke people.

"If you doubt me, s-send me away," Gerek said. "My lord. As you must kn-know from my history, it would not be the first time."

Those wide eyes settled on him, and Kosenmark's expression changed subtly. No longer bland, nor edged with bitter humor. Gerek thought he detected a wincing moment of painful memory, chased by sympathy for Gerek himself.

"Very well," Kosenmark said in that disturbingly high voice. "Let us discuss our true business. You seek employment as a secretary or assistant. I have need of one as you undoubtedly heard."

Gerek bowed his head. This was the nearest Kosenmark had come to mentioning the woman who had served him as secretary, before she became his lover. Gerek would not make the mistake, however, of betraying how much he knew. Just before their interview ended, Mistress Denk had offered one piece of pointed advice. *Whatever you say or do, never mention the name Ilse Zhalina to Lord Kosenmark. He will not forgive that.*

"Your credentials are adequate," Kosenmark said.

Again, Gerek nodded. He had worked over those credentials for precisely that impression.

"I'm curious about your university career. You never formally applied there."

A nod would not suffice this time. "N-no, my lord. I-I had not enough—"

"Not enough money?" Kosenmark waved a hand. "Forgive me. I should not interrupt. Speak as you must."

Another double meaning. Gerek drew a long breath and considered his reply. "No money. As well, I could not s-settle on one course of s-study. I wished to explore without cons-straint, my lord."

That caught the man's attention. His eyes narrowed—in humor this time. "Go on."

"History, my lord. It is not complete without the literature of those times. The reverse is also true."

"What about economics? You studied that as well."

"For practical reasons, my lord. Money is an essential element of the world, no matter which century you examine."

He finished the sentence, let his breath trickle out in relief that he had uttered the thing complete. Kosenmark must have noticed that small reaction, however, because he leaned forward and fixed Gerek with his gaze. "You have difficulty speaking, but not when you feel strongly about the matter. Tell me what else moves you."

Truth, Gerek thought. *The bonds of trust and friendship and family.*

He'd known little of them in his life. To say that out loud was more than he could bear—not to this cold, clever young man.

"You are thinking hard," Kosenmark observed.

"The s-subject is n-n-not an easy one, my lord."

Kosenmark stared at him a longer moment, but when Gerek said nothing more, he leaned back with a disappointed sigh. "You speak several languages, yes?"

So they were back to the formal give-and-take of the interview. "Old Veraenen," Gerek said. "Erythandran. Enough to read texts from the empire days. And s-some Immatran."

"Károvín?"

Gerek suppressed a tremor of excitement. "Yes, my lord."

"Fluently?"

He hesitated. "N-not as well."

"But enough to puzzle out a letter or essay."

"Yes, my lord."

A brief silence followed. Kosenmark tapped his fingers against each other. Gerek waited, trying to keep from shifting nervously on the hard wooden chair. Off to one side stood an enormous hourglass, an extraordinary creation with several globes that worked together to measure minutes and hours. Even as he noticed it, the globes revolved slowly around to begin their measuring anew. Outside, bells rang the hour.

Kosenmark leaned forward again and slapped his hands on the desk, startling Gerek. "You know the salary? Mistress Denk explained that to you, of course. Is that acceptable?"

Gerek nodded dumbly.

"Well, then. Consider yourself hired."

"M-M—"

"No need to hesitate, Maester Hessler. You are moderately qualified. I have moderate needs. If you agree, we can begin our work at once. What do you say?"

Gerek met Kosenmark's gaze as directly as he dared. He saw nothing but boredom in the man's expression. He was not fooled. Dedrick had told him once that you could never trust Raul Kosenmark's outward appearance. It was only by truly listening—by measuring the silences between words, catching the swift tension in his full mouth, the change of brightness in those golden eyes—that you began to understand the hidden man and his moods.

There was only one means for doing so.

He bowed his head. "Thank you. I will begin my work at once."

CHAPTER TWO

AT ONCE WAS a relative term in Lord Kosenmark's household. It could mean that same moment, when a courier arrived with urgent news from his father, or from Duenne's Court. For other matters, one could interpret the phrase to mean *soon enough*.

Raul chose to use the second meaning today. Summoning a runner, he delivered Gerek Hessler into Mistress Denk's hands for a few hours. Let the man grow accustomed to the house and its inhabitants. Later that afternoon, he could initiate Hessler into his new duties.

And decide exactly what those duties would encompass.

The runner took Raul's new secretary away. Once the door closed, Raul raked his fingers through his hair. He could sense the stiffness melting away from his face. How arrogant had he appeared to that poor man? Very, he suspected. He could tell by Hessler's increased stammering.

I was not fair or kind to him. She would have scolded me, and with good cause.

She, meaning Ilse Zhalina. He laughed silently, thinking of just how Ilse would lecture him. Felt a catch in his chest, just under his ribs, where he thought his heart must lodge. Ilse, Ilse, Ilse. Ever present, like a thorn creeping through his flesh.

My beloved. I should not have agreed to your scheme.

Five months and three days since she left. He felt as though he were a grain of sand within his hourglass, and could feel the moments rasping over his skin. He had a sudden vivid memory of standing in deep warm water, the sand ebbing beneath his feet as the tide ran out. It was not from this life. No, this was a waking dream from some previous life, a previous love between him and her.

. . . her hand brushing his cheek. The scent of her favorite perfume, of smoke and sandalwood. Her dark eyes pinning him with a gaze that left him breathless. It had been the same throughout the centuries . . .

Raul pressed his fingers against his eyelids, weary to his bones from unwanted memories. That last unpleasant interview with Markus Khandarr. His exile from court. The news of Dedrick's death. The moment when Ilse first proposed a different kind of exile for herself. He would be free of Khandarr's threats, she had declared. Free to revive his shadow court, to seek an alliance with like-minded nobles in Veraene and other kingdoms. Whatever he chose.

He had thought himself brave, but Ilse's courage left him breathless with astonishment. It was very close to treason, what he and she planned. But they had seen no other way to stop Armand of Angersee's mad plans for war.

A sharp rap at the door interrupted him—the special pattern used by his runners. Raul shuddered at the break from memory to the present. He ran a hand over his face, took another moment to breathe in a semblance of calm.

"Enter," he said.

It was his senior runner with a large flat packet, wrapped in brown paper, which he laid upon Raul's desk.

"Which messenger?" Raul asked.

"The man Haas in Vlôch District."

Haas was a bookseller—one of the few agents from Raul's old network he still trusted. A few months ago, Raul had arranged for Haas to collect all his letters from sources outside Tiralien. Haas delivered them once a week to Lord Kosenmark's pleasure house, along with selected antique volumes for his review. The latest delivery would be waiting below. What would it be this time? Popular novels from the late empire? Historical tracts? Raul ought to have the new secretary inspect the volumes and give his opinion of their value. It would be a good test of the man's judgment.

"Does he expect a reply?" Raul asked.

"No, my lord."

"Ah. Then that will be all."

He waited until his runner withdrew, then took a knife from his desk and cut away the outer covering. Inside were three envelopes, all of them addressed in very different scripts. One was a square of ordinary paper, folded over several times and sealed with yellow wax. Very plain. No magic. The only writing was Haas's own name, and a few curious marks along one edge. Without unfolding the letter, Raul knew at once that it came from Danusa Benik, his best agent in Károví's closed and often dangerous court.

She will have important news. She never dares to write otherwise.

Not yet, he told himself. He was too distracted to give her report proper attention.

Am I? Or am I making excuses?

Let us pretend I have good reason. There is time enough tomorrow to criticize my motives.

He scanned the other two envelopes, which were markedly similar except for the handwriting. Both had outer sheets of expensive parchment. But unlike Benik's, these were sealed with wax and magic. One came from a minor noble in Veraene's capital, an old friend of Raul's who often sent him the latest gossip from Duenne's Court. He set that aside for later.

The second was addressed in a foreign style, without any of the usual signals or marks he associated with his own spies. For a moment he stared at the paper. His name, written in brushstrokes with several flourishes, said that the writer was more accustomed to a different script, and different language.

Karasek. He has answered me.

He snatched up the envelope and felt the buzz of magic over its surface. During his years in Duenne, Raul had studied all manner of spells useful for a court obsessed with intrigue—spells to make and un-make locks, spells to seal a room against intruders, even spells to detect the presence of poison. He was no great mage, but he could sense the layers and pro-tections Karasek had employed. It was an interesting combination. If he read the signs correctly, the spells did not prevent anyone from breaking the seal, but they would leave traces if someone had.

There were no traces of any such attempt. Raul ran a finger along the letter's edge. Magic and wax cracked, and the sheet fell open.

Lord Kosenmark. I thank you for your invitation to your estates. Alas, my duties require me elsewhere.

The letter was signed Duke Miro Karasek and dated six weeks before.

Raul laid the sheet on his desk and stared at it while

he tried to work out the implications of this short, blunt reply.

Miro Karasek belonged to one of the six most influential families in Károví. More important, he and Duke Feliks Markov served as King Leos's senior generals. Markov held more influence at court, according to Benik's reports, where his conservative views were popular. Karasek himself had come to his title only seven years ago, and from all reports, he concerned himself with the kingdom's army, not its politics. His father, however, had advised the king to negotiate less restrictive treaties with Veraene, and to make ties with other kingdoms. Raul had chosen to approach Karasek, hoping he privately shared his father's views.

Apparently he did not. But such an abrupt rejection.

He blew out a breath. This was a public letter, he reminded himself. Karasek had not set any spells to burn the paper, nor to change the letter's contents. His magic would only signal if anyone else had broken the seal. So he had expected spies to intercept the message.

With that in mind, Raul reread it more slowly. He kept in mind that here was a man raised to intrigue and caution. There might be clues hidden beneath each word.

. . . I thank you for your invitation . . .

Mere politesse? He could not tell. The same held for the word *Alas*. Oh, but the next phrase held more possibilities.

. . . my duties require me elsewhere.

Duties. A curious word to choose. It could mean Karasek privately agreed with Raul but dared not say so publicly. And *required elsewhere*. Could he possibly refer to orders from the king? That one short sentence carried a weight of meaning.

He set Karasek's letter aside and opened the letter
from his agent, Benik. It was possible she had news
that would illuminate the matter.

The letter was a single sheet, filled from margin to
margin with densely written paragraphs. Ostensibly, it
came from an old acquaintance now living on the
border between Veraene and the kingdom of Auszter-
lant. In it, the acquaintance detailed his foray into
cattle farming. Number of head, how many herds,
where they grazed, etc. Near the end, the friend gave
a painstaking account of each member of the family,
and asked when Lord Kosenmark might pay them a
visit.

The meaning behind those phrases was clear. Ship
maneuvers along the coast had ended. Troops recalled
from the western border to the Károvín capital, Rastov. Additional ships—the swiftest in the royal fleet—
reassigned and docked at the nearest ocean port. Duke
Miro Karasek temporarily appointed to a special
command . . .

A coldness rolled over his skin as he pieced the clues
together.

Ah, Leos. Now I understand.

Four hundred years ago, Leos Dzavek and his
brother, two princes of Károví, had visited Duenne's
Court. In those days, Károví was a minor province
within the grand Erythandran empire. Though historical accounts from that time were unclear—and indeed, rewritten by subsequent rulers—one point was
clear. Leos Dzavek and his brother had stolen three
magical jewels from the imperial vaults. Lir's jewels,
gifted by the goddess to the Erythandran emperors, or
so the legends claimed.

Whatever their origin, Leos Dzavek fled home to
Károví with all three. He had quarreled with his
brother, however, so when Leos launched a revolt, the

brother led the emperor's armies to retake the province. The brother was killed in battle, Károví regained its independence, and several other provinces broke away in the turmoil.

The empire had collapsed into splinters and factions, leaving only the kingdom known as Veraene. Leos Dzavek, however, had lived. It was the jewels, said the rumors, and their extraordinary magic that taught this man how to live centuries beyond the ordinary life span.

Centuries, yes. It was a hundred years later when the nameless elder brother returned to a new life as Leos Dzavek's trusted retainer. Again the records contradicted each other, but the salient points were clear. The retainer stole the jewels and hid them, then killed himself before Dzavek could extract the truth from him. The jewels remained lost, most likely hidden in the magical plane. Since then, Dzavek had searched for them throughout Veraene, Károví, and all the other known kingdoms.

And now you have found them, Raul thought. *One at least.*

But which one? And where?

"WOULD YOU LIKE to see the public rooms first?" the young man named Uwe asked Gerek.

No, he would not. What Gerek wanted most of all was to sit alone in the dark. With a wet rag over his aching eyes. Then he could think over his interview, and prepare himself for whatever came next.

Raul Kosenmark had not allowed him that luxury, however. Instead, Gerek had eaten his midday meal with Mistress Denk while they reviewed the current household accounts, the monthly schedule, and other necessary topics. Finally Denk had released him to a runner for a tour of the house, while servants fetched his luggage from the freight company. She would arrange to have his office and private rooms ready within a few hours.

The runner was polite enough, but Gerek could not give him proper attention. He followed the young man from the office wing, down one floor, and through a maze of corridors that ended at a wide balcony overlooking the pleasure house's entrance hall. It was all very grand. Tall windows lit the wide-open space, illuminating the many fine paintings and tapestries. The style was deliberately antique, the young man explained. Lord Kosenmark had imported many of the decorations from his father's estates in Valentain. The rest he had acquired through antiquarian dealers along the eastern coast.

Gerek suppressed a yawn. He had risen well before sunrise that morning, endured three hours riding in the freight wagon, then used up his remaining wits and vitality during the interview with Lord Kosenmark. However, he suspected that Kosenmark wanted his secretary familiar with the house, so he dutifully followed the young man down the winding stairs to the entrance hall and gazed around.

Before them stood an arched entryway with a short hallway that opened into a much larger room beyond. Gerek could make out numerous couches scattered about, and several intimate groupings of chairs and low tables. Three maids were at work, dusting and polishing. One knelt on a richly dyed carpet, scrubbing at spots with a cloth. There was a musky scent in the air, an odor that reminded him of his father's quarters on those days when his mother spent the day locked in her private suite, weeping.

"That is the common room," the runner said. "Would you like to see it next?"

The common room was where the courtesans displayed themselves to potential clients. Of course, they were not so crude as to call it that. No, they entertained their visitors with music, conversation, and amusing games. They offered wine and a feast of delicacies from Lord Kosenmark's famous cook. But the purpose was clear. Did the runner expect him to show an interest in the courtesans, then? Most men would. He had no idea if he were like most young men.

"I-I—" His tongue tangled on several different answers.

He forced out a breath to quell the tremors. Was about to try again, when the sight of a familiar figure undid his efforts.

"Let me show him the house," Kathe said. "If Maester Hessler doesn't mind, that is."

Gerek swallowed. "N-n-n-not-not—"

His words came out stuttering and stumbling. Kathe laid a hand on his arm, as if to reassure him that she understood, and turned to the runner. "That is settled, then. Uwe, please go to the kitchens. My mother has an errand for you."

Apparently she had some authority, because the runner immediately vanished through a low doorway Gerek had not noticed before.

Kathe laughed softly and shook her head. Her gaze swept up to meet his, and to his surprise, her cheeks were edged with an embarrassed flush. "I am sorry, Maester Hessler," she said. "I have ordered you and Uwe about most unfairly. Especially Uwe. But you see, I would like to keep away from the kitchens just now. My mother . . ." She drew a deep breath. "Let us say she finds the latest pastry cook unsatisfactory. It's better if I find useful work elsewhere until she's calmer."

"So I-I am useful work?" Gerek said.

Kathe visibly winced. "That was unkind of me. I am sorry again."

"You don't need to be sorry," he said at once. "I-I should—I am sorry. I was rude."

She had removed her hand from his arm. Now she touched him again, but briefly this time, as though she were not certain of his reaction. As though it mattered.

"Come," she said with a semblance of her former cheerfulness. "Let me show you the library first. You will like it, I know. Or would you rather I found you a room where you could sleep a few hours? If I know Lord Kosenmark, he will set you to work at once."

"Or perhaps you should leave him to us," said another voice.

A woman leaned against the pillars of the entryway. She wore a diaphanous robe that left her lean body in shadows, even in the bright sunlight pouring through the windows. She smiled at Gerek, but it was not a friendly smile.

"Nadine, you should not tease," Kathe said.

"I merely follow your example," Nadine replied.

Kathe ignored her pointed comment. "Why are you awake so early? Do you have an appointment?"

Nadine stretched out in one languorous movement. She was like a wild cat, Gerek thought. A panther from the mountains, strong and lovely and dangerous. Apparently his expression betrayed his thoughts, because Nadine paused in mid-stretch and drew her lips back from her teeth, which showed white and sharp against her brown skin.

"Nadine," Kathe said. "I'll tell you again. Do not tease."

Nadine merely laughed. "You eat too many prunes, Kathe."

To Gerek's relief, she flowed back into the common room to join another pair of courtesans—one woman and one man—who were gathered around an expensive-looking musical instrument. As Nadine rejoined them, the man ran his fingers over a series of levers. A bright, rippling melody echoed through the common room.

He let his breath trickle out. His first encounter with a genuine courtesan. Not a very successful one.

"Come with me," Kathe said, as if nothing had happened. "We should visit the gardens."

HOURS LATER, GEREK Hessler sat alone in his new office, one floor below Lord Kosenmark's spacious private suite. After he and Kathe returned from the gardens, Lord Kosenmark had summoned Gerek to his office. There, they had talked—rather, Kosenmark had talked, and at length, while Gerek did little more than attempt to retain the tumbling flow of names and titles and historical events from the pre-empire early days, to the destructive civil wars that fractured the empire, severing Veraene from Károví, Morennioù, Hanídos, and the northern kingdoms.

He rested his head in both hands. He had done it. He had inserted himself into Kosenmark's household.

It was but the first step. In all that excess of talk, Kosenmark had given nothing away. He had not mentioned Armand of Angersee or Markus Khandarr, the king's chief councillor and mage. Nor, of course, anything about his activities since Armand dismissed him from court. There had been one teasing detail—a brief mention of minor Károvín nobility—but then the subject had veered to trading agreements between the two kingdoms, and Gerek had not dared to turn the conversation back.

He wished—again—that Dedrick had confided more during his final visit to Gerek's family. It had taken place directly before Dedrick went for the last time to Duenne and court. Gerek was certain his cousin had gone at Kosenmark's request to spy on the king.

And what shall you do if you can prove it? his brother had asked.

I don't know. But it's not right, what happened to Dedrick. And no one else cares.

His brother had argued, but in the end he had agreed, however reluctantly, to help Gerek with his plans.

Gerek poured himself a cup of water and drank. Kosenmark had given him a small task: *Make a list of the supplies you need. Give the list to Mistress Denk, and she will see to everything. Tomorrow we shall start in earnest.*

He searched the desk first, to see what it contained. Not much. One drawer held miscellaneous social correspondence from a year before. The others were empty, or nearly so. He found a pen in need of mending, a bottle of ink (almost empty), and several sheets of cheap paper, yellowed along the edges. The list would be a terribly long one. What had happened to the supplies for the previous secretary?

Ilse Zhalina. Secretary, then lover. She left. This was her desk; Hax's before that.

Curious, he rummaged through a few more drawers. Nothing. Then, wedged between the bottom drawer and the desk's side, he discovered a half-finished letter. He smoothed out the paper and examined it. The letter was addressed to a Mistress Adela Andeliess in Osterling Keep. It was written in a distinctly feminine hand—however neat and contained—and inquired about a possible post at Mistress Andeliess's pleasure house. It ended in mid-sentence.

Gerek Hessler carefully replaced the letter where he'd found it. He sat back and exhaled, pulse leaping in unaccountable distress. Tricks and traps of memory all over this house. How could he never mention her name when he continued to find traces of this woman wherever he looked? From Mistress Denk's warnings, to Kosenmark's oblique references, to the signs she herself had left everywhere.

Once more he wondered what was the true story behind her departure.

CHAPTER THREE

ILSE ZHALINA STOOD by the window of her study in Osterling Keep. Outside, drifting clouds obscured the stars and darkness lay thick upon the city. Between the inn and bell tower opposite, she could see the lower rim of the crescent moon, dipping toward the watery horizon.

Early spring, almost winter still, and yet the season had turned astonishingly warm. If she closed her eyes, she could almost imagine herself back in Melnek, on a mid-summer's night in the northeast province of Morauvín. There was the same salt tang, the same thread of pine when the breezes curled around from the north.

No. Not Melnek. Not my father's house. It's not the same at all.

She blew out a long breath, wishing she could expel memories as easily as she could the air from her lungs. Any recollection of Melnek always called up more bitter memories—why she had run away from her father's house, how she had sold her body to every man in the caravan rather than return, and how that terrible journey had led her to Lord Raul Kosenmark's household, in Tiralien.

Five months since I left my love. I miss him.

An understatement. She missed Raul Kosenmark as she would miss air to breathe, or salt for meat. As the goddess Lir missed her brother Toc when he died, even knowing he would live once more come spring.

Her heart contracted into a painful knot. Ilse cursed silently as she swiped useless tears from her eyes. She hated herself for being so weak. A strong woman would soldier onward, through loneliness and terror and the ache of separation, to that shining selfless goal of peace between all the kingdoms. She would not mind a part of her self ripped away. Lir had survived until spring, waiting for Toc and their reunion.

Except, except . . .

Except that Ilse knew she was no goddess, just an ordinary woman, and spring would come without any end to her separation from Raul Kosenmark.

It never will, unless we each do our part.

She drew a long breath and willed herself to calm. Stubbornness. That was the key. Raul often told her she was unnaturally stubborn. She could never tell if he meant it as compliment or complaint. No matter. It was a trait inherited from her father, and though she hated any reminder of that man, hated any thought of Melnek and the life that came before, she knew she must use stubbornness to her own advantage.

Because we are bound by blood and flesh, by past lives and memories. Tanja Duhr knew us all, she thought, *when she wrote those words.*

Ilse heard a soft creaking noise—of ropes drawn tight—the sound magnified by night. A moment's anticipation followed, like the infinitesimal pause between a breath drawn and its exhalation, then a muted peal rang out. One, two, three chimes whispered along the breeze, like a song recalling older days and half-forgotten lives.

Another bell tower took up the count, then another,

farther away. Ilse listened until the last bellsong faded, and silence washed over the city once more. In Osterling's fort and along the perimeter walls, soldiers kept watch, but here in Mistress Andeliess's pleasure house, these were the quiet hours. The courtyard below was empty of any passersby. The courtesans and their clients slept, and the servants had not yet begun their day.

It was the hour for magic.

Ilse closed the shutters and set the bar. She locked her outer door and bolted it with sturdy iron. That, however, was not enough. She laid her fingers over the lock's metal plate and murmured an invocation to the magic current.

Ei rûf ane gôtter. Komen mir de strôm ...

The language was old Erythandran, the language of magic. The words she had learned in Raul Kosenmark's household, a place where magical guards were ordinary things. This one augmented the lock itself, so that no one could tweak the pins and levers within. An experienced mage could break these protections, but then, what she did here was simply the first line of her defense.

Once she locked the door and windows, she retreated into her bedchamber. Two lamps burned in their brackets, their scented oil giving off the aroma of lemons and oranges. The walls here were the same pale peach as her study, but with a darker border around the ceiling. Ilse locked and bolted the second door. She paused at the window for one last breath of the warm ocean breeze, then pulled the two shutter panels shut and barred them. The scent of her sweat and the sweeter scent of the lamp oil intensified. Just nerves, she told herself. Nothing more.

She extinguished the lamps and sat cross-legged on

her bed, her back against the wall. She breathed in, felt the air catch in her throat, then slowly released it.

Ei rûf ane gôtter. Komen mir de strôm.

With every exhalation, her thoughts spiraled down to that moment between breaths, to the point where the magic current welled up, like water from a crack in stone.

En nam Lir unde Toc, versigelen mir. Niht ougen. Niht hœren. Versigeln älliu inre.

A heavy silence enveloped her, as though someone had dropped a curtain between her and the physical world. Her rooms were still visible, but the objects outside her immediate circle appeared blurred. That was deliberate. No one must know what she did here.

Now for the next step.

Ei rûf ane gôtter. Ei rûf ane Lir unde Toc. Komen mir de strôm.

Blood pulsed in her ears. She could sense every minute ripple in the magical current against her skin, within her body. Another moment, and her soul would relinquish its purchase on her body, shrug away her flesh, and soar into the magical void between worlds. For over three months, she had practiced just that until the act came easily to her. But not today. Today would be different.

Komen mir de strôm. Komen mir de vleisch unde sêle. Komen mir de Anderswar.

The world tilted away, and she fell into darkness, into emptiness. A feathered hand brushed against her cheek. A harsh familiar voice whispered her name over and over, just like the first time she had crossed the void. She heard the thunder of waves, the gulls from Osterling's shore screaming, *Lost, lost, lost.*

And then, silence.

Eyes still closed, Ilse drew a deep breath and felt an

unnatural weight against her chest. Her face and neck felt slick with sweat, and the soft linen of her gown chafed against her skin. She caught the stink of ashes and burning tallow, overlaid by magic's richer smell. Every sensation was stronger, sharper, than before. Her heart beat faster in anticipation. She opened her eyes.

Osterling Keep and her bedroom had vanished, replaced by a thick fog. Odd sparks and embers floated past her face, and shadows appeared in the milky depths below—darting, hovering, sinking away. Her stomach swooped.

Anderswar. The point where all worlds met. Where lives intersected with lives, and memories with time.

Deep inside, she felt a strong tug from the ordinary world, as though someone had fastened a chain under her ribs. Flesh or spirit did not matter. She was poised on the sharp point of an abyss. One step and she might plunge back into her rooms in Osterling Keep. One minute tilt in any direction, and she'd fall into another world.

Or back to Tiralien and Raul Kosenmark.

Her breath caught at the thought of Raul. To see him once, just for a moment. To hear his voice and feel the warmth of his breath against her skin. His house would be quiet at this hour, with only a few servants about, in case a customer wished for refreshment. She could steal through the empty corridors to the stairway leading up to Raul's private quarters. No one would ever know.

With an effort, she checked those lovely thoughts. She must not go back, not until she found the jewels. The risk was too great. She could not even allow herself the luxury of these fantasies, not in Osterling and certainly not here in Anderswar, whose denizens could read her thoughts and desires.

She blew out a breath and felt an ache spread throughout her chest. Onward.

Onward meant a different thing in the physical world, the ordinary world. There, it meant a difference of distance or time. Here . . . Here it meant a difference of will. She willed herself to creep forward in halting inch-wise steps along the thin edge between worlds and the magical void. Her stomach heaved against her ribs as the sight of lands and spheres flickered into and out of view. There, a city with bloodred towers. Over there, a horizon of stark, straight lines, such as she had never seen before.

With her next step, the fog vanished. Overhead a band of stars streamed past—souls in flight to their next lives. Another step and the streaming stars vanished. A gout of fire burst from the mists at her feet. She leapt back . . .

. . . and stood alone in a brightly lit cave, the walls of which were covered with primitive figures. Lir and Toc. An ancient crone. A maiden and a mother. Others she could not identify. From other worlds or other times? The absence of lamps or candles she did not question, nor that the cave had no exit. This place was not like any other she had encountered. But then she knew from her previous visits that Anderswar delighted in trapping and tricking the unwary visitor with the unexpected.

She made a circuit of the room. The walls felt slick and damp. Smooth, except for patches where it looked as though the stone had melted into rivulets, only to freeze again. The air tasted sour with smoke and magic. Now what?

The light inside the cave flickered. A ghostly warmth brushed against her arm. Feathers. Stiff and likewise soft. Ilse flinched, smelled a rank animal odor, as the invisible presence circled her. Once. Twice. Nails clicked over the stone floor. Then she glimpsed a shadow against the far wall. The shadow darkened into a great hunched beast, with beak and wings and four thick legs ending in claws. A huge ruff of fur grew from its neck. The rest of its body was covered in a mad patchwork of feathers and more fur. As it stumped around to face her, she saw the creature's sex, which hung stiffly between its hind legs. The sheath angled toward her like another threat.

You came back, it said.

Ilse drew a shaky breath. She had encountered this creature before, on her journeys in the spirit. Philosophers claimed Anderswar guarded its entrances with monsters and tricksters. Others argued the guardians were fabricated from the traveler's own dreams and expectations.

The monster laughed, a rough, grating noise from deep within its throat. *You remember me. Are you still afraid?*

She recovered her voice. *I'm always afraid of you.*

Good. Then you aren't as stupid as you look. It leaned toward her, its eyes glittering silver in the unnatural illumination. *You want to find the jewels.*

Of course it knew. There were no secrets in Anderswar.

Can you take me to them? she asked. *Lir's jewels, I mean. I know they are somewhere in Anderswar.*

I can. For a price.

It spoke the truth—she sensed it. A giddy exhilaration filled her. This monster could lead her to Lir's jewels, to wherever Leos Dzavek's brother had concealed them centuries ago. Once she had them, she and Raul could end the threat of war between Veraene and Károví. They could end this miserable separation.

Show me, she said, *and I will pay that price.*

It regarded her for a long moment. There was no

depth to those opaque eyes, which reminded her of a
pair of old silver denier, the edges and impressions
dulled by centuries.

Take hold of me, it said.

Ilse reached out and gripped the ruff at the creature's neck. She stilled a shudder when it rose onto its
haunches and wrapped its legs around her. Its strong
scent made her gag, its sex prodded her belly. She
shivered and felt the creature's body shake with laughter. Oh, it knew all her terrors and nightmares. She
had only a moment to wonder what other torments
lay in wait for her when it sprang forward.

*. . . and they were hurtling backward through a
pitch-dark tunnel, so fast that Ilse could not catch her
breath to scream. Starbursts blinded her. All around,
voices rose into keening howls, broke off, burst out
once more in a staccato chorus.*

Where are we going? she gasped.

To find the jewels.

You know where they are?

I know where all Lir's creatures are.

*Without warning, it bit deep into her shoulder with
needle-sharp teeth, then spat out a mouthful of blood.
Ilse felt the creature's grip loosen. She scrabbled to
hold on, digging her fingers into its fur and feathers. It
gave a rasping laugh and thrust her away.*

You promised, Ilse cried out.

*From afar, she heard the slow heavy beat of its
wings.*

And I have kept that promise.

*Its voice faded as she plummeted through the void.
Light changed to darkness; dimensions vanished. She
was falling through a dark tunnel, silent except for
the shrill whine of her descent, which echoed from the
walls-not-walls, through the air-not-air that shrieked
in her ears. Ilse cried out to the gods, to the magic*

current. Komen mir de zoubernisse. Komen mir de
wërlt . . .

Her vision went dark.

SENSATION CAME BACK in bits and fragments. A yel-
lowish light. Blurred. Something hard and warm against
her cheek. Her fingers curled, felt the same smooth
surface. Lying flat. Sunlight on wood. Skin, burning.
Her heart beat slowly, erratically, as if unaccustomed
to its purpose.

She drew a painful breath, tasted a ripe green aroma
at the back of her throat. Just as quickly, the scent and
flavor of the magic faded, to be replaced by the staler
aroma of orange oils and smoke. Of paper and ink,
and the memory of salt tang and pine. Melnek?

Her throat squeezed shut at the thought of her father. No, no, no. She'd abandoned him years ago,
never to return. Never. No one could force her to. Not
her father or Alarik Brandt or Theodr Galt. Then more
memory returned. Her father dead. Alarik Brandt, the
caravan master, too, executed by Raul Kosenmark.
She was safe from them. At the thought of Theodr
Galt, her certainty faltered. Galt was a man who never
forgave any slight or insult. She had run away rather
than marry him.

Galt could not find her, she told herself firmly. He
did not know her new name or identity.

She levered herself up to a sitting position and as-
sessed her condition. It was enough to send shudders
through her body. Dark bruises covered her forearms.
Her throat felt tender to her touch, and her body ached
throughout, but especially her shoulder. Remembering how the creature had bitten her, she unbuttoned
her gown.

Four crimson spots, surrounded by darker bruises,

marked where its teeth had punctured her skin. Ilse flexed her shoulder and hissed. These were no pretend bites. She would have to find a healer.

Even as the thought occurred to her, the wounds closed, the bruises faded. She caught a whiff of magic in the air. It had an unfamiliar signature, not like any human one she had encountered. Anderswar and its magic. It wounded and healed without reason. Or rather, for reasons of its own.

A rap at the door startled her.

"Ilse?" called out a voice.

Alesso. One of the kitchen servants. He had come with Ilse's customary morning tray. It was far later than she had guessed.

Ilse lurched to her feet in spite of her aching shoulder. Just in time, she recalled the magical guards. "A moment, please," she croaked.

Her skin felt sticky with sweat, and she still wore the same gown from the day before. She dashed water over her face, and fumbled a robe from her clothespress to cover her gown. A few words dissipated the magical guards, a few more erased all traces of her magic. She hurried, unsteadily, to the outer door of her rooms. More locks, magical and otherwise.

She called up the semblance of a smile as she opened the door. "Alesso. Good morning. Please come inside."

Alesso glanced at Ilse briefly as he passed into the room. He was a young man, slim and dark. She had noticed him the first day, thinking he could be a warrior or a dancer, and wondering why he had chosen to work in the kitchens of a pleasure house. Mistress Andeliess had told Ilse his history. Mother a soldier. Father a cook in the local taverns. Six years ago, the mother had taken a new posting in the next province. The father had followed, leaving the child Alesso behind with his aunts and uncles. Not long afterward, Alesso Valturri had applied to Mistress Andeliess and had worked for her ever since.

Ilse leaned against the wall, watching him as he laid out the dishes for her breakfast and poured a cup of tea. Her shoulder was still sore, and she felt as though something had scooped the strength from her body. She yawned, then realized Alesso had finished his work and was studying her with bright black eyes.

"You look terrible," he said. "What happened?"

Ilse stifled a second yawn and shrugged. "I didn't sleep well."

His eyes narrowed. He was smiling, but there was an unusual alertness to his gaze. "Did you sleep at all?" he said. "You're wearing the same clothes as yesterday underneath that robe, and you can barely stand up—"

"I'm fine," Ilse snapped. Cursing silently, she rubbed her eyes with the back of her hand. Exhaustion had led to her outburst. Perhaps she could use it to undo the mistake. "I'm sorry. That was rude of me. I stayed up far too late, reading, and fell asleep in my clothes."

Alesso appeared unconvinced. However he said nothing more, and when she mentioned the hour, he smiled politely and withdrew. Ilse pressed her ear against the closed door and listened. Alesso did not linger. Still, she waited until his footsteps retreated toward the stairs, then sank onto the nearest stool. Too close. And far too suspicious. What if he knew about magic?

Stop it. He's curious. Kind.

Or someone who wished to gain her trust.

Ilse rested her head on her hands. She was trembling with exhaustion and fear. *I cannot live like this. Not everyone is a spy for Markus Khandarr.*

The thought of Markus Khandarr propelled her to the table and her breakfast. The best way to divert suspicion would be to attend drill practice as usual. Alesso had brought her coffee, fresh flat bread, a plate of soft white cheese, and bowls of fruit and olives. Ilse filled her mug, then nibbled at the bread. The strength seeped back into her body. A warm breeze blew from the ocean through the open windows, carrying with it the strong scent of low tide.

Perhaps she ought to leave off magic for a few days. *Excuses. You're just afraid of that monster.*

It was hard to tell when discretion crossed into cowardice. She was afraid, that much she had to admit. Remembering the monster's rank scent, its jutting sex, Ilse shuddered. *I know where all Lir's creatures are,* it had said. But it had lied, and flung her away into the void.

Then I shall just have to try again.

Outside, the city bells rang eight times. Ilse cursed. It was far later than she had thought. Weapons drill had already started. She raced into her bedroom, unbuttoning her gown as she ran. She had promised the garrison commander diligence. Only then had he permitted her to take part in morning drill.

It took but a few moments to throw off her gown and pull on a loose shirt and old pair of trousers. Next came the belt with its sword in sheath. Ilse was never certain what the soldiers thought of her, a woman with money and education, who chose to drill alongside them, earning sweat and bruises and cuts from sword practice. A pet to be humored, she guessed. A mascot. For some, a potential lover.

Like Galena Alighero.

Young Galena who watched Ilse at drill with her pale green eyes. Who smiled quickly at whatever Ilse said, and who found any number of excuses to visit the pleasure house during her free hours, though she never hired one of the courtesans. Ilse recognized all

the signs of an infatuation. She had tried to discour-
age Galena gently, but without any success. She would
have to speak plainly to the girl, and soon.

No time to worry about Galena now.

Ilse locked her rooms and skimmed down the back
stairs. The side courtyard was empty, but carts and
stalls filled the square in front of the pleasure house.
Most were fishermen who trawled the waters close to
shore, or farmers from the hills just north of Osterling—
men and women with plum-dark complexions, who
spoke in a lilting cadence—but as she squeezed through
the crowds, she heard snatches of dialects from the
central plains.

Beyond the plaza, she turned off the main boulevard and plunged into the labyrinth of narrows streets
and passageways around the ruins of the old Keep.
Osterling was a city of walls, each ring marking its
history over the centuries. The garrison and Keep lay
at the heart, tucked against cliffs rising straight up
to a stony crest where the king's fort overlooked the
city and the sea. Sunlight splashed the walls overhead,
but the streets themselves were still dark and cool. As
she crossed through a small courtyard, her shadow
lengthened unexpectedly, and the strong clear scent of
magic filled the air. She spun around into a crouch,
dagger in hand.

And faced an empty lane.

Her skin rippled, as though she still stood in the
void between worlds.

Just a reflection of the sunlight, she told herself.
Nothing more.

Nevertheless, her hands were shaking as she re-
sheathed the dagger and set off again. The quarter bell
rang out, a single chime. Ilse cursed and ran faster. She
would have to do her limbering exercises alone and
try to catch up with the others. If, that is, Spenglar al-

lowed her to stay. Spenglar had trained with the king's personal guards in Duenne. He'd come to Osterling as drill master and captain ten years ago. A grim, disciplined man who expected the same from others.

She jogged up a set of narrow stone steps to the next level. The Keep's wall curved around to the north. Ilse followed the lane beside it to the main boulevard. Now the garrison and the fort atop the cliffs came into view. Soldiers patrolled in pairs outside the fort's walls above. A single pair stood outside the gates to the drill yard. Piero and his sister, Marelda. From within came the crash of swords, and Spenglar's voice calling out the rhythm.

She paused for one breath, then sprinted to the gate. "Piero. Marelda. Am I too late?"

Both swung around to face her. Piero flashed a grin. "Can't you hear them already?"

"I can, but—"

"Poor child. You thought Spenglar might have mercy."

Ilse allowed herself a smile in return. Piero, not so old himself, loved to tease the younger soldiers. "I only hoped, my friend. We both know the gods extracted all pity from Spenglar twenty years ago, when they made him captain."

"Hush," Marelda said. She had gone still, her whole attention elsewhere.

They all went silent. Inside the drill yard, sword rang against sword as Spenglar counted the drill. Then Ilse heard the peal of bells from the harbor towers. Not the slow peal of the hour bell, but faster and more urgent. The next moment, the fort's bells broke out even louder.

"Warning!" Piero shouted. "It's the warning bells. Raiders!"

A roar erupted inside the garrison. Piero and Marelda

vanished through the gates. She heard Spenglar shouting orders, then another voice calling out for weapons and armor.

Ilse drew back from the entrance. She ought to return home at once. Warn Mistress Andeliess and the others—the pleasure house had a secret room dug underneath for just such emergencies—but she stood, frozen and breathless, listening to the tumult inside the garrison.

With a crash, the gates swung open. Men and women in armor poured out, file after file, all the patrols from the morning weapons drill and more. They marched in double time into the boulevard leading down directly to the harbor, the patrol leaders shouting the time above the clanging of the bells. Ilse pressed back to keep out of their way. *An entire wing's worth. Or two. And that's not counting the fort's soldiers.*

"Ilse!"

Galena Alighero swung away from her file. Mail glinted under her leather tunic. A high color edged her cheeks, and her eyes were alight with excitement. She looked tall and strong and impossibly young. "It's going to be a battle," she said.

"Who is it?" Ilse asked. "Raiders or—"

"Alighero!"

Captain Spenglar's voice cut through the din.

"Alighero, you useless chit! Stop flirting! Get moving!"

Galena spun around and pelted after the other soldiers. Spenglar shot a disgusted glance at Ilse, then stalked away. Soon the last file of the last patrol marched through the gates. Piero and Marelda were gone, each to their own file, to be replaced by another pair of soldiers, but otherwise the boulevard and surrounding streets had emptied, while the bells from the garrison and the fort above continued to ring out their warning.

CHAPTER FOUR

A HIGH WIND was blowing long before they reached the harbor walls—strong cold gusts that swept away the spring. Galena sniffed and caught the strange scent of something ripe and green. It was not seaweed—it had a land smell. It reminded her of the pine-forested hills north of Osterling, but that was impossible—the wind came from the wrong direction.

"Watch where you're stomping, Alighero. Or were you daydreaming about Zhalina again?"

Ranier Mazzo shoved her with an elbow. Galena staggered to one side and fell against Lanzo, who swore at her clumsiness. Galena muttered an apology and sprinted to regain her spot next to Ranier.

"Bastard," she hissed.

"Handsome bastard." His dark eyes narrowed with laughter.

She struck back the only way she knew. "That's not what my brother said."

Ranier's reaction was swift. He clamped onto her wrist and dug his fingers into the tendons. Galena yelped and swung out wildly with her fists. He dodged one blow; she aimed another at his throat, but a broad hand closed over her shoulder and yanked her away.

It was Spenglar, angrier than she had ever seen him,

his lips pale against his seamed brown face. "You idiot," he breathed harshly. "Stop brawling. We have an
enemy to fight."

"But he—"

"No excuses. You keep your mind on soldiering,
girl. Now move. Fast. Both of you."

Ranier had already taken off. Galena suppressed
the urge to argue and raced after him. It would do no
good. Spenglar was right. Soldiers who didn't pay attention got killed. All the veterans told her that. She
knew it herself just from living in a garrison city. Oh,
but Ranier had such a bitter, sharp tongue. Her
brother Aris had said the same thing, right before he
left Osterling.

Wing and file marched in through the next market
square (now deserted), down a flight of shallow steps,
and into the wide empty space before the harbor towers. Soldiers were already forming into lines. Galena
spotted her father, the senior officer for the morning
sentry watch, conferring with Commander Adler of
the city garrison and Commander Zinsar from the
king's fort. Two riders stood nearby, next to their
horses.

If it were pirates, those riders would be gone. Her
heart beat faster as she ran through all the possible
reasons why they remained, and why Commander
Adler was glaring at Commander Zinsar.

"... no evidence of attack ..."

"... twenty ships sighted last week ..."

"... duty is to defend the city ..."

Adler's face went stiff. She snapped out a string of
curses that made even Galena's father wince. Zinsar
drew his lips back in a predatory smile. Then he said
something too soft for Galena to hear, but Adler and
Lucas Alighero both went still and blank. The next
moment Adler was screaming for the archers to mount

the walls. Lucas Alighero spoke a word to the two couriers. Within a moment they had mounted their horses and were galloping through the open lane toward the eastern and western gates—taking word to Leniz, Kostanzien, Ostia, and Klee, and from there to all points north and west along the coast.

Two entire wings were marching out the northern gates to the highway. Marelda and a squad of archers mounted ladders. They spread out along the arcs and catwalks over the harbor entrance, to the towers guarding each side, and further to the perimeter walls that encircled the city. That wasn't all. A team of large draft horses followed their handlers into place. They were going to close the harbor gates, Galena realized with a thrill of excitement. It was serious. Not like two years ago, when pirates skimmed past the outer shoals, laughing at the soldiers on watch. No, this was more like the real pirate invasions of fifty years ago. Today, for the first time, she would be a part of those famous legends.

More jabbering between Adler and Zinsar. Then Adler made a rude gesture with both hands. Zinsar grinned again, but in triumph. So he'd won the argument.

Confirmation followed. Orders rippled from the wing commanders to the patrol captains, down to the file leaders and then the soldiers themselves.

"Formation, face left and north," Falco barked.

His two file leaders repeated the orders as they swung around. Galena stamped in time with her file mates. She thought she heard Ranier mutter an insult but she ignored him. Ready, yes, and forward march, companions. Left and right and left. The pattern drummed into her bones since she was twelve and could copy her brother Aris, newly admitted into the wing under Captain Spenglar. As the horses swung into their harnesses, and the massive iron harbor gates groaned along the tracks, Galena marched out the southwest gates and onto the highway.

Dark blue-black smudges blurred the entire southern quadrant. Closer to shore, rain fell in sheets, illuminated by bursts of lightning. And then Galena saw them—three ships flying straight toward land, their sails filled to bursting. Her skin prickled, as though touched by the storm's electricity.

"Where are we going?" she murmured to Lanzo. "Where are *they* going?"

"Western sands."

She wanted to ask if he meant the ships or their wing, but Spenglar was barking and snapping like a wild dog. The winds blew harder. She had to shield her eyes from the whirling sand. Now they were off the hard-packed dirt and gravel highway and onto the flat lands between the lower hills and the sea. Two patrols split off and took up positions along the highway. Falco and the other two patrol leaders shouted for theirs to keep going, damn it, or the Károvín would be landing in the middle.

Károvín. But that was impossible.

Galena stopped in surprise, her gaze yanked outward to sea. The storm had leapt closer to shore, driving the ships before it. Then she hurried to catch up with her file. But she had not missed that hideous rending noise she knew too well. It took a master navigator to clear the shoals off Osterling's shores, and these ships . . .

Like a bubble burst, the storm vanished. The clouds faded into gray wisps, and the towering waves rolled outward until their force died away. Beneath the roar of the surf, Galena heard three strange tones, like midnight bells.

"March, you idiots!" Falco shouted. "Faster, keep time, turn about. Halt!"

From months and years of practice, the two files in his patrol swung about as one.

"Weapons ready!"

Galena and her companions drew their swords.

"Watch and wait!"

The clouds had vanished. The sun's rays now beat against Galena's back and shoulders. Only a damp wind, rising from the south, and the clear scent of pine, reminded her of the storm. From her position in the file, she could not see much except the sky and the thin line of ocean horizon.

"Pirates?" she whispered to Lanzo.

He shook his head. "You heard them. Károvín."

She'd heard but not believed. "All that fuss for three ships."

He grinned, as though he saw beyond her indifference. "It's not just the three ships. Last week, the king's patrol sighted twenty ships with Károvín flags off the northern coast. They were sailing east. If they followed the current 'round, these could be the point of that entire fleet."

Twenty ships. Galena's mouth went dry at the thought.

"What happened to the others?" she asked.

"We don't know. I'm worried they decided to double back and take us by surprise—"

"Hush," whispered Tallo, their file leader.

Muttering died away at once. This was no drill, Galena thought as she examined her blade's edge. Her sword was sharp. Her other hand rested on her dagger hilt. She was as ready as she knew. But would they fight? And why? Oh, sure, she'd heard rumors about tensions along the border between Veraene and Károví,

and her father had muttered about how Armand of
Angersee wanted any excuse to launch a war. But Ar-
mand hadn't declared war, and neither had Leos of
Károví done anything to provoke one.

She strained onto her toes to see more. All three
ships were closer now. She could see dozens of figures
hurrying over the decks. The glint of sunlight on metal.
The masts broken and trailing in the water, dragging
the ship to one side. There, they'd cut the mast free. The
ship righted itself momentarily. She could see some of
their faces. Definitely Károvín.

Several boats launched from the nearest ship. Soldiers and sailors dived from the railing into the water.

"What do we do after they land?" Lanzo whispered
to Tallo.

"Wait for orders," Tallo said. "What else?"

Two of the leading boats skimmed over the waves
to shore. The Károvín tumbled out and dragged their
craft up the sands. As Galena watched, five more shot
from behind the other two ships, which tilted heavily
to one side. By now, fifty or sixty Károvín had landed.
Soldiers, all of them armed and clad in heavy armor.
One of them was a tall man. He carried in his arms a
young woman clad in layers upon layers of soaking
wet robes, which dragged in the receding waves.

The man deposited the woman on the shore above
the water line. She struggled, then jerked around to
vomit onto the sands. The man placed a hand on her
forehead. The air around them shimmered.

Next to Galena, Lanzo uttered a soft exclamation.
Magic.

Her skin prickled with remembrance of that unnatural storm, the scent that could not possibly be
land-borne, riding the sea wind. She watched intently
as the Károvín soldiers gathered on the flat sands.
Over a hundred had reached shore. More were land-

ing from the second and third ships. They matched the Veraenen soldier for soldier. And, she noticed, they all wore armor, as though they expected a battle. Or as though they'd come from one.

The man she'd noticed before spoke briefly with his companions. Then he addressed the Veraenen, first in Károvín, next in Veraenen. Galena could not quite make out his words, but they sounded soft and conciliatory. A dissatisfied murmur rose behind the officer. He barked out a command. His soldiers subsided, but she could tell they were unhappy. She wished her file and patrol stood closer, but Falco had mentioned something about not provoking the enemy.

But if they *were* the enemy, why bother about provoking them? Why not attack?

Commander Zinsar stepped into the clearing between the two parties. Galena had never liked his manner, and she disliked it now. He smirked and smiled and spoke in oily tones. The privates all called him the king's worm. Galena's mother, living outside the barracks and working as a scribe, spoke of the man in blunter terms.

The Károvín officer shook his head at something Zinsar said. He made his own reply. Galena could tell by his gestures, and how quickly he spoke, that the Károvín officer wanted something. No, demanded something. Zinsar shrugged. Next came a swift negotiation. She wished she knew what it was about. Her skin itched from sweat and the chafing of her leather guards.

The Károvín soldiers looked no happier than she felt. All of them were sodden from the storm and seas and dragging their boats to shore. Worse. Their eyes were hollow pits in dark lined faces. Many were bruised or bandaged. Underneath the weariness, she sensed a bright tension.

"They look like pirates," Ranier murmured to Lanzo.

"More like pirates who lost their treasure," Lanzo murmured back.

". . . five hundred gold denier . . ."

The Károvín's voice carried across the sands. Galena choked back an exclamation. Was that a bribe?

"A thousand," Zinsar said. "Provisions extra."

"For the hire of a single ship?"

"We don't run a service for marooned foreigners," Zinsar said. "Pay us, or send word to your king to supply your needs."

Ugly murmurs broke out among the Károvín soldiers. The officer gestured sharply toward another woman, who rapped out orders in their own language. Galena stirred uneasily. She glanced up toward the fort, wondering if they would send reinforcements down the side roads. Or had they decided to set up their defenses in the fort and the city be damned?

Falco eased back along the files, speaking softly to each soldier. "Did you bring your flask?" he said to Galena when he reached her. "Good. Drink all your water."

"Do you think we'll fight?"

He glared at her. "Don't sound so happy about it. Fighting isn't—"

He broke off and spun around. The Károvín had crowded forward, their voices raised in angry protests. That officer shouted back, but their voices drowned his out. Galena was about to ask Lanzo if he understood their language, when sunlight glinted off a swiftly drawn sword among the Károvín.

" 'Ware!" cried out a soldier from the front.

A feathered shaft hissed through the air—an arrow shot from the city walls.

"No, you fools!" Zinsar shouted.

Too late. A patrol leader from the wing opposite

waved his arm. Soldiers surged forward from both sides. Back in the rear of her file, Galena could see nothing as she marched forward, but she heard the thundering crash as the front patrols met up with the leading Károvín. "*Move, move, move*," she chanted under her breath, trying to see her way clear to the enemy.

And then, almost before she realized it, the first Károvín broke through. Automatically she swung up her sword to parry and strike. It was just like the drill and nothing like it at all. She deflected a sword that grazed her forearm, brought the flat of her blade against another's helmet, barely escaped a dagger thrust. Her head rang from the noise, and sand dust choked her throat. There was no time for terror, and yet she could feel it pulsing, just beneath her consciousness.

She killed her first opponent with a stab into his belly. Blood spilled onto the ground, bright and red in the sunlight. For a moment, her vision wavered. Then she gasped, pulled her blade free.

Just in time. Another Károvín stepped over the dead man and swung his sword around in a short deadly arc. Galena beat away his first attack, but though she made a thrust or two, he was much faster and stronger, and she could not break through his defense. For every time she pressed forward, he drove her back twice as far. Soon they were beyond the mass of fighting. Behind her lay the narrow spur of the highway leading west and north.

The Károvín swung at her neck. She leapt back and crouched, waiting for his next attack.

He hefted his sword and approached. "Let me pass," he said in Veraenen.

"No." She swallowed back the bile in her throat. Surely the fort would send reinforcements, but they had to battle through the enemy before anyone could reach her.

The man lunged toward her. Galena brought up her sword barely in time. Their blades met in a jarring crash. With a wrenching twist, the Károvín bent her wrist to the side. Galena jumped away before he could thrust against her undefended body. She turned his attack—just—but the next one nearly gutted her. He was faster than any of her drill partners. Stronger. He would kill her—

Again he swung his blade under her defense. Again she twisted hers around in time. Before she could jump away, he hooked his hilt with hers and pressed forward until her sword touched her own throat.

She had all the time to memorize that face—the swift sharp angles of cheek and jaw, the black eyes with the faintest cast of blue, a full mouth drawn tight in what might pass for anger, but what she knew was a soldier's grim expression in the face of war. This close, too, she caught the rich scent on his clothes. It was the same green scent the wind had carried in from the storm. Magic.

"You should have let me past," he said.

"Why?" she whispered. "You would have killed me anyway."

His expression went blank, as if her words had struck a wound. With a grimace, he thrust her to one side. Galena fell hard against a rock. Stunned, she lay breathless and motionless, waiting for him to run her through with his sword.

The blow never came. With a gasp, she rolled over to see the man's shadow as he rounded the highway leading north.

Galena staggered upright. *Follow him. Stop him from getting away.*

Her feet refused to move.

He's too good a fighter. I don't want to die.

A scream yanked her attention back to the fighting. She twisted around in time to see Piero falling to the sand. Lanzo rushed to Piero's defense. Another Károvín intercepted him; a second one stood over Piero with his knife raised. Galena snatched up her sword and sprinted toward the battle. Her indecision had vanished: she felt reckless, invincible, as if she could live forever or die that same instant. Either would be perfect.

CHAPTER FIVE

LATER, MANY HOURS after she watched the soldiers march from the garrison, Ilse bent over her desk, hard at work on her quarterly report for Mistress Andeliess. She wrote steadily, rows and rows of numbers, in the neat hand she had learned as a merchant's child. Light from the dying sunset streamed through her open windows, casting long sharp shadows across her desk.

A woman's voice sounded loudly in the corridor outside. Another woman answered—one of the courtesans. It was a busy evening in the pleasure house. From the rooms beside and below hers, she heard murmurs, faint laughter, and the more intimate sounds of lovemaking. Usually she could shut these out—they reminded her too strongly of Raul's pleasure house in Tiralien—but not today.

Ilse laid down her pen and rubbed her eyes. *I'm tired. That's all.*

Tired and distracted by the day's extraordinary events. In between her duties as steward, she had gathered details—the three Károvín ships, the storm which drove them onto the rocks, the outbreak of violence and the bloody skirmish that followed. Rumors flowed through the corridors and bedrooms, delivered from visitors to courtesans in private, then dispersed throughout in murmured exchanges. Even better, Falco had visited the common room that afternoon. Ilse had stationed herself close by his chair, and overheard his comments about the fighting. The captains and commanders were still dissecting what happened, he said.

Ilse thought she knew. Last summer, she and Raul Kosenmark had received word from their Károvín spies about strange maneuvers on land and in ships. Today's events had to be connected. Would the regional governor see that? Would he send word to Raul?

A year ago, she would have said *yes* with assurance. Now, she wasn't quite as certain. Lord Nicol Joannis had once been a member of Raul's shadow court. He had served as a conduit for information from Fortezzien and the southeast. Well before she left Tiralien, however, Joannis had withdrawn from their regular correspondence. A matter of precaution, Raul had said in passing, though whether the caution came from Raul or Joannis, she had never learned. Nevertheless, Raul had trusted Joannis enough to suggest that Ilse come here for her temporary exile.

In case Markus Khandarr did not believe our fiction.

In case of other eventualities she and Raul could not foresee.

Their plan had been a good one, a sensible one. But those dispassionate discussions last autumn seemed far removed from today, and this crisis. She had not dared to approach Lord Joannis since her arrival. Why should she? She was nothing more than a commoner, a discarded lover who now earned her wages as a steward.

Useless, useless second thoughts.

Ilse wrote the last sum, blotted the page, and set the

sheet aside. She was still sifting through the details
she'd learned when she heard a scratching at her door.
Ilse paused, almost certain she'd imagined the soft
noise, when there came a tentative knock. One of the
courtesans with gossip? A runner from Mistress Andeliess?

But it was Galena Alighero who stood outside, a
tall pale ghost. "A few minutes," she said quickly.
"That's all I want."

Ilse hesitated.

"Please," Galena said. "It's not about— Please."

Even in the corridor's half-light, her distress was
obvious. Reluctantly, Ilse stood aside and motioned
for Galena to enter. Instead of taking a seat, however,
Galena circled the small room. Her gaze flickered over
the walls and bookshelves as though tracking an invisible enemy.

"What's wrong?" Ilse said.

"Nothing."

A lie. Ilse let it go. "Sit down," she said. "We'll have
some wine."

She filled two wine cups and offered one to Galena.
Galena took it and abruptly sat down on the couch.
Her hands were shaking so, the wine rippled in the
cup. She wasn't acting, Ilse thought. Was it battle
fever? She tried to recall if Galena had ever seen action before.

She took a seat on the same couch—but not too
close—and waited for the girl to speak.

The quarter hour rang outside, a thin soft peal. Galena shivered, as if the bells had stirred unpleasant
memories. "You know about the Károvín," she said
softly.

"I heard. There were three ships. Or was it four?"

"Three. They sank. Foundered on the rocks." She

gulped down some wine. "You heard all that from Falco already. I should go."

Ilse laid a hand on her arm. "Stay. I've heard a few stories, but not yours."

Galena flinched, but sank back onto the couch. "It's the storm," she said. "Or that's part of it." Her voice went breathless, higher than usual. "It was magic. The captains think a mage on the ships called up the storm for cover. The Károvín sent at least twenty ships into the eastern current just last week. If the storm had hit us earlier, we might not have sighted them at all. They could have taken the city."

"With just three ships?"

"No, with all twenty."

Ilse felt cold wash over her skin. Károvín soldiers, here in Osterling, after centuries of calm. Falco had not mentioned that detail. "How did you know they were the same ships?"

Galena hesitated only a moment. "My father said the report came from the king's patrols. No other ships were sighted in those waters. They're certain it's the same fleet. The captains think they meant to head around. Except they haven't, not yet. Commander Adler doubled the watch just in case."

East from the Veraenen coast lay the open seas— there were no known islands, no continents. Nothing, Ilse thought, except an impenetrable magical barrier, and the lost kingdom of Morennioù. Again she had a shiver of premonition.

Legend said that Lir had drawn a curtain around the island province. After the second wars, when Dzavek had invaded Veraene in his search for Lir's jewels, Veraene had sent ships to contact the islands. None had returned. Fishermen brought wild tales of a burning wall in the open ocean to the east. Lir's Veil was its name. The Károvín had their own name for it, most likely.

"Did you take prisoners?" she asked.

"Yes. Thirty-four. Soldiers and sailors."

Ilse did not miss that last phrase, or the pause before Galena had answered. Falco, too, had been strangely reticent when asked about prisoners.

"Thirty-four soldiers and sailors," she repeated. "And who else?"

Galena's fingers tightened around her wine cup. "Who told you?"

"No one. I guessed. Can you tell me anything, or did you swear to secrecy?"

She hardly needed to hear the answer. Galena's panicked expression was enough. "We didn't swear an oath," Galena said. "But Lord Joannis was there. He told us to be discreet."

So the matter was important enough for the regional governor.

She offered more wine to Galena, who refused. "I promise not to spread any rumors," Ilse said. "Or would you rather talk about the fighting?"

"Yes. No. I don't know." Then she added, "They fought hard in spite of everything."

"What do you mean?"

Galena's gaze flicked toward Ilse and away. "Just what I said. They'd fought at least one battle already that day. And they were exhausted from the storm. Still, they didn't want to yield. When we tried to take them prisoner, a dozen or more fell on their swords. The ones we did take—Ranier and Tallo knocked them over the head. Then there was that woman . . ."

She drew a long breath and fixed those unnaturally bright eyes on Ilse. "I'll tell you. But you must promise not to tell anyone else. My father thinks that woman is not Károvín. He says she answered in Károvín, but slowly. As if she had learned it from a book."

The notes of a flute drifted up from the common room, and one of the courtesans, Luisa, began to sing. Ilse could not distinguish the words, but she knew the melody. It was a popular ballad, recounting the history of two lovers separated by chance. Several verses described their anguish, but toward the end, the song spoke in minor keys, how their grand passion died, extinguished by nothing more than neglect. Ilse released a sigh, and drank deeply of her wine. *I wonder why Luisa chose that one.*

Galena, too, was listening intently, her empty cup finally at rest. "Commander Zinsar died," she said softly. "Lanzo lost an eye, and Piero took a sword thrust beneath his mail. The surgeon said he lost too much blood, and the herbs haven't taken hold."

Ilse knew the surgeon. Aleksander Breit was more skilled and conscientious than most. If his patients had any chance, he would give it to them. Still, his best herbs and spells might not be enough. "How is Marelda?"

"Angry. Frightened. She went back to the hospital as soon as our captains dismissed us." Galena's eyes narrowed. "I hated the fighting. I wish—" She broke off with a frown.

Ilse waited through a long silence. Luisa had reached the last section of the ballad. Someone joined in with a guitar, drowning out the flute. Another moment and the new musician gained control of his playing, the two instruments blending into a seamless harmony. Above them, Luisa's sweet contralto swelled to pure and unfaltering tones.

"I heard Lord Joannis wants to celebrate your victory," Ilse said.

Galena shifted uneasily, but said nothing.

I've struck close, Ilse thought. "Would you like more wine? Or coffee?" she asked.

Galena shook her head. "Water. Just . . . water."

Ilse fetched a carafe of water and filled Galena's cup. She watched as the girl drained it, then wordlessly refilled it when Galena held out the cup for more. Around them, the pleasure house was quiet for the moment, but Luisa's song, of love and lovers lost, still ran through Ilse's mind.

"Ilse, why did you come to Osterling?" Galena said softly.

The change in conversation took Ilse by surprise. She sent a covert glance toward Galena, but saw nothing in the girl's expression except ordinary curiosity. What would Galena say if Ilse told her the truth? That she had come to teach herself magic, to find Lir's jewels so that these endless wars between Károví and Veraene would end. So that one day, she and Raul Kosenmark might marry.

But the reasons started long before she met Raul Kosenmark. She had come to Osterling by a series of hard choices, each seemingly inevitable, that had led her from Melnek to Tiralien, from Raul Kosenmark to Osterling Keep. Galena would not understand, and so Ilse gave the simplest answer. "I came because I needed employment, and Adela offered me a position as her steward."

Adela Andeliess had been delighted to hire a steward with experience at pleasing a duke's heir. So she told Ilse, proving it by raising Ilse's salary twice in the past four months.

"I remember the day you came here," Galena went on. "Marelda saw you at your window. You waved back to her."

Ilse nodded. That had happened her first hour in

Osterling, while she stood poised between her old life and the new. "You were walking through the court-yard with Marelda and Piero and Aris," she said. "I met all of you a week later, when the garrison commander allowed me to drill with the others."

"We thought you were a rich woman, playing at soldier. At least, that's what Aris said at first. He said later he'd been wrong."

Exactly the words Aris had used, when he later came to Ilse seeking her advice about the northeast borders, where Ilse spent her childhood. Ilse had told Aris what she knew about the garrisons and patrols. A week later, Aris had secretly applied for a transfer and vanished from Osterling Keep.

"I'm sorry he's gone," she said.

"So am I. I thought— I thought at first he left because of you."

Ilse shook her head. She knew why Aris had left, both the reasons he gave, and the one he kept secret. But she doubted Galena wanted to know about her brother's relationship with Ranier Mazzo. In Galena's uncomplicated mind, love and desire were the same. It would be too difficult to explain that Aris had desired Ranier, but could not love him, even though Ranier desired him in return. Not because a man should not love a man, but because Ranier himself made trust, and therefore love, difficult.

"My turn," she said. "Why did you come here to-night?"

"To talk."

"We did talk. About everything except what bothers you. Was it something you saw today in the battle?"

Galena's breath caught in a laugh. "You could say that."

One beat, two, and three. There were no bells to count the passing moments, but Ilse heard them in the pulsing at her temples, in Galena's shivering as she fought to bring herself under control. Oh, there were secrets unfolding here. She wished she didn't need to listen to them. They would do Galena no good. Nor her. It was for Veraene and the peace that she kept still and waited for the other young woman to speak.

"It was after the fighting started," Galena said at last. "One of the Károvín— We fought hard. He drove me back, away from the others. Then he knocked me down. I hit my head against a rock."

"But he didn't kill you."

"No, and I don't know why. Or maybe he thought he had. Killed me, I mean."

"What happened to him, Galena?"

"He got away." That in a whisper.

So. A Károvín soldier had escaped into Veraene. He'd head directly for his homeland, no doubt, but the patrols would intercept him long before he reached any border. Strange that Falco hadn't mentioned this particular detail. Had Joannis required them to keep the news a secret? Then her breath deserted her when she realized where Galena's confession headed. "Galena, did you tell your father? Or the commander?"

A heartbeat of silence followed. "No."

Ilse closed her eyes, silently cursing Galena's folly. "Why tell me?"

"Because you know Commander Adler and Captain Spenglar. You could—"

"Lie to them?"

"No! But you could tell them you heard a rumor."

Ilse thought briefly of striking Galena with a very hard object. That would do no one any good. No, she had to tell one of the garrison commanders—or better, Nicol Joannis, so they could send out patrols and track the man down.

Galena had begun to weep silently, tears pouring

over her face. Ilse put her arms around the girl and held her close, stroking her hair. When Galena relaxed against her with a sigh, Ilse stiffened. No, she told herself, the girl was too distressed to mistake kindness for desire. She continued to stroke Galena's hair, which was a springy mass of brown threaded with silver, barely contained by the many cords she wore.

"Why are you so kind to me?" Galena murmured.

I am not kind, Ilse thought. *But it's best you believe that I am.*

VALARA BAUSSAY WOKE in a suffocating darkness that reminded her of Autrevelye, of the void between worlds and lives. Panicked, she tried to fight her way clear, only to roll over heaving and retching. Through the roaring in her head, she heard shouts and the clang of metal against metal. It was a battle. Károvín soldiers swarming up the stairwells and through the halls, cutting down her guards as she tried to escape from Morennioù castle.

Gradually the thundering in her skull subsided. There was no battle, only the memory of one. She spat out the bile and wiped her mouth with the back of her hand. Filthy. Stained with muck from the bottom of the ship, with dirt and salt and sand. Her wrists were bruised from the manacles they'd used, even after they had subdued her with magic.

Her treacherous stomach heaved again, but there was nothing left inside her aching body. Valara collapsed onto the stone floor. It was cool and damp against her fevered skin. Fragments of her surroundings intruded. She smelled damp straw, overlaid by crushed herbs and the sickening reek of stale vomit. Her guts pinched harder. She bit her cheeks to stop another bout of retching.

She was a prisoner, taken by the Károvín invaders.

That much remained clear. They must have landed safely, then. She dimly recalled being roused from a magical stupor and hauled onto a ship's deck. Winds were howling with unnatural ferocity and the scent of magic had overpowered her. There'd been a coastline in the distance—Károví, she'd thought. But that general, that duke, Miro Karasek, had roared out orders to the ship's captain, demanding they steer north, north, damn it, even while the shore rushed toward them. Then came a terrible rending noise. The shock of water closing over her head. After that her memory blurred.

It took her several tries before she could stand up. She shuffled over to the cell door. The corridor was empty. Torchlight stippled the stone walls. It reminded her of another prison, from another life.

She wanted to break open the doors, flee the prison, but she remembered enough from those previous lives to make her cautious. She ran her fingers over the iron bars, then the lock and keyhole, probing for traps and alarms. Slow, slow, slow. She approached the magic and the bars as she would a wild deer in the mountains. As she had first approached magic five years ago.

Needles pricked at her skin, as though the dead iron could read her intentions. So. They had placed a magical guard on her cell. That argued for Károví and Leos Dzavek. The last time he had taken her prisoner, many lives ago, she had escaped by slashing her wrists and throat with magical fire, drawn to a sharp burning edge. It had been a painful victory. Leos would have remembered that incident and prepared against it.

Not that death is my choice. Not with Lir's emerald in my hands.

She touched the ring on her second finger. Magic

hummed at her fingertips, the only trace of the emerald's true identity. How long before Leos Dzavek discovered the jewel his duke had stolen was false? How long before he thought to strip her of all possessions and force the truth from her throat? Then he would possess two of the three jewels. Morenniwhere would be helpless against a second invasion. (And he *would* invade a second time. She knew the man who was, who had been her brother. He did not suffer disappointment.)

She had to escape, before he found out her secrets.

There is only one way. Only one choice.

It was a gamble, attempting to make a leap across the magical void in the flesh. She had managed the trick dozens of times in previous lives; she had done it last summer when she recovered the emerald from Autrevelye, and again that last fateful time when Dzavek confronted her. But she had never tried to when so drained of strength. She would have to concentrate hard if she wanted to land in Morenniwhere and not lose herself in other worlds.

Ei rûf ane gôtter. Ei rûf ane Lir. Ei rûf ane Toc. Komen mir de strôm.

Magic rippled over her skin, clearing her head and easing the cramps in her gut. She murmured the phrase again, her sight narrowing down to a point on the stone floor, to a single speck of water gleaming in the torchlight.

Komen mir de strôm. Komen mir de vleisch unde sêle. Komen mir de Anderswar.

The world tilted away. A narrow edge, a bright sharp line, arced through the darkness. She glimpsed a hundred worlds refracted in all directions. Just as she caught sight of Morenniwhere, of Enzeloc Island and her home, a force, like a massive hand, struck her backward.

The shock of return drove the breath from her body.

She lay there, gasping. (There? She had no idea where.) Eventually she coughed, spat out a mouthful of blood. Her ribs ached sharply. Her throat felt bruised and sore. Voices yammered inside her skull. Outside, too—voices shouting curses in Károvín and another language. Veraenen.

Valara hauled herself to sitting. Just as she feared, she was still a prisoner in that same dank dark cell. Off to one side stood a bucket and a tray with a loaf of bread. Valara dragged herself closer. The bucket was half full of water. She drank a handful, then another. When her body stopped its shivering, she crawled back to the iron bars of her cell.

Magic roused at her touch. She moved her palms to the walls. Here the magic beat a slower, deeper rhythm. *Hush*, she told it. *Let me read the past, nothing more. Nothing more.*

She closed her eyes and focused on her hands. When her breathing had slowed, she narrowed the focus to her palms and then to the point where flesh met stone. The current welled up around her; she felt its electric presence rolling over her skin, rippling through her flesh, between her palms and the air—to the region between body and mind.

Ei rûf ane gôtter. Ei rûf ane Lir. Ei rûf ane Toc. Komen mir de strôm.

Her breathing slowed, her thoughts stilled to match the barely perceptible rhythm of the stone. Rock and mortar used no words, but human speech had echoed here in days and weeks and decades past. *Where am I?* she asked.

Sunlight glinted from the faceted granules; a man's voice echoed one word. *Osterling.*

Yes. Osterling. The early kings of Fortezzien had

built a series of castles along the coastline as watch points. The Erythandran emperors had taken over those castles and turned them into forts, manned by soldiers from the imperial army.

Slowly, the rocks yielded their memories, and the trickle of words had become a flood of human speech. Fragments of conversation. Oaths and curses whose meaning had disappeared into time. Valara sank deeper into the past, to the first settlers. Digging. A castle built by common laborers overseen by mages. A remnant of that castle formed this prison. Slowly the voices faded into silence, and she heard only the gulls crying, the wind sifting through sand, and the distant surf, unimpeded by walls or towers or other works of mankind. She had come to the end, which was the beginning.

She withdrew her hands. So she was in Veraene, not Károví. But still a prisoner, and half a world away from her kingdom. Karasek had left seventeen ships behind—nearly a thousand soldiers. Morenniwhere had only a small militia for each city. They had forgotten to guard against an enemy from outside.

No, it was not them. I did this. I destroyed my homeland.

She sank to the stone floor. Her eyes were dry of tears. She had foresworn grief to keep her strength in the face of an invasion. But now, in the quiet of this cell, memory recited a relentless litany of faults and errors and grave mistakes.

Five years ago, she had thought nothing of breaking the conventions against exploring magic. Or rather, she had thought a great deal about it. Her life dreams had pressed upon her nights, then her waking world. Eventually, reluctantly, she had to accept that she was Leos Dzavek's brother in a former life. She had helped him steal Lir's jewels from the emperor. Later, in yet another life, she had stolen the jewels again, and hidden them in Autrevelye.

It was a matter of curiosity, she told herself, unconnected with her life as a princess in Morennioù, the younger daughter, not even an heir. Then her mother and sister died in that shipwreck. Valara had become the heir. Whatever excuses she had made to herself before were worthless. She had sworn before her father's council to obey Morenniou's laws.

And yet, she could not resist the pull of curiosity. So she had poked and prodded at her memories, had explored Autrevelye in flesh and spirit, until her life dreams finally yielded enough clues to help her find the first of Lir's jewels.

Only one. The oldest of the three, the first to speak as a separate creature after the emperor's mage had divided the single jewel into three, many centuries ago. It was the emerald, of course. Daya was its name. She remembered reaching for it, her fingers digging into the dirt in some far corner of the magical plane, when a voice startled her. Leos Dzavek, conducting his own search.

Shouts. Her own frightened response. Then Leos striking at her with fist and magic. She had fled, bleeding from a dozen wounds and fevered by her too-swift passage between worlds.

Her own magic healed her wounds, but Valara had spent a terrified month convinced that Dzavek would follow her between worlds, or that her father's council would strike her name from the rolls of nobility. As summer passed into autumn, she told herself that she had escaped discovery. She began to experiment with the jewel Daya. That had proved frustrating at first. Then, one night at the end of winter, as she worked alone in her rooms, the jewel had woken to her touch.

It spoke. In colors and song, as though Autrevelye itself lived inside me.

The next morning, Dzavek's ships had broken through Luxa's Hand to attack. An impossible deed, according to all her father's mages. Well, they were probably dead, too, along with her father and his chief mage.

Her eyes burned with unshed tears.

No. Not yet. She could not afford the luxury of grief. She had to escape this prison and fly homeward. She knew her father's council too well. They would quarrel—even the best of them—while Dzavek's soldiers plundered the islands and made them helpless against a second attack.

And he will attack a second time. I know it. I must go back.

Propelled by desperation, she stood and shouted. "Help. Anyone. Can you hear me?"

She called out in Károvín and Veraenen, until the other prisoners shouted at her to shut her mouth and die. She didn't care. She had to get word to Veraene's king. She needed an ally.

One of the guards flung the outer doors open and stalked down the corridor, cursing. "What do you want?" he said in stilted Károvín.

"Send for your king," Valara said in his language. "I can tell him about the Károvín ships."

His eyes narrowed in suspicion. "You tell me this news first."

Three hundred years in hiding. It took an effort to break such a long and perfect silence.

"The Károvín," she said after a brief inward struggle. "The Károvín have a new enemy. The enemy could be a friend to you. To Veraene."

"Might?"

"I'm sorry. I don't know the words."

"You know enough," he said. "Why aren't you sure about this friend?"

Careful now. She had to satisfy his curiosity without giving too much away. Her awkwardness with the language helped her there. She made a show of searching for the words, and when she answered, she let herself stumble over the pronunciation. "I didn't— don't. I'm not certain because I do not know your king. Does he want a friend? Does he need one?"

The guard studied her thoughtfully. She wasn't entirely sure if he believed her.

"If you're lying, I could lose my position," he said. "The captain doesn't like tricks."

Valara shook her head. "I'm not lying. Please, tell him. Blame me if you like. Anything. But the king must hear what I have to say."

She held his gaze with hers, willing him to believe her, until the man sighed and tapped his fingers against the bars. "Very well," he said. "I'll tell the captain. It's up to him whether he passes the word higher. I can't promise more than that."

"I understand. Thank you."

Valara watched him walk back through the corridor, his shadow fluttering in the torchlight. The other prisoners flung questions and demands at him, in both Veraenen and their own tongue. He ignored them and slammed the outer door shut.

An uproar broke out. Prisoners cursing their interrupted sleep. Prisoners demanding to speak with the officers, to have word taken to their king. Valara covered her ears and sank to the floor. Even if Veraene's king listened to her, then what? Would he grant her passage home? Would he agree to ally his kingdom with hers?

Hers. Not her father's. He was dead, murdered by the Károvín invaders.

Grief pressed like a fist against her throat. She resisted a moment, then let the tears break free.

ON A BARE ridge, miles away from Osterling Keep, Miro Karasek dropped to his knees. He could almost taste his desire for sleep, stronger than his craving for water. From below came the hiss and roar of surf against the rocky shore.

You will suffer great weariness, King Leos had warned him. *You will live each week twice over. That should inspire you to haste.*

He'd left the coastal highway within a mile of Osterling and its fort, scrambling up the hillside, into the pine-forested ridge that ran the length of the peninsula. Luck was with him so far. No pursuit. There were a few fishing villages on the coast below, but the hills and ridges themselves were bare of population. If he could find some shelter, he could risk a few hours of sleep, then take off once the moon rose.

The swiftest passage home lay on the roads between worlds. But he was too weary to risk that. And the king had warned him against such measures. *They will watch all the borders for any sign of the jewels. Including those of Vnejšek.*

He sucked in the dust-filled air and pushed himself to standing. It was the time between sunset and twilight. The sky had turned dark blue, and a few stars glimmered overhead. Far to the west, a wine-red ribbon marked the line between sea and sky. Already the ground lay in shadows. Risky, to keep walking over rough terrain. He could stumble and fall to his death on the rocks below. Or lie wounded, unable to escape, when the patrols finally tracked him down.

A thousand ways to die, he thought, moving cautiously forward through the tide of dusk. He had tried most of them in this mission.

A flicker of movement at his feet sent him leaping back. He caught himself before he fell, then laughed a wheezing laugh. Just a mouse. The creature darted through the weeds and vanished into the shadows underneath a large boulder.

And if a mouse, why not a man?

Karasek eased himself into a crouch—his knees cracked and protested—and discovered a man-sized opening, choked with rubble. He cleared away the debris and peered inside. The air smelled rank, as though a wild dog had denned there recently. Nothing stirred inside now, however.

He unbuckled his sword from his belt and lay down on his back. The gap was narrow, but the rocky floor gave him enough purchase. He grabbed on to a hand-hold and shoved himself through. Dirt and grit showered his face. He coughed, wriggled deeper into the opening until he reached the farther wall.

Here the niche widened, and its ceiling angled upward. He had enough room to crouch, so he twisted around and slid the knife from his boot sheath. His shirt and jacket made a pillow. The pouch containing Lir's emerald, the reason for his mission, he tucked underneath. As he laid knife and sword within easy reach, it came to him that he was like the renegade warriors of old Károví.

As many brigands as nobles, his father had commented, in an unguarded moment.

His mother had glanced up with a frightened angry look. Karasek had expected another quarrel, but her mouth had inexplicably softened, and she'd murmured, "Be careful, love."

He recalled the moment vividly, though he'd been only seven. One rare gesture of tenderness between his parents—the last one.

Karasek shook away those memories. His father

was dead, secure from accusations, and his mother had deserted Taboresk for her homeland. Only the present concerned him.

Yes, the present. He smothered a painful laugh. He had no gear, no water. Only ten or twelve miles separated him from the garrison city. Disaster had carried him long past Dzavek's original schemes, past the fallback plans the king had devised, and the ones Karasek had decided on himself. Now he was running on instinct alone. Like the old warriors from Károví's founding, he would have to flit like a shadow, using magic and cleverness to regain his homeland.

Brigands and nobles. Which am I? He yawned, curled up on the hard ground, and within a heartbeat, slept.

He woke to the thick dark of full night. Karasek rubbed the sleep from his eyes. His throat felt clogged with thirst, and his stomach had squeezed into an empty knot. *Live and you will eat and drink,* he told his body. One by one, he gathered up his possessions. The pouch he tied around his neck. He covered the sword and its sheath with his jacket, but kept his knives handy. First to check for patrols.

"*Ei rûf ane Lir unde Toc,*" he said. "*Ei rûf ane gôtter.*"

The dusty air stirred into life, brushing against his cheek like a lover's breath. A wisp of current, its scent like pine trees in winter, revived him, and for one exquisite moment, he could forget his weariness and a thirst so profound that his throat felt like sand. It was a risk, using magic, but less of a risk than stumbling into a pack of Veraenen soldiers. He would make a brief reconnaissance and then be gone.

"*Komen mir de strôm unde kreft. Komen mir de zoubernisse.*"

The magic current flickered stronger then weaker as

his concentration wavered. *Magic was like the ocean's currents. Like the inexorable rhythm of life and death. Magic was Lir's sweet exhalation, as she lay with Toc. Magic was completion.*

"*Lâzen mir de sûle. Vliugen himelûf. Ougen mir.*"

The magic current spun through the narrow opening. A thread of perception connected magic with its wielder, and as the current rose toward the sky, Karasek saw the black expanse of night, a brilliant spangle of stars, a raptor floating high overhead. Higher yet, and he could pick out the buildings and walls of the garrison city, now washed in moonlight. Within, the souls of the inhabitants glowed. A few bright points, like suns among the stars, caught his attention. He recognized Valara Baussay's magical signature.

I knew her before, in lives past.

The knowledge had come to him like a shock when his soldiers first brought the Morennioùen queen before him as a prisoner. She had been queen in that previous life, and he, he had been a representative of the empire.

The memories served no purpose, he told himself. He turned away from Osterling and commanded the magic to lift him away.

The current whirled him back toward the hills where his body lay. A blink, a shudder, and spirit rejoined flesh. Karasek drew a last breath of the magic current and savored its taste and smell. Then he spoke the words to wipe the surrounding area clean of his signature.

So. There were no patrols yet. Would there ever be? He had killed the only witness to his escape. Or so he had thought. He remembered throwing the girl to the ground, her head striking a stone. She lay so still, he thought she must be dead. But he had killed so many in the past few days, he might have misremembered. A careful soldier would have run her through with a sword. He used to be careful, before this mission.

Karasek rubbed his eyes with the back of his hand. A month of dangerous travel stood between him and the border. From there, it would take him another ten days of hard riding to reach Rastov. Was that fast enough to satisfy the king?

You must make haste, Leos Dzavek had commanded.

He had, sailing three hundred leagues in twelve days using magic. Time spinning backward through the barrier, then leaping forward on the return trip. It was as if his time in Morennioù existed in a bubble, like a soul's multiple lives, compressed into a single short month.

The king is a thorough man, his father once told him. Karasek had seen the proof—the months of planning and maneuvers, all for an unknown enemy, in an unknown land.

It had started last summer. The king had summoned Miro Karasek to his private interview hall. Karasek had found him immersed in reading.

"You have new orders, your majesty?"

Dzavek looked up from his stacks of books. His gaze was diffuse, as though he saw images beyond Zalinenka's white rooms. "I found him. I found my brother, Andrej."

Karasek felt a river of cold pass over his skin, as though Károví's brief summer had vanished into winter. Andrej Dzavek had died centuries ago, in the wars between Károví and the empire. Apparently that did not matter. Perhaps that was the key to understanding Leos Dzavek. All moments, past or future, were equal. All lives were now. It would be, he thought, like swimming in time.

The king explained. Andrej had returned to another

life as a woman. His brother—this woman—was searching for the jewels in the magical plane of Vnejšek, just as Dzavek himself was.

What followed anyone might have predicted. The two brothers, no longer brothers, quarreled again. Andrej escaped before Dzavek could do anything more than injure him. In the aftermath, Dzavek had discovered more clues, which led him to the second of Lir's jewels, the ruby.

But he was not satisfied with one. He required all three. His health had ebbed in the past ten years. It was a sign that, even with the greatest magic, he could not evade death much longer.

And so, in meetings with Karasek, Markov, and Černosek, Dzavek set out detailed plans for an undiscovered destination, an unknown enemy. Duke Miro Karasek would lead the invasion, Dzavek said, while Duke Markov would take temporary command of all the armies.

Drills and preparations followed throughout that summer. Karasek had thought their plans would come to nothing, when Dzavek summoned him a second time. Andrej had proved careless, had woken the jewel. Emerald had spoken to ruby, one magical creature to its other self. Through their speech, Dzavek discovered where his once-brother now lived.

More preparations and meetings followed. The final week passed in a blur of lists and reports and maps. Letters dispatched to his home in Taboresk. The ships stocked. The final troop selections. Weapons and supplies and gear. Dzavek wanted no blunders with this undertaking. He would not be denied again, he said. That explained several points in retrospect, Karasek thought. The contradiction between Dzavek's meticulous plans and his extraordinary decree that Karasek should return the same day he located the emerald. It also explained the inclusion of Anastazia Vaček.

The last day at sunrise. They were on the point of launching the ships when Dzavek appeared with Anastazia Vaček at his side. "Your second in command," he'd said.

Vaček had smiled and bowed. "My lord, I look forward to serving you and our king. We have the most satisfying orders."

Two commanders. Two sets of orders. What promises had Dzavek extended to Anastazia Vaček that gave her such an expression of hungry delight?

Dzavek's shuttered face had yielded no clues. After dismissing Vaček, he took Karasek to one side. "Remember the spells I gave you for launching the ships through the barrier. Do not discuss them with anyone. Not even Anastazia Vaček."

Secrets within secrets within bloody secrets.

At departure, Dzavek passed along the lines of soldiers and sailors and touched his hand to each person's mouth, Karasek's last of all. Eyes closed, he still felt Dzavek's dry fingers on his lips, still heard the king's inarticulate murmur. His thoughts winged back to his companions. Whoever survived the battle would die before they betrayed their true mission. Discretion at a cost.

The moon had already reached its zenith. The night was spinning toward dawn. Karasek rose to his feet. Once more he checked the emerald's pouch. All secure. With one last glance toward the south, he set off for Károví.

CHAPTER SIX

❋❋❋❋❋❋❋❋❋❋❋❋❋❋

AFTER GALENA ALIGHERO left, Ilse collapsed onto the couch and stared at the ceiling.

Oh, Raul. We never expected this.

All their plans had centered around Armand of Angersee and his ambitions. Even Raul's newest idea—to approach certain Károvín nobles and enlist their support—had at its heart the goal of dissuading Armand from war. They had not taken into consideration Leos Dzavek's plans separate from Veraene. More important, they had forgotten about Morenniou.

I wonder if Leos Dzavek has forgotten anything in four hundred years.

She tried to imagine such a life. His brother killed in the first war. His promised bride reportedly executed as a spy. All his subsequent attempts to build a family ending in their death, while Dzavek lived on for centuries. What must he be like now?

She rubbed her knuckles against her eyes. Dzavek was not her concern. His ships and their mysterious mission were.

I have to get word to Raul. He must know before he talks to anyone in Károví.

The regional governor immediately came to mind. Nicol Joannis had corresponded with Raul in secret for years. Surely he could revive those channels. Surely he would want to, for such important news. The only difficulty was how to speak with him, without provoking suspicion, but Galena herself had provided the means. Ilse could pretend to plead her friend's case. Once there, she could tell Lord Joannis about the escaped officer, then turn the discussion to Raul.

Abruptly her weariness left her. She hurried to her desk and dashed off a note to Lord Joannis, asking for a private interview. She sealed the message with wax and magic, gathered up her report for Mistress Andeliess, and took them both downstairs.

Mistress Andeliess kept her office on the ground floor, in a quiet wing opposite the various public rooms. Ilse delivered her monthly report and spoke a few moments with her employer. On her way back, she stopped one of the house runners and gave him the letter for Lord Joannis. Watching the man disappear through a side door, she felt a flutter beneath her ribs.

There. I have done it.

She had no idea what his response might be. Of all the members of Raul's former shadow court, she knew him the least. Raul had always said that Nicol Joannis disliked the court's secrecy, however much he agreed with its motives. Still, he might consent to send a message to Raul, if only as a favor to an old and trusted friend.

Restless, she turned into the common room, which was bright and noisy at this hour. Gilda and Ysbel had started a drinking game with some wealthy farmers. Several younger men lay entwined on a couch—she could not tell client from courtesan there—and off in a corner, Luisa attempted to strum her guitar, in spite of two soldiers who took turns trying to unbutton her gown. Kitchen girls and boys appeared like swift small birds to take away the dirty dishes and to replenish the wine and ale jugs. Ilse could name a dozen ways this room differed from Lord Kosenmark's elegant pleasure house, but in the essentials, the two were alike. Laughter. Games. Music. And always the presence or potential of pleasure for those with money to pay.

"What tempts you here?" said a voice at her elbow.

Alesso Valturri knelt at her side. He had a tray stacked with dirty dishes balanced on one knee. There was nothing unusual in his appearance—just an ordinary servant engaged in ordinary work—except that Ilse knew Alesso worked the early-morning shift. All her suspicions buzzed into life. "I might say the same to you," she said lightly.

"Ah, me." He stood up and handed the tray off to another kitchen worker. "I am here for the company and to observe our courtesans at work. Would you like refreshment from the kitchen? A cup of wine?"

He plucked a cup from a passing servant's tray and, with an unnecessary flourish, offered it to Ilse. The cup was a deep iridescent blue, which echoed the painted murals of the walls. Both were purchases Ilse had recommended. The wine was a sweet golden vintage, imported from the southwest.

Ilse accepted the cup and settled into an empty couch in the corner. Alesso lingered next to her. "You didn't answer my question," he murmured.

"Neither did you."

He smiled, a slow easy smile that probably charmed all the kitchen girls and boys, and half the courtesans. "Your suspicions wound me, Mistress Ilse. I am working tonight because Daria took ill, and Mistress Andeliess asked me to take her shift. For extra pay, of course."

"Of course." She could check his claim later, easily enough.

"And you?" he said.

Ilse sipped the wine, letting the flavor linger on her tongue before she swallowed. The wine had an oddly tart edge. She took another swallow, trying to decide if she liked the taste or not. "No reason in particular. There were reports to deliver . . ."

". . . and messages to send off."

She pretended not to hear that comment, and kept her attention on the courtesans while she drank more wine. Stefan was mock-wrestling with Ysbel over the favors of a grain merchant from up the coast. The grain merchant was a full-faced, round-shouldered man of middle years, his muscles loosening into fat from too many hours in counting houses. He'd come to Osterling to petition the governor for lower highway taxes. Earlier that afternoon, he'd sat grim and silent, having been refused entry to the governor's presence. Tonight, however, his eyes were nearly lost in folds of flesh as he laughed at the two courtesans.

"You do not trust me," Alesso said.

"Should I?" Ilse replied.

"Friends should trust each other."

"Is that what we are, friends?"

He shrugged. "Acquaintances, then. Colleagues in business."

She glanced up sharply then, but his gaze was on Stefan, who had won the wrestling bout. He and the farmer were now locked in an embrace, indifferent to their audience. Ysbel had disrobed entirely. She lay on her back and beckoned to Luisa and the soldiers. It was the hour of abandon in the pleasure house. The air smelled of wine and musk and sexual spendings. Deep within, Ilse felt the tug of unfocused desire, the tremble of panic.

No one will force me here. None. I am free of Alarik Brandt, of Galt.

A hand brushed her shoulder. She jerked around to find Alesso's face close to hers.

"You are tired," he murmured. "And distressed. Anyone can see it."

"I am not—"

"You are," he repeated. "It's not necessary to wait here. Go and sleep. I'll keep watch for the runner and bring you any reply at once."

She *was* tired. Her eyelids were drooping, her limbs felt like warm water. She wanted nothing more than to lie down and lose herself in dreamless sleep. It was true that she hadn't rested well or long in weeks. Alesso himself had noticed this morning when he brought her breakfast tray . . .

She reeled to one side, nearly fell over. "You. You poisoned my wine."

Alesso smiled. "Hush, no. Merely added a few pinches of valerian powder. You will sleep better and wake without harm."

"But . . ." Her tongue tripped over the word.

He shushed her again. Gently, he took her by the elbow and helped her to stand. No one noticed their departure. Courtesans and clients were absorbed entirely in each other, in the giving and receiving of pleasure. Ilse made an attempt to shake free of Alesso's hand. He laughed and drew her close with an arm around her waist. *No,* she thought. *I do not want you. I only want Raul.*

Her body admitted the lie, however. When Alesso adjusted his hold, his hand shifted downward to her hip. A bright burst of warmth flooded her body. She sucked in a quick breath. He paused, and she could tell he was looking down at her, because his breath feathered her hair. "All well?" he asked.

She shook her head. It was a false desire, born of weariness and fear and the drugged wine.

Outside her rooms, Alesso produced a key and un-locked the door. A part of her protested. How had he obtained a key? But her tongue felt too clumsy, and the words slipped away from her, even as she tried to form them. Alesso paid no attention to her distress. He guided her easily into her bedroom, where he laid her on the bed and loosened her clothes. This close, Ilse caught the whiff of his scent, a mix of bergamot and ginger, and another, a warmer scent, one she knew very well. It was the scent of a man not entirely immune to desire himself. As Alesso spread the quilt over her, Ilse tilted up her chin and kissed him on the lips.

Alesso went still. His expression was invisible in the darkness, but she heard his quick intake of breath. He muttered something—a curse or prayer, she couldn't tell which—then pressed his lips against hers.

He tasted of wine and bittersweet smoke. She opened her mouth to his, and another kiss followed, slow and expert. His lips were hot against her skin as he im-printed more kisses along her cheek to the corner of her jaw. One hand drifted down to her breast.

The touch shocked her into awareness. "No," she whispered hoarsely. She placed both hands on his chest and pushed him away. "No."

Silence between them. Then Alesso said, "As you wish."

He laid a hand over her forehead and spoke a string of syllables. Erythandran, but with an accent she had never heard before, softer and more fluid, the harsh syllables overlaid with tones of Fortezzien's own an-cient tongue. That was all that registered before the magical current wrapped her in sleep.

DOWN AND DOWN, into a sleep so immediate, so pro-found that she did not respond at first to the hands

shaking her. She stirred, mumbled a protest, and tried
to bury herself in sleep once more. The hands, however, were persistent. "Ilse. Wake up. You have a letter."

That was impossible. A letter? What letter? Raul
would never commit any message to paper. It was too
dangerous. Markus Khandarr had spies everywhere.

Hands gripped both shoulders and shook harder.
"Ilse, wake up. Now!"

With a gasp, she came awake.

Moonlight poured through the open shutters of her
bedroom. A salt-scented breeze brushed her face, sweet
and cool. Ilse sat up. She saw a shadow retreating
through the door. "Who—?"

The shadow paused. "You will find the letter on
your desk. Don't worry. I promise to lock the doors
behind me."

Soft footsteps padded over the tiled floor. Moments
later, she heard the door shut. Only then did she recognize Alesso's voice. What was he doing here?

Oh. I kissed him.

All the details returned with hideous clarity. She
stumbled from bed and into her study, but he had already vanished. Outside a gibbous moon hung low in
the sky; bells rang whisper-soft through the night. It
was well after midnight. Now she recalled how Alesso
had promised to wait for any messages. He must have
seen her give the note to the house runner. He was a
spy. Or did he think he might blackmail her?

Letter first. Speculation later.

She found an envelope waiting on a serving tray on
her table. There was also a carafe of fresh hot coffee,
brewed strong, and a small drinking cup filled with
water. She sniffed the water. It smelled sweet and aro-
matic. Not plain water then.

It was then she noticed a scrap of paper, which the
cup had hidden. Printed in anonymous letters was the

message: *No poison. Merely an antidote for the vale-rian in the water. There is nothing in the coffee except coffee.*

Ilse set the water aside, untouched. She didn't trust Alesso's claim. The coffee smelled ordinary, however, so she poured a cup and took a tentative sip. It tasted normal enough, so she drank down two full mugs and felt her head clear. Then she turned her attention to the letter.

The envelope carried no inscription except her name. Joannis had sealed the edges with plain yellow wax. Very ordinary. Very convincing. Anyone might think him too busy to bother with other precautions. Ilse knew better. She tested the paper and detected several layers of spells, keyed to her touch. Ah, interesting. Someone had attempted to break the spells, but failed. Probing deeper, she sensed two magical signatures, one strong and intoxicating, as bitter and pungent as alcohol. The second was warmer, softer and thinner, like a ribbon of worn velvet. She was not certain which belonged to which man.

Wax and magic remained intact, however. She touched her thumb to the wax and felt the magic ripple over her skin as the spell yielded to her identity.

Inside was a single sheet of fine parchment, with one line in Joannis's distinctive script. *I can spare you half an hour tonight. Come directly to the palace.*

Ilse brushed a hand over her face. Alesso was still on watch, no doubt. She could do nothing about him today, however. It was more important that she speak with Joannis.

She made herself as presentable as possible in a few moments, then went below. The halls and common room were silent. Only a few maids moved about, picking up dishes and wine cups from the tables. The scents of stale incense and smoke hung in the air. One of the maids fetched a lantern for Ilse. The girl was plainly curious, but of course she asked no questions. Mistress Andeliess hired only those who proved discreet.

Outside, the steady ocean breeze cleared Ilse's head. She crossed the market square, and turned onto the boulevard leading toward the garrison. The moon and stars illuminated her way, but in the darker alleys around the old Keep ruins, she was glad for her lantern. Osterling was a different city in the night. Lonelier and stranger, with hints and whispers from centuries gone by.

She rounded the Keep's old walls and followed the main avenue to the governor's palace. Dozens of windows in the palace blazed with lamplight. So, too, did the city garrison, while the fort above was mostly dark. Odd.

The palace guards expected her. One of them escorted her across the outer courtyard and through the gaudily painted grand entrance hall, all rose-pink and bright gold, up the winding stairs to the governor's office. As she followed, Ilse noted the guards at every intersection, the many runners who passed them in the corridors, the glances directed at her then away. If tension had a scent and flavor, it was here.

"Mistress Ilse Zhalina to see Lord Joannis," her escort announced to the guards outside.

A look passed between the two guards. Both glanced uneasily at the closed door. Ilse heard voices inside. She was about to say she could wait elsewhere, when the door swung open and Ranier Mazzo exited the room. He stopped when he saw Ilse, and his eyes went wide.

Commander Thea Adler appeared immediately behind him. Fatigue lined her face. Her mouth was set in a thin angry line. The moment she saw Ilse, however, her expression smoothed to a blank. "Come with me," she said to Ranier.

She stalked down the corridor. Ranier followed his commander. Ilse could almost hear the vibration from their passage. More bad news from the invasion? A difficulty with the prisoners?

"Lord Joannis will see you now," the escort said, ushering her inside.

Her first reaction was surprise. She had expected a grand official chamber, such as Lord Vieth's in Tiralien, filled with cold empty air and expensive statuary. Or an old-fashioned office like the one she had visited in Melnek as a child. Chandeliers swarmed like twisting snakes from the ceiling, making the room seem low. A huge desk occupied one entire side of the office, and tables crowded the floor, all of them stacked high with scrolls and books and leather-bound volumes. There were no windows—no distractions—only bookcases fronting every wall. A few patches of plaster showed between the shelves, but these surfaces were painted a rich yellowish-white, the color of skimmed cream. Nothing like the vivid colors she had grown used to over the past months.

Joannis stood with his back to her, gazing at a large map that showed the surrounding region. It reminded Ilse of the maps Raul used. "You've come about Galena Alighero," he said, without turning around.

"Yes, I have." She paused. "You already know what happened."

He nodded. "I know what happened in the battle, and I can guess in part what you've come to speak about. But I'm curious, too. Curious why Galena Alighero failed to report a missing enemy. More curious why she chose to tell you and not her senior officers."

His tone was light. Detached. Unsettling.

"Galena came to me because she trusts me," Ilse answered.

"Trusts you to lie for her?"

Warmth flooded her cheeks. "No. I came to tell you about the Károvín officer. And that Galena Alighero regrets her actions. She is understandably anxious about admitting her fault."

Joannis turned around. His dark face was creased with lines, and the skin beneath his normally bright eyes looked puffy. He gestured to one of the chairs. "Sit. Please. We need to talk."

They sat, he behind his massive desk, and she in the ornately carved chair placed before it. A supplicant to her master. She dismissed the thought as unfair and accepted the cup of coffee Joannis offered.

"It was Mazzo who reported what happened," Joannis said. "He saw Alighero engaged in a single combat. Alighero went down, and Mazzo tried to fight through to her side, but failed. When he saw her next, Alighero was charging into the battle. Naturally, he assumed she had killed her opponent. It was only later, when he and Tallo were talking over the morning, that he realized the man must have escaped."

"My interview is useless, then."

He tilted a hand to one side. "Not entirely. I am happy to know that she expresses regret, though I wonder if her regret is for her mistake—a very grave mistake—or for the punishment that must follow."

Ilse could not answer that one. "There is another reason I asked to speak with you," she said. "Galena mentioned a prisoner, a woman who was clearly not Károvín. I thought you might—"

"There are many things I might do," Joannis said. "And many subjects we might discuss. However, you

must know that certain subjects, certain acts, are
fraught with difficulty."

So. A clear warning against mentioning Raul Kosenmark.

She considered his position as a representative of
the king—a governor of Fortezzien, a province that
turned restless from time to time. Baerne of Angersee
had hoped to quell that restlessness by appointing a
nobleman of Fortezzien ancestry to this high post.
Amazingly, his grandson had not overturned that appointment upon taking the throne.

*He knows Armand watches him. He must tread
carefully.*

"I understand," she said. "Would it be possible to
discuss Galena Alighero's punishment?"

"You do not intend to plead for mercy?"

She hesitated. "Not exactly. I understand you cannot overlook what she did. But I would ask you to
match her punishment to her character. If you strip
her of rank and hope, she becomes nothing to Veraene. With the right handling, she could mature into
a valuable soldier."

Joannis leaned back in his chair. One by one, he
touched his fingers together. Counting. Calculating. "I
see. Well, I will take your argument into account."

His tone indicated that their interview was over. Ilse
stood, reluctantly. Joannis had explicitly warned her
against the subject of Raul Kosenmark. She could
hardly ask him to forward the news about the Károvín
ships, never mind the possible link to Morennioù.
"Thank you for speaking with me."

Joannis smiled briefly. "Thank you for trusting me."

Her gaze flicked up in surprise. He nodded. She
started to speak, but he motioned her to silence. "You
should know that I've sent word about today's events

to Duenne. No doubt you heard that we took prisoners. Consider that our king might send a trusted representative to oversee their interrogation. It makes for an interesting situation," he added.

Meaning that the king's representative would investigate all aspects of the invasion, including her involvement. She, too, would have to tread carefully.

"I see," Ilse breathed. "Thank you for the information."

Back in her rooms, she found someone had taken away the tray. The door had been locked, she was certain. Nevertheless, she made a circuit, checking all her belongings, from books, to any records she kept for Mistress Andeliess, to her weapons and clothing. Nothing missing. Nothing misplaced.

Except one kiss.

And my sense of honor.

GALENA WOKE AT sunrise, to chimes signaling the quarter hour.

She had been dreaming again, the vivid dreams called life memories. An enormous raptor had swooped down and snatched her away from a blood-soaked battlefield. She remembered the stab of its claws, her hands losing hold of her sword, which spun down to the field below. Her ears still rang with screams from the dying soldiers, with the raptor's harsh cry as it bore her upward, ever upward.

You were a soldier then, too. You served the king. You were good and brave.

Or was I?

Galena veered away from that question. She knew very little about her previous lives, only that she had fought and fought again. She never knew the end of the battle though, no matter how much she wished to see that moment. Perhaps it was Toc's will, to keep soldiers brave in the face of death.

The thought comforted her.

Eyes closed, she lay still, listening to the rattle of the reed blinds, like an echo of wind from the raptor's flight. A rose-red light pressed against her eyelids. It was early yet. All around, the rest of her wing and file slept in their cots. Many of them snored. Marelda, in the cot next to Galena, stirred restlessly. On the other side, Ranier murmured, as if talking to himself in a dream.

Soon the watch bells would ring. Soon her companions would burst into motion, flinging themselves into another day. Oh, but not like yesterday. Nothing could match the thundering of her pulse, the crash of swords as she joined with the others against the enemy. Adler might even choose her for a patrol to hunt down that Károvín officer. Tallo had mentioned that her tracking skills were better than average.

The barracks door creaked. Galena sat up in time to see Falco stalk noiselessly into the room. His gaze caught hers. He gestured sharply for her to come outside. Galena rolled from her cot and peeled off her nightshirt. She struggled into her tunic and trousers. With boots in hand, she hurried into the hall where Falco paced, scowling. "Adler wants to see you," he said.

"Do I have time to wash?"

"I doubt it. She said she wants you sooner than now."

Galena grinned. It was just as she had imagined. Adler wanted to tell her first, in private, about the patrol. She saluted Falco, then pulled on her boots and was racing across the garrison yard to the officers' quarters. The guards admitted her at once. Clearly they had expected her. Encouraged, Galena jogged up the stairs to the commander's office. She paused in the stairwell long enough to smooth her tunic before she presented herself to the guards outside Adler's door.

"Send her in," came Adler's reply to their announcement.

Galena marched into the room, stopped, and felt the blood drain from her face.

The regional governor stood behind the commander's desk. She'd only seen Lord Joannis from a distance before. He looked older, plainer, despite the silk tunic with its gold embroidery. Next to him stood Thea Adler. Her close-cropped hair gleamed silver. A thin scar ran the length of her jaw. She had fought in the ranks, decades ago. When Galena saluted, Adler glanced in her direction, her face blank of emotion.

"Tell us about the Károvín officer," she said.

The room closed around her, hot and stifling. *Ilse lied to me* was her first thought. Her second was to explain everything. She choked back those words. Adler hated excuses. Her only chance was to give a straightforward report. Right. She swallowed once to wet her throat—it did no good—and gave a brisk nod.

"I was part of the troops ordered to the western shore," she said. "When the fighting started, we pressed forward to join the rest. A man came at me. He was very strong. He drove me back. Before I knew it, he'd knocked me to the ground. When I looked up, he had disappeared, but then I saw one of my companions in need. I went to his assistance at once. By the time the battle ended, it seemed clear that we had killed or captured all the enemy."

There, that was the truth. She had not actually yielded to the man. She had tried to hold him back. She wasn't a coward. And he might have died in the fighting. It was possible.

Adler leaned close to Joannis; they conferred in an inaudible murmur.

"He made no attempt to kill you," the governor said to Galena.

"No. I-I think he believed he had."

Again, Adler and the governor spoke in whispers. Adler seemed unhappy. She argued in a fierce undertone until Joannis cut her off with an abrupt gesture. "The decision is mine," he said. "And the responsibility. If you disagree, file a formal complaint with our new senior commander. Meanwhile, I want you to have that patrol readied and out before the next hour. I will talk to our soldier here."

Adler gave a stiff salute. "As you wish, my lord."

She shot a penetrating glare in Galena's direction as she marched from the room.

The door clicked shut. They were alone now, she and the governor. Galena's mouth turned dry. Joannis, in turn, studied her in silence. She wished he would offer her water, or even cold tea, but he only continued to observe her with those calm dark eyes, eyes that reminded her of the raptor in her dreams.

"We know what happened," he said softly.

She started. "What do you mean, my lord?"

"You let him go. You failed to report that to your captain and your commander. You betrayed—"

"My lord, no—"

"Do not lie to me, Galena Alighero."

"I'm not lying. My lord, I—"

Joannis cut her off with a wave of his hand. "For all your bravery afterward, you let that man go. Then you failed to report the matter to your captain and your commander. Then you asked another person to plead your case with me. Which act makes you the coward, Galena Alighero? The first one? Or the last? And do not tell me that you acted by impulse. You deliberately withheld information from your officers. I cannot overlook what you did. So. Your punishment."

In a soft, level voice, he detailed that punishment. She was to lose a step in rank. She would report every night for the dark watch at the harbor, followed by the dawn cleanup detail. That would last six months, after which the commanders and Joannis would review her situation. Gradually she took in that she had not lost her post, nor would they whip her, or lock her in prison. It was a far kinder punishment than she would have expected.

When he finished speaking, Joannis stood. Galena saluted, thinking he meant to dismiss her, but the governor shook his head "We are not yet done."

He took a cloth from a drawer. It was a square of gray cotton, with a single word painted in black dye. Even though she couldn't read, she saw the characters were different. Set in reverse, she realized. Her pulse gave an uncomfortable leap. He had it ready. It never mattered what she said. He had her punishment set.

"What does it say?" she demanded.

Then cursed herself. Stupid, stupid. You never spoke to a lord and governor like that. Even she knew better.

Joannis seemed indifferent to her response. "The word says *Honor*," he said. "Come here."

She took a halting step forward. Joannis closed the distance and laid the cloth over her cheek. It stung, like hot needles. Frightened, she started to pull away, but he gripped her arm firmly. "It's magic," he told her. "Hold still or it will hurt more."

He spoke a few words in some strange harsh tongue she'd never heard before. Her cheek burned. A sharp green scent filled the air, so strong she could taste it in the back of her throat. It was the same scent she'd

detected the morning of the battle—a scent of wood-
land and earth and resin, as if she were drowning in
pine needles.

The magic vanished. Taken by surprise, Galena staggered. Joannis caught her by the elbow and pulled her
to standing. His grip was stronger than she expected.
He gave her a shake. She drew a shuddering breath.
Felt the strange numbness recede. Lord Joannis studied her face with narrowed eyes before he released his
hold.

"What have you done?" she whispered.

"This." He took a polished square of brass from his
desk and handed it to her. It was just like the mirrors
she had seen inside Mistress Andeliess's pleasure house,
though the images from this one were blurred. She
tilted it this way and that, until she caught the reflection of her own face.

And hissed in surprise.

Strong black lines marked her cheek. She touched
her fingertips to them. Felt a buzzing under her skin, as
though the magic had imprinted something inside her.

"The marks are temporary," Joannis said. "If anyone asks its meaning, you are to tell them that you
chose your safety and your comfort over your honor.
Those words exactly. If you fail to repeat that speech,
the punishment is expulsion and prison."

Temporary. That was some relief.

"How long then? A month. Two?"

"A year."

"But—" Her hand flew up to her cheek. "My lord.
Please. Not that long. I can't—"

"You must. Or you will resign your post as soldier
and spend that year in prison."

One year. Galena bit down on her protests. It was
more than she deserved, she told herself. Still, it took
all her self-control to keep the explanations from

rising up like the spring floods. She kept silent until she was certain she could speak steadily. He would expect that. And he would remember how she received this punishment.

"Thank you, my lord," she whispered. "For giving me a chance."

He nodded. And in his grim expression she realized it was a chance, however difficult the next year might prove.

THAT AFTERNOON, TANGLED in unwanted and unfamiliar sleep, so that she would wake in time for her new duties, she dreamed another life dream—a long and grueling battle, where smoky figures wielded flames as their swords. The battle had endured for centuries. Death was its sole release. Yet death meant dishonor. So she labored on and on with that heavy sword, knowing she obeyed the king.

CHAPTER SEVEN

ILSE WOKE HOURS past the usual time.

She lurched upright in her bed, panicked. She had missed drill practice. Spenglar would not tolerate idleness. She'd heard him lecture the junior soldiers often enough.

Bellsong vibrated through the air, a loud ugly clanging. She clapped her hands over her ears. A sour taste coated her mouth, and her head felt stuffed with dust and cobwebs. Eight, nine bells. Not as late as she feared, but too late for weapons drill. She wondered why no one had awakened her before. Usually Alesso—

Alesso Valturri. He was a spy. And she had kissed him.

What have I done?

She groaned, sick at the unwanted memory. Oh, there were any number of excuses she might give—the sleepless nights, the anxiety of the moment, the wine and drugs. He had used magic, too. As if that mattered. She had kissed him willingly. That was the truth.

And from that single day, all has changed, Tanja Duhr had written. *One word spoken, one suppressed. One hand clasped, let go. And so the future spins away from us, transformed. Though all we possess remains the same, we gaze upon each thing with different eyes.*

Ilse rubbed her aching head until the throbbing stopped, and the bellsong faded. Her stomach felt queasy, but not from the wine or the late hours. *Regret,* she thought. Even that was too simplistic an answer.

She threw off her covers and stumbled into the next room. It looked so ordinary in the daylight. No mysterious notes tucked beneath her water jug. Her writing desk appeared just as she'd left it when Galena had come to her door. A thin film of dust covered her desk, blown in from the open shutters. Ordinary, yes. And yet, she had the sense of stepping into a false world, painted with shadows and not substance.

Ilse rang for a maid to bring her a fresh water jug and a breakfast tray. By the time she returned from the baths, the maids appeared with her water and breakfast. There was the freshly grilled sunfish, as well as the bread, olive oil, and soft white cheese. One of the girls sent her a sidelong glance as they set out the dishes and cups.

She knew that kind of look. *They've heard rumors. Someone saw Alesso half-drag me to my room. Someone else knows I went out late last night.*

The bread and coffee went down more easily than she thought, and soon the last traces of the drug and the long night vanished. She dressed in a clean gown. Her hair she bound back in a loose braid. Her eyes were like dark smudges, but her appearance would do well enough. They might suspect her of a dalliance, but nothing more.

After several false starts, she settled into her ordinary routine.

She sorted through her notes for the house's expenses. Reports had arrived from the capital about new taxes and fees, which she incorporated in the file. Soon after that, the house agent came by with the receipts for the current month. Ilse spent the next two hours comparing them against the estimated income from the previous year. She usually found these tasks soothing and absorbing, but today she could not concentrate. All the breezes had died. Her rooms were entirely too still and hot. With nothing else to distract her, Ilse's attention wavered between the rows of numbers and the previous day's events.

If only she could pretend yesterday had never happened.

Oh, but it did.

Finally, she set aside her papers and set off for the kitchen. No sign of Alesso. If he had changed shifts with Daria, he might still be asleep. She made a circuit of the pleasure house, starting on the top floor where the servants had their dormitories, then down and around through the bedchambers and parlors, and to the common room.

Here, the kitchen boys and girls were laying out the first refreshments. Courtesans were just appearing for the day. Ysbel lounged on a couch, dressed in a filmy gown of transparent white, under which her nipples showed a rich ruddy brown. Stefan, too, was bathed and perfumed for an early appointment. Perhaps the grain merchant had requested a private audience.

Ilse paused, wondering where to search next, when she caught a glimpse of Alesso across the room. The next moment, he disappeared into the servants' corridor. Ilse caught up the skirts of her gown and ran after him.

She overtook him outside the kitchen doors. Alesso spun around. For one moment, she had the impression of a leopard cornered by the hunt. The look vanished, and he smiled—a warm and friendly smile that would have convinced anyone of his delight in seeing her.

You would almost convince me, Ilse thought. *Except for last night.*

"We must talk," she said.

His eyes widened. "What about? The sweet spring day? About Cook's temper if I dally with you? I fear that I cannot risk—"

"Stop it," Ilse said in a low voice. "You know exactly what I mean. We must talk. Unless you wish me to tell Mistress Andeliess how you drugged me last night. The choice is yours."

The light in the corridor was dim. On the other side of the kitchen doors, Ilse heard the rising activity of kitchen workers as they prepared refreshments for Mistress Andeliess's customers, but for the moment, she and Alesso had privacy. She could not read his expression, disguised by the shifting shadows, but when she laid a hand on his arm, she felt his muscles go tense. His chin jerked up. He glanced right and left.

"Come with me," he said.

He led her through the kitchen, already hot and noisy. Scullions were hauling in vast buckets of water from the wells, while kitchen girls and boys stood around several worktables, washing greens, chopping leeks and onions, or stirring sauces. Ghita Fiori, the chief cook, stood in one corner, shouting directions. Alesso waved in her direction, but never paused when she called to him.

Alesso led Ilse through the outer doors and into the maze of narrow lanes behind the pleasure house. They passed a series of miscellaneous shops, whose upper stories were let as single rooms. Three steps led down to a small courtyard. Several rain barrels stood against one wall. Wind-blown trash had lodged in the corners, and the walls were water-stained, giving the place a desolate air. "Here," he said.

Ilse scanned for open windows or doors. None were

visible. A second gate marked a narrow passageway between two houses, but a quick examination showed that it ended in an even smaller courtyard, entirely surrounded by houses. It was private here, more than she would have expected so close to the pleasure house and the very public squares nearby. And their meeting here would only confirm the gossip about last night's supposed dalliance. Perhaps that was a good thing.

Meanwhile, Alesso had leaned against a wall, his arms folded. Despite his seemingly warm smile, she could tell he had slept no better than she had. Still, his expression was guarded, and seemingly alert enough that she would not find it easy to trap or trick him.

"You have questions," he said. "Ask them."

She started with the obvious one. "Tell me who you work for."

"I work for Ghita the Cook."

Ilse rolled her eyes. "Oh really. I would never have guessed. You gave me drugged wine. Why?"

"Curiosity at what you might say or do. An unrelenting desire for mischief. What do you think?"

It was a challenge. She took it.

She threw out a string of suppositions, each one more outrageous than the last. Alesso shrugged, indifferent. Ilse paced back and forth in front of him. Clearly he would not succumb to threats. She had to surprise him. She threw out a number of names, some of them true, some entirely invention, but he merely yawned. She nearly admitted her connection to Raul, but that was a trick she would have to save for a last and desperate throw.

"You have an extraordinary imagination," Alesso said, when she paused.

"Angry," she replied back. "I dislike being spied upon. You are someone's minion, however sweetly you smile at me. Perhaps not Lord Khandarr's, but what about the garrison commanders'? They might keep a watch on strangers to Osterling, especially after the past few days."

"I would hardly work for the king's commanders."

Ilse swung around. "Why do you say that?"

"No reason."

"You always have a reason," she said softly. "You pretended friendship, kindness. I almost believed you. How foolish of me."

His lips curled into a mocking smile. "Oh dear. How terrible of me. My heart bleeds like Brother Toc for Sister Lir. For surely *you* would never lie to me. That would be unforgivable between colleagues."

Again that word *colleagues*. Was he one of Raul's spies, then?

Impossible. She and Raul had agreed never to risk any contact. This had to be a ruse. Very carefully she said, "I have never lied to you."

"Nor have you spoken the truth." He pushed off the wall and came toward her, with the slow easy grace of a stalking leopard. "You are too much of a coward to admit the truth—that you are as much a spy as I am."

"I am not a coward."

He laughed, deep in his throat, and pressed onward until she retreated to the opposite wall of the court-yard. There he pinned her, a hand on either side of her throat, his face inches from hers. Heat shimmered between them. The scent of bergamot and ginger, of the possibility of more than a single kiss, hung in the air. Ilse's pulse leapt to a faster pace. She considered a dozen tactics to disable Alesso. No doubt he would counter those tactics with his own.

"*Do* you work for Markus Khandarr?" she said.

"No."

She grasped his wrist and pressed her thumb between the fine bones. His pulse beat as quick and light as hers. Even as she counted the beats, she heard his breath catch as he tried to control himself. So he was not as calm and self-possessed as he wished to appear. That pleased her. She loosened her grip and tilted her chin up. No invitation today. Her mouth was tight and angry. "Then you work for nothing and no one. A child playing games."

"Is that what you think?"

He bent down to kiss her. Ilse swung both hands up and snapped them to either side. Before he could react, she punched her knuckles into his chest.

He gasped and stumbled backward. Good. She'd meant to hurt him. Swiftly, she sidestepped him and made for the gate. Alesso grabbed her by the wrist and swung her around. He checked her before she could twist under his arm to free herself. "Listen to me."

"Let go."

"I will. After you listen." He glared down at her, his expression so grim, she hardly recognized him. "What I do and who I work for is no business of yours. But for your own sake, you should understand that not everyone is like your Lord Kosenmark. Not all *games* concern the Veraenen king and his court."

With that he released her and stalked through the open gate.

Ilse stared after him, absently rubbing her wrist. No, he was no spy for Markus Khandarr—of that she felt certain. But definitely a spy. She would have to act even more carefully in front of him, in front of everyone else, from now on. She could only hope her caution did not come too late.

CHAPTER EIGHT

ONLY A WEEK had gone by since Gerek Hessler came to Lord Kosenmark's pleasure house. On the surface, his days passed easily enough. He dealt with an abundance of correspondence and invitations. At times, Lord Kosenmark ordered him to research obscure points in history, or to confirm a quotation by a particular poet for a letter. All very ordinary tasks, some more interesting than others.

And yet he felt a curious displacement from his surroundings. Not in his office, where he spent most of his hours. He had made the office into a home of sorts, filled with comfortable, useful things, much like his private quarters in his father's household. Mistress Denk had assisted Gerek with choosing furniture from the pleasure house's stores. Lord Kosenmark had offered several antique maps. And Gerek himself had arranged everything to his liking.

But whenever he ventured beyond the narrow confines of his duties, and into the common rooms or public parlors, he felt as though he were a lost soul, barely visible to the more substantial inhabitants of this enormous and mazelike house. Fortunately, Lord Kosenmark kept Gerek too busy to worry about such things.

Today, for example.

An open crate sat on the floor next to Gerek's desk. Six more waited in the corner, still bound with leather straps, and sealed with locks bearing the insignia of House Valentain. The crates were filled with books, and had arrived the day before from Duke Kosenmark, a gift to increase his son's already substantial library. Gerek's task was to record each book by title, author, and probable date of publication, then compare the list against an existing catalog drawn up several years before by the old secretary, Berthold Hax. Any duplicates would return to the ducal estates.

Gerek took the next book and carefully unwrapped the layers of cloth protecting it. *An Account of Morennioù, written by Hêr Commander Dimarus Maszny.* It was the man's personal memoirs of leading an expedition to annex the island province of Morennioù. Inside, Maszny himself had written an inscription to Duke Andreas Koszenmarc, in memory of their friendship. A truly valuable book, which dated from almost a hundred years before the civil wars.

Resisting the urge to leaf through the delicate pages, Gerek recorded the necessary information. Outside, the bell towers tolled the hour, followed by three quarter hour chimes. Almost noon. Hanne or Dana would come by soon with his dinner.

He laid his pen down and blew upon the paper. Eighteen volumes accomplished. Two hundred more remained. He stretched to ease the ache in his shoulders and arm. It was quiet at this hour. Most of the courtesans were still asleep. Elsewhere, the chambermaids were freshening the private suites and parlors, and making the common room ready for the clients. Lord Kosenmark himself had risen well before sunrise for weapons drill. He had spent the usual two hours

with Gerek, going over the week's schedule and this
latest delivery from Valentain. Now he was out riding
with Lord Vieth and several other nobles.

With another flick of his attention to the door, Gerek slid a small diary from inside his tunic. Here was
where he recorded his observations about Kosenmark
and the household. It was a habit left over from his
university days, when his professors had recommended
the students keep journals for lecture notes, findings
in their research, anything to help sift through the de-
tritus of history.

He thumbed through the book, scanning the notes
he had accumulated so far.

> . . . House located in an exclusive neighborhood,
> midway between the merchant district and the
> governor's palace. Numerous servants, as you
> might expect for a man of his station. More
> guards than the usual complement, however, and
> nearly all chosen from his father's private men.
> Then there are the courtesans. Sixteen. Men and
> women equally. Two followed him from Duenne.
> The rest he recruited after his arrival in Tiralien.
> None openly acknowledge his political connec-
> tions though they are all aware of the listening
> devices built into the house . . .
>
> . . . Lord Kosenmark rises early for morning
> weapons drill. Day divided between his own con-
> cerns (house, staff, etc.) and visits to other nobles
> in the city. Note: of the names D. mentioned as
> especial friends—Lord Benno Iani, Baron Rudol-
> fus Eckard, Lady Emma Theysson (memo: Lady
> Iani by recent marriage)—none visit the house,
> not even for the general evening entertainment,
> nor does he accept invitations from them. What
> invitations he does accept are of the most unex-

ceptional kind, completely unlike the stories D.
told me . . .

That was not entirely accurate. He had found all the
luxury and decadence Dedrick had described. There
were the perpetual feasts and games and a pervading
air of the sexual. He'd met the famous courtesans:
Nadine and Eduard, Josef, Tatiana, and the astonishingly beautiful Adelaide, who had pleasured the old
king, Baerne of Angersee, himself.

Adelaide's name recalled the latest scrap of
information—that Adelaide intended to leave the pleasure house for Mistress Luise Ehrenalt's establishment.
Ehrenalt was a high-ranking member of the silk weav-
er's guild. She was also a former member of Kosenmark's shadow court. Gerek wrote that down, too.

He paused, pen hovering over the page as he tried
to fit all these disparate clues into a single coherent
picture. He had come here to uncover the treasonous
actions of a self-indulgent lord. Instead he had found
an almost ordinary household. If one could call courtesans and their clients ordinary.

Which reminded him. He blotted his last comment,
turned the page, and wrote:

> *. . . And there is the cook's daughter, Kathe*
> *Raendl, whose position is higher in the household*
> *than I had first estimated. It appears she is her*
> *mother's chief assistant, and more. The girl*
> *Hanne tells me Kathe had befriended Ilse Zha-*
> *lina even before IZ worked in the kitchens. It*
> *was she Lord Kosenmark chose to attend the*
> *young woman through her illness, and she who*
> *trained her in the kitchen. Even after IZ turned*
> *secretary then lover, she retained KR as a trusted*
> *friend, until her own break with Lord K. . . .*

"Maester Hessler?"

Gerek dropped his pen, spattering ink over his note-book and the desk. Cursing softly, he mopped up the spill with his sleeve. His notebook page was smeared, but the script was clear enough. He could copy it over later. He slid the book inside his jacket. "Yes?"

Kathe Raendl backed into the room with a heavily laden tray. Gerek drew a quick breath at the sight of her face. It was too much of a coincidence, his notes, her arrival moments later. He could almost believe she'd used Kosenmark's spy holes, except it was so unlike her character.

"I knocked three times," she said. "And it is after noon."

"I-I-I—" He stopped. Forced out a breath. "I am sorry," he said with deliberate slowness. "I was distracted. So much work."

"Ah, distracted. How often have I heard that explanation? It's as common as mold and dust. Perhaps I should talk to Lord Kosenmark about airing this office, if not the entire wing."

Gerek shot a suspicious glance in her direction. She had never teased him before. Unlike Kosenmark, she never finished his sentences for him. She waited until he mastered his wretched tongue, forcing out syllable after painful syllable, then helped him work his way back to simple conversation.

Kathe coughed and nodded at his desk. "Do you wish to take your meal here? Or shall I find a parlor elsewhere in the wing?"

Hurriedly he cleared off a space. Kathe set down the tray and laid out several covered dishes, a carafe of fresh cold water, a second of strong coffee brewed just as he liked. From her demure expression, he might have believed her yet another kitchen girl, but he had seen her name throughout Mistress Denk's accounts.

She had lately taken over reporting the kitchen expenditures. She also shared the responsibility for designing the splendid feasts given in Lord Kosenmark's pleasure house. Denk had commented that Kathe could command a position in any noble's household as chief cook. He wondered why she lingered here, as a mere assistant.

His attention on these speculations, he reached for his water cup. His hand accidentally brushed Kathe's. He felt the brief warmth of contact, heard her intake of breath.

Gerek jerked his hand back. "S-s-s-sssorr— Oh damn it!"

He thrust himself away from the desk with both hands and shut his eyes. He could not bear to see her shocked expression. Because she would be shocked. They always were. They never understood his shame.

Kathe remained silent, still. He could sense her presence, however, just on the other side of his desk. He wanted to order her away, but he could tell his tongue would not obey him, not for many long moments. Nor did he dare to open his eyes and meet her gaze. He could not tell what he might do if he saw pity on her face. He'd had enough of pity.

"You have nothing to be sorry for," Kathe said softly.

So she had understood. He opened his mouth to speak, felt a betraying tremor in his throat, and shook his head. After another long silence, he heard her quietly exit the room.

He let his head sink onto his hands. It was always the same. *My father and grandfather are right. I am a fool. Oh Dedrick. You needed a bolder, braver cousin than I.*

From far away came the soft chimes of the quarter hour, echoed by the house clocks. He drew a long breath and glanced at his meal with distaste. The delicately spiced fish, the rice dotted with leeks and peppercorn, all cooked and presented with care, turned his stomach. He drank his cup of water slowly to ease the nausea. Tomorrow was his first full holiday. He wished it had come today. He badly wanted to escape this house for a few hours.

He stacked the dishes onto the tray and carried it to the sideboard for later. Back at his desk, he picked up the next book from the crate. Another set of memoirs, from a member of court in the late empire days. Gerek sighed. The task reminded him of the few, vague life dreams that visited his sleep. *I have always been a clerk, writing down others' deeds.*

"Hessler."

Lord Kosenmark stood in the open doorway. Had he knocked? Gerek couldn't remember. He curbed the urge to touch the diary, hidden inside his jacket. "My lord?"

"There's been a change in my schedule," Kosenmark said.

He still wore his riding clothes from this morning—a sober costume of dark blue wool, edged in darker blue silk, and speckled with raindrops. Blue, the mourning color of Károví. Was that a subtle signal, or merely coincidence? Then Gerek took in more of Kosenmark's appearance. The tense, straight line of his mouth. How the man's eyes had turned opaque, as if the eternal golden sun behind them had set.

"Well?" Kosenmark said. "Why aren't you writing this down?"

"My lord?"

"A visit to Lord Demeyer's country estates," Kosenmark said, with the tone of repeating himself. "Expect me to be absent three days. Make my excuses to anyone who requires it. That is one of your responsibilities, no? Never mind. I do not need an answer today."

He swept from the room, leaving Gerek teetering between apology and outrage.

WITHIN THE HOUR, Lord Kosenmark had departed on horseback. A carriage with trunks and servants and outriders followed. It was all so unnecessary, Gerek thought, as he returned to his office and his untouched meal. A great deal of show for nothing at all. He nibbled at the rice, then forced down a few mouthfuls of fish and a sweet pale pudding. With food, his headache eased, and he was able to concentrate on the current situation.

Kosenmark had left. He would not return for three days—the number of trunks guaranteed that. So. Yes. It was time for the next stage of Gerek's long-laid plans.

No one would notice anything he did. They all expected him to hide in his office or his private chambers. Gerek set the dinner tray outside his office for the kitchen maids. He locked his door with keys and magic provided by Kosenmark himself. (A sign that Kosenmark did not entirely trust his household. Gerek reminded himself to note this later in his book.)

Up the silent echoing staircase he padded, past the bright-lit windows overlooking the grounds, to the landing outside Kosenmark's private rooms. With the lord absent, no runner waited in the alcove beside the door. Gerek had prepared an excuse just in case, but he breathed in relief that he didn't need to explain himself.

The door to Kosenmark's office was locked. Gerek had expected that. He withdrew a bloodstained handkerchief from his pocket, which he laid against the keyhole.

The idea had come to him six months ago, soon after he learned about Dedrick's death. He'd been researching the early empire days, and the closer relationship between mages and rulers, when he came across the spell. It involved hiding the user's identity, their magical signature, behind another. Used without embellishment, it created a blank in place of the signature. Tricky. And not necessarily foolproof. A trained mage could detect its use. But the only mage among Lord Kosenmark's friends was Lord Iani, and his later investigations confirmed that Lord Iani had not visited the house for months.

There was a second variation of the spell. If you added the physical traces of a second magic worker, the spell would imprint that other person's signature atop your own. The older accounts spoke of flesh or skin. Gerek had dismissed that as too difficult. But then Kosenmark had come to Gerek's office with a fresh-bleeding cut from his morning weapons drill. Gerek had offered Kosenmark his own handkerchief, then accepted the cloth back with barely concealed excitement.

Ei rûf ane gôtter. Komen mir de strôm.

The air pulsed, turned thicker and more pungent—a clear sign that he had deflected a portion of magic's current into the ordinary world. It was a sensation he had grown used to over the past few months. He was no expert magic-worker, of course. But he had a scholar's stubbornness and the luxury of solitude, which had allowed him to study and to practice until he had achieved success with a handful of spells.

Ei rûf ane gôtter. Ei rûf ane Lir unde Toc. . . .

Now a strong fresh scent washed over him, like grass crushed underfoot, or the traces of pine carried by the mountain breeze. He breathed it in, sensed a

new fluency in his poor lame tongue. There were a
thousand descriptions of how magic tasted and smelled.
None of them were right, all of them were true. Gerek
continued to recite the spell, words of the long-dead
Erythandran language, which rolled from his mouth
with an ease he'd never experienced before.

*Lâzen mir drînnen Lord Raul Anton Maximilian
Kosenmark.*

His skin rippled, as though he were a metal speck
caught halfway between two powerful magnets. Then
he felt an inward ping. The current vanished, and the
latch gave an audible click of release.

Gerek had to stop himself from laughing out loud.
The spell had worked, mangled tongue and all. Then
the urgency of his position overtook him. He stuffed
the handkerchief into his pocket and pushed the door
open.

Eight days. Twice or three times each day, he had
entered this room. Today, he saw everything with fresh
eyes, and a mind undisturbed by the presence of others.

It was a place of beauty and quiet and light. Polished red tiles lined the floors. Shelves with books and
fine rare statuary covered nearly every wall. Here and
there were tables with carvings in ivory or gemstones,
done in the modern style. Off in the corner stood the
sand glass he'd noticed that first day, an expensive
contraption built from pulleys and weights, fashioned
from rare metals and pure blown glass of enormous
size. Through the windows of the opposite wall he
glimpsed the rooftop garden—as yet unexplored territory. The scent of sandalwood hung in the air, like a
memory of the man who ruled here.

Gerek went immediately to the iron letter box next
to Kosenmark's desk. His key opened the top lid. Inside was a wide slot where Kosenmark had instructed

him to insert any letters that arrived during his master's absence. He laid the handkerchief over the hinges and lock.

Ei rûf ane gôtter. Ei rûf ane Lir unde Toc.

The magic current sighed into existence. Faster now, he recited the words for the spell and spoke Lord Kosenmark's full name again. The current flickered with a short-lived tension. Disappeared almost before he could register its presence. A long moment passed before he could take that in. Less confident now, he tried the spell for his own letter box, but substituting Kosenmark's name. Nothing, not even the faintest buzz of magic, as though the current itself recognized the futility of his attempt.

Gerek blew out a breath, disappointed.

Well, and if the first interpretation of an old document yields nothing, we try another theory, another approach.

Or another room.

Two more doors opened from Kosenmark's office. One led onto the rooftop gardens. Gerek would explore that region later, if necessary. If he had time and opportunity. The second door was the key, he decided. It led into Kosenmark's inner rooms—to his bedroom, and other secret chambers that Dedrick had mentioned to Gerek alone, and then only briefly, almost reluctantly.

He turned the chosen door handle. It gave way at once—unlocked. Not surprising, he told himself. The man employed dozens of guards to patrol the grounds. Still, his pulse beat faster as Gerek stepped cautiously over the threshold.

It was a dimly lit world of branching corridors that he faced. One lamp burned low in its bracket just inside the door, and farther off, a shaft of light penetrated from a window set in the ceiling, but for the most part, he had to pick his way through darkness. As his eyes adjusted to the gloom, he took in the details—a miniature reading room off to one side, a closet with rich costumes, another closet with clothing wrapped in herb-scented covers. He passed by these, then paused beside a long narrow corridor, fitted with grills in the floor and along its walls. That had to be the listening room, where Kosenmark could spy on his own courtesans and guests, if he wished. Dust covered the floor, untouched.

The bedroom itself offered more surprises. From Dedrick's comments, Gerek had expected an unrestrained opulence—a room swathed in silks and pearls, to use the fanciful words of the more romantic poets. Perhaps he had banished the excessive luxury along with Dedrick, because though the room was furnished with items of good quality, it was hardly a sybaritic vision.

He started with the superficial and the obvious—the clothes-presses, the vast trunk in one corner, the closets, and underneath the bed itself. Off in one corner stood a small desk. Gerek lifted the lid to find the usual writing materials, a few half-finished letters about nothing. If those were coded, they were beyond him. Maybe the next time he visited, he could make copies.

He had a momentary burst of excitement when he discovered a series of recessed buttons behind the desk's main compartment. He pressed one. The bottom of the desk's interior slid back to reveal a small space. Inside, however, was nothing more than a single book.

Gerek picked up the book. A volume of poems, by Tanja Duhr. An antique, judging by the worn leather cover and old-fashioned lettering. Tucked between the pages was a thin strip of paper, with writing in Kosenmark's hand.

To Ilse Zhalina. A gift in return for your gift of conscience and truth. Thank you.

Carefully he replaced the book and shut the desk. It took him several moments to recover his outward composure. His inward composure was another matter. Clearly the book was a gift from one lover to another. And she had returned it. Did that mean their break was genuine? If it was, why did he keep the book in a desk by his bed?

Questions and more questions. He'd come for answers.

A further, more careful search revealed no secret compartments in the bedposts, nor any loose planks in the floor. The few other spells he'd mastered revealed nothing.

After an hour, he worked his way back through the various chambers and rooms and closets, to the outer office once more. Though no fire burned on the fourth floor, his clothes were soaked through with sweat, and he itched from the dust coating his skin. He sank into the chair behind Kosenmark's desk and surveyed the room.

Imagine yourself in the writer's skin, one of his professors had said. *Use their words to see and smell and taste the world they lived in. History is not an abstract. It is blood and passion. It is real.*

Gerek tried to imagine being Lord Raul Kosenmark, a man born to wealth and privilege. Someone ambitious enough at fourteen to have himself emasculated, just to retain his family's position as councillors to the king. *Impossible. I cannot imagine it.*

He made a second, more perfunctory search of the desk and drawers. Nothing. Either Kosenmark was entirely innocent, or he'd hidden everything in that damned letter box, locked with a spell Gerek could not begin to guess at.

He hauled the letter box onto the desk and began to examine its surface. It was square, its width and height no longer than his forearm. The polished iron surface showed a blurry reflection of Gerek's face. Much like Kosenmark's eyes.

He ran his fingers over the surface. There were no obvious signs of magic, but he knew Kosenmark would have protected this box with magic set into the iron itself. Any attempt to break through the sides would trigger another set of spells to destroy its contents. Still, for every spell to safeguard a box, there existed another to breach those protections. He was no mage, but he could hire one to do the work. Or he might risk everything and simply carry the box to Duenne. He was calculating how he might smuggle himself and the box from the house when he heard footsteps. He heaved the box off the desk and tried to erase all traces of his activities.

Not soon enough.

The door crashed open. Raul Kosenmark appeared in the gap. He stared at Gerek with a hard unblinking gaze.

"So," he said. "Maester Hessler. No, let us use your proper name. Lord Haszler. Lord Gerek Haszler. Have you found what you were looking for?"

CHAPTER NINE

GEREK FROZE. ONE hand still gripped the letter box by its handles, the other the edge of the desk. He considered a mad dash for the door. Quashed the urge before he'd done more than make a convulsive movement to stand. A far deeper silence had dropped over the room, and he distinctly heard the sand hissing as it fell from one globe to another in the vast hourglass behind him.

"Don't bother answering," Kosenmark said. "I doubt you could just now."

Blood rushed to Gerek's cheeks. He released his hold on the letter box and straightened up. "I-I can s-speak, my lord."

"Then explain."

Kosenmark's voice was high and light. Gerek did not mistake that for fear. Anger. Certainty. An arrogance greater than any king's. Was there anything that frightened the man?

A moonless midnight in the soul. A shadow over hope.

Words from a poet who lived centuries ago. Strange how they eased the tightness in his chest. He took his time, however, releasing each syllable in order.

"You s-set a trap, my lord. I fell in."

Kosenmark's lips parted in silent laughter. "Lies. Though very pretty ones. The trap was yours, Lord Gerek. *You* fashioned it when you wrote me two months ago, inquiring about a position as my secretary."

He glided into the room. The door swung shut behind him, cutting off all sounds from outside. Kosenmark paced toward the desk and set both hands on its surface. Gerek fell back into the chair. It took an effort of will just to breathe. For the first time, he noticed the weapons Kosenmark wore at his belt. The sheaths at both wrists. The glint of chain mail under his shirt.

He goes nowhere unprotected, not even when he rides with his guards.

That was a clue. He would understand it later—if there was a later.

Meanwhile, Kosenmark was speaking in a soft, quick voice. "I did not guess right away. Your résumé and letters of recommendation proved well constructed, and the further inquiries I sent for confirmation were answered just as one might expect. You must have associates, yes?"

Gerek glanced up and away from that bright, intent gaze. He pressed his lips together.

Kosenmark leaned over the desk until his face was only a few inches away. This close, Gerek could see fine lines radiating from the man's eyes. Caught the aroma of horse and sweat and leather. The scent of the man himself. He felt a tightening in his groin, in spite of the terror yammering inside his skull. Perhaps he had more in common with Dedrick than he'd thought.

"Do you work for Lord Markus Khandarr?" Kosenmark said.

"No," Gerek said shortly.

"The king?"

"No." And then, before he thought better, he added, "Do you?"

He regretted the words at once. Kosenmark made a sound, a growl deep in his throat. "You think I'm a traitor?"

What else should I believe? But he could not say that. Not when this man could summon a dozen guards. How easily could they dispose of his body? Far too easily, he decided. Dedrick had talked about the fortified household, the men and women chosen for their loyalty. Gerek had assumed the measures were a defense against robbers, not a private army, but now he wasn't so sure.

"You are thinking too hard," Kosenmark said. "Truth requires but a moment . . ."

"Except in the face of deception," Gerek replied.

And to his surprise, he caught a smile of recognition on Kosenmark's face. The book of poetry, of course. But then he remembered the slip of paper inside. Any quote from Tanja Duhr would surely call Ilse Zhalina to mind.

Do not mention her name, Mistress Denk had warned him.

He loves her beyond reason, Dedrick had said.

Meanwhile, Kosenmark's smile had faded, and he studied Gerek with a new intensity, as though looking beyond the mask of flesh and into Gerek's hidden thoughts. There was no sign of amusement, nor mockery, in that handsome face.

"You think I am a traitor?" he repeated. "Is that what Dedrick told you?"

At the mention of Dedrick's name, Gerek started. "Who told—"

"No one told me. Not outright. Your papers were very good. But you have a slight resemblance to Dedrick, and though Dedrick was no scholar, you both

shared certain turns of phrase. Baron Maszuryn was
another member of the riding party today, and a few
questions told me who you were. So I ask a third time,
do you believe I am a traitor to the kingdom? No, a
better one. Why did you come here?"

No more lies. No more subterfuge. I cannot stand it.

"I came for the truth," he said.

"Ah. That." Kosenmark exhaled and closed his eyes.
"Truth is a chancy thing, soft and dangerous, armed
with sudden sharp edges."

He straightened up and turned around. Clasped his
hands behind his back in a knot. Bookcases and tapestries lined the opposite wall, but Gerek could tell
Kosenmark saw nothing of these, only some vision
within.

"I killed him," Kosenmark said quietly.

Gerek stilled the quiver in his throat.

"Oh, I did not draw the knife myself," Kosenmark
went on. "He came to me several months after we
broke off. Offered to observe matters at Duenne's
Court and send those observations to me, by whatever
means I thought wise. Though he didn't admit it, I
knew he wanted to revive our friendship. For that
reason alone, I nearly refused. But Dedrick was right.
I did need a friend at court—a secret one. I told myself
that Markus Khandarr would not suspect Dedrick
after our very public break. Deception," he murmured,
half to himself. "It was easier to deceive myself than
admit I sent Dedrick into danger I dared not face."

There was a pause. Then, "Do you know how he
died?" Kosenmark said. "Did they tell you that much?"

If Gerek had not believed the room empty of air
before, he did now. "Only what the king's letter said,
my lord."

"Do you believe it?"

The official letter from court stated that Lord

Dedrick Maszuryn died from a fall while riding in the hills north of Duenne. His companions had reported that he'd been unable to control his mount—a stallion that Dedrick had insisted on buying in spite of its wild character. The horse had been destroyed the same day. Dedrick's ashes had been returned in a small silver box, fitted with priceless jewels.

He died by order of the king and his councillor. And no one grieved for him. No one. They uttered the most ordinary of platitudes and then continued with their lives, grateful that they were untouched by the scandal.

"No, my lord."

"Your voice says you guess, however. He died . . ." Kosenmark drew a shuddering breath. "He died at the hand of Lord Markus Khandarr. It was magic. Lord Khandarr demanded the truth. Dedrick gave it to him, but his answer was not the one Lord Khandarr desired. He wanted proof of my treachery and used magic to force a different confession from Dedrick's mouth. And so Dedrick, my friend, my once lover, died for his honesty."

Kosenmark turned around. The brilliance had faded from his complexion. He looked older, and the late-afternoon sunlight, slanting in from the windows by the garden door, threw the lines beside his mouth and eyes into sharper relief than in days past. His cheeks were wet with tears.

"So," he said, "you have the truth. My truth. What now?"

The question caught Gerek by surprise. "I . . . do not know."

The other man smiled. "A fair answer. What do you want, then? What *did* you want?"

"Justice."

He flinched, expecting laughter, but Kosenmark was

nodding. "Justice for the dead. I can understand that. How do you propose to achieve it?"

No explanations. No long tirades to justify himself.

"I don't know," Gerek said. "I-I thought— I meant— Dedrick was very trusting, my lord. Too trusting. He loved you."

There. He'd said it.

"You believe I convinced him to commit treason."

Gerek dared a soundless *yes*.

Kosenmark blew out a breath. "Words are useless. Mere sound of flesh and air. Yes, the poets were right, as always." In a softer voice, he said, "I knew someone who felt as you do. She— They argued against my convictions—called me arrogant and— Well, never mind what they said. Their disbelief was good for me, urged me to do better, at least for a time . . ."

Silence filled the room, except for Gerek's pulse in his ears. The groan of pulleys, the hissing of sand as the hourglass turned end over end, its luminescent grains spilling through the narrow aperture. *Time, time, time slides away from our fingers, even as we try to grasp the moments and seconds.*

"We are at an impasse," Kosenmark said. "So let me propose a new idea. Let me tell you my intentions. Believe me or not, but listen. Stay in my household a few weeks longer and share my work. Judge for yourself if I am a traitor to the kingdom or not."

He went on to speak of the kingdom, of old Baerne of Angersee, and his son who died of drink and despair. Of the present king, Armand, who desired to outshine his grandfather's deeds. And how Lord Markus Khandarr fed the young king's desire for glory, provoking him toward war with Károví without regard for the kingdom's welfare.

"Armand is not the first king to disagree with his councillors," Kosenmark said. "Nor is Lord Khandarr the first councillor to use his position to further his own ambitions. However, I would not see thousands die. Nor can I stand silent while another man drives the king toward such a war, so that he might seize the kingdom for himself. If that is treason, then I am a traitor."

Without another word, he walked to the farther door and onto the rooftop garden. As the door swung shut, a breeze filtered through, carrying the scent of warm air, of green growing things bursting free of the earth. Of the outer world.

Gerek stared at the blank desktop for several long moments. Considered the man Dedrick had spoken of with such admiration. (And love. Let us not forget they loved each other once.) Considered what he'd observed himself over the past eight days. Kosenmark trusted no one. And yet he had offered to open his secrets to Gerek. Was that proof enough of his good intentions?

You came for truth and honor.

I did, Gerek thought.

He stood. Entered the garden and carefully shut the doors behind him. Twilight had fallen. A dusky violet veil covered the sky, brushed by smoke-black clouds. Light speckled the rising hills; lamplight illuminated the city spreading toward the shore. From there, the seas were only visible as a dark expanse.

Gerek made his way between the rows of budding trees, the beds of newly sprouted flowers. Spring had arrived without his being aware.

Kosenmark sat on a bench at the far end of the garden. His hands were clasped, one within the other. He stared outward to the seas, but his eyes obviously saw nothing of this world.

Gerek stopped and thought through the words he wished to say. He did not want to falter.

"Tell me more," he said. "So I might do the work properly."

THEIR CONVERSATION CONTINUED to midnight, first in the rooftop garden, then in Kosenmark's private rooms over a supper of bread and cheese and triple-watered wine.

Gerek had known before that Kosenmark allowed him to see only the most unexceptional of his correspondence, but the number of names—the names themselves—left him breathless with astonishment. Lord Iani and Lady Theysson he knew about. Also, Luise Ehrenalt. When he heard the names Eckard, Vieth, and Nicol Joannis, he drew an audible breath. These were all high-ranking members of Veraene's nobility. Two of these men were regional governors, appointed by the king.

"A shadow court," he murmured.

Kosenmark's hands stilled, his expression turned momentarily remote. "Someone else thought that a good name for what I do. I cannot agree entirely. I am not king, and the only true court resides in Duenne. However, the thought behind the name is true. We are nobles and commoners who care deeply about Veraene's welfare."

It was after Dedrick's death that Kosenmark ended his shadow court. Instead, he had begun to approach certain members of Károví's Court, to negotiate an alliance across both kingdoms to work against the war. So far, he'd had little luck, he told Gerek.

"Their court is smaller, but their factions just as numerous as ours. I had hoped to win Duke Miro Karasek to our side, but friends in Károví tell me King Leos recently sent Duke Karasek on a mission overseas. And other friends told me today of the end to that mission."

He went on to describe that end. It happened in Osterling Keep, he said, nothing in his expression betraying Ilse Zhalina's presence there. The king's patrols had sighted twenty ships heading east. Three returned, only to founder on the shoals off the peninsula. During the skirmish that broke out, Duke Karasek had escaped. So far, he had evaded capture.

From there the conversation turned to the minor nobles in Károví, King Leos's probable choices for an heir, and the possibility of approaching Ryba Karasek, cousin to that same Miro Karasek. He was only a baron from a minor branch of the family, but if his cousin did not return from his mission, Ryba Karasek might inherit the duchy.

Well after the bells rang midnight, they ended their session. Gerek went off to a restless sleep, crowded with dreams that might have been life dreams, they were so vivid. He woke much later than his usual time. He was overtired, but with excitement bubbling underneath the weariness. Before he left his rooms, however, a note came from Lord Kosenmark, reminding him that today was his weekly holiday.

But I don't want a holiday. Not yet.

He picked up his pen to protest this interruption, then stopped. Any break in routine would be remarked, especially after Lord Kosenmark's precipitous departure and return the previous day. He studied the note again. One line that served as a warning, a suggestion, an act of newborn trust, all at once.

Gerek folded the note and dropped it into his private letter box. (Because it was a sign of trust, which he wanted to preserve for the future.) He ate his breakfast without appetite. Spent an unsatisfying hour in the library. Soon his restlessness drove him outside, onto the streets he had not visited since the freight wagon dropped him in front of Kosenmark's house.

Nine short days. The sky and city had changed in that interval. A green haze covered the trees. He sniffed and smelled the scent of newly blossomed flowers and more, of something born of the sea, as if the oceans themselves had seasons. Above, the cast of winter gray had vanished entirely and the sky was now a soft and vivid blue.

His feet took him to the nearest market square, where he bought a plate of grilled fish and rice from a street vendor, hot tea from another. He ate, then wandered onward, remembering more of the city from those past two visits. There, there was the Little University. There was the old bridge to the tenement district, where he'd lived with his tutor, and the rows of cook shops where he took his meals.

By midafternoon, he had circled back to a small park, a niche of greenery with several stone benches that overlooked a vast market near the coast. He settled there with a cup of hot tea from another vendor, grateful for the steady breeze blowing in from the seas. From here, he could see the entire harbor, a grand sweep from the northern hills, inward to the wide mouth of the Gallenz River, then south in a more gradual curve. Ships of all sizes dotted the dark blue waters, their white sails like flecks of foam at this distance. Farther off, a dark line of much larger vessels moved steadily northward. The king's fleet? A convoy of merchant ships? He could not tell.

Gradually he became aware that someone stood nearby, watching him.

It was Kathe, with a large basket over one shoulder, a smaller one in hand. "Hello," she said. "I'm glad to see you found the outside of your office."

Gerek ducked his head. "I could s-say the same about you."

She laughed. "Not everyone locks themselves in the

house like you, Maester Hessler. Besides, there are times I like to visit the market myself, instead of sending out one of the girls."

She shifted her loads. Recalling himself, Gerek asked if she would like to sit down. He slid to one end, and Kathe sank onto the bench with a happy sigh. "Thank you. This is my favorite bench in the city, I think. I can visit the harbor, shop in the market, then rest a bit and look at the waves before I go back to the house. Unless, of course, I bought fish. It spoils so easily, even in winter."

She set the larger basket on the ground between them. It was stuffed high with bundles wrapped in paper, and the sharp scents of several different spices tickled his nose when he bent over to inspect the contents.

"N-no fish, then?" Gerek asked.

"None worth buying today. But I did find a new spice shop. I think they might have connections to smugglers. I know it's nearly impossible to find red peppers at such a cheap price. No doubt they will be gone before my next visit, so I bought all their stock."

She chattered on about spices, which provinces or kingdoms produced the best quality, and how the recent increase in tariffs had driven the prices to unbearable heights. There was talk of war, even. That could only make things worse. Gerek listened, happy that she did not insist on replies. So it took him by surprise when she asked him, "How do you like working for Lord Kosenmark?"

"Good." He thought of several things to add, but decided against them. "Good," he repeated, then cursed himself silently for such a stupid reply.

Kathe didn't seem to notice. "I'm glad to hear that. I know—" She hesitated. "I'm going to say what I shouldn't. You see, I've been with Lord Kosenmark almost six years. Before that my mother and I saw him at court when he visited our old mistress. Even though he's told me nothing outright, I can guess what he does. We all do, of course, but there are times he's trusted me with, well, certain things."

"What are you saying?" Gerek said.

Her cheeks darkened. "I know he doesn't give you all his letters. And I know he pretended to leave yesterday, then came back right away. I was worried for you. I was worried for him, too, though he thinks he's invincible, the great idiot. And if you ever tell that I called him a great idiot, I shall smack you with a fish. Anyway, I'm not asking you to tell me your secrets. I'm just glad that you've found the right way with him. If . . . if that is what makes you happy."

"I had n-no idea I was s-sso obvious," Gerek muttered.

Her cheeks dimpled in a pensive smile. "You aren't. But I was curious about you. And you remind me of someone I knew before."

Unsure what to say, he fixed his attention on the harbor and the seas. The fleet or convoy was already much farther north, heading between a scattering of islands. The pattern of ships and boats in the harbor had shifted, too. It was like a secret code, transparent to those familiar with waves and tides and water craft, but to strangers such as him, the language remained opaque, unsettling.

"You are angry with me," Kathe said.

"No. I am n-n-not used to people watching me."

"You aren't?" A pause. "They should. I don't know you very well, but I see much to admire."

He made a quick gesture of denial.

"I do," she insisted. "You work hard. You are clever with words. No matter what you think," she said, overriding his second and more vocal objection. "Words are not just sounds, spoken prettily. They are shapes on the page and in our hearts. I've always thought—" She broke off and shook her head. "I'm sorry. I'm babbling again."

I like your babbling. But he didn't dare say that out loud.

They lapsed into another silence, an easier one this time. Gerek pretended to be absorbed in an altercation in the marketplace below—a man driving pigs through the square had lost control over his animals. The pigs were dashing between carts and stalls, upsetting wares. Others were screeching at the hapless swineherd.

Kathe's unfinished sentence teased at him. He wanted to ask what she thought about words. He wanted to ask what she'd meant the day before, about not needing to apologize. But words were more than flesh and air, no matter what Kosenmark claimed. If he spoke, he might disturb the easy silence between them. It should be enough, he thought, to sit companionably with a friend.

Down below, the swineherd drove his pigs from the marketplace. A few shrill grunts floated up on the breeze, then the noise died off, leaving just the dull, indistinct roar from the crowds. Kathe touched his arm. "I must go back to the house. Will you come back for supper? Or shall I tell them to expect you later?"

Several different answers hovered on his tongue. In spite of what he thought earlier, he had the impression of a rare chance offered. Gerek swallowed and made a silent prayer to Lir. "Would you— Would you like me to carry your basket for you?"

There was just the briefest hesitation from Kathe. The pause lasted long enough that Gerek cursed his impulse. But then she smiled. "That would be kind of you. Thank you."

Gerek slung the larger basket over one arm and made certain its contents were secure. He took the second from Kathe's hands. They felt as light as a bundle of cotton. *I am an ox,* he thought, recalling his mother's words.

His mother had always used the name with affection. Even so, Gerek hated how it made him feel— large and awkward, a lumpish beast. But today the sky was bright, the breeze clean and brisk. And there was Kathe, holding out her hand.

CHAPTER TEN

WHEN SHE FIRST arrived in Osterling Keep in winter, Ilse Zhalina thought she had unraveled the days and miles to a summer's day in Melnek, where she had lived as a child. The sky was the color of pale blue ink suspended in water. Dusty green trees fringed the cliffs above the city, and only at night did she sometimes light a brazier to warm her bedroom.

As the season turned into spring, the seas glittered beneath the sun, and fishermen spoke of the coming summer storms. Fleets of merchant ships hurried down from the northern ports to complete their passage before those same calm seas turned rough and wild. Those with a few hours of leave visited the pleasure house, and Ilse worked into the night to keep the house well supplied.

Still, for all the orderly, ordinary succession of her days, she had the impression of a smothering weight over the city. Riders had taken word of the battle and the escaped officer to garrisons along the coast, and Lord Joannis had sent word to Duenne by ship and land. The effects were immediate—more guards in the harbor and around the city garrison. Rumor also talked about an influx of reinforcements due from Konstanzien, up the coast.

Ilse herself stopped using magic entirely. *Be cautious,* Nicol Joannis had warned her, in his oblique fashion. No more journeys to Anderswar. No more searching for Lir's jewels. She even stopped using the ordinary spells for lighting candles.

Nor did she meet with Alesso again.

That, however, was not her doing. Two days after their confrontation, Alesso transferred to the late-night shift. Ilse learned about that from the kitchen maids. Interesting, she thought. If he had frightened her out of complacency, perhaps she had done the same with him.

This day and hour, however, her attention was wholly on the pleasure house and its books, not the far-off doings of armies or kings. She sat with the chief cook in the woman's office, reviewing the monthly accounts. It was midafternoon. The sunlight was white and unforgiving, and the room echoed with activity from the kitchen next door.

The cook, used to the noise, pitched her voice louder. "Fish," she said.

Fish, hook, net, snare. The old game of word links came effortlessly to Ilse's mind. She smiled to herself. Ghita Fiori was an utterly plain woman, unimaginative except when it came to her cookery. She would not appreciate a game about words.

"Fish," Ilse repeated. "I never knew how many kinds of fish lived in the sea, until I came here."

Ghita snorted. "We only care about the edible ones. Speaking of which, fish needs salt, and the king has raised the salt tax again."

Taxes. Ilse sighed. "How much?"

"Thirty copper denier for a hundredweight."

A small sum, except when you considered how much fish and meat the customers consumed in one year. Ilse calculated the probable increase in expenses and sighed again. "That means higher taxes for freight and shipping. Mistress Andeliess might have to increase her prices, too."

"That is her business, not ours."

"True. But she'll want the numbers from me. So, then. We require fish, bought fresh from the wharves, in all varieties that you have so helpfully noted in your expenses and projections. Three hundred silver denier for the past month, including taxes. Next is beef . . . Yes, Rina?"

It was one of the house runners—Mistress Andeliess's grandniece, recently hired to begin her internship in the family business. The girl bounced on her toes. Her eyes were shiny with excitement. "I came for Mistress Ilse," she said. "You have a visitor. In your rooms."

Ilse frowned. "You took them to my rooms?"

"It wasn't *me*." The girl's voice squeaked high. "Fredo took them up. But come. You'll see he had no choice."

Fredo was the house's senior runner, old and trusted and wise in discretion. If he had elected to bring this unnamed visitor directly to Ilse's rooms without notifying her first, it argued for someone both important and well-known to Fredo.

Lord Joannis. He was the only person who could produce that kind of reaction. But why would he come to *her*? Perhaps he'd sent word to Raul in spite of his own warning to her.

She blotted the page with shaking hands, all too aware how Ghita and the runner watched her. "We can work together later," she said. "Tomorrow morning is best for me. That gives me a chance to speak with Mistress Andeliess about the salt tax. Will that suit?"

Ghita answered, but Ilse hardly heard the woman.

She gathered up her books and writing case. Murmured a reply that surely made no sense, but all she cared about was the visitor and what news he might bring.

She sped to the stairs at the back of the house. By the time she reached the second-floor landing, she was out of breath. She paused at the door to smooth her hair and recover her poise. If her visitor was Lord Joannis, she would have to act her part in case anyone overheard them. Then she rounded the corner from the landing into the hall.

Her first warning was the sight of two armed soldiers outside her door.

Both men glanced in her direction. Light from an open door beyond cast their faces in shadows. Then one man rested his hand on his sword. The movement sent a ripple of sunlight over the metal studs of his leather glove.

Ilse continued forward, her heart skipping to a faster beat as she took in more details. Royal insignias. Full armor despite the heat. Someone important, then. Given a few moments, she could probably guess the identity of her visitor. She laid a hand on the latch to her door, felt the warmth of recent magic, the hint of a signature she almost recognized.

Inside, a tall man dressed in a dusty drab cloak stood behind her desk. He held a paper in one hand. A dozen more were scattered over the floor, as if he'd tossed them to one side. A wide-brimmed hat shaded his face, but Ilse felt a stir of fear. Something about his height, the dismissive manner with which he flicked aside the paper and took up another.

Markus Khandarr, King's Mage and chief councillor, glanced up. "Mistress Ilse Zhalina. Formerly Mistress Therez of Melnek. Good day."

Her mouth went dry. "Lord Khandarr. I remember you."

Oh yes, she did. She had met him only once, for a few terrifying moments, two years ago. He had infiltrated a secret meeting between Raul Kosenmark and his shadow court. Or rather, he had intended to. Suspecting a spy, Raul had arranged a false meeting, with only those associates already known to the king.

"I am glad you do," Khandarr said. "That will make our interview easier. Lord Kosenmark tells me you've broken off all connection with him."

A lie. Raul would tell this man nothing. With an ease that she did not feel, Ilse turned toward the sideboard and indicated the waiting carafes. "Would my lord care for wine? Or I might send for coffee."

Khandarr smiled faintly. "No, thank you. A few answers are all that I require. Tell me what you remember about the Károvín ships—the ones that foundered offshore last month. What did you see that day?"

"Nothing," she said. Too quickly, because Khandarr's smile deepened.

"Nothing at all?" he said.

She made a show of considering her answer this time. "Nothing, my lord. You might know that Captain Spenglar allows me to drill with his wing. That day I came late, so I was outside the yard when the alarm bells rang. The wings and files marched out. I waited until they passed, then returned here to my work."

"You were not curious?"

"Very curious. And frightened. There were rumors of pirates, you see."

"But they were not pirates."

"No, my lord. They were not. I learned that later."

Khandarr regarded her for several moments. It was hard to read his expression—he'd placed himself between her and the window, and shadows covered his face—but she had the distinct impression of strong emotions running just beneath the surface. Disappointment. Fury. A mixture of the two. She wished she knew more about current doings in the royal court.

"Tell me what magic you know," Khandarr said.

Ilse suppressed a flinch. "I know very little magic, my lord."

"False," Khandarr whispered. "Your first mistake."

"But my lord—"

"Shut up, you miserable girl. You know magic. Kosenmark taught you. Your own books betray you." He dropped the papers onto her desk and curled his fingers into a fist. The magic current stirred, drawing her skin tight. "I'm glad to see you have not forgotten me," he said. "Consider what you know. What Kosenmark told you. How Lord Dedrick died. Because tomorrow we shall talk again."

He brushed past her on his way out the door. Ilse held still. She counted to ten after the door closed, then moved swiftly to the sideboard and poured herself a generous cup of wine.

He came to interrogate the Károvín prisoners, of course. That was the meat of Nicol Joannis's warning. She had misunderstood him. She had expected the king to send a military officer. The incident was a military matter, after all. But it was the short interval since that warning that frightened her the most. Only a month had passed since the governor sent word to Duenne. How many horses had Lord Khandarr and the courier killed between them?

Her thoughts veered back to her other encounters with Markus Khandarr, the reports from trusted agents, even Lord Iani's own account of Dedrick's death.

Khandarr raised a hand. Ilse's skin pulled tight across her forehead. Her throat clamped shut, and her vision went dark . . .

. . . he shouted and the air turned bright and heavy. Then came a wind. Then a burst of fire. Then I saw

the soldiers along the perimeter wall burning, burning, and yet they did not die . . .

. . . Khandarr was furious, Iani told them. He called up magic so thick that I could hardly breathe. Dedrick fought hard against it. Gods, I thought his throat would burst. And then . . . And then it did. . . .

Her stomach heaved at the memories.

I should have sent word to Raul myself, she thought. Alesso might have helped, if she offered him enough money.

What if. Might have. Ought to.

All those second guesses were worthless.

She heard a soft scratching at her door. Ghita the cook? One of the runners? Her pulse gave a start when she heard Alesso's voice instead. Interesting that he would be awake at this hour. Except that true spies never slept.

She drank off the wine and went into her bedroom.

The signs of Lord Khandarr's search were few but telling—the bed quilt rumpled, her bookcase with several volumes pulled out, one trunk with its lid propped open, the scent and texture of his magical signature heavy in the air. He had not rifled through all her books, however. The books of poetry and history remained as she had left them. She removed one thick volume of Tanja Duhr's poetry and let her breath trickle out in relief.

He had not discovered her most secret weapon, then.

Ilse took out the scroll from its hiding place. It had come from Lord Iani, from her last few months in Tiralien. He had not liked her request, but he had given in to her insistence. He was right to be reluctant. With these spells, she might erase her mind completely. She could lock her memory against all probing, sealing her thoughts away forever, or locking them with a particular key.

For a long while, Ilse considered the spell and its implications. Once invoked, she would forget Raul Kosenmark and everything between them. His shadow court would be safe. She . . . she would be a mindless puppet. She could use the variation with a key. The right person with the right key could recover her self. But then she risked the key being lost or misunderstood.

Or understood by the wrong person altogether.

Not yet. Better to wait and see what Khandarr does next.

VALARA BAUSSAY LAY on her back, staring at the ceiling. A spider had begun a web in one corner, near the window. The web shook from an unseen breeze, a breeze so weak it did nothing to relieve the suffocating heat inside the prison. Nor the smell. The guards were late emptying the slop buckets today, and the air smelled ranker than usual.

In the weeks since her capture, she had come to know every detail of her cell. It measured four feet by five—an enormous, luxurious space. Other prisoners slept two or three together, their straw pallets crammed close along one wall, as far away from the slop buckets as possible. And hers had an actual window—just a foot-square opening, blocked with iron bars, but through it, Valara could see a patch of sky. If she stretched onto her toes, she could even make out a thumb-sized smidge of wall from some other part of the garrison. Once the summer storms came, the guards told her, she would get a bit of tarpaulin to keep out the rains.

Summer. She could hardly imagine a season hotter than this one.

In Morennioù, on the island Enzeloc, the lilies and orchids in the castle gardens would be ripe with new blooms. Outside the grounds, the trees in Louvain's orchards would be shedding their blossoms. She loved riding with Jhen Aubévil through the blizzard of petals.

Not this year. This year, soldiers burned those orchards.

Her chest squeezed tight in grief and anger. She remembered—could not forget—that terrible first day of spring. The alarm bells, her running to find her father and his chief mage. Her confession about the jewel. Their panicked attempts to conceal Lir's emerald, only to have the emerald awaken and change itself with its own magic. Valara absently rubbed the wooden ring on her finger and felt a dull prickle of the current, uninspired and nearly imperceptible. Once she had imagined the jewel spoke to her. Or was that a memory from old lives? An image from ordinary dreams from long ago?

The hour bells rang out, followed by a softer quarter bell.

Valara stirred, restless and hungry. It was two hours past the usual time for supper, but no guard had come with her meal. She heard one of the Károvín complaining to his cell mates. She understood them much better, six weeks later. At times, she practiced Károvín and Veraenen, whispering the words to herself. The languages had changed in the past three hundred years, but not beyond recognition. She had spoken both fluently in previous lives. She could do so in this one.

A loud crash brought her alert and to her feet. Six guards marched through the outer doors and down the corridor. One of them unlocked Valara's cell door and seized the overflowing slop bucket, cursing at the mess. Another tossed her straw pallet to a companion.

"What are you doing?" Valara demanded. Fear made her reckless. For a moment, she forgot she was only a prisoner and grabbed the guard's arm. "What is happening?"

The guard shook her off. Before she could fling herself after him, another guard carrying a bucket of soapy water shoved her into a corner. He pinned her against the wall with one arm and scrubbed her face with a rag. "Finish yourself," he said, dropping the bucket at her side. "And hurry."

He slammed the door shut. Valara choked and spat out a mouthful of soap. All down the corridor the other prisoners shouted curses. The guards ignored them and continued to work at a feverish pace. Torches lit. Pallets and blankets taken away. A hasty scouring of the floors and prisoners. Something very strange was afoot. A visitor?

My message to the king. They finally delivered it.

She snatched up the rag from the floor and washed her hands, her neck, behind her ears. She wore the same threadbare clothes as the other prisoners. It was not how she wished to appear before a king or his representative, but she could make herself presentable at least.

The senior guard marched past the cells to make one last inspection. Once he completed his circuit, he shouted an order. Immediately a squad of soldiers poured inside. Half of them peeled off to line the corridor, the rest marched down, almost to Valara's cell and swung about, blocking her view. The din was unbearable—boots ringing off the stones, the clatter from several dozen swords drawn in unison, a great shout like a panther's coughing roar.

The guard captain barked an order, bringing an instant hush.

Valara held her breath and in the stillness heard a

single pair of measured footsteps. The footsteps paused.
A murmured conversation followed. She could not
make out the words, but she could guess. The king
had sent a man to question the Károvín prisoners. The
guards in Osterling had tried that once or twice. Valara had overheard them whispering about a cruel
magic laid upon the Károvín soldiers.

The murmuring changed to raised voices. The argument was conducted in Karóvín, but she could not
make out what they said. The exchanges grew louder,
more abrupt. Then . . .

"Ei rûf ane gôtter. Gaebe mir alle werrit."

A rank smell swept through the prison. Valara bent
over double, overwhelmed by the harsh magic. Beyond the thrumming in her head, she heard the whine
of voices. Erythandran. Károvín. But the Erythandran
grew louder, more insistent, commanding the other to
speak, speak the truth, no matter what spells were laid
upon them, while the other voice rose into a shriek.
Valara pressed both hands over her ears, but she could
not shut out the cry until—

Abruptly the shrieking stopped. Valara slumped to
the floor. She heard the soldiers outside her cell muttering softly. Even they were troubled.

A metallic clang echoed down the corridor. The
muttering stopped at once. Now movement flowed
through the crowd of soldiers. They were making way
for someone's passage. Before Valara could stand up
and recover herself, the guards outside parted and
two men came forward to the door of her cell.

Both were clothed in dark blue robes and trousers.
One had a complexion that was blacker than a moonless night, and silver hair, cropped close. She had seen
him once before, the day after the battle. He was Osterling's regional governor, Lord Nicol Joannis. The
second man was taller, his spare frame stooped as if

from a heavy burden, and he wore a broad hat that cast shadows over his face.

Joannis produced a key and unlocked the door. The second man walked past him into Valara's cell and signaled for his companion to remain outside. As he turned to face Valara, he removed his hat, revealing a gaunt face and pale brown eyes. Torchlight reflected from the silver in his long thin hair.

"My name is Lord Markus Khandarr." The man spoke in strongly accented Károvín. His voice was clear and deep. "I am a councillor to the king and his chief mage. The commander sent word that you wished to confess. Here I am. Speak."

Valara glanced from him to Joannis. One to question, the other to watch. She had planned to announce herself plainly, but the conflicting signals of magic and violence made her wary.

"I have no need to confess," she said in Veraenen. "My message was to Veraene's king, not a minion."

Khandarr waved his hand, as if dismissing her words. "Reliable witnesses have sighted Károvín ships in our waters. Such news worries Armand of Angersee; therefore it worries me. He has sent me to question all the prisoners. And you. Tell me your name, and what you know about Károví's plans for Veraene."

He had answered in Veraenen, at least, but his abrupt tone unsettled her. *You are my prisoner,* it said. Valara ran through her answer twice before she could speak. "I will tell you as much as I am able. Remember, I asked to speak with your king. I believe we can help each other."

His eyes narrowed. "Then answer my questions. Six weeks ago, the king's fleet sighted a large number of Károvín ships bound for the east. Not long after, three of them foundered off our coast. Tell me where Leos Dzavek sent those ships. And why."

Valara hesitated, glanced toward Joannis. No sign of what he thought. It was clear, however, that he would not interfere with the king's chief councillor and mage. And Khandarr was obviously impatient for her to answer. Oh, but it was so hard to break the secrecy of three hundred years, especially to this man.

He is the voice of the king. I must work through him.

Choosing her words carefully, she said, "Leos Dzavek has discovered how to break through Luxa's Hand—what you call Lir's Veil. He sent those ships to invade our kingdom."

Khandarr watched her, his pale eyes unblinking. "Go on."

"His general took a number of prisoners for questioning, but he left behind most of his troops. I am a member of the court. I requested an audience with your king so we might discuss the possibility of an alliance. I would offer a great deal for safe passage back to my homeland."

She heard a soft murmur from one of the guards. Joannis leaned closer, his eyes bright with anticipation. Khandarr, however, did not change his expression. "One of the Károvín sailors mentioned an island kingdom before he died," he said softly. "He died from choking. Another one said the word *magic* before her throat burst open and she bled to death."

A chill went through her at this flat recitation of violence. "So you see I'm not lying."

"Nor have you told me the entire truth. For example, you are a trained mage. The guards tell me you attempted to break free using magic your first night here. And there are traces of your signature in this cell, though you tried to erase them. Did you help the Károvín to break through the barrier? Is that why Leos Dzavek sent ships to Morennioù? You call it an invasion. To me, it looks more like an alliance—"

"There is no alliance," Valara broke in. "Leos Dzavek sent twenty or thirty ships against Morennioù. He
gave them orders to murder the king and—"

She stopped at the eager look on Khandarr's face.

"And did he?" he asked. "Did he murder the king?"

Valara said nothing. She had already said too much.

"I believe he did," Khandarr said softly. "So Morennioù's king is dead, and the barrier no longer quite so
formidable. And you, you know far more than you
admitted at first. Yes, my king must hear what you
have to say, but everything, not just what you choose
to reveal. You will not be bound by Leos Dzavek's
spells."

He raised his right hand and murmured the familiar
invocation to magic. The current gathered around his
fingers. Another spell and the air crackled with a bright
electric charge. She swallowed with difficulty.

"Ei rûf ane gôtter. Ane Toc unde sîn kreft . . ."

Valara felt her gorge rising. Her tongue, like a creature alive, moved to speak. She clamped her mouth
shut, but the magic had gripped her like a hand and
was prizing her lips open. "He came . . . He came because I . . . because I . . ."

With an effort, she choked out a spell to counteract
his. The current wavered—a temporary reprieve. Khandarr had far more skill than she. Already her mouth
was twisting open again. She would tell him about the
emerald. He would take it and—

*"Wenden dir sîn zoubernisse. Nemen îm der wâr
unde kreft. Nemen îm der sprâche."*

With a loud crack, the current rebounded. Khandarr sprang backward, clawing at his throat. Valara
scrabbled into the far corner as guards streamed into
the cell. Her skin burned with magic; the current bub-
bled through her veins. Dimly, she heard an uproar.
One of the guards shoved her against the wall. His

sword was a bright blur of motion; its point stopped inches from her throat and poised to strike.

"Stop! Do not kill her!"

Joannis's voice broke through the din.

"Get back. Everyone. You, hold the prisoner. Nothing more."

"But my lord—"

"I said, *Nothing more.*"

Joannis's mouth was drawn tight. He looked angry, appalled. With obvious reluctance, the guards retreated from the cell, except for the one who held Valara. He did not loosen his grip, nor did his sword waver.

Joannis knelt by a motionless Khandarr. He touched the man's throat, ran his fingers over the man's body, murmuring in Erythandran. A sheen of sweat covered Khandarr's face, and his skin had turned gray. Valara watched with sick dread. She had tried to stop Khandarr's magic with her own—that much she remembered—but then her recollection failed. There had been another voice, like an enormous bell, inside her skull. Was it her imagination? Khandarr's magic?

"Send for the chief surgeon," Joannis said to the guard captain. "Fetch a litter and carry Lord Khandarr to my quarters. Clear the streets first. But do nothing to this woman. We need her alive. Lord Khandarr's orders."

Guards appeared with a litter. Nicol Joannis motioned them forward. As they carefully shifted Khandarr onto the litter, his throat gave a convulsive twitch. He turned his head toward Valara and met her gaze— one penetrating look—before Joannis signaled the guards to take him away.

CHAPTER ELEVEN

HOURS LATER, VALARA Baussay sat in the corner of her cell, knees drawn up to her chest. Her stomach had contracted into a hard painful knot. The guards had not brought supper, nor had they returned her slop bucket. A small grate in one corner would do, but she wished the men outside her cell would look away, just for a few moments.

They wouldn't of course. These were the second pair to take the watch. They were awake, alert, and angry. She heard them discussing what punishment Joannis or Khandarr would order for her. If they meant to frighten her, they had succeeded.

I trusted too soon. I promised too much.

She had expected Veraene to welcome Dzavek's enemy. She had hoped they would negotiate with her. Whatever the cost, in money, in concessions, she would have promised it. Once back in Morennioù, she could have renegotiated the terms of their alliance.

They don't want an ally. They want a hostage. And why not? I would do the same.

The hour bells rang—six clear soft tones. Midnight. Five more hours until dawn. Khandarr would return tomorrow. She was sure of that. Any competent mage-healer could restore the man's wits. Khandarr himself

could do the rest. Once he had recovered, he would
bind her with magic and rip the truth from her throat.
She had to escape before then.

You tried once. You failed.

Then I must try again.

She had panicked before, that was all. The spells
guarding this prison were strong and complex, but
she had made a delicate examination of them over the
past several weeks. Only the bars and floor stones
were steeped in magic. Unless she misread the signs,
she could escape to Autrevelye before her magic trig-
gered the prison's spells. She had been too slow before, too befuddled from the magic Karasek had used
to drug her.

She counted to ten to steady her nerves. Her heartbeat slowed as her gaze turned inward.

*Ei rûf ane gôtter. Ane Lir unde Toc. Ei rûf ane gôt-
ter. Ane Lir unde Toc.*

Magic coursed over her skin. She no longer saw the
torchlight or prison walls, no longer felt the stone
floor beneath her. She was rising slowly through a
viscous ocean. Far above, she saw a vast empty cavern,
where shadowy hills rolled and surged toward the horizon. Higher still, a glittering band of lights streamed
through the sky. The void between lives, which lay
upon the edge of magic.

Noandnoandno.

A force struck her chest. The current scattered. She
was falling, falling, falling through darkness while
monsters shrilled and the ocean roared.

"—thought that blessed magic was supposed to
stop—"

"—if we hadn't watched—"

One of the Osterling guards hauled Valara up from
the floor and pinned her against the wall. The other

flung a bucketful of water over her. She coughed and sputtered and cursed.

"Good enough," the first guard said. He drew a knife and laid it against Valara's throat. "I'll stay with her. You go for the governor. He said to report anything."

Valara struggled to speak. Not Joannis, she wanted to cry. Tell Joannis and you tell Khandarr. It was Khandarr she feared. Khandarr would rob her of the emerald and turn its magic against Morennioù. She knew it.

She had to summon the magic again. She had to call the spells laid down in the prison stones. It might give her a chance to escape. *Ei rûf ane gôtter . . .*

. . . ei rûf ane Lir unde Toc unde strôm unde mir.

The words rang in her skull like the great bells of the Morennioù castle. An unknown signature overwhelmed hers, and the scent of magic rolled through the air. A brilliant light exploded in the cell. Valara's sight blurred into white and then shadows. Magic drenched her, and her skin burned. Pure magic—she would have one taste, and then it would consume her.

. . . a river of shadows. An inhuman voice. A burst of light. Nothingness . . .

She knew nothing except darkness at first. Moments trickled away, unnumbered. Then a change to the blankness surrounding her. It was like emerging from a deathlike sleep. Or even death itself, she thought. Perhaps a newly reborn soul had one moment of awareness such as this before the knowledge of all previous lives faded into nothing.

More slowly she became aware of her surroundings. She lay stretched out on a hard stone floor. Her skin felt hot and sensitive, as though she'd handled fire, and the wooden ring on her finger buzzed with magic.

Groaning, she levered herself to sitting. Someone had hung a lantern on the cell wall. She blinked to clear her vision.

And sucked in a breath of surprise.

Both guards lay motionless, one inside the cell and one in the corridor. The open door swung on its hinges, creaking. The rest of the prison lay in deep and unnatural silence.

Valara released a shaky breath. What had happened back there? She had called on the magic current. It came and—

She stopped and sniffed. Her own signature hung in the air, like a fox slipping through the bracken. But another, much stronger and more vivid, overlaid it. A signature as bright as star showers. No, something far more alien. A signature that belonged in Autrevelye.

Was it you? she asked the emerald.

No answer. She crawled over to the nearest guard and touched his throat. His skin felt cold and stiff. His mouth, half open, looked dark and cavernous in the dim light. She bent closer and realized with a shock that his mouth was filled with blood. She examined the second guard. He was dead, too.

Unnerved, she ventured from her cell. Torches burned at the far end of the corridor. Their light cast a ruddy glare on the walls, sending rippling shadows over the stones, but nothing moved, and no voice broke the silence.

She peered into the cell next to hers. There was just enough light to make out three bodies. Two men lay motionless on their pallets. A third sprawled over the floor, as if felled in the act of standing. Valara's throat tightened in dread. Had she killed them as well? She couldn't tell if they breathed.

It didn't matter. Here was her chance to escape. She hesitated a moment, then hurried back to her cell and rifled the guards' pockets, thinking how she had always been a thief in all her lives, whether queen or prince or a common soldier in the service of Leos Dzavek. Her search yielded a handful of coins, two daggers with wrist sheaths, and an oversized tunic, which she wrestled off the smaller guard. She wanted shoes, too, but their boots were too big. In the end, she settled for what she had. She could steal shoes later.

Valara fastened the sheaths to her wrists, stowed the money in a knotted corner of the tunic. It wasn't nearly enough to bribe a ship's master to take her home, but it might feed and clothe her until she could get far enough beyond Osterling's cursed magical guards. Then she wouldn't need any ship. She could walk home through Autrevelye.

The scent of magic and a bright signature welled up around her. *You must not go home. Not yet.*

The great voice penetrated her bones. Now she recognized it. She'd heard it speaking on the ship just before the storm. She'd thought it a fever-dream from the magic used to subdue her. But now she understood. It *was* the emerald—Lir's emerald. It was alive. She had not imagined it.

City bells rang the next hour. There was no time to question or explore. She ran.

GALENA HAD DREAMED of the bells long before she woke. Bells and more bells, the count leaping from one tower to the next, as though time chased itself through Osterling's dark streets. Their voices rose in volume, until they became the shrieks of winged monsters, so high and pure her bones ached and terror gripped her stomach. *Coward*, Ranier Mazzo had whispered. *Go fight them and die. Do you dare?*

She woke to a single bell ringing the first hour past

midnight. It was quiet in the garrison sleeping quarters. Moonlight slanted through the reed blinds, and a warm salt-fresh breeze filtered through the room, carrying with it the scent of rain and the coming summer.

I am a coward, she thought, lying in her cot.

A coward without honor. Ranier had said that outright the day before. He'd stepped into her path as she trudged from harbor watch to cleaning duty. *Tell me what that word on your face means, Alighero. I know you must.*

She told him, in exactly the words given by Lord Joannis. It had been hard. Her voice choked, and the mark on her cheek buzzed with magic. Worse, much worse, was the sight of those she had called her friends. A few others from her file—Marelda, Tallo, Falco—averted their eyes, but she noticed that no one defended her, even when Ranier went on to mock her viciously in the low sweet voice that Aris had loved at first, then had come to hate.

They think the same as him. They just don't say it.

Harbor patrol had turned out to be a kindness. She bunked in different quarters. She stood guard with almost-strangers who ignored her. She could almost pretend that she'd transferred to a new garrison, far away from Osterling Keep, where no one knew about her shameful past. If they asked about her mark, she could claim it was a badge of honor.

Except you know you can't. The magic won't let you.

It was a pleasant dream, nonetheless. So she lay there, eyes closed, imagining herself with new friends, a new regiment. A chance to prove herself . . .

The garrison bells tolled. Galena's reverie broke. She sighed. Two hours until watch. No more sleep tonight, that was certain. She could lie here in misery, dreaming of the impossible. Or she could report to the harbor early. Old Josche wouldn't mind. He'd set her to work cleaning weapons or some other useful task. He might even tell Commander Adler.

She dressed in silence and gathered her weapons and gear. Outside the garrison, moonlight washed over the streets and towers. The prison building was dark, except for one window. The fort above was little more than a looming presence on the cliffs. A quiet night, the guards outside the barracks gate told her.

Quiet and empty. She had come to love the night watch, though she had not expected to. Osterling had a different face, painted in moonlight, inked in shadows. As she jogged down the main avenue, she spotted a few lamp-lit windows, but otherwise the city slept. Harbor duty wasn't much, Josche told her the first night. Except when it was. Then he told her stories about when raiders swooped through the shoals to attack.

She had just crossed the second market square— not far away from Mistress Andeliess's pleasure house—when a movement off to one side caught her attention. She stopped, hand on her sword, and peered into the darkness. Runners often carried messages between the city walls and headquarters, she told herself. But a courier or runner would not hide in an alleyway.

The stranger darted from one doorway to another. Suspicious now, Galena sprinted toward the alleyway's entrance and peered down its length. Tall buildings blocked out the moon. All Galena could see were shapes and movement. And one tall lanky figure. A young man, judging from his height.

The boy glanced over his shoulder and took off at a run. That decided her. He *was* a thief. Galena launched herself after him. The boy dodged right into the next street, then right again. The chase took them back toward the main square, past the inn and the pleasure house, and into the merchants' quarter, where the boy veered into a side alley. Galena followed, laughing to herself, because she knew how this chase would end.

She rounded the corner into the courtyard. There were no exits, just one door chained shut. The boy was scrabbling at the latch, muttering strange words, but swung around to face Galena, hair swirling in a dark cloud. A forgotten lamp burned in a window overhead, casting a dim circle of light over him.

No, her.

Galena stopped, her heart thudding faster. *I know her.*

It was the woman she had sighted on the beach, the day of the battle. She was bone-thin and nearly as tall as Galena. Her eyes were dark and narrow above flat cheeks, her complexion like the dark golden sands of Osterling's shores. She wore a prisoner's uniform underneath a shapeless tunic with a guard's badge sewn at one shoulder. Her feet were bare.

The woman raised both hands. The sleeves fell back, revealing two wrist sheaths and their knives. Galena paused, wary. She drew her sword and rocked on her feet, ready to defend or attack as she needed to.

"*Ei rûf ane gôtter,*" the woman said. "*Komen mir de kreft.*"

The air turned dense, like the morning fog rolling in from the sea. Galena scrambled backward, but not quickly enough. The cloud swept over her, and the world went blank.

When she came to, Galena lay at full length on the hard paving stones. Her head throbbed, her eyes refused to focus. She groaned and stirred. That was a mistake. Pain lanced through her skull. She choked back a surge of bile and groaned again.

Cool fingers pressed against Galena's temples. A

woman murmured in an unknown language. The fresh green scent of pines filled the air, taking away the nausea. More words spoken in that unknown language, like water trickling over stone, then a command delivered in Veraenen.

"Stand up."

Galena blinked and focused on the woman standing over her. The prisoner. She fumbled for her knife, only to find the sheath empty. Sword gone. Both knives missing. The woman had taken everything.

"Stand up," the woman repeated. She held a knife to Galena's throat.

"What do you want?" Galena croaked.

To her surprise, the woman gave a soft laugh. "What do I want? Too many things." Then all the humor vanished from her face and she leaned over Galena. "I want a way out of Osterling. Get me past the gates."

Galena noticed she hadn't promised to release Galena after she escaped. So she was smart, too. "What if I say no?"

"Then I make certain you can't warn anyone else."

Her tone was cool and composed, but the hand gripping the knife shook slightly. *Desperate enemies make dangerous ones,* her father always said. "What did you do to the others?" Galena asked.

A heartbeat of hesitation. "They sleep."

She killed them.

Galena squeezed her eyes shut against renewed dizziness and considered her situation. This young woman knew a great deal of magic. She'd killed a dozen guards or more. She'd broken free from a prison with strong magical shields. Even if Galena took her by surprise and wrestled the knife away, the woman could probably murder her with a single word.

"I can't help you alone," she said. "And I need my weapons."

"No weapons."

"Very well. But I can't get you away from Osterling by myself. I know someone who can, though." When the other woman hesitated, she added, "If you don't believe me, you can kill me now."

The woman frowned, tight-lipped. "You promise? You promise to get help?"

It was not exactly a lie, Galena told herself. "I promise. Come with me."

CHAPTER TWELVE

MIDNIGHT. ILSE STARED at her ceiling, hardly more than a pale square above her, illuminated by moonlight. Her thoughts remained frozen. No, not exactly frozen. More as though she had succumbed to useless panic, which robbed her from any useful activity. So she lay there, counting the slow thump of her heartbeat. Waiting, waiting, waiting for the day to begin and her enemies to come.

One quarter, two, three.

As from a distance, she heard the next hour bell ring. A single soft peal. They had entered the interval between one day and another. *Like the void between lives,* she thought. *Like the moment between one breath and the next.*

Tomorrow Khandarr would question her. It was too much of a coincidence, her presence here, where the Károvín ships had foundered. She could tell from his manner that afternoon. She knew too much about Raul Kosenmark. She only wondered why he had not bothered before.

She rubbed her hands over her face. No use lying in bed. She rose and stalked into her study, scowled at the map of southern Fortezzien, spread over her desk, which she had abandoned earlier. Its contents were not encouraging. Osterling sat on the point of the peninsula. A spine of rocky hills extended its entire length, and into the mainland. On both sides, the shores were narrow, populated with small towns and fishing villages, which were connected by a single highway. There were garrisons, too, each within a day's ride of each other. Besides, Khandarr would have notified the fort and harbor watches the moment he arrived. They would stop her at the gates.

She could attempt to cross into Anderswar, and from there to Tiralien.

Another questionable choice. Even if she could dare such a thing, Khandarr could track her to Raul's doorstep.

No, there was no escape. Except one.

Her gaze flicked toward her books. The scroll from Lord Iani hid between two massive dictionaries of the Erythandran language. Not yet, she decided. Not until she was certain about Khandarr's intentions.

A small voice whispered, *Coward*.

I am a coward. I like my life and my self.

The candle flame shuddered, sending a cascade of shadows over her desk and hands.

Shadow, ghost, death. A link of words came too easily. It was a child's game, she told herself. She had left the game behind when she escaped her father's house in Melnek. Briefly, she wondered about her childhood friend Klara, with whom she had so often passed an afternoon with such pastimes. They had talked about lovers, years ago. Ilse hoped Klara had found her artist, someone who loved beauty as much as she did.

The thought of Klara brought her other friend to mind, Kathe. Kathe who had tended her through sickness. Who taught her how to mince garlic, and stir a sauce to the smoothness of silk. Who stayed her friend even after she left the kitchens to become Berthold Hax's assistant, then much later, Raul's beloved.

I lied to her. I told her I left Raul because I wanted children. She thinks me selfish.

Or was it a lie?

Ilse folded the map together and set it aside. Walked over to her bookcase and knelt. Her limbs felt numb, her body removed at a distance, as she commanded her hands to seek out Lord Iani's scroll and extract it from its hiding place. It unfurled at a touch, revealing a foot of thick dark parchment with the words of the spell written in old Erythandran. Ilse glanced over it. She had only to speak those words to take herself beyond Khandarr's questions. They would save Raul Kosenmark and all his shadow court. She didn't even need to provide a key for unlocking her memories.

The shutters beside the bookcase rattled. Pebbles and dirt flew through the slats and onto the floor. Then, she heard a hoarse shout. "Ilse!"

Galena?

Ilse swiftly coiled the parchment and tucked it behind her books. She rose cautiously and peered through the window slats. Moonlight splashed over the roof and the center part of the courtyard, but the perimeter lay in darkness. Then she sensed a movement by the far wall. Galena Alighero emerged from the shadows. She wore her uniform and armor, but no helmet. Moon and starshine silvered her brown hair. And she limped.

Ilse had not talked with Galena since the girl received her punishment. She knew Adler had transferred Galena to harbor duty at the dark watch, between three bells and dawn. What was she doing here, at this hour?

Galena glanced over one shoulder, bent, and gathered another handful of pebbles. This would not do.

One of the house guards would hear the noise. Ilse opened the shutters. "Galena," she whispered loudly. "What is it?"

Galena immediately let the pebbles fall. "Ilse. Can you come outside?"

"Why? And why aren't you at the harbor?"

"Not time yet. Please, Ilse. It's important."

"Then come inside. We can talk—"

Galena shook her head. "No. Out here."

A trap, Ilse thought.

She considered notifying the guards. Her instincts warned against that. It might be nothing more than Galena wanting reassurance.

"Go to the side door," she said. "The one directly below. I'll meet you there."

She pulled on a robe and took up the candle from her desk. Its dish was deep enough to keep the wax from spilling over her hand, but she could only walk swiftly, not run as she wished, down the stairs. Luckily, no house guards or runners were about.

She opened the door. Galena stood a few feet away.

"Come outside."

"Why? What did you do?"

"Nothing!"

A lie. Ilse was about to shut the door, when she sensed a change in the night air. A whiff of green. An impression of a furtive wild animal.

She threw the candle onto the stones and flung up both hands. *"Ei rûf ane gôtter. Komen mir de strôm."*

Magic sparked against magic, an explosion of bright cold fire. Ilse staggered backward. A double signature washed over her. A hunting fox. A silver blaze far brighter than the cold fire she had summoned to protect herself. She whispered Erythandran through numb lips. Her tongue unlocked and she could speak the words to release the magic flooding her veins.

The fire faded, the current ebbed away. Ilse rubbed a hand over her eyes. The door into the courtyard swung on its hinges. It was silent in the pleasure house. No one had raised the alarm. Cautiously she approached the open door.

Outside, moonlight spilled over the paving stones. The heavy scent of magic hung in the air. Shards of broken pottery littered the ground, and a coil of smoke still rose from the candle wick drowning in a pool of wax. Off to one side, Galena crouched on hands and knees. Farther away, a figure lay at full length.

Ilse hurried past Galena and knelt by the body. The throat felt warm to her touch. The pulse beat steadily. And yes, here was the source of that first magical signature, the one that reminded her of a wild dog or a fox. Long loose hair covered the face. Ilse brushed the hair aside and drew a swift breath. A woman. Not anyone that Ilse recognized. The stranger wore a thin cotton shirt and trousers beneath a much-too-large tunic.

"Who is she?" she said.

"One of the prisoners," Galena answered. "I caught her in the streets."

She said it so casually—too casually. Along with realization came another.

"One of those from Károví?" Ilse said. "Why did you bring her to me?"

Galena seemed oblivious to what she had revealed. She answered in a disgusted tone, "It was that damned magic. She caught me by surprise and knocked me out. Took my knives and sword. Wanted me to smuggle her past the soldiers on watch. You know magic. I thought you could help. And you did."

One of Dzavek's soldiers who knew magic. Ilse took the woman's hand and ran her fingers over the palm. Smooth. No sign of calluses. Hands fine-boned. Wrists like reeds. This woman had never wielded a sword. She wore leather wrist sheaths with knives, but the sheaths were far too large, loose and clumsily tied so they wouldn't fall off. Was she some kind of adjutant, a mage assigned to the army?

Galena lurched to her feet and grunted in pain. "Damn. Ilse, we need to send a runner to the garrison. I can walk, but I can't carry her back myself."

"Wait," Ilse said. "Don't call anyone yet."

Galena stared down at her. "What?"

"Bring her inside. I want to talk to her."

"Are you mad?"

She was mad to ask such a thing. But instinct said if she could question this mysterious prisoner, she might discover the reason behind Dzavek's mission to the east. She could send word to Raul Kosenmark.

"Bring her inside," she repeated, "and I'll pay you back in whatever favors you like. Talk to Lord Joannis. Beg him to commute your sentence. Convince him to transfer you to another garrison. Anything."

Lies. She had no influence. Tomorrow she might be dead or witless. From Galena's long silence, Ilse suspected the young woman had guessed the truth. If persuasion didn't work, she would have to use violence. She was about to whisper the magic words to summon the current, when Galena jerked her chin to one side. "You promise? You'll speak to Lord Joannis?"

"I promise."

Galena met Ilse's gaze fleetingly. "Then . . . I'll do it. But only for a few moments, Ilse. After that I *must* send word to the garrison. Where do we take her?"

"My rooms. Quick. One of the house guards might pass by."

Between them, they dragged the woman into the pleasure house. The stairs—narrow and steep—almost undid them. Their captive was limp and unresisting, and her legs thumped loudly over the steps. Finally Galena slung the body over her shoulder and hauled herself and her burden up the stairs in spite of her injured leg. Ilse ran ahead to make certain no one was about.

At last Galena staggered through the doors into Ilse's rooms. She slid the woman onto the rug, while Ilse fastened the door with lock and magic, then lit a branch of candles with a whispered word of magic. She turned to find Galena tight-lipped with pain. "It's nothing," Galena told Ilse. "Just, I slipped when she took me by surprise. We better search her for weapons. I know she took my knives. She might have more surprises."

They examined their captive, working methodically from the obvious to the hidden. The wrist sheaths came off first. "Thief," Galena muttered. She extracted two more knives from inside the woman's tunic, which she restored to her belt and boot.

Ilse made a cursory search with magic, but detected no traps or set spells. Nor did she uncover any more weapons. To her surprise, she found a handful of coins tied into the tunic's bottom hem. She deposited the money to one side and examined the body a second time, this time searching for clues to the stranger's identity. With a touch, she turned the woman's face toward the candlelight. Their captive was young—far younger than Ilse had expected, given her powerful magic. Only a few years older than Ilse herself. Her complexion a clear golden brown, much like Raul's. But with those flattened cheeks and nose, hers was clearly not a Veraenen face. Nor was it Károvín. It belonged to no province or kingdom she could think of.

She's no soldier. She's the foreigner. The prisoner from Morennioù.

Except for the weapons and money, the woman had

nothing out of the ordinary except a polished wooden ring on one finger. Odd that the guards had not removed it before. Ilse tugged the ring off and turned it over in her hands. Very plain. Carved from a dark wood, which felt silk-soft to her touch, the ring felt strangely heavy for such a small object. And there were clear traces of magic.

The woman's eyes blinked open. With a strangled cry, she lunged toward the ring. Galena grabbed the woman's wrists and shoved her back to the floor, her elbow pressed against the woman's throat. Ilse threw the ring aside and snatched up one of the knives. She pressed its point under the woman's ear. "Do not attempt any magic," she said. "You would be dead before you spoke a syllable."

The woman opened her mouth. Galena immediately leaned closer, cutting off her words.

"Don't kill her," Ilse murmured.

"Why not? She'd kill us."

Possibly. The woman glared at them both. Her lips were drawn back from her teeth, and she breathed in quick, noisy breaths, like a ferocious animal brought to bay. Terror and desperation. A dangerous combination.

Ilse bent over the woman, until her face was inches away. She noted a tattoo on the woman's cheek, on the outside corner of her eye, drawn in a reddish-brown ink. Another under her bottom lip had faded into near invisibility. She wished she knew what they signified.

"I have questions for you," she said slowly in Veraenen. "You will give me answers. But first, let me tell you what I already know."

She waited. The woman's eyes narrowed in obvious suspicion. Interesting that she could be so self-possessed, in spite of the situation. But she was listening. Good.

"You came with Károvín soldiers," Ilse went on.

"But you are not Károvín. You are Morenniòuen. A mage, obviously. Someone very important. A member of their court, I would say. Leos Dzavek sent his ships to your kingdom to recover a particular item of great value to you both."

Guesses, all of them. But she had the satisfaction of seeing confirmation in the woman's reaction. The signs were few—just a flicker of her eyelids, a sudden still remoteness. It was enough to tell Ilse she had guessed correctly.

She smiled at their captive, keeping her satisfaction deeply buried. "You do not need to speak. I know my information is correct. Now for my questions. You were a prisoner. Did a man named Lord Markus Khandarr question you? He is tall and thin, his hair is gray. He is a mage. Don't lie. If he spoke with the other prisoners, he would not neglect you. Tell me what happened. Let her speak," she said to Galena.

As Galena relaxed her hold, the woman swallowed audibly. Her irises, wide in the dim light, contracted as she turned toward Ilse and the candlelight. "Who are you?"

Her voice was low, rough. She spoke Veraenen with a lilting intonation.

"My name isn't important," Ilse said. "Answer my question."

Silence.

"Do you wish me to send for Lord Khandarr? Galena—"

"No!" The woman made a convulsive movement. "No. Please."

"Speak, then. Your name?"

A pause. "Valara Baussay."

Ilse suspected the woman possessed quite a few more names. She had not admitted to a title either, but those omissions might be caution, not outright lies.

"You came from Morenniwhere. Are you a member of their court?"

Another pause. "Yes."

Her tone sounded high, restrained. Nothing close to natural. But then, this was no normal conversation. "Tell me what happened between you and Lord Khandarr," Ilse said. "Tell me everything. The truth, or I send you back to prison."

Valara Baussay closed her eyes. The pulse at her temple and throat beat visibly faster. Arranging her lies? Reviewing a horrifying memory?

"It was Leos Dzavek," she said at last. "He sent ships to invade my homeland. We have only a small army, and it's scattered around our islands, but we do have guards at the castle. They were not enough. The soldiers took the castle and murdered my . . . murdered everyone at court. The king. His councillors. Everyone."

"Except you."

"I was to be a hostage." Her voice sank into a bitter whisper.

"Why?"

Valara's eyes opened. They were dark, so dark a brown they appeared black. Slight folds at the corner of her eyelids were like a brush from the artist's thumb, softening an otherwise sharp-featured face. Again the similarity to Raul Kosenmark struck Ilse—the lines and angles an echo of those old portraits from the empire days. Valara Baussay was not a beautiful woman by ordinary standards, but hers was a face not easily overlooked or forgotten.

"He came for the jewel," she said. "Lir's jewel. He did not find it. So he left an army behind to savage the kingdom until he did."

"And Markus Khandarr knows this?"

"No. But I could not risk his questioning me again."

Ilse wished she could have witnessed this interview between Valara Baussay and Markus Khandarr. She wondered what had transpired afterward and what means Valara used to escape the prison. Too many questions. She could not ask them all tonight, only the most important ones. "Where is the jewel, then?"

Those bright dark eyes closed, and Valara's face pinched in remembered pain. "Home. That is why I must go home. As quickly as I can. Don't you see?"

Her voice broke on the last word. She was trembling. Not with terror, though. Valara Baussay was more than simply desperate. She spoke as though she were the only one who could save . . .

Ilse's breath went still with insight. "You. Your father was the king. You are the heir. The queen."

Galena made an astonished noise. Valara's expression smoothed to a blank.

"It's true," Ilse went on, more confident now. "With you as his hostage, Leos Dzavek can threaten all of Morennioù until he gains the jewel."

It explained so much. The mysterious fleet sent into the east. Their almost immediate return a few days after the first sighting. She rapidly reviewed all she knew of Leos Dzavek and Károvín politics. A strong king who held absolute control for four hundred years. A council fractured by that knowledge and their own agendas. She knew, with certainty, that Raul would have no success in forming an alliance abroad.

We must do the work ourselves.

She laid the knife aside. "I can help you. Galena, let her go."

"No," Galena said. "You can't trust her."

"Trust is a gift. You cannot ask a bondage price for it."

Valara's eyes blinked open, and she stared hard at Ilse. It was not a warm, open gaze. Those great eyes held secrets behind secrets. *She will lie to me,* Ilse thought. *I cannot trust her at all, but I have no choice. I cannot allow Markus Khandarr to learn about Morenniou's jewel.*

"I have a friend," she said softly. "A powerful friend. He has great influence in Veraene—unofficial influence. You must speak with him, and explain your situation. There is one requirement. He will want to know more about your connection with Leos Dzavek."

Another pause. Then, "Does your friend want the jewel?"

Ah. Here was the heart of the matter. The truth was simple enough. Almost too simple for a royal princess used to the intrigues of court.

"He wants peace," Ilse said. "Our king insists on war. The fewer weapons he and Leos Dzavek hold, the more likely my friend can achieve his goal."

She met Valara's gaze steadily, willing the other woman to trust. Moments were sliding through the hourglass. If they delayed too long, it wouldn't matter what Valara believed. Galena gave a whispering sigh, as if she, too, were calculating the time.

Finally Valara said, "So you will help me get away from Osterling Keep? To meet with your friend?"

"Yes."

"No," Galena said. "Ilse, you promised to talk to her. Ask her questions. You didn't say anything about helping her to escape. That's *treason.*"

"I know," Ilse said quietly. "I can't expect you to—"

A soft rapping interrupted them. Galena started to her feet, knife held ready. Ilse motioned for her to stop. "Go into my bedroom," she whispered. When Galena frowned, she added, "Do it. Unless you want to explain yourself to the house guards, and after them, Lord Joannis."

Galena scowled, but she lowered the knife. She and

Valara hurried into Ilse's bedroom and eased the door shut. Ilse waited, hoping her unwanted visitor would leave, but another knock sounded, louder this time. "Ilse? You're awake. I know it."

Alesso. Ilse cursed softly. Anyone else she could easily send away without an explanation. She went to the door and opened it a crack.

He was little more than a shadow and a scent in the darkness, but she caught the tension in his attitude. "You have visitors," he said softly. "And before you deny it, I saw you admit them through the side door. Or rather, you admitted one visitor and the two of you carried the other. Let me in, or I will cry to the watch that robbers have invaded your rooms."

This was no bluff. He would do it. Ilse stood aside and motioned for him to enter. Alesso glided into the room, glancing to either side. His gaze paused at the lit candles, the map of Fortezzien spread over Ilse's desk, then the closed bedroom door. He sniffed, as though he could scent the mystery in her rooms.

Or the magic.

Ilse stole behind him. She could take him down with a hold and a sweep, then silence him with a blow to the throat. Alesso whirled around and seized her wrist. "Please," he said. "We are two old friends. We do not betray each other."

She tested his grip. It was too strong to break without making noise. "How sweetly you talk," she said. "I wish I could believe you. Speak plainly."

Alesso laughed. "This is why I adore you. Very well, I shall speak plainly. You have two visitors. One illicit, if not dead. Tomorrow, you face an interrogation with Lord Markus Khandarr, who is recovering from a rather strenuous interview this past evening. My guess is that these two incidents are connected. Let me help you in your endeavors."

"For what payment?"

His eyes were bright with amusement. "You are so blunt. I shall return the favor. I want you to plead my cause—Fortezzien's cause—with your beloved, Lord Raul Kosenmark."

Her skin went cold at Raul's name. "I left him and his house."

"You did, but rumor tells me your heart did not. What is your answer?"

Ilse thought quickly. She did not trust Alesso. But he had proved discreet. He had not gossiped about her letter and visit to Lord Joannis. He clearly knew more about Osterling Keep than she did. And she had not forgotten his words about political games, how not all of them concerned the king and his court.

"Do you want money?" she asked. "Or influence? You must have many friends in need. Shall we call them rebels, or do you have a more polite name?"

"Our names are not important. Nor do I want money. I want your promise of Lord Kosenmark's assistance in the future. We can discuss the details later. Introduce me to your friends and tell me your plans."

He smiled easily. Ilse wanted to slap him. "Galena," she called softly. "Bring our visitor, please."

They emerged from the bedroom. Both of them stared at Alesso with open curiosity.

"A prisoner," Alesso said softly. "And a soldier of the kingdom. So I guessed correctly. You should know that I could overhear your argument. You want to smuggle this woman out of Osterling. I can help you with that."

Galena hissed and drew her knife. "I told you no, Ilse. I meant that."

She darted toward the door. Alesso grabbed her arm, but Galena was as tall and strong as Alesso, and she had a knife. Ilse darted forward and disarmed Galena with a blow to her finger bones, which distracted

Galena long enough for Alesso to complete a sweep and throw her to the ground.

Ilse bent over her, the other knife in her hand. "Galena. I am sorry. I cannot let you report to your officer. Not yet."

"You lied."

"I did. I'm sorry."

"That is your mistake," Alesso said. "Being sorry, that is. Do we kill her?"

"What? No." But she eyed Galena uneasily.

Galena lay there, her eyes wide and pale. Valara had circled around and observed the scene with her arms folded. Her lips twitched in a smile when Ilse glanced in her direction. "Let her live," Valara said. "She will hate that worse than dying. Won't you?" she asked Galena. "Betrayal is a coward's weapon."

Galena flinched. "I am not a coward."

"Nor a friend," Valara said. "You have no reason to like or help me. But her"—she nodded at Ilse—"you care a great deal about her. Do you want her dead? Locked in prison and tortured? Better you let us go tonight and salve your conscience tomorrow."

Bells whispered through the open shutters. Three quarter chimes. Ilse glanced at Alesso. He nodded. He, too, understood they had little time before the watch changed, before someone sent a runner to the garrison prison and Valara's absence was discovered.

"Choose," Alesso said to Ilse. "Death or—"

"Forgetfulness," Ilse said. "I know magic to lock her memories."

He shook his head. "Not good enough."

He pressed the knife's edge to Galena's throat. Ilse reached for Alesso's arm, but it was Valara who intercepted him before he could do more than make a shallow cut. "One moment." Her voice was calm, dispassionate, as though they were not discussing murder. To Galena, she said, "Help me and I will take away the word on your face."

Galena's eyes went wide.

Ilse held herself still, watching them both, but especially Valara. *Oh, she is perceptive. Even at such a time as this.*

"Can you?" Galena asked.

"Of course."

"They'll see," Ilse said. "Your captain and everyone else will notice if that mark disappears overnight."

Valara shrugged. "I can make a spell with a lock. Your friend may wait a day, a year, then speak the words to complete the spell and set magic free to do its work."

Leaving Galena free to join her brother at the borderlands, or farther west. But Ilse did not dare to interrupt. She, too, needed Galena's cooperation.

Galena licked her lips. "I will then."

Once more the scene rapidly changed. Alesso helped Galena to sit up. Ilse fetched a wet cloth to clean the wound on her neck. Valara murmured a string of Erythandran, and the wound closed to a bright red scar.

"Now," Alesso said. "We make our plans quickly. You can't slip past the city gates, or by sea. Those soldiers keep a strict watch by the harbor as well as the highway. Even if you could, there's the fort. They'll snatch you up within two miles of Osterling. No, the only possible way is through the tunnels."

"What tunnels?" Ilse said sharply.

But Galena nodded slowly in recognition. "From the old days before the empire," she said in a wondering tone. "The kings of Fortezzien had them built in case of a siege. They could send messengers past the enemy, to summon aid from another city."

"You know where the entrances are?" Alesso asked her.

"Inside the Keep's ruins. They used to set guards outside, but not anymore. But I don't know anything else about them."

"How far do they run?" Ilse asked. "Far enough?"

Meaning, would the tunnels take them past the first circle of patrols. Alesso seemed to understand because he nodded. "Back in the old days, the tunnels ran halfway up the coast. Most collapsed years ago, but it's still passable for a few miles, if you don't mind rats and rubble. Is that acceptable to my lady?"

He left a great deal unsaid, but Ilse could piece together the clues. Alesso and his colleagues used the tunnels for their own activities. Which meant the regular soldiers did not. "It is," she said. "What if they decide to follow?"

"Then we make certain they don't. You and your friend go to the tunnel. Soldier girl reports to her harbor duty. Certain of my friends will arrange a distraction, while I handle things here in the pleasure house to explain your absence."

Ilse gazed into Alesso's eyes, wishing she could read what lay behind them. *Trust was indeed a gift. You could not ask a bondage price for it.*

"Give us until the next hour bell," she said.

Alesso's eyes narrowed, as if he were calculating a great many things. "When are you due at your post?" he asked Galena.

"At the hour bell after next."

"It will have to do," he murmured.

He rose and made for the door. Ilse followed him into the corridor. "Alesso."

Alesso turned. His lips curled in a sardonic smile. "What? You wish a kiss in farewell?"

She ignored his banter. "No. A favor. You must have the means to send messages to your colleagues. Send one for me to Lord Kosenmark, as quickly as you know how. Tell him . . ." She paused, wishing she knew how much she could commit to Alesso and his unknown associates. "Tell him to expect word from me through the usual means. Tell him that we need a ship for passage to a far foreign port. I can only tell him more once . . . once we meet."

The smile faded as she spoke. He studied her a moment with a strange, unreadable expression. "I will send word to your love. And you, you remember your promise to me."

She nodded. "I will."

"Then we are friends indeed." He bent down and kissed her on the cheek. The next moment, he was hurrying toward the stairwell.

Ilse closed her eyes. Her pulse danced far too fast for comfort. *I do not love him. I love Raul. Oh, but in a different life . . .*

No time for self-doubt. She spun back into the room.

"We need provisions," she said in an unsteady voice. "I'll fetch as much as I can from the kitchens. Galena, go to my bedroom. Help her to find better clothing for our journey."

She didn't wait for their reply, but sped outside and down the stairs. Once on the ground floor, she slowed her pace. It was quiet below, in these hours between midnight and dawn. A few lamps burned in their sockets, but otherwise the house was dark. Ahead, a bright light shone from the kitchen itself. She paused to collect herself, to think what she absolutely needed.

I need a guide, horse, provisions, and weapons. But salt and water will do for a start.

Only two scullions and a single senior girl sat by the open windows. They glanced up at Ilse with little interest. It wasn't unusual, after all, for those in the pleasure house to fetch a carafe of wine or water themselves. Ilse found a tray and loaded it with a jug of water and a loaf of bread. When she was certain no one watched her, she added a saltbox, tinder, two small metal pots, and a water skin. On her way back, she stopped by a storage closet for a lantern.

Back in her rooms, she found Valara dressed in one of Ilse's old baggy tunics. She had kept her prison trousers, though. "Yours were all too short," Valara said. "So were your shoes. Could you find me a pair of boots? Sandals even."

"We don't have much time." She noticed that Valara had found her ring. "You value that."

Valara's cheeks darkened. "I do. My brother gave it to me, years ago. I would not wish to lose it."

Yes. She had lost all her family to the Károvín. She would value any memento.

In her bedroom, Galena had pulled heaps of clothes from Ilse's trunks. She had separated the trousers and shirts Ilse used for drill from the others, and was folding them into bundles. "Do you have any packs?" she asked.

"None in my rooms. We'll use blankets instead."

Ilse gathered her weapons together—knives, her sword, the sheaths that went with them. That done, she pulled out the locked chest she kept under her bed. Her hands shook as she transferred money and jewels into a leather purse. They had made too many assumptions, left too many clues scattered through the past hour. She could only hope Alesso had told her the truth about the tunnels.

Galena uncovered a pair of oversized boots and took them to Valara to try on. Ilse changed rapidly into more practical clothes—trousers, a plain shirt, the boots she had not worn since her journey from

Tiralien to Osterling. She buckled on her belt, slid her sword into its sheath. Knives came next. One went into her boot, another into the sheath she fastened to her arm. She packed the leather purse among her clothes in one bag. On second thought, she added her map of Fortezzien and a map of Veraene's coast around Tiralien and Gallenz. She also packed her scroll from Lord Iani. *In case we fail,* came the fleeting thought. She shook away that idea and slung the blanket over her shoulder.

All ready.

Galena had packed the supplies from the kitchen into another blanket, which she gave to Valara. With a last glance around her bedroom, Ilse led her companions down the back stairwell and into the courtyard. "You go on to the harbor," she said to Galena. "You don't want to be late for watch."

"Not yet." Galena glanced meaningfully toward Valara.

"Take us to the tunnels first," Valara said. "Then I will do my part. I promise."

Galena studied Valara with a searching gaze. Then, with obvious reluctance, she said, "Good enough. You wouldn't find those doors without me anyway."

They took off through the dark, deserted streets of Osterling. The moon had sunk in the past hour, and clouds masked the stars. In Melnek and Tiralien, city watches patrolled the streets, but not here, where a fort overlooked the circling highway. With Galena leading the way, they stole through court and lane and avenue, across the main market square, where they recovered Galena's sword and shield, then on to the opposite side of the city.

"Not much farther," Galena whispered.

"What is that?" Ilse whispered back.

Footsteps rang off the paving stones. A voice called out, "Who goes there?"

A squad of soldiers marched toward them. Galena gave a sharp cry and drew her sword.

We are lost, Ilse thought. She had her own sword ready, but it was nothing against a full squad of trained soldiers. She took Valara by the hand, intending to drag her into the nearest alleyway. They still had a chance—

Ei rûf ane gôtter. Komen de hôchkelte.

Bitter cold and green magic flooded the air. It buzzed against Ilse's fingers, enveloping her hand, and crawling up her arm. A strange darkness, thicker than night, had dropped over them. She could no longer feel Valara's hand. She tried to summon the current herself, but her lips refused to work. It was that same otherworldly signature from before. It reminded her of Anderswar, of its alien creatures and the guardian who met her each time she dared to enter.

The magic receded. She blinked. A short distance away stood a dozen still figures. The one in the lead had turned his head to call out orders.

The soldiers.

They did not move. They could not, she realized with a sick feeling. They all remained in the same rigid stance, their swords raised and mouths opened to speak. But their faces had turned gray, and heavy ice weighted their clothing. Even as she watched, water trickled from the ice to run in rivulets over the cobblestones. But the men did not move.

"What did you do?" she asked Valara.

Valara herself appeared stunned. "I am not certain."

A dull boom sounded. Ilse dropped into a crouch just as a second and third explosion followed. Bright sparks hovered overhead. A sulfurous stink rolled up from the harbor, and a bloodred light bathed the city. More explosions, these from a different quarter, followed by a bright gout of fire that rose toward the sky. Alesso and his distractions.

Galena stared in the direction of the harbor. "Old Josche," she whispered. "Giann. He killed everyone on the watch. He would have killed me, too."

"We don't know that," Ilse said.

"We do know that. And you wanted me to trust him."

I warned you about me, Ilse thought. *That night you asked for my help.*

She reached for Galena's hand, which felt cold and clammy, in spite of the warm night. "Come with us. My friend can help you, too. You can find another place, without the words on your face, without any pledge."

Galena shivered, but with another tug from Ilse, she turned away from the terrible spectacle below.

"One moment," Valara said. "We need to remove the evidence."

She spoke more words in Erythandran. Again came the scent and image of a fox. Then the frozen bodies of the soldiers shivered into dust. More words erased the spells and all traces of their presence.

Another quarter hour and they gained the old Keep's ruins. It was Galena who pointed out the entrance, guarded by an old wooden door between two massive blocks of fallen stone. Soon they were inside. Ilse climbed down the stairs first, followed by Valara. Galena came last and shut the door, sinking them into darkness.

CHAPTER THIRTEEN

VALARA LEANED AGAINST the damp stone wall of the
tunnel's entryway. Darkness pressed in upon her; a
sour smell permeated the air. The other two, the soldier and her friend from the pleasure house, spoke in
soft tones. Something about the wisdom of setting a
wooden beam across the door. Valara hardly cared.
The exhilaration that had carried her from the prison
through Osterling's streets, to that strange confrontation with the soldier and its aftermath, had vanished
completely. Her bones were like water and a dull ache
centered between her eyes. Hunger, no doubt. Thirst.
Later, she might remember to be terrified. Right now
it was too much trouble.

The emerald's voice vibrated deep within her. It
sang without words, a stream of notes in a minor key,
like a ship's ropes keening in the wind. Daya, the oldest, the emerald. Rana was the ruby, which Leos Dzavek
had reclaimed. She couldn't recall what the third jewel
called itself. In older lives, she had known them all.
Known them even longer ago, when the three jewels
were one.

Before my brother divided them.

No, that was the life before they were brothers.
Leos had told Andrej once about his life dreams. Daya

and its siblings had been one, a milk-white jewel, the chief treasure of the empire. He had been a priest charged with safeguarding the imperial treasury.

And I was a queen of Morennioù. And Miro Karasek my beloved.

Daya's music stopped abruptly, and Valara realized the woman named Ilse had addressed her.

"We must go on," she was saying. "Can you?"

Valara brushed aside her wish for sleep and nodded. "I can."

Galena lit the lantern with their tinderbox. The light flared. Hundreds of beetles scattered in all directions, like dry autumn leaves before the wind. Valara caught a glimpse of broken furniture, old casks, and heaps of trash, all overlaid by a coating of dust, before she ducked under the low brick arch and followed her two companions.

For the first hour or so, the tunnel was a broad straight road. They picked their way through the dust and trash, startling more beetles and rats with their presence, but they made good progress. Then a set of steps led them down into a much narrower passageway that stank of dead things. Here the paving stones were broken; in places the brick-lined ceiling sagged dangerously. They jogged along bent over at first until the ever-lower ceiling forced them to crawl.

Valara soon lost count of the moments and hours. She ignored the patches of slime. The rats skittering over her hands or the tickle of spiders and their webs against her face. Whenever she slowed, Ilse poked her from behind. They had placed her in the middle, which meant they did not entirely trust her. She found she didn't much care. As long as they reached this mythical exit Alesso had promised them. Once beyond Osterling's magical shields, she could make the leap into Autrevelye and, from there, to Morennioù and home.

Home. To her people. To her father's advisers and his army, now hers.

She paused and closed her eyes tight against the darkness. Felt a surge of grief she had not expected after all these days.

A hand smacked her on the buttocks.

"Don't stop," Ilse hissed.

It took all her willpower not to round on the woman and curse her with magic.

"Yes," she breathed. "I understand."

And she did. This was no time for grief. There wouldn't be time, until she regained her homeland, took her throne, and drove the enemy from her shores.

She shook away the tears and hurried to catch up with Galena, now several feet ahead. Only another few hours, a day at the most, and she could escape this kingdom entirely. But she had to be certain before she made such an attempt. Ilse Zhalina knew a great deal of magic. Not as much as Valara, but enough to make escape difficult. No matter what the woman claimed, Valara did not trust her and her so-called friend with influence. If they suspected she held the jewel, they would do the same as Markus Khandarr.

The same as I would.

Their lantern sputtered and died. Galena abandoned it, and they continued forward through a suffocating darkness. The broken tiles gave way to rubble and trash and loose dirt falling from the ceiling. From time to time, Ilse called for a brief stop so they might each drink a mouthful of water, but neither she nor Galena suggested a longer halt. Valara didn't argue. She did not want Markus Khandarr's soldiers to trap her here.

At last, they reached a sharp turn, which emptied into a large chamber. Valara stumbled, her muscles cramped from the hours and hours of crawling. Galena

caught her by the elbow to steady her. Valara muttered a thanks. Her throat was clogged with dust, and
her voice came out as a feeble croak.

"Water," Ilse said. Her own voice creaked. "Drink."

Valara accepted the water skin and took a great
gulping swallow. The water was warm; it carried a
tang of earth and the slightly flat quality of cistern
water. She took another swallow and handed the water skin back to Ilse, who drank deeply before she returned it to Galena.

"Do you know where we are?" Valara asked.

"The end of the tunnel, I think," Galena said. "As
far as we can go at least."

"You think? You mean you don't know?"

An uncomfortable pause followed.

"No," Ilse said. "Unless you remembered to bring
the map. Did you?"

Her tone was light, almost amused—a courtier's
voice, and very much out of place in this miserable
dirty hole. Valara felt unaccustomed laugher fluttering
beneath her ribs. If she gave way, she might start
weeping from terror and exhaustion. She had the impression Ilse might do the same. "No. I forgot. My
apologies."

"A pity. Perhaps we ought to explore this chamber
carefully. Alesso claimed we should find the way
straight and easy, but he might have misspoken."

A delicate way to say she had not trusted him completely, Valara thought.

They felt their way forward through the dark, keeping to the edge of the chamber. It was much larger
than Valara had guessed—an irregular cavern made
even more irregular by hundreds of crevices and al-
coves. At one point, Galena discovered what must
have been a continuation of their tunnel, but its en-

trance was blocked by an enormous spill of dirt and stones.

"Never mind," Ilse said. "What we want is the exit to the shore."

"What if he lied?" Galena said. "He lied about other things."

She and Ilse began a soft-voiced argument about what to do next. Valara turned away from them. Was it her imagination, or had the light in the cavern brightened? She rose onto her hands and knees. Air puffed against her face. She sniffed and smelled salt tang and grass.

Without waiting for the other two, she felt her way toward its source. Her hands encountered a spider-web, an outcropping of rock, then a gap where a steady breeze filtered down from an unseen opening. She lifted her face and saw a wedge of light far above. "Here," she said. "I've found our exit. An exit. Look."

The argument behind her stopped. Galena came to Valara's side and craned her neck, trying to see what Valara meant.

"Do we try to go on, or do we try this exit?" Valara said. "If it is the right one."

"We have no choice," Ilse said. "Galena, what about patrols?"

Galena shook her head. "It depends. We're supposed to be dead. Or sailed away in boats before fire took. But if the commanders think we headed north, they'll make sweeps all the way up the coast and inland."

Not a comforting answer, but Ilse was right. They had little choice.

The tunnel slanted upward gradually for a distance. It was slow miserable going. They had to crawl on hands and knees, scrabbling through loose dirt and debris. The dirt filled their noses and choked their already dry throats, but the sight of the sunlight far above encouraged them. As the passage narrowed, they had to crawl on their bellies. The last section was the worst, the floor of the tunnel covered in thick layers of filth and bones.

At last, the entrance loomed ahead, a bright patch of sky and sun.

Galena crawled out first. She paused to scan her surroundings, then signaled to her companions to follow.

Ilse and Valara tumbled out of the passage into the open air. They were high above the shore, on a narrow spine of rock. A fresh breeze, sweetened by rain, washed against Valara's face. She blinked, dazzled by the light darting off the green waters of a bay to her left. Down below, a highway followed the larger bends of the coast. "Where are we?" she said.

"Two or three miles from Osterling," Ilse said.

Not nearly far enough.

Ilse and Galena began a swift discussion on what direction to take. Valara collapsed onto her back. Her hands were bleeding from cuts. Her trousers were ripped and her knees raw from scrabbling through broken rocks and paving stones. It didn't matter. She was out of that miserable tunnel and breathing clean air. Off in the distance, she heard a gull cry, the soughing of waves against a shore. Galena was saying something about patrols and magic sniffers. It took all her self-control not to make the leap into Autrevelye right away.

Tonight or tomorrow. Once I've eaten and slept. Then I won't make any mistakes.

A mistake would be fatal. She might fall into the wrong world. Or into the gaps and voids between them. There were accounts in the old histories of companions who dared to journey between worlds. One came home. The other remained lost forever.

They drank the rest of their water and started off along the ridge. By noon, they came to a cleft that snaked down the ridge into a ravine choked with pine trees and coarse grass. A stream gave them water to wash and to refill their water skin, but then they marched on. Soon the ravine opened into a wider valley surrounded by low hills. They plunged into a forest of yellow grass, which swelled from short clumps to a thicket that rose above their shoulders. Warm rain spattered them throughout the rest of the afternoon. The ground had turned into a treacherous bog, and they made slow progress along a narrow path.

A cluster of lilies, its blooms like russet stars against the pale grass, was the first sign that they had crossed the marshes. Beyond, a stand of pines made an island in the muck. As the land rose from the marsh into new slopes of red clay, the filament of a breeze washed against Valara's face.

Galena called a halt under a stand of pines. "We'll camp here."

Valara slumped onto the bare earth. She cautiously touched her swollen feet, chafed by the miles in too-small boots. "How far have we come?" she asked.

"I don't know," Ilse said. "Five miles?"

"Ten," Galena said. "I used to hunt here with my brother. We should make the next valley tomorrow afternoon. Then come hills and more hills until we reach the Gallenz River."

Ilse refilled their water skin from a nearby stream while Galena gathered pine branches and covered them with their blankets. When she had done with their bedding, Galena washed her hands, then picked a heap of marsh grasses, which she started to braid together.

"What are you doing?" Valara asked curiously.

"Making snares. With luck, these will bring us lunch tomorrow. For tonight, I'll have to forage a bit."

So many things she had not considered before her desperate flight. Valara absently rubbed the wooden ring. She'd not heard anything from the emerald during their long trek. Even now, the ring felt lifeless to her touch.

Daya? Can you hear me?

A wisp of magic's green scent, then Valara felt a cool wind against her face, heard the shriek from a startled gull, tasted the heavy tang of salt from the bay. Below her, she saw a figure running through the underbrush. He stooped, threw a glance over his shoulder, before he darted across the bare patch. Something in the man's height, the way his night-black hair swung around, reminded Valara strongly of Karasek.

Impossible. He died. I know it.

She blinked and found herself back in the swamp. The sun had already sunk beneath the hills, the sky had darkened to violet, and the full moon shone bright and sharp against it. Once more, time had sifted away.

Karasek dead. She felt a pang of regret, which puzzled her. She had known about his death weeks before. Or rather, she had guessed it. No one, not guards or prisoners, had mentioned him in Osterling. He would have been a prominent prisoner there.

I knew him, though. Long ago.

She wiped away the images from her past and glanced around. Ilse had built a small fire. When Valara stirred, she asked, "Did you discover anything?"

Of course the woman had recognized the magic.

Valara shrugged. "Nothing dangerous."

Ilse tilted her head, as if she wanted to ask another question, but returned her attention to the fire without speaking.

Not long after, Galena returned with a woven basket of provender. They dined on stale bread and turtle eggs, served with cattails and fresh water. She insisted they douse the fire right away, and went on to list the many dangers they faced, from dogs to magical spells to the patrols themselves. Her voice had taken on a nervous quality, and Valara remembered she had not wanted to come at first.

Finally Ilse laid a hand on Galena's arm. "We should sleep. We have a long march tomorrow."

Galena twitched away from the other woman's touch. "I'll take first watch."

Interesting, Valara thought. So much revealed in a few gestures.

They had assigned her a bed in the middle. She lay down on the mattress of pine branches, which creaked underneath. The rich tang tickled her nose; it reminded her of the hills above Rouizien on Enzeloc. From far off, she heard a bullfrog's deep-throated song, the rill of water. Her thoughts winged back—as always—to Morennioù and Vaček's soldiers. To her father's council, now hers by default. If she could have transported herself back to Morennioù that instant, she would have done so.

SHE WOKE IN the middle of the night. Ilse was shaking her arm. "Your turn to watch," she whispered. She said more, about keeping time by the moon's angle, but Valara paid no attention. Here was the opportunity she needed.

She took her post beside the stream and waited for her companions to settle into sleep. It was the first quiet moment she had to observe her surroundings. The trees and marsh looked far different under the moonlight, their colors bleeding to silver and gray. Shadows blurred the distance, changed perspective.

Sounds were different, too. Rain had fallen while she slept. Now she heard a constant silvery trickle from the trees onto leaves, a stronger rill from the stream.

She counted the moments to herself, well into the thousands, until she felt certain Ilse slept. Then, she rose silently onto her feet. The moon had reached its midpoint in the sky, and she could easily see the best path, but she moved cautiously nonetheless. Even one careless step might bring Galena awake.

The hillside dipped into a fold, not far from their camp, then rose steeply into a forest of pine and oak. Valara climbed until she reached a small clearing. Here the moon was hardly visible, and the musty smell of old leaves filled the air.

She sat with her back against one enormous oak. With practiced ease, she turned her focus inward, folding her thoughts upon themselves until she brought her mind to a single point, to a single moment.

Ei rûf ane gôtter. Ane Lir unde Toc.

The magic current breathed to life around her. Its scent was fresh and sweet. Valara continued the invocation, to the gods, to the magic. From a distance, she heard Daya humming a discordant song, but she did not pause to wonder.

Komen mir de strôm. Komen mir de vleisch unde sêle. Komen mir de Anderswar.

The trees around her dissolved into a diamond-bright mist. Beyond the mist lay a thick darkness, almost a presence. It was like a fog-bound night on Enzeloc's coast, when stars and moon were veiled and invisible.

The mist thinned to wisps and curls, for all the good that did. She stood in the midst of nothing, a void illuminated by a brilliant light. Even as the thought came to her, the light shifted, changed to an impossibly vibrant prism of color. She paused, uncertain. Though the familiar green scent saturated the air, this place was like none she had ever visited in Autrevelye, not even in lives before. No wheeling worlds beneath her. No sense of instability. All was too quiet and still, as though she stood in a bubble outside all worlds.

Because you do stand outside them all, Valara Baussay.

A tall figure strode into view—a woman with silver hair and a gleaming black face. When Valara fell back, the woman held up her hand. A long slim hand with eight fingers and nails curved into claws. *Stop,* the woman said.

Who are you? Valara whispered.

You know me.

There was magic in her song, a rainbow of hues in her words, and sharp sweet flavors with every syllable. She was a creature of Autrevelye, but unlike any Valara had ever encountered.

No, I am not of Autrevelye, though you abandoned me here a dozen lifetimes ago.

Cold trickled through Valara's veins. *Daya? Why did you stop me? We cannot stay in Veraene. They will take you and use you—*

And you will not? I was captured and tormented. My soul was divided. You . . . you promised me freedom, all those years ago, but you lied. You left me and my brothers-sisters. And now you would battle your brother again over us. We are not things, Valara Baussay. We are one.

But you helped me escape the prison.

I did. You will go home. I swear it. But not before you deliver us all.

What do you mean deliver?

But Daya had resumed humming.

. . . rûf ane gôtter . . . rûf ane zoubernisse . . .

The mist streamed around them, once more a thick and brilliant white.

Wait, Valara cried. *Tell me what you want. I'll do it.*

Deliver me. Deliver my brothers-sisters-cousins-self. Promise me . . .

Her words ran together into a chorus of silvery notes, high and clear and precise, the rill of water singing over stone, of raindrops cascading from the trees . . .

The crackle of thunder brought her back. She started, found herself gripped by both arms. Galena on one side. Ilse Zhalina on the other. They were dragging her back down the hillside, which was awash in heavy rains. Valara twisted away to break their hold, but Galena smacked her across the face. "You filthy lying bitch."

"No more, Galena," Ilse said, but she didn't protest when Galena struck Valara again.

When they regained the camp, Galena flung Valara onto her mattress. Ilse stepped between them. She leaned over Valara. "You lied to us," she said in a low angry voice. "You said you needed our help to escape Osterling. Now we find you can walk between worlds. At least, you tried to. What happened?"

She could not admit what happened. That meant explaining about Daya and the other jewels. Valara pressed her lips together and met Ilse's gaze with stubborn silence. Galena laid a hand on Ilse's arm, but Ilse shrugged her away. She stood and stared down at Valara, her face a blank mask in the night.

"Never mind. She will speak or not as she wishes. If she does not, we leave her behind."

A bluff, Valara thought. *Or not,* as Ilse turned.

"I—" She stopped and licked her lips. Ilse did not turn around, but she was clearly listening.

"I did try to escape," Valara said. "I tried before and couldn't. I don't know why."

It was the truth. Even so, she didn't expect Ilse to believe her. She waited, not certain what the others would say. In the end, Ilse shrugged and told Galena that she would keep the next watch. The two of them would take turns after that.

Valara released a shaky breath. No reproach. No ultimatum. Just a choice.

UNACCUSTOMED SUNLIGHT WOKE her early the next morning. She rolled over and groaned. Her body was stiff from the previous day's march. Her clothes were still damp, and clung to her in patches. She levered herself to standing, biting her tongue against the painful blisters that rubbed against her borrowed boots.

The previous day came back to her in sharp, uncomfortable detail—the escape, the long trek through the tunnel, her failed leap into Autrevelye.

I shall have no chance like that again. Not soon.

Galena and Ilse were eating a breakfast of raw fish and more turtle eggs. They said nothing as Valara approached, nor did they acknowledge her beyond a glance. She noticed, however, that they had left her a mug of water and a share of the eggs and boned fish. She should have taken satisfaction, but she was too hungry.

Breaking camp took more time than expected. Ilse scattered the pine branches. Galena covered the latrine with dirt, then leaves. She had snared two rabbits, which she skinned and gutted before hanging the bodies from her belt. The two of them repacked their belongings in the blankets. Then they set off with Galena in the lead.

Valara waited a few moments before she followed. They climbed the hillside to the next ridge, circled around the clearing where Valara had attempted her escape, then followed a narrow track between the trees, which led them over the ridge and into a low range of hills. A hush lay over the forest, and already the air felt thick with summerlike heat. As they climbed higher, they left behind the dense patch of trees for another clearing, where sunlight filtered through a web of shadows. A breeze drifted between the trees, carrying the rich scent of pine. *Relief,* Valara thought, as she tilted her face to meet it.

A movement to one side caught her attention. She went still, her heart beating faster. Was that a soldier, an animal? As she stared through the dust-speckled sunlight, the patterns of light and shadow slowly resolved into human features.

A woman stood underneath the pine trees. She was of ordinary height, her coloring a pale brown, much like Galena's. Oh but this was no ordinary human. With a shudder, Valara realized she could see the blurred outlines of the trees through the woman's body, lines that fluctuated and eddied, then hovered still.

Daya. Watching her.

CHAPTER FOURTEEN

MIRO KARASEK BRUSHED the snow from the ground with one gloved hand. More snow dusted the mountainside, in spite of the advancing season, and his breath blew in white clouds. Light was fading from the sky. He needed a fire or he would not survive the night.

In spite of the gloves, his hands were stiff from the cold, and he felt light-headed in the thin air. It took him several tries before he could arrange the layer of bark and twigs properly. If only he hadn't lost his tinderbox in that gravel slide. But he had, along with half his gear. He still had magic, of course, but the cold made it difficult to concentrate.

It could be worse, he thought, beating his hands together. *I could be starving. Or dead.*

He wasn't. Not yet.

Wind sang through the peaks high above. The keening made him think of souls crying for release. Ghosts, the Veraenen called them. It was possible. Dzavek's first armies had fought in these passes. According to legend, some chose to remain here as guardians instead of passing to their next lives. The Erythandran armies had called those rebel soldiers goats—stubborn and crude. Károvín poets had turned those insults into praise. But even goats could not survive without warmth.

He tucked his hands underneath his arms and closed his eyes. *"En nam Lir unde Toc. Ei rûf ane gôtter."*

Magic washed over his face, and his skin stung with returning sensation. Miro continued his summons until the current enveloped his entire body. Then he removed his gloves and bent close to his pile of tinder. *"Komen mir de viur,"* he commanded.

He cupped his hand around the spark to shield it from the wind. It brightened as he continued to speak magic, and smoke coiled up from the bark. At last, the flame caught, and a thin sliver of fire crawled along the tinder's edge.

Magic. Lir's gift of breath. Precious beyond telling.

He fed the flame with more bark and twigs, then added branches one by one until he had built a sizeable pile. Once the fire burned steadily, he took up the two marmots he'd snared that day. With swift sure strokes, he skinned the carcasses and cut the meat into strips, which he laid on stones beside the flames. Leaving those to cook, he filled his one cooking pan with snow, to which he added a treasured handful of late haws, and set that to boil.

As he worked, the sky had faded from indigo to black. The nearest mountains had become dark silhouettes, and he could no longer see any trace of sunlight on their upper peaks. For all he knew, the world had vanished, leaving only his firelit hollow.

More than a month had passed since his landing on Veraene's shores. He'd stolen an old shirt and a mule from a small farm on the peninsula. The shirt covered his Károvín uniform, and the mule carried him as far as the Gallenz Valley. When the beast went lame, he abandoned it near another farm and took to his feet.

North and north he marched, keeping well away from town and village. When he sighted the mountains on the horizon, he doubled inland to avoid the border armies, and made a great sweep west and around until he came to the plains just south of Ournes Province. There he had turned east toward the Železny Mountains and a little known pass into Károví.

Miro scooped up a handful of snow and scrubbed the blood from his hands. He rubbed another handful over his face, shuddering at the cold like a dog. Another week—maybe less—would see him through these mountains and into the province of Duszranjo. Once he located a garrison, he could command supplies and a fresh mount. He could reach Rastov and the king before the season turned.

To report my success. And my failures.

The greasy smell from roasting marmots filled the air. He stabbed the chunks of meat with his knife and ate them quickly, washing them down with gulps of hot tea. The meat was rank, the tea weak, but he didn't care. He ate until only bones and guts and sinews remained, then sucked the bones dry of their marrow.

Once there was nothing left, he buried the entrails, cleaned his knife and cook pot with more snow, banked his fire for the night. Once more the solitude pressed against him. He bundled himself in his blankets and stared at the night sky, where stars glittered like flecks of ice. Each one could be a soul in flight. How many were those of his soldiers, lost in Morennioù, or the ocean storm, or on Veraene's shores? How many had died because of his mistakes, his miscalculations and assumptions?

A breath of magic stirred. Once more he felt the touch of Dzavek's fingers against his lips, willing him to silence.

I am the king's chosen weapon. I execute his will.

The day's fatigue overtook him at last, and he fell asleep to that thought.

HE ROSE AT sunrise and drank the cold dregs of his tea. It took only a few moments to break camp— tamping dirt over the campfire, brushing away the more obvious signs of his presence. Wind and rain would take care of the rest. He worked more by habit than from any sense that others still pursued him. Then, his few possessions wrapped in a bundle, he marked out his next goal and started on the day's journey.

He marched until midmorning, then stopped for a brief rest. He refilled his water flask and gathered what provender he could find—handfuls of pine nuts, lichen scraped from stones, and puckered cranberries that were dusty and bitter with age. When he finished his meal, such as it was, he brewed a pan of tea and drank deeply. After a moment's hesitation, he took the leather packet from his shirt and unwrapped the long-guarded treasure he had carried from Morennioù.

Dzavek's prize.

The emerald lay dark and inert in his palm. For weeks, the jewel had tormented him with possibilities— sparking at his touch, inundating him with magic's powerful green scent. Gradually, that powerful response had faded, and its pulse turned elusive.

Do not call its magic, Dzavek had said. *Do not yield to its temptations. And be warned, I will know if you have tampered with my treasure.*

He wants to wield the jewel in war. Another war. Possibly our last.

Miro held the emerald up to the clear morning light, reconsidering the host of choices that faced him. He could defy Leos Dzavek and take its power for his own. He could bury it in the wilderness and hope no one rediscovered its presence. He could take flight, just as Dzavek's trusted adviser had done, three hundred years before.

To die for one's kingdom demands courage, his father had said. *But to live for one's kingdom . . . that requires endurance.*

Miro closed his fingers around the emerald. He had sworn allegiance to his kingdom. He would not break those vows. With a sigh, he tucked the emerald back into its pouch and set off once more. By midafternoon, he sighted a notch in the mountains—just a hazy golden smudge against the endless gray rock—but as he mounted higher, a thin ribbon of green showed beyond. Duszranjo. Károví. Home.

He marched faster. Had the captains written his name in the dead lists, or had they waited for infallible proof? He'd surprised the scouts more than once, returning from the impossible assignments his father had awarded him. His father would not witness this homecoming, but still Miro bent himself to the trail.

An hour before sunset, he gained the notch and a clear view of Duszranjo Valley. He dropped to his knees and sucked in a shuddering breath.

Duszranjo, the pearl within a granite sea. The Solvatni River wandered through the valley's golden fields and dark green stands of pines, a thin silver ribbon far across the valley floor. A town had settled on its banks—a neat square of gray stone and muddy red bricks. That would be Dubro, judging by the nearby garrison. Closer by stood a shepherd's hut. Herds of sheep moved across the slopes toward their enclosures, little more than blurred white shapes in the falling twilight.

He had lived here once, against his will, from eight to thirteen, after his mother fled his father's household.

At thirteen, he had made his own escape, taking the wilderness roads east to rejoin his father at Taboresk. But somewhere in Duszranjo, Pavla Karasek still lived—an anonymous woman of means, her identity kept secret by unspoken agreement between his parents, now between him and his mother. *Was she happier,* he wondered. *Did it matter?*

On impulse, he lifted his hand to capture whatever magic would answer his summons.

"*Ei rûf ane gôtter. Komen mir de strôm de zoubernisse.*"

The darkening air glinted with magic, and its thick scent overpowered the pine resin, the fresh scent of new hay. Was it his imagination, or did magic shine more brightly here, along Duszranjo's border? The touch comforted him, warmed him, but could not fill the clefts and voids within his contrary mind.

He released the current and it sighed into nothing. Still troubled, he made his way cautiously through the gloom toward the shepherd's hut. Within a short while, he came to a low square building with light seeping around its shuttered windows. A dog barked loudly. Beyond, hidden in the darkness, bleating sheep milled around on the edge of panic.

Miro stopped. He heard voices whispering within the hut. They must think him a robber.

"I've lost my way," he announced loudly. "I would ask the favor of your fire."

The dog whined, then fell silent. The door opened. By the lamplight streaming through, Miro saw a young man, square-built and dark, one hand nervously gripping a long knife.

"Who are you?" said the man. "You'll get nothing but a fight from us."

Miro held his hands out to show they were empty. "My name is Duke Miro Karasek of Taboresk."

A second man pushed to the front and held up a lantern. He was older, with a high forehead and iron-gray hair. The old man took in Miro's appearance with a searching glance. His frown smoothed into surprise— and recognition. "Your grace. Welcome." He beckoned Miro inside. "Fedor, stand aside for the duke."

Miro stumbled. Someone caught hold of his arms— Fedor, most likely. The young man helped him into the cottage and onto a stool. Miro found a mug of hot tea in his hands. The tea was bitter and keen and hot. He drank deeply, grateful for its warmth, and for the presence of others.

"I need a message taken to Dubro," he said. "I must let them know I've returned."

"At once, your grace."

There was a murmured conversation between the old man and his grandson, then Fedor was gone, tak-ing the lantern with him. The old man refilled Miro's mug. With more tea, he felt the cold melt away from his bones; his muscles relaxed. He was in danger of falling asleep, when he remembered the shepherd's curious expression of recognition.

"You know me," he said.

The old man hesitated, and his glance slid to one side. "I recognized your father, my lord. Thirty years ago, it was. I was a soldier from the conscripts. Matus is my name. Your father ran the garrison tight, he did. Kept the smugglers and bandits tame. He left a good name for himself here."

Yes and no. There had been a minor scandal, when this king's officer and nobleman had married a Dusz-ranjen woman. Did the shepherd know the ending to that story?

The old man Matus looked nervous, as if he feared he had angered the nobleman's son. Miro roused him-self from memories to ask about Matus's family, and about life in this remote province. He drank cup after cup of bitter hot tea and listened to tales of marauding wolves, mountain panthers (Miro's father had died, hunting one), and the illicit trade between the northern kingdoms. The old man mentioned rumors about war. News about troop maneuvers had filtered to the populace, obviously, and so they worried, imagining more and less than what actually happened.

They were still talking about those rumors when hoofbeats sounded outside. The garrison must have sent an escort back with Fedor. Matus opened the door to a lean gray-haired man, who ducked under the doorframe. Not just any escort, this man wore a captain's insignia stitched over his heart.

"Donlov."

Grisha Donlov crossed the room and knelt at Miro's feet. "Your grace."

There was profound relief in Donlov's tone. So others had expected, or hoped for, Karasek's death. Those speculations could wait. Miro stood and gestured for the man to rise, saying, "No formalities, Grisha. We're not at court."

Donlov grinned, a wolfish grin that creased his weathered face. "Not yet, your grace." He nodded to old Matus. "Grandsir, I left your son with a full plate and a full mouth. One of my men will ride him back when he's done. He eats like a soldier, that one."

After some argument, Miro persuaded the old man to accept a handful of coins for his hospitality. Then he and Donlov went outside to where Donlov had left two horses tied to a post. Donlov relit the lantern he'd brought along. By its light, they picked their way between the sheep pens into the fields leading toward the river.

"You made good speed," Miro commented.

"I'd've made better in daylight, your grace."

"Next time, I'll wait until morning. What brought you to Dubro?"

"Orders. Duke Markov wanted a firsthand account of our garrisons in Duszranjo. The king agreed."

Markov, Dzavek's other general. Interesting. "Any news then?"

"None. Unless you bring us some, your grace."

Miro glanced at his companion. Grisha Donlov's attention seemed wholly on their path, but Miro could tell by the tilt of his head the man listened intently for his reply. Rumors about his mission must have percolated downward.

"Whatever news I have belongs to the king, Captain."

"Of course, your grace." Donlov's tone betrayed no disappointment. He was a good soldier, and a loyal one. "So you go directly back to Rastov?"

"Tomorrow. I'll need a fast horse, provisions, and an escort."

Donlov saluted. "That you will have, your grace."

THEY REACHED THE garrison without incident. The commander, an old friend of Miro's father, provided Miro with a generous supply of new clothes and weapons. He had also arranged for an escort, mounted and fully provisioned, with Grisha Donlov at their head.

The following afternoon, they set off.

The company rode hard for eight days. Miro felt a peculiar haste driving him onward, through the narrow mountain roads, to the highways leading to Rastov and Zalinenka. Once they reached the open plains, they could gallop from garrison to garrison, taking fresh mounts at each stop. Overhead, the pale blue sky stretched into a dizzying arc, and at night its black expanse glittered with stars brighter and colder than

Miro remembered. With every mile north, he had the impression he rode just ahead of the greening spring.

Soon the highway rejoined the Solvatni River. Cities replaced the farms and outpost villages, and within another week, Miro sighted Rastov's dark red domes on the horizon. They gained its outer gates that same evening. Guards saluted Miro as he rode past. He returned the gesture absently, his thoughts now fixed on Leos Dzavek and his own report.

He touched a hand to his breast. Success. And failure.

Streetlamps dotted the avenues, and in the larger squares, the buildings were bright with candles and more lamplight. Despite the approach of dusk, Rastov's streets were crowded with merchant caravans and cargo wagons. The wine shops, taverns, and inns also looked busy with customers, whose faces might appear angry or sullen or carefree, but none was anxious. The rumors of war might be unique to the borderlands.

Solvatni Square was empty, and its many government buildings were dark. The previous year, lamps had illuminated every window past midnight. That was before the invasion.

Miro and his company crossed the bridge to the king's castle. Word must have preceded them, because the guards were already at attention, and attendants waited inside the courtyard. Miro gave his horse over to a stable hand. With a brief farewell to Donlov, he crossed the final distance to enter the castle.

More guards saluted, and servants approached to take his cloak and gloves. Across the marbled entrance hall, Miro saw Duke Šimon Černosek and Duke Feliks Markov walking together toward the audience halls.

The Scholar and the Brigand. He paused, disconcerted by the unexpected encounter. Černosek hap-

pened to glance in his direction. He leaned toward
Markov and spoke. Markov shrugged, as if indifferent to the news, but Miro noted how the man's mouth
tensed briefly. Subtle signs from a subtle man.

We shall have to speak honestly, one of these days.

Not today, however. A runner in the royal livery appeared at Miro's side. "Your grace. The king awaits
you in his private offices."

"At once," Miro said, with a last glance toward the
pair.

He hurried after the runner, up the several winding
staircases, and through the broad public halls, until
they reached the king's private wing. There the runner
withdrew. The guards outside the king's chamber announced his arrival.

In spite of the late hour, the king was immersed in
the business of his kingdom, and surrounded by a
host of servants, retainers, and members of his court.
A scribe knelt at his feet, taking notes. Others hovered
nearby, and several courtiers stood at the edge of the
room, which blazed with light from the enormous
fireplace. A chandelier hung from the ceiling; its dozens of candles, each enclosed in glass globes, poured
more light over the room. The glass divided the light
into a pale rainbow, scattering a suggestion of color
over the white marbled floor.

At Miro's entrance, Dzavek waved a hand. The
courtiers and servants withdrew, and the guards shut
the door, leaving Miro alone with his king.

Dzavek gazed at Miro, his chin resting on the curve
of his wrist. Like the room, Dzavek was dressed without true color—in gray robes trimmed with darker
gray. His long white hair was bound with a matching
ribbon. His dark face seemed drawn tight with anxiety, and the cloudy veil over his eyes was more impenetrable than Miro remembered.

Miro knelt and took the packet from his tunic. "Your majesty, I have both good and bad to report."

Dzavek accepted the leather packet and hefted it. "You took the castle."

"Yes, your majesty."

The king nodded. He set the packet to one side and extended his hand toward Miro. Silver rings covered every finger. Miro kissed them. Their gems felt cold to his lips.

"Tell me what happened, Miro. Leave nothing out."

Miro's relief drained away. So, here was the test.

Head bowed and kneeling, he delivered his report as he had imagined it while marching through the wilderness. Starting with the moment of departure, he recounted the rapid journey over the seas, through the barrier, and the first sight of Morennioù's coast.

"We arrived at dawn," he said. "As you predicted, we found the castle and its docks on the northwest point of the main island. But someone must have given alarm, because we met defenders at the castle gates."

"The barrier," Dzavek said. "I warned you that breaking through signaled anyone who listened. So you overcame these first obstacles."

"Yes, your majesty. Their soldiers fought hard, but we outnumbered them. I ordered the castle surrounded and any fugitives detained for questioning."

"Then you took the castle and recovered this emerald." Dzavek nodded toward the leather packet. His tone—cool, almost indifferent—unsettled Miro Karasek. To his ear, it sounded as though Leos Dzavek already knew the invasion's details.

"The king and his chief mage died in the attack," Miro continued. "We captured the princess before she could escape. Our search uncovered this emerald. As you commanded, I left Anastazia Vaček to extend our hold on the island, while I returned with Lir's emerald."

"Two months ago, Miro. What happened?"

Miro raised his gaze to Dzavek's face, hoping to read whatever minute reaction the king allowed to escape. He saw nothing but intense curiosity.

He dropped his gaze to Dzavek's hand, which still clasped his. "A storm sank our ships off the Veraenen coast, your majesty. We brought our launches on shore, to Osterling. I was negotiating with their commander for transport when a . . . disagreement broke out."

"But you escaped."

"I did. Unfortunately, I had to leave the Morennioùen princess—the new queen—behind. The Veraenen took her prisoner."

He looked up to see Dzavek gazing at him with those strange and clouded eyes. The impression of age was stronger now, lamplight shining through the man's almost transparent skin, sending shadows of lines cascading over his face.

Like a death mask. Immediately, he quelled the thought.

With a sigh, Dzavek stirred, and the flush of life replaced that mortal stillness.

"I am glad you did not choose to lie, Miro."

He touched his other hand to Miro's mouth, his lips moving in a whispered spell.

"En nam Lir unde Toc, komen mir de kreft unde zoubernisse."

The king's fingers were hot—unnaturally so. It took all Miro's discipline to remain still while Leos Dzavek continued to draw the magic into a thicker cloud.

Komen mir de strôm. Nemen mir de swîgen.

Dzavek was releasing Miro from the magic seal that he had set upon him two months before. A green scent filled the room, strong and invigorating. The miles of marching and riding dropped away like the snows in summer. Dzavek spoke another word to release the current, which faded into nothing, taking the spell with it. Only by its absence could Miro tell the difference.

Then it struck him. *He knew already what happened in Veraene.*

"Your majesty, has Anastazia Vaček returned?"

"No." Dzavek smiled briefly. "Though she did try to send a messenger. They failed to break through the barrier, Rana tells me. You may stand now." He retrieved the packet from the table and untied its leather strings. Within, the emerald gleamed with a dark green fire. "Do you believe this is a true jewel? One of Lir's children?"

"I believe so, your majesty. It has the touch of magic."

"An equivocal reply. If you weren't certain, why did you guard it so long?"

Because you ordered me to. Because I vowed obedience.

Dzavek did not seem to want an answer, however. "Listen," he murmured. "Watch."

He held the emerald up to the firelight. His gaze went diffuse. Miro detected an electric quality to the air as the magic coalesced around them. He listened, every sense trained on the emerald, thinking that at last he would hear the same musical speech his ancestors had, when Károví had first claimed Lir's gifts for its own.

The room seemed to grow smaller, the walls pressed inward, and in intense weight pressed against Miro's chest. Still Dzavek did not stir, but continued to stare at the emerald.

Ei rûf ane gôtter. Ei rûf ane juwel. Sprechen mir.

Dzavek was commanding the emerald to speak, bidding it as he might a servant.

Ei rûf ane . . .

Miro's ears roared as the air thickened to an impossible heaviness.

. . . ane gôtter. Sprechen mir. Iezuo.

A loud crack echoed through the room. The emerald vanished in a burst of light, leaving a tiny heap of gray dust in Dzavek's palm. Dzavek glanced from Miro back to the dust. "A counterfeit," he said softly.

Miro blew out a breath. *All those months, all those lives, gone. For nothing.*

The king scattered the dust with a flick of his hand. "Never mind the mistake. You lost the Morennioùen queen, but I found her. She has the true emerald. She used it to escape her prison. Or it used her."

More surprises. Miro licked his lips and considered what he might safely say. "It appears you had no need for my report, your majesty."

"Yes and no. You brought me news of the battle and its aftermath. And yourself. I need both for the next stage of my plans."

He turned toward the table beside his chair. He unlocked a drawer and retrieved a wooden box, not much larger than his hand. Dzavek lifted the lid and took out a small dark ruby, which flared bloodred in the lamplight.

Miro knew this one. It was Lir's second jewel, Rana. The one the king had recovered from Vnejšek the previous summer.

As Dzavek turned the jewel over in his palm, the ruby cast a red sheen over his skin. Miro suppressed a shudder. Anastazia Vaček had been quoting Leos Dzavek when she had told Miro her true orders for Morennioù. By blood and bone and magic, Vaček would prepare the ground for Dzavek's second invasion. Leos Dzavek had not forgiven his brother's treachery even though lives and centuries had passed.

"We can plan the next assault later," Dzavek said. "Once we secure the emerald, Morennioù cannot resist long, not with hostages. We will hold the new queen against their surrender. And their welfare against hers."

I loved her once.

But those were lives and days past. With an effort, Miro returned to the present.

"She might be difficult to locate, your majesty," he ventured to say.

Dzavek made a careless gesture. The gems on his fingers flashing in the lamplight. "Not at all. Whenever the queen speaks with her emerald, she must use magic. When she does, I will hear her."

CHAPTER FIFTEEN

OVER THE PAST several months, Gerek Hessler spent his holidays wandering the streets of Tiralien, reacquainting himself with the districts from his student days. Today he browsed through the warren of secondhand booksellers in the Little University. Here one might find dozens of cheap novels, or second-rate poetry from the previous decade, but it was also possible to find a genuine treasure. Some of the vendors were iterant, much like the spice dealers Kathe mentioned, selling their wares from carts or baskets in the street.

He picked up a crumbling edition of Alberich Wieck's essays from one such cart. The copy itself was not valuable—the binding had cracked and several pages were missing—but he had always liked Wieck's observations on the accepted forms of scholarly interpretation. He handed over a silver denier, received his change, and moved on with the book in his satchel. The next stall carried only mathematics textbooks. Interesting, but not worth the price. He drifted past more shops and stalls into a square populated mostly by butchers and chandlers. One lone vendor, however, had set up a cart by the entrance. Without much confidence, Gerek looked over the man's wares. Political

treatises. Erotic engravings. An occasional tract spec-
ulating about spiritual matters.

He turned over a few leaflets without much interest,
then paused.

A cookbook?

Gerek glanced back at the other shops, as if considering whether or not to move on. Pretending boredom, he sorted through the bin a second time. It *was*
a cookbook. The title—engraved in thick woodcut
letters—mentioned ornamental dishes from the court.
He dug past the book to an assortment of heroic poetry volumes, then back to the cookbook itself.

Its condition was better than he would have expected. Water stains covered several pages, but the
parchment showed no signs of worm or decay. If the
date was correct, the volume dated from the later
empire days. If not . . . well, it made an interesting
curiosity.

"Ten silver denier," the vendor said immediately.
"Which is a true bargains for such a rare—"

"Ten copper," Gerek countered.

The vendor wailed about his poverty, the wife and
ten children he fed from his meager earnings, etc., etc.
They dickered back and forth a few more times, until
Gerek finally handed over two silver denier. The price
was robbery, but he thought Kathe might like the
book. He knew she studied all manner of cookery.
Sometimes Lord Kosenmark liked to hold historical
feasts for his noble friends.

He ordered the book wrapped in clean brown paper
and added it to his satchel. And because he liked the
man's looks, he added a third silver denier to the sum.

My father was right, I am a fool, he thought, as he
accepted the man's thanks.

But the thought of Kathe's pleasure overrode everything else. He spent most of the walk back to the plea-

sure house imagining her delight when he presented this gift.

Except he was not entirely certain of her delight. To be sure, Kathe smiled whenever she greeted him. But she smiled at everyone, including the rag and bones man. *Well, she might like the book, even if it comes from me.* He could write a note. Say he'd come across the book by chance, which was true.

It was late afternoon when he returned. Guards nodded as he passed through the front doors. Inside, he heard the maids at work in the common room. Gerek was fumbling at the door latch to his rooms when a runner came round the corner. "Maester Hessler. Lord Kosenmark requires your presence."

"Right away or—?"

"Now, sir."

Kosenmark never acted without reason. And Gerek had noted how Kosenmark had withdrawn into a deeper privacy over the past week. Could there be a crisis with the kingdom? Gerek thrust the book into the runner's hands and asked him to deliver it to Mistress Kathe. He would write a note later, he told himself, as he jogged up the stairs to Kosenmark's office.

Two guards stood outside the door, and another inside—Detlef Stadler, the house's senior guardsman. But it was the pair farther inside the room that captured Gerek's attention.

Kosenmark sat at his desk. A stranger stood in front of him—a young man with thick black hair tied in braids. Dressed in salt-stained clothes and carrying the strong scent of fish and tar, he appeared to be a common sailor. At Gerek's entrance, the young man glanced toward him. His face was marked with bruises and what appeared to be a half-healed burn, which showed bright pink against his dark complexion.

Kosenmark gestured for Gerek to take a seat. "Tell

us your report," he told the young man, adding,
"Names are not necessary just yet. You came with
news about Osterling."

The young man nodded. "I did. Three months ago,
the royal fleet sighted Károvín ships sailing east. A
week later, three of those ships foundered on Osterling's reefs. In the skirmish that broke out, the garrison troops prevailed. They took a number of prisoners,
including a young woman the Károvín had drugged
with magic."

"You have spies within the prison."

A shrug. "That follows, yes. I learned this woman
made several attempts to escape. None succeeded. The
old prison uses particular spells to guard against particular kinds of magic. Unfortunately, those spells did
nothing to prevent Lord Khandarr—"

"No names," Kosenmark said.

The young man regarded Kosenmark with evident
curiosity. "Very well," he said slowly. "Then let us say
a certain man questioned this woman about her identity, her allegiances, and so forth. The young woman
did not cooperate. As is usual with a man of his character, he resorted to forceful magic. The woman defended
herself with even stronger magic that struck the man
insensible. He had not yet recovered when the woman
escaped in the night, leaving the entire garrison, including the other prisoners, either dead or unconscious."

He paused and drew a deep breath. "I cannot continue without using names, my lord."

"You can and you will."

The young man's lips parted in a bitter smile. "Are
you afraid of names, then?"

Kosenmark merely stared at him. Gerek knew that
stare and he wasn't surprised when the young man
lowered his gaze. "No names," he repeated. "Very well.
She escaped, this nameless woman. Her path crossed

that of two other nameless women in the city. As you can understand, that attracted my attention."

"Yes, I do understand that," Kosenmark murmured.

His comment seemed to provoke faint amusement. "Yes. Well, as you can also understand, I offered my assistance. My colleagues organized several distractions. We fabricated evidence that more prisoners had escaped from the garrison. A supposed murder took place in a certain pleasure house. In the confusion, I sailed here by a convenient boat. Your friend—I gather she is your friend—sends a message. She desires a ship for distant ports. She will send further word by the usual channels."

If he had not known Kosenmark, Gerek would have missed the brief flicker of tension in the man's mouth. There and gone, like a speck of snow in a fire. *He is afraid,* Gerek thought. *Not of this stranger, but for Ilse Zhalina.*

Kosenmark's voice, however, betrayed nothing. "Did she mention which channels?"

"The usual, my lord. Just as I said."

"I see. Thank you." Kosenmark signaled to Stadler. "Please escort our guest to quarters until we can confirm the details."

Stadler took hold of the man's arm, but the man pulled away. "You will remember your promises?" he said to Kosenmark.

"You have my word."

The answer seemed to satisfy, because the stranger gave a curt nod and followed Stadler from the room without any further argument. Once the door closed, Kosenmark rested his head on his hands. "I leave tomorrow," he said. "Two days at the latest."

"But my lord, I–I—"

Gerek swallowed the spasm in his throat. Kosenmark kindly did not pay attention to him. "Our friend's report is not entirely unexpected. I've heard rumors that the king's mage is too ill to leave Fortezzien, and deprived of its usual ruler, the court in Duenne is in disarray. The two might be connected or not. I dislike making assumptions about anything connected to Markus Khandarr. However," he said, "the matter of the King's Mage and his health are not our immediate concern. The news this young man brings from Fortezzien is. There are a dozen usual channels a trusted friend might use to contact us. Over the last half year, several have proved unreliable. I suspect that Markus Khandarr has bought their loyalty. In spite of his recent indisposition." In a softer voice, he added, "They were always more devoted to profit than any particular cause. I cannot blame them, considering past events."

Meaning Dedrick's death, along with Lothar Faulk and other trusted associates.

"If anyone inquires after me," Kosenmark went on, "tell them I am grieving for an old friend's unexpected death. That should please Markus, once he revives enough to inquire. And I know he will. Have Mistress Denk keep the house open to our oldest clients, but no one else and absolutely no festivities. Meanwhile, I want you to find a ship built for deep sailing. Buy it or lease it, I do not care. Hire a crew. Found it with provisions for a six-month cruise. But do not allow anyone to make a connection between that ship and my name. Use that list of special agents I gave you. I believe I can trust them still . . ."

It was like those first days, when Kosenmark spoke on without pause about all manner of arcane subjects, while Gerek mentally scurried to keep up. If Gerek had not watched Kosenmark over the past few days—had not noted the sudden deeper reserve, the broken-off invitations, the hours spent alone in his rooms—he would have said that Kosenmark knew about Zhalina's message even before the stranger brought it.

He did not know. He thought her dead. Murdered.

And this flow of words was a burst of relief that he could at last stop the endless wait and act.

So Gerek listened and burned these instructions upon his memory. Not once did he ask, *Where are you going with this ship?* Because he knew without asking that even Raul Kosenmark could not know the answer.

THE JOURNEY TO the Gallenz River lasted over twenty days, far longer than Ilse and Galena had first predicted. They had agreed to act as though Markus Khandarr would send patrols after them, and so they kept well away from the coast and any tracks or trails inland. Instead they struggled through thick pine forests among the hills, and slogged through grassy bogs in the dells, sweating in the close heat.

This morning, they marched in single file through a grove of aspen. Rain had fallen in sheets over the past few days. Their clothes were drenched, their make-shift packs soaked through and heavy. Now the sun shone hot and unforgiving through the trees; steam rose from the damp forest mast. Ilse lifted her face to catch a few drops falling from the leaf canopy and caught a glimpse of Valara's amused expression.

The expression quickly vanished. Once more hers was the bland, blank courtier's face of the past weeks. Ilse wiped the raindrops from her face, tasted their clean woody flavor, and continued marching. Ahead, Galena had not even paused. She strode through the wet, a rough-cut staff in one hand to switch away the underbrush.

Three weeks together and we are still strangers.

Oh she was glad for Galena's presence. It was

because of Galena they had enough to eat. Galena knew about building shelters, coaxing fire from damp wood, and how best to disguise their tracks without using magic. She didn't even complain when Ilse explained that avoiding magic meant a longer delay before Valara could remove the mark from Galena's cheek.

Even so, Ilse did not miss the many signs of her distress. Galena in Osterling would chatter and laugh, even if the chatter was too quick, and the laughter sometimes brittle. The Galena of the wilderness was a quiet young woman, and when she spoke, it was only about necessities. Galena in the wilderness frequently glanced southward, her lips pressed together.

I wish Lord Joannis had listened to me, Ilse thought. If he had, Galena would be in Osterling still, a very junior soldier in Veraene's army. She would have a black mark against her name in her records, but with the promise of a better future.

And yet, if Nicol Joannis had listened, Galena would not have encountered a runaway prisoner in the night. And Khandarr would have recaptured Valara Baussay within a mile of Osterling, if not sooner. Ilse ran her hand over her face. If she were master of time and the world, would she undo the past three weeks? Would she set Galena back in her former life?

She knew the answer and did not like it.

Valara was another matter. Ever since her attempted escape, she had marched in steady silence. She obeyed Ilse's orders, but she never volunteered to do more, nor had she attempted any conversation with either of her companions. She was not sullen or troublesome. *She was,* Ilse thought, *resigned.*

Galena's pace slowed. She pointed with her staff toward a break in the trees. Ilse came up beside her and shaded her eyes. She could just make out a swath of blue sky and a darker horizon, low in the distance.

They had reached the Gallenz Valley at last.

Another hour brought them to the edge of the valley where they paused. To the north and west, the hills rolled up to the sky, and Ilse noted golden bands alternating with russet and green. Farmland, she remembered from her previous trek through the wilderness, years before. What interested her the most were several towns along the river. She thought she recognized the particular configuration of river bends and settlements, but she couldn't be certain. And for this next step, they could not afford any doubt.

"Where next?" Valara asked.

"We stop for today," Ilse said. "I want to review our map."

Galena found them a campsite in a thicket of birch and thorn bushes, near a small stream swollen from the spring rains. Dinner consisted of an insufficient amount of dried rabbit seasoned with wild currants and handfuls of clover. Afterward, they boiled pot after pot of water and stripped to scrub themselves clean.

Ilse brewed a cup of tea and settled down with her maps. Rain had soaked through the thick parchment, and she had to unfold the sheets carefully to avoid shredding them, but the mapmaker had evidently used ink imbued with magic, because the letters and lines were as crisp as when Ilse purchased the maps three months before. She traced the outline of the Gallenz River with one newly scrubbed finger, then peered down into the valley to match the drawing to their surroundings.

The river narrowed between two high banks. Two distinctive bends, with settlements on either side. Those would be Aschlau and Gutell. She knew from conversations with Raul that Aschlau was an overgrown village, founded by a miller and an ironsmith, which lay at the intersection of several large farms. The iron-smith sometimes passed along information to Raul. Gutell was a sister settlement across the river.

Both were too small for their purposes. Villagers noticed and remembered strangers. She scanned the map for other, larger towns or cities, where three wanderers might pass unnoticed. Ah, there—a small city named Emmetz. Measuring with her thumb, she calculated that twenty miles separated Emmetz from Aschlau, sixty miles from Tiralien. Far enough that Khandarr would not keep a watch on them.

"Three more days," she murmured. "Four at the most, and we shall come to our first test."

THEY ROSE AT dawn and shared out the cold remains from supper for breakfast. Galena covered their fire pit and latrine. Valara and Ilse refilled their water skin from the stream, before they set off for the valley below.

At noon, they paused to rest and eat wild onions dug from the ground. Then it was onward through a meadow of new grass and wildflowers, to an almost invisible footpath that turned into a muddy trail rutted with wheel tracks. They filched vegetables from the fields outside Aschlau and ate them raw as they circled around the village for the highway beyond.

And now we are among people again, Ilse thought.

Her stomach tightened from nerves. It was like her first encounter with the river and its highway, after she had escaped from the caravan, but then she had lived for weeks alone, starting at every sound because she feared Alarik Brandt. This time it was Markus Khandarr. Strange how she could not measure the distance of terror between these two.

It was late afternoon of the fourth day, the sun slanting toward the horizon, as they approached the outer buildings of what Ilse decided had to be Emmetz. They passed a blacksmith, then several sizable animal pens, crowded with goats, sheep, and ponies. Beyond these stood a wall of brick houses and a paved street. Passing between them, Ilse saw that the banks of the river were much higher here, and most of the town perched on the slopes leading down to the water.

They asked directions from an old woman carrying a basket on her head. The woman's eyes narrowed at their clothes and knapsacks, but she answered politely that, yes, they had reached the town of Emmetz and they might find an inn or tavern if they followed the main street. Soon enough they found a cheap-looking inn where they bought bowls of porridge. For a few denier more, the innkeeper filled a tub with hot water so they could bathe. He even offered them a scrap of soap for a small price. They scrubbed themselves as well as they could and beat the dirt from their clothes, but it was obvious they had spent weeks traveling through the wilderness, and Ilse felt as if a dozen eyes watched them as they made their way through the main square.

The late-afternoon sky was darkening, and the air was thick with golden light. Many of the shops had closed, but Ilse found a baker still open. She asked for directions to the street where Raul's chief agent lived. The baker's mouth settled into a disapproving line. Not a pleasant neighborhood, Ilse guessed. But the woman gave her directions and even offered her a drink of water after Ilse bought a half loaf of bread.

"Where next?" Galena asked when Ilse came outside.

"Minnow Lane. Once we deal with my friend's friends, we can find a room and bed for tonight."

Galena shrugged wearily, as if she hardly cared any longer about inns or friends. Valara shook her head but said nothing. She limped from blisters, but she offered no complaints.

Ilse led them back to the main avenue. From there, they hurried along the edge of the riverbank to an open square. A smaller lane at the bottom of the square, mentioned particularly by the baker, looped down the slopes toward the river. Now Ilse understood the woman's distaste. An air of neglect overhung the neighborhood. Damp stained the plaster, the air smelled of urine, and paving stones changed to ankle-deep mud and filth.

Her companions followed her silently to the house Lothar Faulk had once described to her. Ilse motioned for them to stand to one side. She knocked.

Nothing. She knocked again and set her ear against the door.

"You won't find 'em home," said a rusty voice.

Ilse turned to see an old woman peering down from an open window in another house. "Not at home," the woman repeated. Then she laughed, a high creaking laugh. "Sold up three months ago. Said that business turned bad here, and he'd try his luck elsewhere."

"Do you know where?" Ilse said.

"No. But for a man with such terrible business, he whistled and sang a great deal. Are you wanting a room for tonight, lady?"

It was tempting. She might question the woman about Raul's late agent. But it was equally likely the woman had been set to watch any visitors. She gave a friendly smile and shook her head. "Thank you, but no."

The old woman muttered something about dirty beggars and slammed the shutters closed. Ilse skirted around the corner, to where Galena and Valara waited out of sight.

"Your friend's friends were not so lucky for us," Valara said.

"He has other friends. But I think we should try another town. We can find a bed for tonight, then head for Gutell tomorrow." They would buy new clothes and good packs before they left Emmetz. They didn't want to attract more attention.

They retraced their path up the hillside. In the brief interval since they arrived, the sun had disappeared behind the hills. Twilight flooded the streets, making them appear all alike. Ilse thought she remembered the way back. There had been a couple quick turns, then a pair of stairs leading up to the more public avenues.

A wrong turn brought them into a maze of passages, overhung with looming blank walls. Not their first wrong turn, Ilse thought as she surveyed their surroundings.

"We should have followed that other street to the left," she said.

Galena sniffed. "We're close to the river. I can smell it."

"Do we go back?" Valara said.

"Yes, and quickly," Ilse replied. "We don't want to spend the night in the streets."

Especially these streets. She disliked their emptiness, and her hand found her sword hilt.

Her suspicions were confirmed when she turned around to see a shadow blocking their path. It was a boy, all bones and ragged hair. Scars stood out pale against his dusky complexion, and he had the scattering of a beard. He held a knife in one hand, its blade pointed upward. His gaze flicked over Valara, then settled on Ilse. "I saw your money," he said. "Drop your purse on the ground, and you won't mind what comes next."

Ilse exchanged a glance with Galena.

"Thieves," she murmured, drawing her sword.

Galena already had hers in hand. "Hungry ones."

What happened next came so quickly, Ilse could not separate cause from result.

Half a dozen figures swarmed from the building on their left. Six or seven more blocked the street behind them. Most of them were older boys, but several were hardly more than children, and there was one girl with a swollen belly. All of them were skinny, their eyes like dark pits in their faces. All of them carried sticks and knives.

Galena slashed at the gang leader's face. The boy flung his arm up and ducked away in time. The others charged. Ilse parried with her sword and backed up against the closest wall. All her old drill patterns came to her without thinking. Block. Parry. Block again and thrust. Twice she took hard blows that made her gasp and lose the pattern, but these were not trained fighters.

Merely desperate ones. Their numbers could make up for skill. One blow to her head, one slash at her eyes, and she would die.

She glanced around, trying to find her companions. Valara had called up a wall of fiery magic. A double signature hung in the air—the dark of a fox, the cold bright of starlight. Good. Ilse whispered the summons, but she needed all her concentration for the fight, and the current wavered.

Off to one side, Galena's blade flashed through the twilight. The youngest of the children scattered. One boy fell in a heap, stunned, another boy dropped, clutching his stomach. "Run!" Galena shouted.

With a flurry of blows, Ilse drove through her attackers. Together she and the others pelted toward the next street. If they could gain a few moments alone, she and Valara might combine their magic. They skidded around another corner. Valara stumbled. Ilse dragged her to her feet, but the gang was already upon them.

Galena gave a shout for help. Several shutters overhead were flung open. They immediately shut with a bang. Ilse swung around, looking for her companions. A hand grabbed her by the shoulder and flung her backward. The gang leader, blood streaming from his face, swung his knife high to strike.

Five strangers burst onto the scene. Four plunged into the mass of boys, sending them scattering with blows and sword thrusts. One—a powerfully built man—leapt past his companions to seize the gang leader's arm. His knife arced through the air. The boy crumpled into a bloody heap. But the man did not release his hold until he'd bent over the boy and touched his throat. Then he lifted his gaze to Ilse's.

It was Raul Kosenmark.

CHAPTER SIXTEEN

FOR A MOMENT, Ilse could only stare at Raul. *Seven months. More than seven months since we were last together.*

There was nothing of the lord about him today. His hair was tied back into a tight queue. He wore loose mud-stained trousers; dirty, scuffed boots; and a dark gray shirt that made him almost invisible in the twilight. Utterly plain. Very practical. He might have been a soldier, a robber, or a pirate. She wanted to walk directly into his arms and never leave them again. With a sickening effort, she controlled herself.

Raul sheathed his knife and came toward her in three swift strides. He touched her cheek as if to reassure himself that it was truly her, then glanced around at his guards and the street. "We should go at once," he said. "There is a watch of sorts in the town. Eventually they will notice us."

Only now did Ilse realize the fight had ended. The leader was dead, so were three of his companions. The pregnant girl sprawled on her back, groaning. Several others lay motionless. Ilse could not tell if they were dead as well, or unconscious. She glanced down at her bloody hands. Her shirt was bloody, too. She vaguely remembered stabbing one of the boys.

One of Kosenmark's people pulled Galena to her feet. Galena looked dazed, her clothes were bloody and torn, but she was alive. Valara appeared untouched, unmoved, as she observed the scene. Ilse shivered at the blood and Valara's indifference. Her own pulse beat erratically, and she tasted a sourness at the back of her throat.

I've killed a man before. Blood should not make me so squeamish.

A man, but not boys.

The warmth of Raul's hand on her shoulder steadied her. He took a flask from his belt and handed it to her. It was good red wine, undiluted. She drank and felt warmth flood her body. She took a second, smaller swallow and gave the flask back. When he tilted his head in question, she nodded. *I am fine. I will survive.*

Raul turned back to Galena and Valara. "Are you wounded?" he asked Galena. She stood slightly askew with one hand held over her ribs.

Galena's chin jerked up and she stared. It was his voice—a woman's contralto voice from the throat of a man. Ilse could see the clues fitting themselves together from the girl's rapidly changing expression. A noble's accent. A man whose reputation had spread throughout the kingdom. Even Galena had heard of Lord Kosenmark. She straightened up with a wince and saluted. "No, sir. I mean, my lord. One of them knocked me in the ribs. It hurts, but not so bad."

Raul smiled at her. His gaze passed over Valara as he turned back to speak with his guards.

"Your friend came just in time," Valara said quietly to Ilse. "He is your friend, yes?"

"Who else would rescue us?"

Valara did not answer. She was scanning the guards and Raul Kosenmark with an assessing gaze. Ilse thought Valara did not consider herself to be rescued.

She looked as though she was preparing herself for another interrogation.

She is not so wrong. Raul will not trust her easily. He cannot afford to.

Raul signaled to his guards. They scattered to their posts—two in the lead, two more to guard the rear—and set off through the dark streets. Their pace was soft-footed and quick, but not so quick that Galena could not keep up. They must have scouted the entire town, Ilse thought, because they never hesitated once. Within moments they had left the alleyway behind and were gliding between silent buildings, then down a series of shallow steps to the waterfront.

Raul paused in front of an old wooden building. He scraped his knuckles over the door and whistled a lilting tune in a minor key. After a brief wait, another whistle answered. Raul rapped sharply in a one-two-one rhythm.

The door swung open to show a bulky man whose body filled the frame. Ilse recognized his face. His name was Gervas, and he had come to Kosenmark's household five years ago. Like the rest of the guards, Gervas was dressed in dark gray and black clothing, and in the twilight, he was little more than a looming silhouette except for a thin edge of light reflecting from the short sword in his hand.

"My lord," he said. "Trouble?"

"A bit. Nothing terrible."

Raul led his party inside, past Gervas and a second armed guard. Ilse had the impression of a vast empty space, the air dank and smelling of wood rot and sludge. She could hear a sucking noise—water against pilings—and the rill of a free-flowing river. In the distance, she made out a pattern of faint gray lines. Cracks in the walls? Shutters? She couldn't tell. They'd reached an abandoned warehouse of sorts. Alesso had delivered her message—that much was clear. When Raul had arrived, and how he had discovered her whereabouts, was not.

She reached out for Raul's arm, only to find he had moved on. He stood a short distance away, speaking to one of his men in a soft, high whisper.

"We have a temporary shelter," Raul said as she came to his side.

"How temporary?" she asked.

"A few hours, no longer. As I mentioned, Emmetz does have a watch of sorts. One of them will eventually discover a few bodies . . ."

"And those thieves will report us for the reward," Valara said.

Raul regarded her with a slight smile. A leopard's smile, neither safe nor friendly. "They might," he said. "Would you rather I had killed them all?"

"Perhaps. Does that prove your moral superiority?"

He laughed. "An interesting question. Let us discuss the matter in more comfort."

An open staircase in the middle of the room led up to a trapdoor. Raul whistled a different tune. There was an answering whistle, then the trapdoor creaked open. "My lord," said a woman's voice. "We didn't expect you so soon."

"Does that mean Barrent doesn't have our supper ready?"

"He says nearly, my lord. Give us another quarter bell."

She heaved the door to one side, and they climbed through into another empty cavern of a room. Farther off, two men stood around an iron kettle filled with burning coals. The scent of leeks and fish and olive oil wafted toward the newcomers. Raul indicated to Valara and Galena that they should join the others. Ilse was about to follow, when he touched her arm.

"One moment," he murmured in her ear. "I need a word alone with you."

He took her through another door into a smaller chamber lit by moonlight from an open window. Blankets and gear were stacked in one corner. Outside, a balcony ran the length of the building, and stairs zigzagged down to the alleyway below, where another pair of guards patrolled. The sight reminded Ilse of the previous summer, when Raul had hired scores of new guards because of his private war with Markus Khandarr.

That war never ended. It never will, until one of them dies.

And even death was no guarantee.

Raul shut the door and whispered the invocation to magic. A sharp green scent rolled through the air, the scent of crushed grass and wildflowers. He spoke a second phrase and silence closed around them.

Ilse turned. In the moonlight, Raul's eyes were like shining golden disks. Underneath the scent of magic came the sharper scent of blood, both from his clothing and hers. Ilse felt a tug deep within. There was something wrong in this painful spurt of desire, but she had no wish to suppress it just now. And yet she found it impossible to move, to do more than stare at him from across the room.

His mouth curved into a smile. "Are you hungry?"

Ilse laughed weakly. "Oh yes."

His words, her laughter, released her from inaction. She walked toward him into his embrace. It was not necessary to kiss. The warmth of his body, the pressure of his arms around her, the scent of wood smoke and cedar and sweat, a scent that was entirely his. She held him tightly. The shirt's cloth felt wonderfully rough against her cheek. Through the fabric, she heard the rapid beat of his heart. *I love him. I always have. In lives before and times long ago. Today and now. Through all my future days.*

Raul buried his face into her hair. "Your message came to me last week. Unfortunately, Khandarr set a watch on my house. It took several days before I could arrange matters to escape without his notice."

At first she could only take in his presence, his arms holding her tightly, and his voice, which was like an invocation to a different kind of magic. But then the meaning of his words broke through. "It came only last week? But—"

"Last week," he repeated. "Six days before that came a report you had died."

She pressed harder against him. Felt him trembling. *Oh my love.*

His lips brushed her cheeks. His breath feathered her hair, as he continued. "I had word that our usual channels were not to be trusted. I went immediately to Aschlau, then sent my best trackers to sweep the hills. They sighted you when you came into Emmetz. As soon as I got word, I . . . I hurried."

Hurried. Such a lovely, ordinary word. She wanted to laugh again, but tears choked her voice, and it took a few moments before she could say anything close to sensible. "I am so glad you did," she said. "Let me tell you more."

He gave her the flask again. She drank sparingly, because she did not want the wine to muddle her thoughts, and quickly told him about Valara, from their first encounter in the pleasure house, to their flight through Osterling's streets, to their confrontation with the soldiers and how Valara killed them with magic. She went on to describe Valara's attempted escape and her subdued behavior since.

Throughout, Raul listened without interruption. When she was done, he considered a moment, then asked, "What about the ship? Do you still believe we should give her aid?"

She blew out a breath. "I don't know. But I believe it would be a terrible mistake to leave her to Khandarr or Leos Dzavek. Morennioù has one jewel. Dzavek and Khandarr both would use this woman as a hostage to obtain it, which means war between all our kingdoms. However, I've promised nothing so far, only that you would listen to her. In return she must listen to you."

"Fair enough," he said. "What else must I know before we return to the others?"

What warning could she give? All her impressions, beliefs, and second thoughts flashed through her mind. There was so much she wanted to tell him, but in the end one quality stood out from the rest. "She lies," she said simply. "Every moment. You cannot trust her."

"How interesting." He shook with silent laughter. "We should deal famously then. What is the truth behind her stories, do you think?"

She shook her head. "Better that you listen and make your own judgment."

"Which is a judgment itself. Nevertheless, I see what you mean. I shall be cautious."

His hand brushed against her hair. Ilse tilted her face up to see him studying her. Moonlight picked out silver at his temples. She wondered what other changes the past seven months had worked within and without the man. She wondered what changes he had remarked in her.

I shall have to tell him about Alesso.

Not yet. Not when they had found each other again.

She laid a hand on his chest, closed her eyes, and tried to reach for a calm and focus she did not possess in the moment. Raul had sensed the change in her mood, because he loosened his embrace. "Come," he

said. "We'll eat our supper and head north. Then we
can talk with our queen."

WITHIN TWO HOURS, they had crossed the river by
the nearest fording and left Emmetz behind for the
rain-wet fields beyond. They marched in single file
along a muddy goat track, which rose slowly from the
riverbanks to the lower slopes of the northern hills.
The company kept to an easy pace, with frequent
stops, but Raul did not call a halt until several hours
later, when they had gained the edge of a pine and oak
forest.

The guards went to work at once to set up their
new camp, fetching water and deadwood, stretching
lengths of canvas to make shelters. Ilse leaned against
a tree trunk, overtaken by weariness. The moon had
set an hour before. Far to the east, the first pale bands
of dawn showed, but the river valley below was overrun with shadows. The air smelled fresh and cool,
with a foretelling of rain.

"Do we go on tomorrow?" she asked Raul.

"Not until we talk with your queen," he said. "I
want to make certain we agree on the essentials."

One of the guards approached. Raul turned away.
Ilse listened to them discuss the watch rotation. She
rubbed her palms against her eyes. The brief spurt of
joy at seeing Raul had faded hours ago, during the
long march into the hills. She had not removed the
reason for their separation. She had merely changed
the direction of their plans. What came next depended
on Valara Baussay.

Raul and the guard were still deep in conversation.
Ilse took herself to the edge of camp. Galena and Va-
lara had disappeared. Another guard, Ada Geiss, told
Ilse that Galena had volunteered to dig latrines.
Valara had retired into her tent for the night. Ada's

expression was bland, but Ilse caught a hint of amusement in her voice, and she wondered just what Valara had said or done to provoke that.

Most likely she was herself.

She asked where she ought to sleep, and Ada pointed her to Raul's tent. It was the largest of the camp, with a portable writing desk in the corner and a small metal box layered in spells, a miniature of the one he used in Tiralien. Several packs stowed in one corner. Two mattresses, she noted, both made from blankets tucked around pine branches.

On the bed to her left, someone had laid out clean clothes and other necessary items, all of them sized for Ilse. Next to the bed she found her old gear from Tiralien—leather armor, wrist sheaths, even the metal helmet she used for weapons drill on those days when Benedikt Ault pushed her exceptionally hard. *I love him,* she thought. *All over again. He does not come to rescue me. He comes to deliver me weapons.*

Ilse changed into a new shirt and trousers, and lay down on her pine mattress. The crushed scent of needles reminded her of magic's green scent. Magic, that rare and dangerous current, and yet the ordinary world was filled with reminders of its presence. Crushed grass, the tang of forests, the rich perfume of new blossomed wildflowers. Was it, as the old scholars insisted, only a matter of setting your gaze in the right direction? And if that were true, why were so many blind to it?

Rain pattered against the tent ceiling, a rhythmic tap-tapping that emptied her thoughts. Eventually, she slept.

SHE DREAMED OF rain drumming against canvas, against doors and windowpanes. Gradually the rain faded away and she walked in silence through dreams

of a milk-white palace. Narrow windows showed a
night sky salted with stars. Snow hushed against the
stone walls outside. And everywhere hung the scent of
magic.

*A prince of Károví sat opposite her, his lean dark
face intent upon the book between them. It is a matter
of discipline, he said.*

*His eyes were large and bright, like a bird's. He
wore a ruby in one ear, a sapphire set into his cheek.
She touched the smaller emerald in her own cheek. Its
presence chafed, but she willed away these thoughts
and concentrated on the text, an antique volume that
one of the diplomats from the Erythandran Court had
brought as a gift to her, in recognition of her position
as the affianced bride to the Károvín heir. She had
showed it to Leos because she respected his opinion in
scholarly matters. As usual, they had begun to argue.*

*Discipline is but one ingredient, she said. You know
that, Leos.*

Talent, he said with a dismissive gesture.

*Not talent alone, she replied. Honor plays a role. So
does heart. No, do not scoff, Leos. There are cases
throughout history that support my theory that magic
is both act and consequence. Imagine if you were that
wizard who discovered Lir's jewel—except "discovered" is too soft a word for what he did.*

It doesn't matter what he did. He served his king.

*No, she said. He captured the magic for himself. He
took the gift of magic and entrapped it inside a dead
stone for his own glory. He paid a terrible price—*

*She stopped at his expression. You know nothing
about him, he said coldly. He rose, taking up the book
as he did so. Thank you for the gift. I will treasure it.*

*He stalked away, his gait unnaturally awkward. She
did not have the courage to remind him the gift had
been intended for her. She glanced out the window, to*

the vista of rooftops and the plains beyond. Clouds
passed before the sun, casting the room into shadow.
It had begun to snow, in spite of the spring season, the
flakes coming down large and wet against the expen-
sive glass panes of the window.

She woke to the trill of running water. The air inside the tent was warm and close. The scent she smelled
was crushed grass drenched in rain. Ordinary things
from an ordinary world, but still her pulse beat an
uncomfortable tattoo as she took in the implications
of her dream. She and Dzavek, together, in the days
before Károví broke away from the empire. Why had
she never dreamed of him before?

Oh. But I have.

She recalled the image of Dzavek's face as he turned
away—an image she had dreamed a hundred times
without understanding its import. And another dream,
of darkness and torchlight and a blade flashing toward her throat. There was even the moment when
she had glimpsed her grandmother's life dream, to see
herself in the same white palace. Fragments only, and
yet if she had had the wit to piece them together, she
might have understood her part in this spectacle.

But no, I only thought how my life had intersected
with Raul's.

The thought of Raul drove away all dreams.

She sat up. His mattress was empty. His clothes
from the day before lay folded at the bottom, and the
mattress showed signs he had slept beside her. The
blankets themselves held none of his warmth, but a
faint trace of Raul's unmistakable scent lingered in the
cloth, the same she had breathed in the night before in
the deserted warehouse. It was like finding traces of a
ghost.

Then she heard voices not far away—a man's and a
woman's.

She crawled from the tent into the twilight. The ground was wet through, and more rain dripped from the trees. Clouds mottled the sky. A red smudge ran along the western horizon. She had slept the day through.

Raul sat alone with Valara Baussay by a low-burning fire in the center of the campsite. A kettle of venison stew hung from a metal rod, set between two stakes. There was also a pot of coffee set beside the fire to keep warm. It had a burnt smell, which told Ilse the others had been awake an hour at least. None of the guards were in the camp.

A bucket of water stood by the tent. Ilse rinsed her mouth and splashed more over her face. Then she approached the other two.

"Have you held a conference without me?" she asked.

Raul smiled tightly. "Hardly. You are the linchpin of our discussions, after all."

His voice was high and edged. And Valara's face was too deliberately bland.

"I am no linchpin," she said. "Merely a participant."

Raul smothered a laugh. Valara shook her head. Interesting.

Ilse took a seat on the third side of the campfire. Raul sorted through a collection of mugs, plucked the cleanest of them, and poured her a cup of coffee. She accepted it with caution. His mood was clearly sarcastic, Valara's furious. It was easy to see they'd already had at least one unpleasant exchange.

"What have you decided so far?" she asked.

"Nothing," Valara said.

"And everything," Raul added.

Ilse sipped her coffee, which was bitter, and observed them both. Valara's mouth was set in a hard, angry line. Raul appeared amused, but she read tension

in the tilt of his head, the way he flexed his fingers as
he refilled his own mug.

"Would you like to know what we've discussed?"
he said to Ilse. "Your companion is not Károvín or
Veraenen. Her accent confirms that. She claims to be
Morennioù's newest queen. An outrageous declara-
tion, but let us accept it for now—"

"You said you wanted peace," Valara broke in.
"You lied."

"How so?"

"If you truly wanted peace, you would not demand
a price in return."

Raul shrugged. "Our queen believes we should provide her with a ship on her word alone. To ask for any
assurance is unreasonable."

"I said nothing like that. You want too much."

"I want your promise that you will not involve
yourself in our wars."

"And what if I refuse? Would you deliver me to
Lord Khandarr?"

"No, to King Leos Dzavek."

Ilse went still. The coffee roiled in her empty stomach. "Raul—"

"Hush," he said. "Let me continue the part our
queen expects."

A role, then. Her misgivings, however, did not
abate.

Valara was glaring at Raul. "You speak of treason
to your own king."

He seemed impervious to her rage. "I've committed
treason already, by certain lights. I learned of your
escape last week. And yet I said nothing to anyone in
authority. If I had, you would be in Lord Khandarr's
gentle custody."

A long pause followed while Valara studied Raul.

The tattoos on her cheek and under her lips stood out against her pale brown skin. Ilse thought she saw traces of a third. Again, she wondered at their significance.

Finally, Valara said, "You mentioned the jewels before. Does that mean you are searching for them?"

"No. I wish to secure peace between my kingdom and Károví. The jewels are a hindrance."

"Or a provocation," Ilse murmured.

Raul shot her a keen glance. "Yes, or a provocation. They are rare and powerful objects, which any kingdom might find useful in war. Do you deny that?"

Valara's eyes narrowed—almost an obvious clue to her thoughts, except that Ilse believed nothing obvious about this queen. Was she calculating the risks to any answer? Or possibly weaving a new and more plausible story?

"You wish me to be honest," Valara said at last. "Very well. I have said we in Morennioù possess one of the jewels. I discovered it myself in Autrevelye— what you call Anderswar. It was last summer."

Ilse suppressed a flinch of surprise. Last summer was the time when she and Raul had received disquieting news from their spies. Károví had begun naval maneuvers off the Kranjĕ Islands. Not long thereafter, Dzavek had recalled high-ranking officers from Taboresk, Duszranjo, and Strážny. She glanced toward Raul, whose expression had not changed, but she knew the same thought would occur to him.

"Did Dzavek know of your discovery?" he asked.

Valara hesitated. "He did. But he did not know my identity until much later. That was when he launched a fleet of ships through Luxa's Hand."

"How?"

Another pause, almost undetectable, but Ilse was

watching Valara closely. She did not think the woman was lying outright, but she suspected carefully selected gaps in her story.

"He used magic," Valara said slowly. "Spells locked on the ships, which remained dormant until unleashed by a matching key. It— I am not certain I have the words to describe it, but those spells translated the ships and everything inside them to light."

"You saw that?" Raul said sharply.

She shook her head. "I heard the soldiers talk about it, after they took me prisoner. One set for all twenty ships bound to Morennioù. Another set for those who returned."

Ilse let her breath trickle out. So, Dzavek had found the means to break through the magical barrier set by Morennioù's great mages three hundred years ago. It would require equally great magic to do that, but Leos Dzavek had the knowledge and skill—centuries of it.

Raul refilled his mug with more unpalatable coffee. Such a casual gesture, but Ilse thought she could read great tension underneath, like a panther that has sighted its prey. "Interesting," he said mildly. "Leos Dzavek achieved what no other mage could these past three hundred years. Are you as skilled as he is?"

Valara's gaze never wavered. "No."

"Then how do you propose to return to your homeland? Unless you have Lir's jewel and can use its magic to support your own."

"I have no jewel with me," Valara replied quickly. "It stays hidden in my homeland. The Károvín did not discover its presence, because we gave them a counterfeit wrapped in magic. This is what I told her before." She nodded toward Ilse. "But with a good ship and crew, it is possible to circle around the barrier. Luxa's Hand does not extend infinitely. I've studied

the maps left by the old mages. Far south, near the
great ice fields, the barrier ends."

Raul sipped his coffee, grimaced, and set it aside.
"A dangerous voyage."

"Yes," Valara said. "But remember, a fleet of ships
and their soldiers remain in Morennioù, Lord Kosenmark. I might be queen, but I am a hunted queen, far
from home and with the enemy at loose in my lands.
That is the reason behind my desperation. So I ask
again, will you give me passage home?"

Raul said nothing for a few moments. Ilse didn't
need a magical spell to read his mind. He was casting
over what Valara told him, sifting through her words
and silences for the truth.

"What about us?" he said at last. "More important,
what about the third jewel?"

"What about it?" Valara asked in turn.

"You have one jewel. Leos Dzavek has recovered
the second. Do not bother to deny it. I have confirmation from several trusted sources. So far you are well-
matched. Veraene has nothing."

"Not exactly nothing," Valara replied. "You have
tens of thousands of soldiers more than I. You have a
mage councillor of great skill—"

"Leave him aside," Raul said. "One jewel—one
creature born of Lir's breath and love and passion—
that can overturn any advantage we have. We need a
better assurance."

"What kind of assurance? Your famous peace?
Your word is not enough, Lord Kosenmark. You
might say I have nothing to bargain with. But I would
gladly bargain my life against my kingdom's security."

The firelight gave the other woman's face a ruddy
cast. Her eyes were like dark strokes of ink against a
sheet of parchment, aged to the color of honey, her
face like the face of stone monuments from ancient

times. It was in that moment that Ilse saw why Valara was the heir and now queen. She did not speak empty words.

I have met this woman before, in lives past. Which ones?

She glanced toward Raul. He gave slight nod. *My turn*, Ilse thought.

"Are you ready for war, then?" she asked Valara. "Are you ready for all your people to die, not just you?"

Valara blinked at the question. "Why should that matter to you?"

"Peace matters to me. Unless we agree, Veraene faces a bloody, unnecessary war. Unless we agree, you face a thousand or more soldiers and mages from Veraene or Károví."

"More threats," Valara said. Her voice sounded rougher than before.

"No, merely observations about the risks following your decisions. You might believe that a war between Veraene and Károví protects you. It will, for a time. We haven't ships or soldiers or mages enough to battle two kingdoms, especially one so far away as yours. Or you might believe that Morennioù could ally itself with either of us—"

"I don't."

Ilse tilted her hand to one side. "Then you believe that Lir's Veil protects you. Also wrong. Morennioù is no longer the lost kingdom. One fleet of ships found a way through the Veil. Others will follow. War here simply means a delay."

Valara stared at Ilse a long moment. "So what do you propose?" she said at last.

"A balance between the kingdoms," Ilse said. "You pledge to keep Morennioù neutral. Lord Kosenmark gives you passage home, and pledges to use his influence to forestall any difficulties between our kingdom and yours."

Valara frowned. "A pledge of influence? From a man dismissed from court? I cannot—"

"And I give myself to you as a hostage," Ilse said.

A thick silence dropped over the campsite. Ilse wasn't certain why she had offered herself. It was impulse, and the knowledge that unless Valara gained a true advantage over Raul, she would never agree to anything he proposed.

But the sight of Raul's masklike expression was like a knife stroke.

She drew a breath. "Let me explain."

"Please do," Raul whispered.

"Yes," Valara said. "You would offer yourself as my hostage. How does that benefit me?"

"Two ways. You are assured that Lord Kosenmark will keep his promises. And you may use my presence should you need to bargain with Armand of Angersee and Lord Khandarr. King Leos remains your concern. In return, you will offer us all assistance to recover Lir's third jewel."

Valara stared at Ilse. Again Ilse had the impression of a hunting fox—and that impression strengthened when the other woman drew her lips drew back from her teeth. "I agree."

A longer pause followed before Raul said, "I would like to discuss certain points with Mistress Ilse before I pledge my word. Please," he said, cutting off Valara's incipient protest. "You will have weeks or months to discuss the matter with her. I require only until tomorrow."

Valara shrugged. "Very well. Let me know in the morning what you decide."

She stood and deliberately turned away, toward the rows of tents. Ilse watched silently until the woman disappeared into the closest one. All the while, she sensed Raul's unhappiness, his tense stillness, as he waited for her to speak again.

It had been the logical move, she told herself. The only one that gave Raul the advantage he needed against Armand and Khandarr. Valara had studied the jewels. She knew enough to rediscover one. And though Dzavek had taken the second, she must have clues to where the third one lay. If Veraene controlled that one, they could achieve a true balance between the kingdoms—a dangerous one, if any king or queen decided to risk all, to gain all. She did not think that Leos Dzavek would do so, nor Valara Baussay, in spite of her bravado.

"You made a risky throw," Raul said.

He spoke softly, his voice more like a woman's than ever.

"I had no choice," Ilse said.

"Liar," he whispered.

At that, she had to meet his gaze. "I am not lying," she answered, as softly as he. "I am not running away. But if we do not give this queen some advantage, she would die before she agreed to any pact with us."

"You said she lies."

"She does," Ilse said. "That is why I offered myself—to ensure our part of the bargain. She will search for the third jewel, whether I go with her or not, you know. She is a great deal like Leos Dzavek. They both want all three, and not just for practical reasons."

An image of Dzavek's face flickered through her memory. She shivered, thinking of the similarities between him and the Morennioùen queen.

"A risk." Firelight and shadows made Raul's smile deeper than it really was.

"Somewhat," she agreed. "Do you see a better course?"

"That is the simplest question I've answered today. A better course would let me spend the rest of my days with you. No more hiding. No more pretense. But," he went on, his voice high and soft, "that course is not one I'm offered."

"You aren't arguing with me," she observed.

"No." She could hear the briefest catch on that word. "No, I am not your master. I make no cages for you, not even ones of words and wishes." Then he said, "I love you. I have not said that enough lately."

Her throat closed. She had to swallow before she could speak. "We haven't had much opportunity."

"No, we haven't. Would you like to change that?"

His voice turned rougher, deeper. It was more than desire that tugged at her. It was . . . a sense of completeness in his company. More, because she could tell from a myriad of details that her presence wrought the same effect on him.

We need each other.

And she had just consigned herself to yet another, longer absence.

Raul held out his hand. Hers found it without conscious volition.

"What about . . ."

"Don't worry," he said.

He led her back to their tent. Ilse almost cursed him for predicting this moment, but instead she laughed softly as they ducked through the opening. Raul turned and with a quick movement, untied the cord holding the flaps open. Darkness fell over them. The air turned warm and close.

He drew her close and nuzzled her hair. "I love how you smell."

"Of mud and sweat and . . ."

"You."

His mouth closed over hers in a kiss.

Oh. Oh, I had forgotten.

Forgotten how warm and insistent his kisses were. How he liked to pull her tight against him, so that she lost her breath for a moment. And how he drew back, just enough so one hand inevitably traced a path from her hair to her neck to her breast, where his palm cupped her flesh gently.

"Raul . . ."

His answer was a mumbled laugh, a cry.

"Raul, I must tell you something. It's about Osterling."

"Not tonight," he said hoarsely. "Tomorrow."

Tomorrow. It was a promise and a warning.

He touched her cheek with his fingertips. Ilse drew him close into a warm kiss, soon followed by another. Their kisses turned into a hungry feast of caresses, of mouth against skin, until they had shed their clothes and locked themselves in a bubble of passion.

CHAPTER SEVENTEEN

IT WAS A return to their early days in Tiralien—before the affairs of the kingdom intervened and Markus Khandarr executed Dedrick Maszuryn. Before they conceived their separation. If she could put a number to those days, she knew it would be no more than three or four months from the time when they admitted their love, to when Dedrick first approached Raul about spying in Duenne's Court, and yet to memory's eye, the interlude seemed an endless ribbon of pleasure and passion and contentment, which curled back upon itself and so continued forever.

We were Anike and Stefan, she thought. *Two ordinary people without any concerns for the empire or magic.*

Remembering those days, Ilse insinuated her arms around Raul and drew him tight against her chest. His smooth skin—unlike any other man's—was like fire-warmed silk. His heart beat swiftly against hers, a mirror of her own painful emotions.

"I love you," Raul whispered into her ear. "I always have."

"Impossible. You loved Dedrick."

Dedrick, once Lord Kosenmark's beloved. Then his friend and spy. Now dead because of that love. For many months, Ilse had not been able to mention Dedrick's name. Nor could Raul.

We were too new to love, in this life. We had to learn how to trust all over again.

Raul rolled onto his back, a familiar movement that brought her, by habit, to settle under his arm. It was like one puzzle piece fitted to its mate, one word linked to its proper companion.

"No," he said. "I meant that first time in Andelizien. You were Sonja and I was Andreas. Or at least, that is the first I remember us together. Later, I came to Zalinenka from the emperor as an emissary to the court of Károví. You and he were prince and princess together. I was nothing but a messenger, stupid and young and homesick, but you were kind to me. I thought I would kill myself from desire."

Her skin prickled at this host of images from her life dream the night before. "You were there? You remember?"

"Of course I remember. And yes, I have always been there."

Like the earth beneath her feet.

"I've dreamed of those days," she whispered. "Of Leos Dzavek. I had not known . . ."

"Nor had I." His voice, high and fluting, whispered back to her. "But lately I've dreamed more of those past lives."

He pulled her close, but not for lovemaking, only to hold each other in warmth while the stars wheeled overhead and the moon swept down to the horizon. They slept, limbs entangled, as in the olden days, days from just a year ago. Toward midnight, Ilse stirred and woke, to find Raul awake. The sky had cleared and a bright moon shone through the canvas. He rested his head on one hand and gazed upon her with a foolish grin. "I should not have such joy within me," he said.

She kissed him, tasted the salt of his skin, the sweetness of his mouth. "We take joy as we take the sun-bright days of summer."

Joy.

Unexpectedly, a pang shot through her—so sharp and strong, she had to bite her lip to keep from weeping. She shook her head and her unruly hair tumbled loose between them. Later, she would have to braid it fresh for the night. Such an ordinary thought, for such an extraordinary day. She found she could not hold back the tears, and she wept. Wept for their newly rediscovered love, for the new exile she had chosen, for any number of reasons that she and he could not be Stefan and Anike, simply living together.

I chose my new exile, she told herself. *I chose it, and he agreed.*

And yet she could see no other path.

"Hush," Raul whispered into her ear. "We have not reached the end of this life together. Do not give up hope."

"How long?" she managed to say. "How long until the ship comes for our queen?"

"That depends on my secretary."

The words acted like an antidote to sorrow.

"You have a new secretary?"

Raul laughed softly at her surprise. "It wasn't my idea. He came to me three months ago with a raft of well-written recommendations and a story of how he disliked the northern winters and wanted to try a post in the south for once. He was very clever. It took me weeks before I discovered he was Dedrick's cousin."

A cousin? The news shook her unaccountably. She had known about Dedrick's sister in court, and his unrelenting father, but she had not suspected a wider world of relatives. It was a fatal error to think all families were like her own, small and insular.

Raul went on to describe the new secretary. He had given his name as Gerek Hessler, but his true name was Lord Gerek Haszler. He was Dedrick's second cousin, from a minor branch of the family. The man had infiltrated Lord Kosenmark's house, and during Raul's one brief absence, had gained access to Raul's private chambers. Raul described his own discovery of the man's identity, and their confrontation when Raul unexpectedly reappeared.

"He is a good man," Raul said. "Clever with words and languages. Not so clever with his tongue. I believe he cares about Kathe."

Another unexpected bit of information, which Ilse needed a few moments to digest.

"What does Kathe think?" she asked.

"Ah, that I have not dared to inquire," Raul said. "These days, she glares at me as if I were a recalcitrant kitchen girl. Even her mother dislikes crossing her. If I were bold enough to guess, I would say she is disappointed."

"Because of this Gerek?"

"I do not know. That would be prying."

His tone was so prim, she had to laugh out loud. "You. How dare you pretend not to pry?"

He laughed, too, his face buried in her hair. "And you, you are too good for me."

"How, good?"

"Honest, then," he said.

The brief wave of mirth vanished at the word *honest*, and Ilse pressed her face into Raul's shoulder to stop her tears.

Once, she had thought herself honest. Raul had told her he depended on that quality.

Once, she and Kathe had shared confidences. They were friends, from the first days, when Ilse came to the pleasure house, and Kathe had tended her through her sickness and losing the child. She had remained her best friend throughout Ilse's transformation from kitchen girl, to secretary, to the days when Ilse and Raul had become lovers. But Ilse and Raul's plans had required a complete deception of the pleasure house and all their friends. That had included Kathe.

Time, and necessity, had worn away her honesty.

Not quite trusting her voice, Ilse said, "Will you promise me something? Tell her . . . tell Kathe the truth. But only when it's safe. Please."

Raul drew her into a tighter embrace. "I promise. I will tell her the truth the moment I return to Tiralien. Speaking of messages, I have a confession to make . . ."

His voice went high and light, like a bird's.

"What is wrong, then?" she asked, trying to keep the anxiety from her own voice, and failing.

He exhaled sharply, as if bracing himself for an unpleasant confession. "Do you remember a man named Alesso Valturri?" he said.

She was so intent on him and his moods that she missed the name at first, and its import. Then, "You know Alesso? He's the one—"

"—who brought me word of your escape. I know. He also works for me."

It took her several moments to comprehend what he said.

"You sent him to Osterling."

"No. He was born there. I knew him through various reports. Lord Joannis and . . . others."

Meaning his network of spies. Her first impulse was to rage at him. How dare he set spies upon her? Raul must have guessed her mood, because he loosened his embrace and drew back.

"I have no excuse," he said. "None except worry about your safety. After Dedrick—"

Yes, Dedrick. She checked her first furious response. "I understand."

He kissed her, lightly and tentatively. "I doubt it."

She nearly did strike him then. "You—"

"Idiot," he said immediately. "Idiot. Fool. An interfering creature who pretends omniscience, when he wants to hide how afraid he is."

She wanted to laugh again, but her heart was at war with the rest of her nerves, and she could only clutch him tightly while she brought her emotions under a semblance of control.

"Who is he?" she whispered. "Who is he really?"

"Exactly what he seems, but more. He's a kitchen boy and serving man in Andeliess's pleasure house. He's also a rebel who works for a collection of the disaffected in Fortezzien. He agreed to watch over you. Your safety, I mean. In return I promised to consider his cause if ever I gained more influence in Duenne's Court." He added, "He is a persuasive young man."

Oh yes. Even when he did not mean to be. Which brought her to her own confession

"He drugged my wine," Ilse said. "He kissed me. No, let me tell the truth. I kissed him. I'm sorry."

"For what?" he asked. "For kissing Alesso? I would have kissed him, too, no doubt, if he had poisoned my wine. Do you love him?"

"No, but—"

"Do you want to bed him?"

"No," she said, softer than before. "But what does it mean? For us?"

Raul took her hand and kissed her palm. "It means we are human, my love. Flawed and wandering in purpose at times. What else it means is your decision. I love you," he added.

The knots inside her broke. "I love you."

EVENTUALLY THEY GAVE over lovemaking and conversation and slept, slept until morning broke over the Gallenz hills. Ilse rolled onto her back and stared upward. A circle of sunlight illuminated the canvas above. Patches of shadow, however, covered one end of the tent. Midmorning or later, she guessed. Outside, she heard the guards discussing what to forage for the midday dinner.

She closed her eyes and lay quietly, listening to Ada Geiss and Theo bickering quietly over who had responsibility for the latrines. She recalled nothing of her dreams, ordinary or otherwise. Had she traveled beyond them, or had exhaustion overrun any warnings from her past?

Except you dreamed of him, of Dzavek, just the night before.

Raul stirred. His hands reached toward her.

"You are awake."

"I slept enough."

A flicker of tension passed over his face.

"Is that true?"

She wanted to lie, to smile and say all was well, but his proximity, the nearness of himself and their reunion, made that impossible.

"No," she whispered. "How could I? We have a few weeks and then . . ."

His eyes, inches from hers, were wide and bright. "Then we must do our best to secure the right promises from your queen."

He rose and pulled on his shirt and trousers. Ilse dressed in her new clothes and brushed out her hair with a comb he produced from one of the packs. It was, she noted, her favorite comb from her days in Tiralien. She thought she had packed the item before she departed the first time. Its unexpected reappearance unsettled her.

"Are you ready?" Raul asked.

She nodded.

A substantial breakfast awaited them, provided by the morning cook detail. Camp bread. Porridge flavored with spices and dried fruit. The coffee was fresh this time. Most of the guards had eaten already and separated to their various tasks, including Galena, whom Detlef had assigned to a foraging expedition. Valara had not yet shown herself.

She's not certain what to expect from us, Ilse thought.

Her guess was confirmed when Valara emerged from her tent. Her face and manner were wary, and she spoke only briefly in response to Ilse's greeting. However, she politely accepted a plateful of food and mug of coffee from one of the guards.

Raul paid Valara no attention at first. While the three of them ate, he sorted through orders with Detlef. Katje and Theo would hire horses in Emmetz and ride back to Tiralien. "They leave within the hour," he said. "I will write a letter with instructions for Maester Hessler."

Valara waited until Detlef withdrew to the camp's perimeter before she spoke. "You agree then?" she said. "About the ship?"

"It depends," Raul replied, "on our conversation this morning. Whatever its outcome, I will have instructions for my secretary."

Valara set aside her mug and plate. "Speak then. What more do you want from me?"

Ilse felt the air tremble, as if magic's current had

awakened. If Raul sensed it, he gave no sign. He stared at Valara, his gaze as uncompromising as hers. Both had their faces turned in profile to her. It was then she saw, with a shock of sudden recognition, the resemblance between them. The shape of cheek and jaw. The flat nose. The golden brown complexion. Oh, there were differences, too—the folds at the corner of Raul's eyelids were almost invisible, his eyes were golden and hers dark, nor was her coloring as fair as his—but it was like the difference between brother and sister.

Was it possible that Valara's people had sailed west to the continent, centuries ago?

Then Raul stirred and Ilse thrust aside any speculation to listen to what he would say.

"I agree to nearly all your terms," he said. "However, I have several of my own. First, as Ilse stipulated, you will render all assistance to her so that she might recover Lir's third jewel. Do not," he said harshly, as Valara started to speak, "refuse this condition. And do not pretend you can do nothing to help. You spent years searching for the jewels. You recovered one. Even if you could recover the third on your own, your knowledge would aid Veraene to do so. That would ensure a balance between the three kingdoms."

He paused. Valara's cheeks were flushed, her eyes were bright with fury. "Go on," she said roughly.

"You agree?" he asked.

"I say nothing. What are your other conditions?"

"Just two more. In return for your assistance, and to guarantee my part, Ilse Zhalina remains your hostage for one year—"

"That is not long enough," Valara said sharply.

Raul's mouth curled into a smile. "It is more than enough. Agree, or I leave you to wander Veraene alone. Unless you think you can find another ally, Leos Dzavek or Markus Khandarr will eventually recapture you. The consequences you can picture."

"Is that all?"

"No. We require a hostage in return. Once the ship reaches Morennioù, you will choose someone from your court. Ilse Zhalina must approve the choice, of course. That person will sail back with my ship and my crew. It is the only means I have," he added, "of ensuring your cooperation."

As expected, Valara Baussay argued every point. Each time, Raul Kosenmark repeated his willingness to set her free in Veraene to find her own way home. In the end, she conceded the time limit and the need for an exchange of hostages. More argument followed on the logistics for exchanging those hostages. Valara wanted Ilse to come ashore on Enzeloc first. Raul insisted the man or woman from Morennioù's Court board the ship. They bickered over guards and weapons and how to ensure that one side did not gain undue advantage over the other. In the end, Valara agreed that Ilse might remain on the ship until her own candidate boarded. After all, she said, Morennioù's navy could overtake them if his people reneged on Lord Kosenmark's promises.

But the limit of one year she refused to allow.

"You want me to promise my kingdom's neutrality," she said.

It was an hour after they had set aside their plates and coffee mugs. An hour of wrangling and bickering. Of accusations wrapped in polite tones and oblique terms. Eventually, Valara agreed to a limit of three years. After that, depending on the state of her kingdom, she would release Ilse Zhalina to return home, but she would make no promise beyond that about her kingdom's role. At Raul's insistence, she pledged never to release Ilse to Lord Markus Khandarr.

The compromise was imperfect, but it would do.

Raul and Ilse retired to their tent, where Raul would write the detailed instructions to his secretary for securing a ship.

"Do you believe her?" Ilse asked, as she watched him unlock his portable desk and lay out his writing materials.

"No," Raul said. "But she has conceded enough that I do not mind."

He did mind, she thought, observing the tense line of his jaw, the overbrightness of his eyes. She minded, too, if you could use so mild a word, but she also noted that neither of them mentioned breaking the agreement, or proposing a different plan. They had little choice, if they wanted to prevent war between the three kingdoms.

Kingdom. Empire. Shatter. The next word link hovered just beyond her grasp.

She gave that over and watched as Raul wrote his orders to his secretary. "What are your plans, then? Your next plans?"

He answered without a pause in writing. "Gerek will find a ship. He thinks he cannot, but he will. He underestimates himself constantly. Once he does, he will send it to the Kranjĕ Islands. We, however, will march in double time to the coast. There we will hire or steal a boat and sail to Hallau."

The Kranjĕ Islands were part of Károví, but isolated from the mainland by a storm-ridden strait. Hallau was the largest of the Jelyndak Islands, which lay a hundred miles south, off the coast of Veraene proper.

"You don't trust him?" she asked. "Your secretary, I mean."

"I trust him. I do not trust Markus Khandarr."

He was remembering Dedrick's death at Khandarr's hands. She could tell by the way his gaze turned inward.

Deception would not save Gerek if Khandarr questioned him and disliked his answers, but it might deceive the man long enough for Valara Baussay to escape home. Raul knew that, too.

Raul finished his letter, sealed it with wax and magic. He used a complicated spell that Ilse did not recognize. Then he wrote a second letter, which he sealed with ordinary magic. He summoned Katje and Theo, and handed them the two envelopes. "Give these into Gerek's hands directly. No one else's. He will have further orders for you both."

Ilse waited until they had gone, and Raul had packed away his pens and ink into his writing desk. "I have one more concern," she said.

"Your brother?" he asked.

She had not expected that. It took her a moment to quell the old memories of Melnek. "No, it's about Galena Alighero. She risked everything to help us. I would like to know what happens to her after I'm gone."

He locked the desk and laid a hand over its latch. His movements were so slow and deliberate, she decided he was avoiding the question. "Well?" she asked.

Raul shrugged. "Tell me about the mark on her cheek. The word says *Honor*."

"You are ruthless," she murmured.

"Of course. Tell me."

With a sigh, she recounted Galena's story. She told Raul about the girl's infatuation, her quarrels with Ranier Mazzo, the moment of cowardice during the battle, and how she wanted Ilse to lie for her. After briefly describing Galena's punishment, including the mark, she went on to the night when Valara escaped. How Alesso meant to kill Galena, and the moment in Osterling's streets when Galena realized it. She offered more detail about the journey, and how they would not have reached Emmetz without Galena's experience in tracking and hunting.

"She is foolish, impetuous, and far too willing to avoid responsibility," Ilse said. "And yet . . ."

"And yet you think you ought to help her." Raul blew out a breath. "Very well. Let her travel with us. Detlef can give her regular duties. After we accomplish our meeting with the ship, I'll write her a letter of recommendation to a mercenary company. You say our friend the queen has promised to remove this mark?"

"Yes. Or at least she claims she can. We didn't dare use magic before, in case they tracked us with mages."

He nodded. "A good decision. My guess would be that removing it requires extraordinary magic—it would be a glaring signal to Khandarr and any other mage. I'll have Detlef tell the girl we can't do anything for her until the ship."

The ship. Always the ship.

"How long do you think we have?" she asked.

Raul gathered her hands within his. "Ten days. Possibly two weeks. We'll hire a boat and sail to Hallau. The rest depends on how long Gerek requires for his part."

Of course. So much depended on these arcane transactions. She had the important details, however. Ten more nights, possibly a handful more, until she began a longer and more distant exile.

CHAPTER EIGHTEEN

THE MIDDAY SUN streamed through the windows of
Duke Miro Karasek's apartments in Zalinenka castle.
Karasek sat at his desk, writing letters. It was quiet,
the servants momentarily busy elsewhere, and the
scrape of his ink stick against the inkstone sounded
unnaturally loud. He had packed his gear and weapons the night before, and between the silence and
emptiness, the rooms had a deserted air.

... *the king's runner had knocked on his door at
midnight. Come. No delay. He had paused long
enough to scrub the sleep from his eyes, then followed
the messenger at a run. It was not fast enough. Dzavek paced the length of his study, his shadow flickering in the light of a dozen candles. The moment Karasek
crossed the threshold, the king swung around to face
him ...*

Karasek added water to the ground ink and mixed
it thoroughly. A few more lines, rapidly brushed, finished off the letter to his secretary. He dusted the paper and laid it aside to dry, then wrote a second letter
to his steward. He trusted both men to know their
duties, but it gave him a small measure of comfort to
send these last instructions.

The orders had come late the night before.

*. . . You sail tomorrow, the king said. Karasek
bowed his head. What else could he answer? But his
acquiescence was not enough, apparently. You don't
ask why, Dzavek said. Look at me, Miro.*

Miro lifted his gaze to the king's. They were of a
height—both tall and lean, both with dark deep-set
eyes, black with a hint of indigo, like the storm clouds
in summer. Karasek had seen portraits of the king
through the centuries, before the deep lines marked
his face, before his eyes turned cloudy with age. The
resemblance was strong between them. More than
once, he had wondered if they shared an ancestor. Or
was the king himself Miro's ancestor?

*I have found my brother, Dzavek said. The Moren-
niòuen queen. She rides with companions to the
coast where she hopes to take a ship home. You must
stop her.*

Simple orders. Why had they bothered him so?

*Because you once loved her. Because you betrayed
her once before, in the king's name, the emperor's
honor. At the cost of your own.*

Bells from the palace towers rang noon. Two more
hours until they sailed. There was little else to accomplish, to distract himself from worrying. He and
Grisha Donlov had already reviewed the final preparations. A ship waited for them at the city docks—a
swift-sailing craft with room enough for her crew
and a single squad, twenty of Dzavek's best soldiers,
men and women whom Karasek could trust on this
mission.

Miro rubbed his forehead. After he had left the
king, he had slept uneasily, dreaming he had returned
to Taboresk. He was riding through the forests, in the
hills near his estate. No purpose. No guards. He was
alone with the endless pine forests, with the sky like a
clear blue mirror overhead. It was a strangely unsettling

dream for all its tranquillity. Like a final visit with a friend before they died.

He blew out a breath. He knew better than to give into nerves before a battle.

One last letter, then. He took a new sheet, dipped his brush in the well of his inkstone, and wrote.

"From Zalinenka castle, Rastov, to the Baron Ryba Karasek of Vysokná. My dear Cousin Ryba. I write to you with a fresh burden to offer. My duties require my continued absence from Taboresk, and I find myself uneasy about my estates . . ."

Miro reread the first lines. He disliked them. They implied a lack of trust in his secretary and steward. And yet he knew no other way to express his unsettled state, not without making its cause too plain.

I want your eyes there. I want you looking over the portraits and statues, the stables and fields. Capek is shrewd and Sergej Bassar is capable, but I need a friend and brother to oversee my home, once our home together.

Stilted. Awkward. Not at all how they spoke in private, but this letter was a public one, so he continued in the same formal style: "If your own duties and obligations permit, I have a very great favor to ask of you. Vasche Capek himself can run Taboresk with little direction—and I have already sent him instructions for the next month—but my heart would rest easier if you could arrange a visit . . ."

His brush moved easily through the glib phrases. In his thoughts, however, he wrote a different letter, worded as though he were alone with Ryba in Taboresk. *I am afraid,* he wrote in that invisible letter. *For myself, and for the king. I fear the threat to our honor—his and mine. I am a soldier, as he reminded me. I deal in spilled blood and battle cries, in the broken bodies of our enemies, those who face death bravely, and those who weep in panic, even with a new life awaiting them across the rift.*

He paused and looked out the window. The sky had turned a luminous blue, vivid against the pale stonework of the castle. It reminded him strongly of his dream. Not a life dream, he told himself. Nevertheless, the image of those empty silent forests troubled him. It was like a sending from the gods, reminding him that he faced death on this mission.

He stared down at the half-written letter, seeing instead Dzavek's face etched with lines. He remembered the king's soft voice, explaining that he could not leave the kingdom unprotected against Veraene's growing desire for war and a return to the empire. He would sacrifice his honor to protect it. He would willingly sacrifice his brother's kingdom. This was no new turn in his character, Miro thought. The clues had been obvious for centuries, if one examined the records. His father had done so, but no one else, it seemed. Why?

It is because we died and thus forgot. Our king, however, lives on.

He had lived on, gaining strength and youth from Lir's jewels. Later, the jewels gone, Leos Dzavek had continued to extend his life, using the magical knowledge acquired during that first century. He drew the years with a sure hand, like a smith would draw a thread of forge-heated gold, long past all expectation.

But no man can live forever. Not even Toc could deny death. And he knows it, Ryba. I see the terror in his face, when he holds Lir's ruby in his hands. He knows that even with the jewels, he will die someday.

A thought he could not share, even with his cousin, even in a letter never written.

A shadow fell across Miro's desk. The sun had risen higher in the sky. He would need to go soon before the next bell rang. Taking up his brush, Miro continued his dual letter. As he wrote of Taboresk's ordinary concerns, his second letter continued his thoughts about Dzavek's intentions.

We forget, you and I, that Leos Dzavek, for all his achievements, is a man with faults and flaws like any other. He nurtures a bitter hatred toward Morenniou's queen—the woman who was once a man, once his brother. They trusted each other. They betrayed each other—several times over, if the histories are true. And because they did, Leos Dzavek would fashion me into a blunt tool, just as he did with Anastazia Vaček. He would bloody me, wipe me clean with a rag, and cast me to one side. I fear I will never be able to eradicate the stain.

Miro pressed both hands against his eyes. *I swore an oath to Leos Dzavek and Károví. I swore another to my father as his heir.*

He thought of his father, whose conversations remained guarded, even in private interviews with his own son. Alexej Karasek had served Dzavek for a lifetime. He'd spoken of the king's insight in council, of his farsighted plans for Károví, both within the kingdom and in the greater world. *Honor and glory and strength,* his father had said. *He wants a gift for the future.* And yet his father had also spoken of doubts.

Miro sighed and read through the half-finished letter. There was little to add, except a postscript inviting his cousin for the hunting season next autumn. He folded the paper, sealed it with wax, and wrote the address on the cover. That he used no magic would signal to Ryba that the contents were public. And since Ryba knew Miro as well as any brother, he would know to read between the written lines, to the invisible letter Miro had composed in thoughts alone.

It would be safer if he could not.

He summoned a runner and handed her all three letters. "Letters to Taboresk and Vysoká," he said. "Deliver the first two into my steward's hands, the third to my cousin, Baron Ryba Karasek. Use the fastest courier you have."

The letters dispatched, Miro turned to the one remaining trunk of clothing. He removed his fine woolen trousers, the silk shirt, and the loose tunic with its satin trim and embroidered sash. In their place, he donned the knitted undershirt, the tunic of fine-linked mail, the gloves fashioned of the same material. It was appropriate. If he was the king's chosen weapon, he would look and dress the part.

I will make Valara Baussay my prisoner. By sword or magic.

Anything less would be treason.

CHAPTER NINETEEN

THE HOURGLASS SPUN over. As its sands flowed through to the empty glass, Gerek heard the bells from the nearby tower counting the hour. Three, four, five. Late afternoon.

He stretched his arms and shoulders, then addressed himself to the papers on his desk once more. Water casks. Those were like barrels, he guessed. He had not expected barrels to cost so much. Three had sprung leaks during the last voyage, and the captain spoke in strong language about the necessity for replacing them before the new owner undertook any extended voyage.

But how long a voyage? And where?

Not that Gerek knew. He cursed softly. How pleasant to solve an equation with so many unknown factors, especially if you did not have to solve it yourself. Oh yes, he appreciated the elegance of mathematical theory—he had known a number of mathematicians at the Little University during his previous stay in Tiralien—but his appreciation was like an appreciation for cashews, or modern sculpture, or weapons drill at sunrise. Others might adore such things. He did not.

He wrote a note, authorizing the purchase of three

new water casks, then moved on to the next item in the captain's list. Provisions. Specifically, barrels of salt pork. A dull pain settled below his ribs. He had not eaten properly in several days, and the thought of salt pork gave him indigestion.

Many times in the past three weeks, he had wondered why he remained in Lord Kosenmark's service. It wasn't the money. He might be the younger son of an unimportant lord, but he had an independent sum, enough to live on simply without his father, or his brother, or this irritating son of a duke, who gave him orders with such airy assurance.

No, he knew the answer. He remained here for Dedrick's sake. Because Kosenmark had offered him trust, as no one else had.

Then why do I want to bash him with an ax?

A question others undoubtedly had asked before.

Hiring a ship should not have proved so difficult in Tiralien. Hundreds of merchants shipped their goods through this port. The royal fleet had their own dock for refitting and repairs. Then there were the privateers, the pirates and smugglers (operating under the guise of ordinary business), the smaller packets that plied the coastal trade, the courier ships taking messages to Osterling, Klee, Pommersien, and beyond. With all this wealth of seagoing traffic, Gerek expected to find at least one ship fit for deepwater sailing.

No, finding a ship to hire was not difficult. What made the matter complicated was Kosenmark's need for secrecy. *Do not link my name to this ship,* the man had said, more than once, in the hours before he rode off to find Ilse Zhalina. *Markus Khandarr will have set a watch on this city and this house.*

So Gerek worked through a chain of several agents. Within a week, he had located a vessel that matched

Kosenmark's needs—a ship built for deep-water sailing, with only minor repairs needed. His heart thumped, remembering the terrifying moment when he signed the paperwork, authorizing payment of six thousand denier to the old owner, also the captain. At least the ship came with its own crew.

Back to provisions. The captain recommended salted fish, which he could obtain for a good price from certain suppliers. Gerek signed the request, glanced at a second stack of papers. He had spent the past three days buried in paperwork for licenses, bills for provisions, more bills to finish the ship's repairs, the hire of new men to replace those who had left when the ship changed owners, and a mountain of other minutiae.

A rapping at his door interrupted him. "Maester Hessler? You have visitors."

It was one of the house runners, with news that two of Kosenmark's guards had arrived from distant parts. Immediately all Gerek's weariness dropped away. "Send them to me at once."

He gathered his papers into an untidy stack and brushed away the crumbs from his last hasty snack. Just in time, because the runner returned within moments with a woman and man. Katje and Theo, he recalled. Both of them trusted guards of several years' service. He waved for them to be seated, but Katje laid two envelopes on his desk with some ceremony before she took a chair.

Gerek regarded the envelopes with caution. Two messages. Both sealed with magic. He took up the one addressed to *The Captain* and hissed with surprise. Layers upon layers of complicated spells protected it. He recalled his earlier studies of the man, how Dedrick spoke of Kosenmark's skill with locks and other spells used by couriers to ensure that spies could not intercept their messages.

The second one was wrapped in the usual, ordinary spell set to Gerek Hessler's touch. He brushed his fingers over the edge of the paper, and the letter folded. His personal instructions, then.

"Wait," he told the two guards. "Let me know what our lord wishes."

The first part contained a summary of what they had discussed before. Ship. Six-month voyage. Possibly longer. But then Kosenmark went on to say that its first destination was . . . Here came a particular longitude and latitude that meant nothing to Gerek, followed by two names that were distinctly Károvín.

Gerek stopped and reread the location. *Tuř on Osek.* Osek was an island settled by Károví and much disputed during the civil wars, if he recalled his history. Tuř must be a village on the coast. Very odd, he thought, but then, trust was not an absolute. Kosenmark trusted Gerek enough to handle the ship and the money. If he wanted to keep certain details a secret, it was his privilege.

The rest of the instructions were clear enough. Send two senior guards from the household to join the crew. They would need some experience with ships. Equally important, they must have at least two years in Kosenmark's service. Besides observing any suspicious activities, their most important task was to deliver the second letter to the captain with a message.

> *Tell him to read the instructions only after he has left port. And he must read them alone, in his cabin, from beginning to end, without omitting anything.*

There were more instructions about their guest from Fortezzien and for providing money and horses to the two guards. The letter ended abruptly, without a signature or even an initial. Gerek stared at the page, though his mind was on the writer and not the contents. For all the painstaking detail, there were deliberate gaps in the information. *He does not trust me*, Gerek thought. And then, *No, that is not true. He trusts me, but not the situation.*

"So," he said softly. "Do you require mounts this afternoon?"

He had expected them to say no, but Katje immediately smiled. "That would be best."

Which means the matter is urgent. And he told them, but not me.

Gerek suppressed his frustration and smiled. Not very convincingly, because Theo flinched. "Let me arrange everything," Gerek said. "Go to the common room and tell the maids to serve you an early supper. I should have money and horses for you within a few hours."

Alone once more, in the quiet of his office, Gerek rested his head in his hands. He had accomplished much in the past three weeks. He had danced the great dance of secrets. And yet . . . he wanted nothing more than to hide in a quiet room, well away from this pleasure house and Lord Kosenmark's intrigues. To forget all about ships and provisions and which men and women he could trust.

I want— I need a day of peace.

If he were to admit the truth, he wanted to sit with Kathe on that bench overlooking the harbor and listen to her so-called babbling. She was clever and kind and true. In her presence, he had a sense of competence, of completeness.

Kathe had not spoken to him in the ten days since Kosenmark departed. He knew she received the book—Hanne had told him about the episode in the kitchen. How the kitchen girls watched, whispering,

as the runner handed over the gift. Kathe had thanked
the runner, of course, and she smiled at Janna's teasing, but she had said nothing. Not to Hanne or the
other girls. Nor to Gerek himself.

He scribbled out the orders for money for Katje,
Theo, and the Fortezzien man. Then he sent a runner to the stables for two fresh mounts, with tack,
gear, and provisions. Another runner went off to the
agent, alerting him that two new crew members
would join the ship's company, and here was a letter
written and sealed to confirm the order. It was a
risk, this direct contact between Gerek and the captain, but he could not risk the delay with the usual
channels.

Mistress Denk sent back three notes of hand to the
bearer, each for the requested amount, each drawn
from a different anonymous account. Gerek recorded
the transactions and forwarded the notes to their
proper recipients. Thereafter he deposited the true
records in his magically sealed letter box and, as part
of the usual fiction, wrote a new set of receipts for
rare books in the official ledger. If anyone examined
the records for this household, he thought, they would
spend a hundred years untangling the truth.

He trudged down to the guards' quarters and the
office Ivvanus Bek held during Detlef Stadler's absence. Bek was buried in his own paperwork, but he
at once cleared off his desk and made himself avail-
able to Maester Hessler. Two guards with ship experience? He would suggest Ralf and Udo. Both had
served Lord Kosenmark seven years, both had the
requisite skills. Gerek gave directions to reach the ship
and handed over the letter for the captain.

One more transaction, and then he would be free
for the night. He took a roundabout path from the
guards' quarters, to the far side of the house, and up

the stairs to the second floor. His own sense of time said it had to be late at night, but the golden sunlight of late afternoon pouring through the windows gave him the lie. He rounded the first landing and paused to catch his breath. From far off, he heard voices raised in cheerful conversation. Closer by, in one of the private rooms, he heard the sudden cry of pleasure, followed by the whispered words "slower, softer, yes."

Gerek drew a painful breath and continued up the stairs. Usually he was spared such scenes until much later, but sometimes clients requested early visits. *Sex and more sex until we are sated,* he thought miserably. *Until we hardly notice its delights.*

His path took him along a gallery that overlooked the common room. He paused and looked down below. Half a dozen chambermaids were at work, brushing and dusting and sweeping. Several courtesans occupied the couches, while Eduard played at the hammerstrings—his fingers running over the keys in a soft and melancholy tune.

They were all beautiful. All of them trained to pleasure. For a moment, he wondered what it might be like, to be a client of this house, to have a man or woman exert themselves to give him delight. His stomach pinched tight at the thought. No and no. He wanted love, not just passion of the body, and he wanted it freely given.

A door below swung open and a woman entered, carrying a tray of wine cups. She bent over to set the tray before the women playing cards. Gerek didn't need to see her face to recognize Kathe. He knew how she walked, how she swept a hand over a surface, as if to banish dirt and ugliness. As if, he thought, she could order the world into beauty with a gesture.

I love her.

* * *

THE NEXT DAY dawned early and dull, and imminent
with rain. Gerek crouched over his desk, wished Lord
Kosenmark and all his minions to the darkest corner
of the void. He ought to be pleased, he told himself.
Katje and Theo had departed with their horses, money,
and provisions. Ralf and Udo had set off directly for
the ship with the captain's instructions. He had even
remembered to arrange a special signal with the captain, apart from the agent, in case of any emergency.

I should dance with joy, and yet I cannot.

He knew why and did not like to think about it.

Scowling, he buried himself in paperwork. At some
point, Hanne came with his noon meal tray. He nibbled at the bread and drank down his coffee. The
grilled fish he set aside for one of the house cats, a recent innovation by Nadine. Report came back from
Ralf at noon, saying they were signed on with the
crew. Another report, from the captain this time, confirmed that the ship's victualing was nearly complete.
If all went well, the ship could sail in another day.

A loud knock at the door startled him. Gerek hast-
ily covered the ship's paperwork with some blank
sheets of paper. "Come in."

He had hoped it would be Kathe. He expected a
runner, or one of the kitchen girls to fetch away his
tray. Instead the door opened on Nadine.

She wore her finest courtesan's costume—a silk
gown of dark apricot that flowed like a waterfall over
her slim body. Her dark hair swept back from her narrow face and made a second shadow waterfall, which
hung over her bare shoulder.

Nadine remained at the door. Her expression was
one of curiosity and faint impatience.

"Yes," he said at last.

She arched one delicate eyebrow. "I came," she said

softly, "because I am a friend. Also, one day I would like to turn messenger for idiots and fools. I have so much practice in this household. Do not stare so blankly," she went on, "or I shall be moved to violence. The message is not from another. It comes from you, Maester Gerek Hessler. Or rather, it should."

Gerek swallowed to calm his throat muscles. "Who—"

"That would spoil the surprise," Nadine said. "Go to the spider room this instant. Never mind about those papers on your desk. Go. Give your message. You will understand once you have."

She gave a magnificent flourish with one hand—the gesture clearly meant as mockery—and dropped into deep bow. Before Gerek could react, Nadine withdrew from his office with a dancer's grace.

Gerek stared at the closed door. It had to be a prank. What else? Nadine and Eduard were famous for them. But until today, they had ignored Gerek. He had supposed, at first, that his position safeguarded him, but conversations with Kathe soon corrected that belief. Nadine teased and tormented everyone, from Mistress Denk and Mistress Raendl to the newest stable boys, without regard for rank. She had teased Ilse Zhalina and Maester Hax in their days, too. So then he had assumed she found him too ordinary to bother with. Was this sudden change a part of the strange mood infesting the house?

Or was it something else?

Cursing himself for a fool, he put aside his papers. He checked all the locked boxes and set the bolts and spells on his office. If they wanted to make him into a fool, he was used to that, but he would not neglect Lord Kosenmark's orders about discretion, even inside the pleasure house.

The spider room was on the second floor in the east wing. He had passed by its door several times, but had never ventured inside. It was a luxurious room—almost too luxurious. Kosenmark once called it his finest extravagance. Courtesans used the room for special clients. Gerek hurried down the stairs. He noted no one waiting about as if watching for him. He crossed over to the east wing, which was equally empty in the early afternoon.

Pulsing thrumming in his ears, he entered the spider room.

A web of lace fluttered at his entrance. He started, thinking at first someone else had disturbed those hangings. But the lace floated downward into stillness, and the scent of rose petals whirled around him in the empty room.

Gerek released a long breath. *I should be used to this. My sisters. My cousins.*

Behind him sounded a flight of quick light footsteps on the tile floor. He spun around to see the door flung open and Kathe hurrying into the room. At the sight of him, she checked herself. "Nadine said a messenger came for me."

Gerek opened his mouth, but his tongue refused to work. Kathe turned to go. With an effort, he pressed down the trembling in his throat. "Kathe. Please."

She paused, her face turned away from his, only the outline of her cheek, and the clear tense line of her jaw visible in the lamplight. Nadine was right, he thought. He had only one chance to deliver this message. And quickly.

"I— It's about the book," he managed to say.

Her mouth curved into a pensive smile. "Yes, thank you. It was a thoughtful gift."

It was more than a gift, he wanted to say. It was a

curiosity, a moment of pleasure, a thank-you for the kindness she had shown him. It was all the words he could not, dared not utter out loud. Ah, but he had to speak—now. If he did not, she would vanish into the kitchen. And he would never have such a chance again.

"I-I lied to you," he said.

Kathe spun around. "You *lied*?"

Those were not the words he meant to say, but having said them, he realized they were the truth. He gulped down a breath and prayed to Lir to keep his tongue under control. "Yes. My name. My n-name is Gerek Haszler. Dedrick Maszuryn was my cousin."

The dark flush along her cheeks faded. Her eyes widened in surprise. "Lord Dedrick. He was your *cousin*?"

He could not tell if that were a good or a bad thing. He stumbled on, keeping to the truth. It was all he had to offer now. "Yes. He was. I-I came because. Because he . . . died."

Murdered. Executed by the king's order, or at least with his consent. From the twitch of Kathe's lips, she knew the truth behind Dedrick's death, too. "Does Lord Kosenmark know this?" she said. "He does," she went on, before he could answer. "That is what happened that day. When he told us all he meant to stay at Lord Demeyer's country estates. Then he came back for no reason at all. The day you and he talked until almost morning." Then her gaze veered up to his. "You are Lord Gerek, aren't you?"

He did not trust that anxious tone in her voice. "Yes. But it-it doesn't matter. I—" *Hurry. Before my tongue fails me. Before she turns away.* "I wish you would consider me, Kathe. I-I am n-not rich. I am a plain man. Very plain. But I— I would be true."

A long silence followed. Kathe stood motionless, her gaze carefully averted from his. Gerek could not breathe. He wished he could see her face, her eyes. He wanted to say more, but the wisest part of him knew he'd said everything that was important. His heart paused, it seemed, waiting for her answer.

"I must go," she said softly.

She slipped through the door and was gone.

Gerek released his long-held breath. *Nadine was wrong. I spoke too soon.*

Or not. There might be a chance if he could only explain . . .

He rushed through the door, only to run into Kosenmark's senior runner. "Maester Hessler. A message came for you just a moment ago."

The man thrust a letter at him. Gerek muttered a curse in old Erythandran. He saw Kathe at the far end of the corridor, just rounding the corner into one of the servants' passageways.

The runner jabbered at him, insistent. Gerek growled back, but it was no use. He would have to seek Kathe out later. With a curse, he fumbled open the letter, barely noticing the magic that prickled at his fingertips. Someone who knew him. Yes, yes. He was not surprised. It came from the first agent for the ship. The man had written in the house code even.

Then he read the words again. Someone had suborned one of the agents in their chain. The man could not tell which one. He wanted to consult with Maester Hessler himself, to determine what action they could take to repair the damage.

For a moment, he pretended he could ignore this information another hour. But no. Kosenmark trusted him too much. With a last curse for that trust, Gerek jogged to his office and slammed the door shut. He tried to scribble a letter to Kathe, asking her for just a few moments . . . No, that was no good. He crumpled the paper. He could not write what he felt. He needed to speak directly with her, to watch her face, to read the subtle alterations in her expression, some of which he had learned to decipher these past few weeks. He wanted to learn more of them.

In the end, he left word with Mistress Denk that he had errands to run and would return by evening.

He had not lost all sense of discretion, however. He took a guard with him, one particularly recommended by Ivvanus Bek. He and the guard rode to a square within a half mile of the harbor district. From there, they made their way on foot to their destination. He had worked out several meeting places with the agent, in case of emergencies. The first was a wine shop in an alley bordering the wharf district. Gerek stepped into the shadows. His guard moved past him, knife held ready as the man scouted the perimeter of the room. It was impossible to see anything after the brilliant sunlight outside. He could smell the shop. Sour wine. The reek of fish and tar. As his eyes adjusted to the gloom, he could make out a few rough tables and stools, scattered about. Ahead was a plank that served as the counter. No sign of the agent, but Gerek would wait a few moments before he tried the next meeting place.

He ventured forward to the nearest table.

Several things happened at once. The door swung shut. Several tables crashed end over end. Gerek turned in time to see his guard grappling with three men. He spun around and ran into another. Gerek swung a fist and downed the man. He had just reached the door and was clawing it open when he caught a glimpse of a club arcing toward his head.

* * *

GEREK WOKE TO darkness and a ferocious throbbing
in his skull. He sprawled on his stomach, as if someone had tossed him there. The ground felt cold and
damp. Dirt, not plank or stone. The air stank of mud
and saltwater and his own vomit. *Where am I? What
happened?*

Vaguely he remembered entering the wine shop.
Oh, yes. Someone attacked him. His head throbbed
too hard for him to think clearly, but he remembered
a skirmish and a sickening smell he thought might be
blood.

He drew one arm close. First clue: no ropes or
chains. Either his abductors had forgotten to tie him
up, or they didn't think it was necessary. The second,
he decided. Not a good sign.

Very slowly, cautiously, he levered himself to sitting.
Breathed through his nose until the nausea subsided.
When he was certain he would not vomit, he opened his
eyes to slits. Dark, dark, dark, but as his eyes adjusted,
he could make out gray shapes towering over him. Farther off, a thin bright line marked a rectangle. Door, he
translated for the rectangle. And . . . and barrels?

Barrels. Laughter overtook him. Stupid, cursed barrels. He would never be free of them, even when taken
prisoner by enemies unknown. He gulped down the
laughter. Hiccuped. Then nearly wept. It was too absurd. Too terrifying.

Gerek bit down on his cheek. Pain revived him.
Helped him to think more clearly. So. Taken prisoner near the wharves. His abductors had not removed him from that district, however. Belatedly, he
remembered his guard. He called the man's name
softly.

Without warning, the door crashed open. A flood
of sunlight attacked Gerek's eyes. He flung up a hand
to cover his eyes. Another crash, and the door closed.

Gerek blinked, but sparks and specks danced across his vision. Dimly, he made out a monstrous figure approaching, blotting out the sunlight. Another blink, and the monstrous figure divided into three. Two smaller monsters. One leaner, taller figure that stumped toward him in a strange up-and-down gait.

The lean figure stopped. Mumbled a command. Light flared from a lamp, which one of the others hung from a hook on the low ceiling. Gerek blinked several times, took in more details. Directly in front of him stood a tall man who leaned heavily upon a thick walking stick. Thin white hair drawn back tight from a thin face, deeply scored with lines. Pale brown eyes, almost yellow.

With a jerky motion, the man pointed at Gerek. A second man, the largest of the three, strode forward and slapped Gerek across the face. "Tell me about the ship. Where is it bound?"

No need to ask which ship. A dozen different possibilities occurred to Gerek. The agent discovered. Ralf and Udo dead. The house runner taking a bribe to betray Kosenmark. His own mistakes. He shook his head. "I-I don't kn-kn-know."

The man slid a knife from his belt. "You should wish you did."

He slashed Gerek across the chest. Gerek bit back a cry. The man flipped the knife around and sent the hilt crashing into Gerek's cheek. Red washed over Gerek's vision. He screamed, unable to stop himself.

"Now you understand," the man said. "Tell me."

Gerek spat blood from his mouth. The teeth on that side were loose. But there were no broken bones. He could still talk. The man had judged the blow well.

"I-I have n-n-nothing to say."

The man slapped him hard—the same place where

he'd struck him with the knife hilt. "Tell me, or you die in the most unpleasant way possible."

It was not hard to feign terror. He was shivering. Blood trickled from the gash on his chest. He swallowed and tasted more blood. His stomach heaved against his ribs, but he willed himself not to vomit again. "I have nothing to say."

The man shrugged and turned aside. Now the lean figure approached, limping heavily and leaning upon his stick.

"I am Lord Markus Khandarr," he said. "I would know the truth from you."

Khandarr. Gerek nearly fainted. This was the man who killed Dedrick. The king's own mage councillor. But the man's voice was strange—the speech garbled, as if he had an impediment like Gerek's. Then he remembered Alesso Valturri's report, and how the king's mage had suffered injury from his confrontation with the Morennioùen queen.

Injured or not, Khandarr went on to question Gerek closely, though he often needed several attempts to speak. Which agents had Gerek used? Where and when did Kosenmark intend to meet the ship? What was his destination?

"I-I do not know," Gerek said.

Khandarr gave an inarticulate cry. The guards stepped forward to intervene, but Khandarr rounded on them, furious, and gestured for them to keep their distance.

He turned back to Gerek. Mumbled a few words in Erythandran. The air turned cool and crisp, like the mountains above the Gallenz Valley. "Where is Lord Kosenmark? He has a ship. Which one? Where do they meet?

Gerek shook his head.

"Where?" Khandarr struck him with his staff. "Answer."

Then he spoke—a stuttering string of Old Erythandran. The philosophers always said that spoken words were only one medium for magic. If you imprinted the discipline on your mind, you did not need the words. Khandarr proved the theories true, because the air drew tight around them, a thick green cloud that almost suffocated Gerek even as it loosened his tongue.

He had no choice. Even as he realized it, he hated how easily he confessed everything to this man. Yes, Kosenmark left Tiralien weeks ago. There was a ship. A meeting. Where? Tuř on Osek. No, he did not know the ship's final destination, but yes, the matter did concern the recent events in Osterling Keep. The rest he did not know, did not—

He choked. Abruptly the magic released him. Gerek fell to the floor, gasping for breath. He heard, through the thundering in his ears, Khandarr giving orders but he could not make out the words.

Then, unexpectedly, a loud hammering at the door, and someone demanding entry in the name of the watch. One of Khandarr's men doused the lamp, the other flung himself against the door. Gerek scrabbled away from his captors, shouting for help. One man grabbed him by the collar and cuffed him across the face. Gerek wrestled with the man and they both fell to the floor, taking Khandarr with them.

The door burst open. Khandarr gabbled more Erythandran, but he was too late and too slow. A dozen men poured inside, all of them wielding clubs. Gerek ducked under one man's arm, rolled over in time to see another bring his weapon down hard on Khandarr's head. Khandarr collapsed into a heap. There was a brief struggle before the intruders subdued his two men.

Gerek snatched up Khandarr's staff and backed into a corner, breathing heavily. One of the strangers—the new set of strangers, that is—gazed around the cramped room. The others fell into that waiting quiet of soldiers expecting orders. Gerek shifted his grip on the staff.

The stranger's gaze fell on him. To Gerek's surprise, the man smiled. A brilliant, open smile, completely at odds to what had just transpired. He was so taken aback, it took Gerek a few moments before he recognized the man. Alesso Valturri. "You," he breathed.

Valturri smiled, a lazy seductive smile that reminded Gerek of Dedrick. Or Kosenmark. "I am delighted you remember me. However, we do not have time for pleasantries." He turned to the others and gave them a rapid string of orders. Then he held out a hand to Gerek. "Come."

But Gerek refused to trust him so easily. "What happened? How did you find me?"

Alesso sighed. Motioned for the others to leave the room.

"I cannot blame you for mistrusting me," he said. "So, let me begin again. You know Kosenmark and I had an agreement. No? I am disappointed but not surprised. Listen to me then. Your Lord Kosenmark offered certain assistance to me and my associates, in return for other favors. In the spirit of that assistance, I followed these three men to Tiralien's wharves."

Gerek gripped his aching head in both hands. "A very good story. Thank you for the distraction."

Valturri grabbed Gerek by his shirt and shoved him against the wall. "Listen, you stammering idiot. Your Lord Kosenmark expects a ship. I learned that in his own household. What he, and you, do not understand is that Khandarr's agents have taken your agent and all his records. Your man is dead, do you understand?

He killed himself before they could question him. So they decided to arrest you."

Gerek absorbed this news with dismay. So very plausible. Too plausible. "How do you kn-kn-know that?"

Alesso shrugged. "Does it matter how I know? What does matter is that you must get to the ship and tell them to sail at once. Never mind about the stores or all the rest. Leave before this one"—he gestured toward Khandarr, lying insensible at their feet— "recovers and closes the port."

Gerek wanted to argue, but he was too sick to make the effort. And too much of Alesso's explanation made sense. The man might be a questionable ally, but he was right in this matter. He rubbed his aching head. "Very well. I will go at once."

Alesso's grin was unnerving, almost gleeful. "And I will come with you."

IT TOOK THEM longer than Alesso liked, but Gerek only had the name of the ship and the captain, not where they had anchored, and they were both too wary to use these names indiscriminately. Eventually they found the ship—it lay well off shore—and hired a boat to take them over.

The argument with the captain took longer. At first the man would not believe Gerek. But when Gerek repeated the sum of money paid, named the presence of Ralf and Udo, and recited the exact instructions he had written to the agent, and finally remembered the code words passed along by Ralf and Udo to ensure just such an emergency, the captain relented.

"Have you read those instructions?" Alesso asked.

The captain shook his head. "My orders were to read them once at sea."

"Do it now," Gerek said.

The man took Kosenmark's letter from a locked chest. Ran his hands over the paper and tried the wax seal. He shook his head. "No good, sir. I don't know magic, but I know enough that it won't open without the right spell."

"Let me see it," Alesso said.

He, too, tried a few spells but to no effect. While the other two muttered about secret orders, Gerek examined the letter. He was an amateur, he reminded himself. And yet, so was the captain. Kosenmark surely did not expect Gerek or an unknown captain to decipher such a key.

He went through all the instructions. They were simple, short. Read everything. How many ways could a man interpret that? Read the instructions. Every word. Wasn't that obvious?

Oh. Now I understand.

"To the captain," he said softly. "Read everything. Private orders."

The envelope unfolded. Inside was a single short paragraph:

> *Sail to Hallau, Jelyndak Islands. Send a boat with six men into the old city. We will keep a watch for you, but if we are detained, have the men wait ten days. Return once more in three weeks. If that meeting fails, depart the region at once. Send word through the agent for further instructions. Above all else, do not hail any other ships.*

Alesso and the captain were both staring at him. He felt a bit shaken himself. He handed the letter to the captain, who read it through quickly. Gerek watched as a series of emotions passed over the man's face—surprise, curiosity, and a measure of unease. "You have your orders, with one difference," Gerek told him. "If our companions fail to show, you take your further instructions from me."

And Lir help us if that happens.

But he would consider that difficulty later. For now, he only wanted to depart as swiftly as the winds allowed. "How soon can you set sail? At once?"

"The next tide," the man answered. "Within the hour."

"Then do it." To Alesso's unspoken question, he added, "We don't have time to disembark. As you said, the ports will close any moment. Besides, you and I know too much."

THE SHIP'S SURGEON saw to Gerek's injuries at once. After that, though the hour was early, the captain fed them well at his table, while the crew ordered a cabin for their use. After they had dined, Alesso remained with the captain and Kosenmark's two guards to discuss a course that would keep them away from any other ships. Gerek retired to their cabin. It was small—barely wide enough for two hanging cots, and a couple sea chests stacked in one corner. A covered lamp swung from its chain, sending a ripple of light and shadow over the walls.

Gerek climbed awkwardly into the cot nearest the porthole. Dinner and a quantity of good wine had done much, but his jaw still ached, and every movement reminded him of the slash across his chest. Tomorrow he would see the ship's surgeon again for another application of herbs. Now . . . now he wanted nothing more than to lie quietly.

No, that was not the truth. The truth was that he wished himself back in Tiralien, in his own snug rooms. He wished for a quiet dinner, a book to read. He wished . . .

I wish I had one more chance to speak with Kathe.

That would come later. How much later, he did not know. It was the old conundrum of the magical journey, where you could not reach home before traveling through all the rest of the worlds first. Well, he did not have to travel through all the worlds, just to Hallau Island and Lord Raul Kosenmark. It was a long enough voyage, for all that, he thought and yawned.

He fell asleep to the creaking of the rigging and the rush of water against the ship.

CHAPTER TWENTY

THROUGHOUT THE NEXT ten days, Ilse and Raul and their companions traveled as a military company. It was an aspect of Raul that Ilse had never suspected before. She had known him as a sophisticated nobleman, trained in matters of state, someone gifted in both conversation and weaponry. She had not considered he knew anything about wilderness travel and commanding soldiers.

"I learned from my father," Raul said, when she asked. "He had served as a garrison commander in his younger days. Later, he found it useful to maintain a private company. They patrol the more remote regions of Valentain, and deal with smugglers along the coast. I served under our senior officers for a while, then led my own squad the year before I left for Duenne."

"I never guessed," Ilse murmured. "Though I should have."

Raul's mouth tilted into a smile. "It would be terrible, if you had guessed everything about me within a few months. It leaves us nothing for the future."

The future. Which would be delayed for three years.

Her eyes stung with tears. She had not allowed herself to weep these past two weeks. She wanted to remember this interval with joy, a secret treasure to hold tight throughout her exile. Raul guessed her mood, but in silent agreement, he, too, never spoke of their coming separation. For the most part, they kept their conversation on the present—the hills turning green and golden with the advancing season, the logistics for setting up camp. Even that mention of his childhood was brief.

It was too much like their last hours in Tiralien, she thought.

"Until forever," Raul murmured.

She glanced toward him sharply. He did not meet her gaze, but she could tell that his thoughts echoed hers.

Until forever, yes. He had promised that once. He was a man who kept his promises.

They had eight more days together, she told herself. Then a temporary exile. At least its ending lay within her control. She had but to find the third jewel and she could return. Their plans did not end there, of course. Until the exile began, however, she would not dwell upon further obstacles.

FIVE DAYS INTO their journey to the coast, the guard named Katje returned with a letter from Raul's secretary in Tiralien. Valara observed the woman's return from the edge of camp. Two guards sent, only one came back. Interesting. She noted how Kosenmark and Ilse Zhalina vanished for a private conference, well away from the campsite. She also noted how the other guards did not ask about their missing companion. More of Lord Kosenmark's mysterious plans, which he had not bothered to share with her.

The private conference lasted nearly an hour. Valara mistrusted this delay, mistrusted this obvious exclusion. But when Kosenmark at last summoned her to join them, she hid her irritation. He was a king, whether or not he admitted it, and he behaved like one. She could picture her grandfather or father acting just the same. Or herself, once her council installed her on Morennioù's throne.

The letter itself was short. Kosenmark's secretary reported the ship acquired. Outfitting and repairs were nearly complete, and the captain predicted their ship would sail within the next week. The secretary also reported that the watch on the ports continued, with reinforcements brought in from neighboring garrisons. The royal fleet had doubled its patrols along the coast, by direct order of the king.

Which means by order of Markus Khandarr.

"What if your people arrive early?" she asked. "Or late?"

"The captain has his orders to send a boat to the island. The ship itself stands off the coast. If necessary, it sails away to avoid any encounter with the royal fleet. I have given my people a list of alternate plans to meet in case our first attempt fails. Once we come to the last of these, however, the world will rightfully judge us dead."

Valara digested this information. It was more detail than she had requested. He had done her the honor of speaking candidly, at least about this subject. "And if we arrive early?" she asked.

"We wait our own ten days. If the ship does not appear, we must assume they have encountered difficulties."

Difficulties, another word for secrets betrayed and plans come to grief.

"In that case," Kosenmark added, "we must withdraw and devise a new strategy."

She found herself smiling at the phrase, caught him smiling in return. *Ah, he is a dangerous man. Too charming and clever.* She would have to guard against that.

The following morning, they set off at a much faster pace. Kosenmark had rejected Valara's suggestion of horses. They could move more easily, more unobtrusively, without them. So they marched at a punishing pace through the hills above the Gallenz River, angling north and east toward the coast, until they came to a small fishing village named Isersee.

There, Detlef bargained with the local fishermen for a boat and a pilot. The terms were high. The men obviously suspected these tough-faced warriors to be smugglers or brigands. In the end, however, they provided their largest boat, a single-masted cutter, which the village used to fish the outer reaches of the bay.

"What if they betray us?" Valara murmured to Kosenmark, after he finished speaking with Detlef.

"That is my concern," he said. "You will have sailed far beyond pursuit before they can."

An unsatisfactory answer. She would not be beyond Armand of Angersee's grasp until she landed on Enzeloc Island, if then. Luxa's Hand had already proved insufficient to the right spells. She rubbed her throat, remembering how her tongue had become like a separate creature under Khandarr's magic. Markus Khandarr might not be Leos Dzavek's equal, but he had more than enough skill to make him a dangerous enemy.

They sailed at dawn with the turning of the tide. Heavy blue clouds obscured the sky. The clouds thinned toward the horizon, and pale sunlight glanced over the rolling swells. Three fishermen had offered their services to Detlef, and together with Kosenmark's versatile guards, they set the single sail and laid in a course for the southeast.

Rain spattered them throughout the morning, and

as the swells increased, the seas broke over the boat's bow. Valara spent the ten hours tucked in the small cabin. Ilse stayed with her, but the woman remained silent, her gaze turned toward the shuttered hatch. *She has ransomed herself for her kingdom,* Valara thought. A bout of sympathy overtook her, unlike any she'd experienced since she was a small child.

More rain. A muttering of thunder in the distance. The sun breaking through at last. The ship rode more smoothly over the swells. Eventually, Ilse went above. Valara remained by herself in the cabin, counting the miles by the song from the ship's ropes. After a time, she slept.

She woke at the pilot's shout, and the thunder of footsteps overhead. Valara climbed the ladder to the deck. Straight ahead, a great dark shape loomed. The ruddy light of sunset outlined a series of high cliffs. Waves crashed into the rocks below. As she watched, a flock of terns wheeled away, small black dots against the darkening sky.

"Hallau Island," Kosenmark said, as he and Ilse Zhalina came to her side.

"Where is my ship?" she said.

He glanced at her with an unreadable expression. "The ship is not here yet. We land and wait."

The pilot brought them around the northern point of the island, where the cliffs fell away to a narrow rock-strewn strip of land. Around on the seaward side, the shore opened into a broad level expanse. Valara hissed at the sight of an enormous city. She rounded on Kosenmark and Zhalina. "You—"

"We've not betrayed you," Kosenmark said. "Look again."

She gripped the railing and leaned forward, staring, calculating what action she could take if Kosenmark had decided to hand her over to his king. The pilot was steering toward a great stone wharf. As the boat drew closer, Valara could see that the wharf was deserted. There were no other boats in sight. No crews or dockworkers. The city beyond stood silent and empty. Even from this distance, she detected currents of old magic.

"What is this place?" she demanded.

"A trading port," Ilse said. "It fell during the war between Veraene and Károví. The second one," she added.

"I know the story," Valara murmured.

Imre Benacka had hidden the jewels in Autrevelye, or so the legends went. Dzavek had recaptured the man but not the jewels.

Images flickered through her mind. Of a chase through Autrevelye, Anderswar, Vnejšek. She knew the magical plane by all three names. Her brother's scent and signature close behind her. She had tried to lose him by a leap to Morennioù, to that other land on the far side of the world, but he found her, him, each time. It was only by the chance of a few moments she was able to hide the jewels. And then he had captured her. Captured him.

A shout from one of the sailors recalled her to the present. Valara blinked, drew a long breath, and pretended a great curiosity for the shore while she recovered herself. Ilse was studying her with narrowed eyes. Luckily, the boat came to the docks, and everyone burst into new activity to make it fast and transport their gear to shore. Valara accepted a pack from one of the guards, the woman named Katje, then followed her onto land.

At Kosenmark's orders, the sailors hauled the boat into a slip behind a great block of stone. It wasn't hidden, but a ship passing by the shore would miss its presence here at this empty dock. The pilot offered to

remain behind to guard the boat but Kosenmark
shook his head. They would stay together, he said. His
people would know to search inland for them. Meanwhile, he wanted to find water and a less visible place
to camp.

They set off in military order, even Valara and the
fishermen. The closer they got to the city, the clearer
the signs of destruction. What troubled Valara more
was the absence of green growing things. The ruins
remained bare of moss and vines, no weeds grew between the fallen stones.

My brother was a thorough man.

They picked their way through the debris and
across tipped and shattered paving. Eventually, the
avenue they followed fed into an open plaza, where
Kosenmark's hired pilot claimed they would find a
well with sweet water.

Kosenmark gave orders to find the well and set up
camp. They would spend the night here, then recon-
noiter for a better site the next day. He and Ilse vanished for another conference. Or lovemaking. They
were insatiable, Valara thought.

Detlef set a watch and gave orders for preparing
dinner. Freed from their attention, Valara made a circuit around the plaza. Most of the paving stones were
broken into dust. The ground beneath was bare and
hard, in spite of the rains. Here and there, a few walls
remained intact. That one might have been a prince's
palace. That other, a temple to the gods. Valara could
not tell. Dust and wind had completed the war's dev-
astation, and time had reclaimed its own.

She made her way to a series of broken columns,
which marked the entrance to another avenue, and
detected a stronger rill of magic. At a distance, the signatures had merged together, indistinguishable from

each other, but this one she knew as well as her own. Dzavek had come here.

Valara bent down and picked up a fragment of stone from the street. The stone was gray with dark blue motes, its once regular shape cracked and broken. Across the once smooth surface, she noted a rusted stain. When she pressed her thumb against it, a shudder penetrated her bones.

... widerkêren mir de zeît ... widerkêren mir ane rivier de zoubernisse ...

Though she had not summoned it, the current pressed against her skin. A shock ran from her fingers down through her body, and she felt the draw of memory from the stone.

... a mob rushed through the streets, pursued by soldiers wielding axes. One man fell. A soldier swung his weapon downward. Blood splashed over Valara, and its metallic taste filled her mouth. A heartbeat later, the vision disappeared. The city stood empty and blackened.

Not quite empty, she realized. A tall man stood by a broken statue in the now-deserted square. Valara recognized the face from prints in history books, from paintings in Rouizien's Old Palace, and from all her life dreams.

Leos Dzavek crossed the square. His hair was as black as she remembered from their days together, and his eyes were bright and dark, though he had to be at least a century old. Only the fine lines crisscrossing his face, the slackening of flesh along his jaw and at his throat, spoke of the many years he had already lived. She watched as he stopped and touched a wall, a statue. His lips moved, silently, but she could decipher the words. *Ei rûf ane gôtter. Nemen mir de tacen, widerkêren mir de zeît. Ougen mir de juweln.*

He's looking for the jewels.

Dzavek paused and turned around. By chance his gaze met hers.

Valara dropped the stone, and the vision of the past disappeared.

Dizziness swept over her. She pressed a hand over her mouth. No good. Her stomach lurched against her ribs, and she vomited onto the rubble at her feet. Footsteps sounded close by. A hand caught her shoulder before she fell.

"What happened?"

Ilse Zhalina held her steady, offered her a clean cloth, which Valara took gratefully. Her hands were shaking, her skin felt cold beneath a coating of sweat. She wondered how long Ilse had observed her. "Nothing," she croaked. She wiped her mouth with the cloth. "Dizzy. Seasick."

A transparent lie. To her relief, Ilse did not press for the truth. "Try some bread and watered wine. Then lie down. We've set up shelters from the rain."

"YOU SAY SHE lied?"

Ilse leaned into the curve of Raul Kosenmark's arm. They were alone in their tent, which by unspoken command was set apart from the rest of the campsite.

"I could smell the magic in the air," she said. "And she had that look, as if she'd returned from a faraway world."

"But she did not. Try to escape, I mean."

No, she had not. That was what bothered Ilse the most. This woman, a powerful mage, might have dared crossing into Anderswar in the flesh, then from there into Morennioù, but since that one attempt, back in Fortezzien, she had not tried again.

Secrets and more secrets.

She left those secrets aside. One more day. Or more.

They could not tell when the ship might arrive. She would have to take each moment as a gift.

AS USUAL, DETLEF handed out the watch assignments after dinner. He told Galena once, when she asked in a burst of confidence, that he preferred to give unpleasant news to his soldiers when they were warm and well-fed. If he couldn't manage warm, he always tried to manage the well-fed part. It was a trick he'd learned from his old commander, the Duke Kosenmark, in their days on the western frontier. He launched into a story about those days—the harsh winter winds, the spring rains falling in sheets, the sand and mud. Mostly, he talked about the mud and how it covered everything and everyone, including the duke.

Galena found it hard to imagine any nobleman covered in mud. And yet this Lord Kosenmark marched alongside the others. He carried a pack, he stood watch, he even took turns digging and filling in latrines. It was his voice that constantly startled her—high and fluting, like a woman's—no matter how many times she'd heard it before.

"Alighero."

She yanked herself back to attention. "Sir."

He grinned sardonically, reminding her of her old file leader, Falco. "You and I take the midnight watch. I hope you pay more attention then."

She ducked her head, embarrassed. Gervas snorted. Katje rolled her eyes, but that was aimed more at Detlef than Galena herself. The others paid no attention. They all knew her story. Or at least she assumed they did. No one said anything about it to her, except for a few covert glances at the mark on her cheek. At the same time, no one ignored her. They treated her the same as they would treat any junior soldier.

The evening passed quickly enough with chores. Galena spent an hour checking over all their weapons, sharpening the dull blades, scouring away any rust spots. From her vantage point beside the fire, she watched the to-and-froing of the company. Ilse and her Lord Kosenmark went apart for a time. Ada and Barrent patrolled the streets bounding the plaza and returned with their report. Valara Baussay had set off on a circuit of the empty plaza. Detlef sent Gervas after her, but Ilse Zhalina had intercepted the guard and brought Valara back herself. Katje muttered something about the stink of magic, but Galena merely shrugged. The whole island stank of magic. She couldn't tell any difference.

Once finished with chores, she slept. At midnight, Detlef woke her by that uncanny internal clock soldiers possessed. Galena buckled on her sword, slid her regulation knives into their sheaths, and set off with her companion on their rounds. They would patrol the neighborhood around the square first, he said as they picked their way through the moonlit streets. Then they would make a wider loop to include the stone wharf and its surroundings. Although Detlef said nothing, Galena had heard the rumors after Katje returned. They were waiting for a ship to take Valara Baussay home. Ilse Zhalina was to go with her.

After the ship sails, I start a new life, too.

Kosenmark had spoken to her briefly. He had promised her a letter of recommendation and directions to a northern mercenary company, along with money for the journey. Her heart leapt at the news, and she paid little attention to his lecture about assuming a new identity. Her thoughts were entirely on her brother Aris. He, too, had gone north. True, he had joined a regular garrison, but mercenaries and garrisons often fought together.

She and Detlef finished the round of the plaza and set off down the main avenue toward the wharves. All was quiet, empty. She and Detlef avoided the wide bright band of moonlight down the center of the street, keeping close to the shadows next to the walls. When they reached the next intersection, Detlef motioned to Galena to turn down a side lane. Here the shadows were thicker, and their progress slower. They both had their weapons ready, and they paused every few steps to listen and scan their surroundings. It was tedious business, but necessary.

Galena's cheek itched. She scrubbed at it with the back of her hand, but the itching grew worse. *Damned magic.* If only that cursed ship would come so she might be rid of this torment.

"Eyes up," Detlef said softly.

Galena lowered her hand at once and shifted her sword. Detlef silently pointed. Ahead lay a silver-lit square, the entrance to the main avenue. She squinted, saw nothing unusual. But when she held her breath and *listened,* she heard the faint tread of boots over stone. The footsteps ran swiftly, stopped, then others echoed from farther away. It was a pattern she knew well—the scouts advanced, scanned the next stretch, then motioned their companions to follow.

Detlef laid a hand on her arm and drew her close. "Those might be our friends," he whispered into her ear. "I don't know. But I don't like how they travel. Too quiet. You, go back to the campsite and warn the others. I'll make sure of these."

Meaning, if these were enemy, he would try to hold them until she woke the others.

He'll die, she thought. *Unless our enemies sent too few.* She doubted that.

"Let me stay," she whispered back. "You go back to Lord Kosenmark. I'll hold them."

Even as she spoke, her skin rippled in fear. But it only made sense, she told herself. Detlef was the senior guard. Kosenmark needed him the most. Besides, with Toc's goodwill, she could hold them long enough for reinforcements to come to her aid.

"Are you certain?" Detlef said.

"Do you think I won't?"

He tilted his head. His face was invisible in the darkness, but he reached out and gripped her arm. "I trust you. Stand strong."

With that, he turned back into the dark side street and set off in a silent run. Galena hefted her sword, checked her helmet, then strode toward the enemy.

ILSE WOKE TO a shout from Detlef. Instinct took over. She flung the blanket away and snatched up her sword. Raul already had his in hand. He tossed one helmet to Ilse, took another for himself. "Boots and daggers, too," he said. With shaking hands, she buckled on her belt and stuffed her feet into her boots. She thrust daggers into both sheaths. Raul did the same. "Stay close to me," he said. Then they were through the tent flaps.

Outside, the entire camp was awake. Detlef was bellowing, *"To arms, to arms."* Ada had rousted the last of those sleeping, handing out swords and helmets, and shouting for the outer perimeter to draw back now, damn it.

Just in time. A crowd of strangers poured into the moonlit plaza, a swarm of faceless shadows. Kosenmark's guards met them with swords and knives. The pilot and his crew had their clubs. One man caught up a burning brand from the fire. He hurled that in the face of the nearest enemy and struck with his dagger. The next moment, the air went taut with magic, and he went down into a pool of blood.

Ilse had no time to notice more. One of the strangers shouted an order. Immediately the others spread out. Three of them ran toward her and Raul. Ilse swept up her sword to block the first blow. She blocked again and felt the shock of her opponent's blow through her body. He was a tall man. He had a longer reach. She did not dare to press him too closely or he would use his height and strength to overpower her. The years of drill served well enough to keep the man from breaking through her defenses, but he would, soon enough.

Raul charged the man, who turned to meet him. Sword struck sword. Raul pressed the man's sword back to his throat and drove his dagger into the man's belly. One garbled curse, a wet and choking noise, and the man collapsed.

Károvín, Ilse thought. *He spoke Károvín.*

The other clues clicked into place. These were soldiers—Dzavek's men—come for Valara Baussay. She had no more time for thought. Raul plunged into the fight. Ilse followed. Together they fought their way toward the rest of their company. Their only chance was to make a square and work their way to the nearest wall.

It wouldn't be enough. They were only twelve. Their attackers almost twice as many.

Katje went down, run through by a sword. Ada leapt over her body to fill the gap. Ilse sensed Valara's signature, but she could not see where the woman had gone.

Then she spotted her.

Valara had a knife in her hand. She was swiping at those trying to capture her, and shouting in Erythandran. A bright fire hung in the air around her. One of the Károvín soldiers shouted an answering spell. The fire wavered. He plunged through and wrapped an

arm around her throat. Valara twisted away from his
hold. Before he could recapture her, she cried out in
Erythandran.

"*Ei rûf ane gôtter. Ei rûf ane Anderswar.*"

Magic exploded in the air. There was a blinding
bright spot in the middle, which changed in an instant
to the dark outline of a woman's form. Valara. Gone.
Ilse didn't wait to think what to do.

"*Ei rûf ane gôtter,*" she cried. "*Komen mir de Anderswar. Komen uns de vleisch unde sêle.*"

The world split open in a dazzling cloud of magic.

MIRO LUNGED TOWARD Valara Baussay. Moments
before his hand closed over her arm, a blinding explosion of magic swept over him. He stumbled, caught
himself, and rubbed his gloved hand over his eyes. He
could see little more than a smudge of light and shadow.
But then the shadow blinked out of sight.

His pulse tripped and raced forward. *She escaped.*

He knew it. Caught the scent of Vnejšek, of smoke
and burning incense, as though a wisp of its essence
had leaked through the infinitesimal gap required for
her flight from one plane to another. He hesitated a
moment—he had made this leap only a few times
before—then he was speaking the words to follow.

"*Ei rûf ane gôtter. Komen mir de strôm. Komen mir
de vleisch unde sêle ane Anderswar.*"

Hallau Island vanished. But the stink of blood and
fire, the smell of panic—all the scents of battle—filled
his nose. He felt everything ten times over, from the
cold air in his lungs to his blood rippling beneath his
skin. Vnejšek in the flesh.

He spun around, searching for Valara Baussay.
White vapor extended in all directions, shaped in pillars and canyons and shadowy halls of a gossamer
substance. The air smelled of hot tallow and ashes

and a scent he recognized as Leos Dzavek's. Vnejšek was reading details from his secret thoughts and half-remembered dreams.

A wall of blue fire illuminated the horizon. Two shadows stood before it, tiny dark dots before that glaring light. One shadow turned. He recognized Valara Baussay's profile and the way she lifted her chin.

Her gaze met his. Miro sheathed his sword and lifted one hand. Hers lifted halfway. She stopped herself, leaned close to her companion. There was a blur of motion which he could not follow. The next instant, both vanished into the fire.

Miro ran forward along the edge between worlds. Stopped himself. The queen might flee through a hundred different paths, he told himself. In the end, however, she would return to her home. If he pursued her, he might—would—lose a month or longer to magic and its realms.

That decided him. He spun away from the void and into the maelstrom below. *Károví, Károví, Károví,* he chanted.

A muffled chorus of wails and gibbers rose up from the depths. Darkness pressed against him. His flesh turned heavy, heavy, heavier, until he lost his balance and plunged an immeasurable depth, to land on his hands and knees. His stomach lurched against his chest. He swallowed. Gradually took in a few more details. Wet. Mud. (Mud? Such an ordinary thing.) An ache shot up his arms, as though he had fallen a much greater distance than he had first estimated.

It took him even longer to recover his bearings, to focus his eyes. Which world had he landed upon? He might have misjudged, might have plunged into another time or another place far removed from the one he knew.

He drew a deep breath. His sense of smell told him

the truth. The fragrance of clover struck him first, of spring mixed with snow, and far away, the newly flowered památka. These and all the other scents he knew from Károví's northern plains. He rubbed a hand over his eyes to clear them. A muddy plain stretched out before him. Above arced the pale blue sky of his homeland. Károví, yes. He almost laughed with delight and relief. And there, not a mile away, the walls of a garrison.

RAUL SWUNG HIS sword up to meet the next blow. A burst of magic illuminated the plaza. His vision blurred. He saw a mass of shadows against the brilliance. The shadows wavered, separated into three. Two vanished. A moment later, the third and last followed.

Then a bright shape arced upward. He met the blade with his own. For a long moment, he strained to hold his sword against the enemy, while all around, the magic current sparked and buzzed. When his vision cleared, he saw he faced a tall Károvín, a man nearly as tall as he was, but of a wiry build, obvious in spite of the layers of leather armor. The man's dark face gleamed with sweat; gray stubble along his jaw gleamed in the moonlight.

Everyone—Veraenen and Károvín alike—had frozen in momentary confusion. Kosenmark swiftly scanned the immediate area. There were several down, including Detlef. He could not tell if Ilse were among the dead and wounded. An inner voice whispered she had escaped, chasing after Valara Baussay. He almost laughed, until he remembered the third shadow. A Károvín must have dared the leap to follow them.

If he had possessed the skill, he would have done the same that instant. No. He would not. He could not abandon his soldiers on this desolate island.

"Are you stuffed full of battle yet?" he said in Károvín to his opponent. "Or do you want to fight on?"

He caught a passing expression of surprise on the man's face, followed by a studied blankness. "Not part of my orders," the other replied.

It was his voice.

I should be used to it by now, Raul thought. *And yet I am not.*

"So," he replied gruffly. "What were your orders? To start a war with Veraene?"

That provoked a harsh laugh, broken off. "Oh no."

Raul took in the man's military bearing, his reticence, and came to his own conclusions. "You are the king's soldiers. You came here for a purpose, and she is no longer here. Never mind whether I am right or not. Tell me— No, do not tell me anything except this—did your commander give you further orders?"

The other man hesitated, then said, "No."

Kosenmark released a breath—the moment of trust had come—and slowly lowered his sword. "A truce then. Agreed?"

The Károvín nodded. "Agreed."

There was the usual grumbling but soon enough, both sides withdrew, Károvín on one side of the square, Veraenen on the other, the dead and wounded scattered in between. The Károvín leader made a quick inspection of his people, then returned. "My name is Grisha Donlov," he said. "Captain Donlov. Do you need a mage-healer?"

"Mine is Raul Kosenmark. Yes, we do."

The aftermath took much longer than the battle itself. The Károvín and Veraenen worked together to sort out the dead and wounded. Katje had died in the first onslaught, as had Johannes and two of the fishermen. Detlef had taken a sword thrust to his belly. He would not survive the night, the Károvín healer told Raul. She was more a soldier than a healer, older than Raul, but only by a few years. For the dead, she called down the magic current to turn each body into ashes. For those who lived and suffered, she stayed by their sides to give such comfort as she could.

Raul visited each of his own wounded. The tally was less than he had feared. Gervas had taken a blow to the head, but other than a temporary deafness, he would be fit for duty the next morning. Others had bruises or cuts, which he or the Károvín healer dealt with. He checked over the dead twice. There was no sign of Ilse Zhalina or Valara Baussay.

Near the end, he came to the body of a young woman, dressed in secondhand clothes from his own stores, with a helmet set askew. The Károvín had carried her into the plaza from down the avenue.

Galena Alighero.

Her face was slick with blood. More blood soaked her clothes. Raul counted a dozen wounds on her body. She had fought on despite them. It was the deep gash across her throat that had bled her dry.

Raul touched the cold cheek. It was bare of any mark. Even as he took his fingers away, he felt the fading signature of Nicol Joannis of Fortezzien.

Death wipes all dishonor, Raul thought. *Even yours, Nicol.*

"She fought against all of us together," the Károvín healer said. "Back there. We might have taken you if she had not held us back." In a softer voice, she added, "She died bravely."

THE SHIP WITH Gerek Hessler and Alesso Valturri arrived off the coast, five days past the appointed time. They had spent three days, at least, skirting around the royal fleet, another day evading a mysterious single ship, sighted on the horizon. Only after they spent an entire day without further sightings did the captain and Gerek consent to head toward Hallau's shore.

Alesso had borrowed a glass from the captain, and he swept the coast for several long moments before he spoke. "Empty."

His tone was impossible to read. "What do you mean, empty?" Gerek demanded.

"Just that. Nothing and no one on shore."

Gerek snatched the glass and made his own examination. Though the captain warned them what to expect, the sight unnerved him. The city blackened and ruined. Empty. The wharves a desolate expanse of broken stone. As the ship slanted toward the coast, he glimpsed a small, one-masted boat tucked into a hiding spot, but no sign of the promised signals.

"What next?" Alesso said.

Over the past ten days, Alesso and the captain both had showed more respect than Gerek felt he deserved. And yet someone had to make decisions. "We send a launch to shore with six men," he said. "You choose your followers. Make sure they are well-armed." Almost as an afterthought, he added, "I-I should go, too."

It was a strange and silent journey to the wharf. The crew landed them neatly beside the other boat, which rocked in the waves, its single sail fluttering in the breeze. No one was on deck. As a precaution, Gerek sent Alesso over to search the small cabin.

"No one on board," Alesso reported. "But no sign of any fight."

Then one of the crew sniffed the air. "I smell wood smoke."

There were fresh tracks in the dust, too, which another man discovered. Farther on, signs of a scuffle and dark stains in the dirt. Gerek sent the two men ahead to follow the scent and the tracks, while he followed behind with Alesso. "It could be a trap," Alesso observed.

"It could," Gerek replied, nettled. "Do you have a better suggestion?"

Alesso shrugged. "No. Only that we don't go rushing forward with joy at finding your beloved master. After all, that boat might belong to a crew of testy smugglers."

"Then we take precautions."

Precautions meant they kept well behind their advance scouts, gliding through the unnaturally silent ruins. There were no birds here, Gerek noticed. No mice or crickets or toads creaking in the twilight. He almost remanded his order, thinking they should retreat to the ship for a conference, when footsteps ahead brought them all to attention.

One woman, two men rounded the corner from an alleyway. They stopped at the sight of Gerek and his guards.

There was a snick of tension. Both parties shifted into battle stance with weapons drawn.

Gerek tried to speak, but his tongue stuck on the first syllable. Then he recognized Kosenmark's guards—Ada Geiss, Barrent, and Gervas. In the same moment, Ada spotted Gerek. She gave a signal. Her guards dropped back a few steps. A breath later, so did Alesso and the others.

Ada lowered her sword. "Maester Hessler," she called out. "A good thing you came along."

He nodded, not quite able to master his speech. She seemed to understand because she drew him off to one side. "I am glad you came, and not just because we knew you. We've had trouble. I can't say more here, but take care when you speak with him."

He found his voice at last. "What happened?"

"Károvín soldiers," she said. "They came for that woman. The stranger."

"Any dead?"

She shook her head, but Gerek understood her meaning. It was a thing she could not discuss yet, not here in the open. He motioned for the rest to stay behind with Ada and her crew, then hurried forward alone through the avenue, until he came to a wide plaza. More ruins met his gaze, more dust and emptiness. On the farther side of the plaza stood the campsite—several canvas shelters stretched between enormous fallen blocks. One man bent over a makeshift fire pit, stirring a pot filled with bubbling stew. Others were at work with different tasks.

One of the men recognized him. "Ah, Maester Hessler. You want Lord Kosenmark, don't you?"

He pointed out Kosenmark's tent, larger than the rest, which was situated at the edge of their camp. Gerek jogged toward it, taking in the sight of the wounded, the great charred square off to one side, and a lingering burnt stench that hung over everything. By the time he reached Kosenmark's tent, his steps had slowed. He stopped a few feet away. "My lord," he said, tentatively.

There was a pause. Then, that high familiar voice said, "Come in."

Kosenmark's appearance shocked Gerek. The man's face was bruised. His eyes were sunken, as if he'd not slept in days, and the once-faint lines beside them were etched deeper and stronger. It was then that Gerek realized he had seen no sign of Ilse Zhalina or anyone else except the guards from Kosenmark's own household.

Take care when you speak with him, Ada had said.

Gerek bowed. "My lord."

Kosenmark studied him with those great golden eyes. "I did not expect you."

"There were . . . difficulties, my lord."

"Ah." A tiny smile lightened Kosenmark's expression. It vanished quickly. "Just as well. As you perceive, our agenda has changed somewhat."

He pointed to a wooden box with symbols burned onto the lid. The box was clearly a makeshift creation, unpolished and rough, but Gerek recognized the signs for a box of the dead. His breath came short. Ilse Zhalina's?

Kosenmark must have interpreted his thoughts, because his mouth twitched into a bitter smile. "She is not dead. At least, she did not die in battle. No, this was a soldier of the kingdom, who gave her life defending me. I would bring her ashes to her family, except that her family already believes her dead. I shall have to think over what to do."

His voice died away and his gaze went diffuse. He appeared oblivious—or indifferent—to Gerek's presence, and it took Gerek several moments before he could bring himself to speak and break that reverie. "What comes next, my lord?"

That distant gaze went blank a moment and then returned to the present. Kosenmark smiled, almost naturally. "We go home. I have a few promises to keep. And we prepare for the future, whatever it holds."

CHAPTER TWENTY-ONE

FIRE. MAGIC. CONFLAGRATION.

Ilse gripped her sword, ready to ward off the next blow, but none came. The battle had vanished. No, *she* had vanished from the battle, translated by magic into Anderswar's plane. She still heard its echoes in her ears, still saw ghostlike images flickering before her eyes, like memories come to life. *You are not true,* she told them. *You are base illusions, sent to frighten me.*

As if Anderswar heard her thoughts, the images faded. She was alone, with flames and fog and the lights from a thousand worlds wheeling beneath her feet. Ilse swallowed, tasting grit and ashes from that faraway campfire on Hallau Island.

Onward, she told herself.

One step, another. The worlds shuddered and spun. She ignored them. Far ahead—if distance mattered here—she had glimpsed movement in the shadows. A third step and the shadow resolved into a tall figure striding along the bright-lit edge. Valara.

"Valara!" she called out.

Valara paid her no heed. She strode faster, sending the current whirling around her. Fox and stars, the signatures were unmistakable. Impossible, Ilse thought.

No one had a double signature. And then realization came to her—the woman had a magical device. Something powerful enough that it made its own separate impression.

Ignoring the chasm on either side, Ilse raced forward and seized Valara above her elbow. Valara tried to shake off Ilse's grip, but Ilse's fingers tightened around that bone-thin arm. "We must go back," she said. "Valara, do you hear me? We must go back."

Her last glimpse of the fight had been of Raul, his face covered with blood, fighting off three attackers. It was impossible for him and his guards to defend themselves against the Károvín for very long. If they were quick enough, if they hadn't lost hours—or days—they might surprise the Károvín and overcome them with magic.

"No." Valara's voice was rough and quick. "You can go back to die if you like. But I won't. Not this time. Not again—"

She broke off with an exclamation. Her chin jerked up and she had a wild fey look in her eyes. "He came. I should have expected that. He would not let death stop him from pursuing me." Then in a softer voice, "Only an order from his king could turn him aside."

Ilse glanced over her shoulder.

Clouds roiled up from an invisible horizon, a vast expanse of silver and white in constant motion. Even as she tried to make out what caught Valara's attention, a dark shadow appeared against the bright mist, like an ink spot dropped onto snow. The spot grew larger, becoming the figure of a man, holding a sword. A breeze from nowhere ruffled the man's dark hair, sending a trace of his magical signature toward them. She had met that same signature in lives past . . .

"He's one of the soldiers," she said.

Valara's lips drew back in a snarl. "Oh yes. His

name is Karasek. He led the invasion against my
people." She yanked free of Ilse's hold. "Come with
me or not. But I will not let that man take me prisoner again."

She dived into the chaos below. Ilse barely hesitated
before she dived after her.

*. . . their world tilted upside down. A thrumming
filled her ears. She had a vision of islands scattered
over wine-dark seas. She knew them, had sailed to
their shores in a different life. It was the lost kingdom
of Morennioù. Valara Baussay was fleeing homeward . . .*

*A voice rang out, a great harsh bell-like voice, so
loud her bones vibrated. No and no and no, it cried.
You must deliver us all . . .*

An irresistible force plucked them away from the
islands and hurled them through a maelstrom of
fire and smoke. Ilse heard a ragged scream—Valara,
shouting curses to someone named Daya. Just as she
thought they would be lost forever in the void, the
world materialized around them and a cold wind
struck Ilse in the face.

She crouched on a bare rocky plain. Her sword,
dark with dried blood, lay beside her. She blinked.
Her tears turned to ice. She brushed them away with
one stiff hand and shaded her eyes. Snow whirled
through the air. The sun was little more than a white
disk hovering above the flat horizon.

Ilse drew a long painful breath. Her ribs ached. Her
head rang with an echo of the shrieks and curses from
the void. A rill of magic floated past, like a second
current of wind, then vanished.

Where am I?

A dark mass huddled next to her—a woman, whose
hair streamed loose in the wind. Valara.

Valara Baussay lifted her head. Her tattoos stood

out sharply against her cheek and lips, now gray from the cold. She spoke, but her words made no sense to Ilse. The language was neither Veraenen nor Morennioùen. It reminded her of the old text from Károví that her brother, Ehren, brought home from Duenne's University, a time and world so long ago, they could have been a previous life.

The wind shifted, carrying with it a hint of warmth, and the overpowering scent of magic. Ilse squinted. It was impossible to see more than a haze of white and gray. She rubbed the back of her hand over her eyes and blinked. Her vision cleared, and she gave an astonished cry.

A mile away from them, argentine cliffs rose tall and straight from the snow-dusted plain, a vast rippling curtain of stone that interrupted the smooth horizon. And like a curtain, there appeared a gap in the front, where dark sand and gravel spilled forth to the plains below. Above, the air shimmered, as though fires roared inside that fantastical creation.

It was like all the paintings and ink drawings she had seen in books. It was like her own memories of this place, from lives and lives ago.

The Mantharah and the Agnau.

She knew exactly where magic and the void had flung them, as if a map lay before her. They were in the far north of Károví, a hundred miles or more from Rastov. Oh, but this was more than some lonely mountain. Here the gods had feasted upon each other's love. Here they'd fashioned the world, drawing out a never-ending ribbon of life from the Agnau's molten stuff—from the magical creatures of Anderswar to the ordinary beasts and all mankind.

Wind blasted through her thin clothes. She shook Valara's arm. "We can't stay in the open," she shouted.

"We'll take shelter over there." She jabbed a fist toward the Mantharah.

Valara nodded dumbly, but gave no sign of comprehension. Ilse shook her again, hard. The other woman gave a gasp. She snapped her head up to face the Mantharah. Her eyes narrowed in awareness. And recognition.

Ilse didn't need to say anything more. They helped each other regain their feet. Both of them were stiff and clumsy with cold. Ilse sheathed her sword. She drew her hands into her sleeves and tucked her chin into her collar. Valara scowled, as if she could subdue the cold with her fury, but she did the same. Heads bent against the constant wind, they stumbled toward the Mantharah and that narrow gap between cliff and cliff.

By the time they reached its ash-strewn slopes, Ilse's face was numb. She caught a whiff of strong magic, of warmth, from above. She and Valara scrambled up through loose dirt and gravel, breathing in that incredible scent, as though spring had bloomed, invisible, just beyond their sight.

The slope led up to a hard-packed crown of stone. From there, the cliffs swept around a lake of silver, its shore a perfect circle of ink-black sand, washed smooth by the Agnau's waves, which rolled ceaselessly from shore to distant shore. Surrounding the lake, the cliffs rose straight toward the sky. Here and there in the silvery walls, Ilse saw shallow indentations, as though fingers had touched them before they had hardened.

The hands of gods.

It was all too much. She wanted to weep at the impossibility. She sat down hard on the ground and began to curse. Her mad outburst must have frightened

Valara, because the other woman retreated farther along the Agnau's shores.

"You." Ilse scrambled to her feet and drew her sword. "You will tell me the truth, Valara Baussay. No more lies. I am sick to my soul with your lies. Sit over there."

She pointed to a small, broken off boulder next to her—an anomaly in this strangely smooth and perfect setting. Valara glanced from the boulder to Ilse. "You want to kill me."

"No," Ilse said harshly. "I want to hear the truth for once. Sit. And speak."

Gingerly, Valara took her seat on the boulder. Ilse remained standing.

"Where should I start?" Valara asked.

"With you and Leos Dzavek. No, with the jewel you found in Morennioù."

Valara flinched. "Yes. That."

She chafed her hands one within the other, as if searching for the words to begin her story. She still wore that plain wooden ring, Ilse noticed. It had turned darker over the past few days, and its polished surface took on a brighter gleam. A brother's gift. A very strange one, much plainer than one would expect from a royal prince to his sister.

Valara met her gaze. Her lips quirked into a smile. "My ring. Or rather, Lir's emerald. I called it a gift from my brother. In a sense, that is true. I would not have it except for him. Leos Dzavek, I mean. He is not my brother now, but he was, once."

Ilse's pulse took a sudden leap. She lowered her sword and stared at Valara, who glanced away. Of course. It explained so much. The magical storm that destroyed the three Károvín ships. Valara's escape from Osterling's prison. How she killed those soldiers with a powerful magic that seemed to surprise her as much as it did others.

It took her many moments before she could collect her thoughts and focus on the essentials. Even longer before she trusted herself to speak in anything resembling a rational tone.

"When did you find it?"

Valara opened and shut her mouth. Then she wiped a hand over her eyes and smiled, a strange sad uncomfortable smile. "Last year. Shortly before my mother and sister died. When I became my father's heir. You must understand . . ." She stopped a moment, pressed her lips together and sent a glance upward to the cliffs, as if she would find an answer there. "Or perhaps you cannot understand. You were not there, after all, through these past three hundred years. You see, in Morennioù, we have certain conventions. There are magic workers, mages, wizards, whatever you like to call them, but none of them are kings or queens. Even the nobles do not cast any spells other than the simplest ones. Lighting a candle, sealing a letter."

"Those are not necessarily simple spells," Ilse murmured.

Valara gave a soft laugh. "No. Over the years, the definition for ordinary has stretched and twisted and changed. But I can assure you that powerful magic—including a journey to Autrevelye, to Anderswar—is strictly forbidden. I broke the conventions because I was curious, at first. Later, when I discovered that Leos Dzavek was my brother, and I the one who hid Lir's jewels, I studied more magic so that I could reclaim the jewels for Morennioù. I knew that one day, Luxa's Hand would fail us and we would have to face the world. I did not wish to do that without a weapon at hand."

She twisted the ring around her finger. "I had not realized that day would come so soon."

Luxa's Hand. What the Veraenen called Lir's Veil. It had stood so long—three hundred years—they had all forgotten to question its existence.

Except Leos Dzavek. He forgot nothing, whether good or evil. Was that a factor of his long life? Or of himself, his own nature, refusing to take anything for granted?

She knew the answer already, from her life dreams. So did Valara Baussay.

She turned back to her questions. "Dzavek sent his soldiers after you and the emerald. Did Markus Khandarr know?"

Valara's mouth tensed at the mention of Khandarr's name. "No. He would not have allowed me to live so long, I think."

Very true. Ilse could understand this woman's reluctance to speak openly. She was a queen among her enemies.

It would have been simpler if she had trusted us. But then, we did not entirely trust her.

A savage ache had settled between Ilse's eyes. She was hungry, weary, frightened. Angry with herself for not guessing the truth earlier. For trusting too much and not enough, all at the same time. Absently she rubbed her free hand over her forehead. Smelled the lingering scent of smoke and blood, overlaid with the strong scent of magic that permeated the air. *I cannot stop the questions yet. She is speaking at last.*

"Did anyone else in your court know about the emerald?" she asked.

Valara shook her head. "Not at first. I had not decided when, or how, to introduce the matter. It is a delicate subject."

And you were not certain you wished to share this information.

Ilse kept that thought to herself. "You say not at first . . ."

"I told no one at first. It was too dangerous—dangerous the way I used to understand such things. Court dangerous. Politically dangerous. There were several factions who— Well, never mind about them. I told my father and his mage councillor, but not until that very last day. They are both dead now."

More glimpses into the woman's life and Morennioù's Court. Ilse had the impression of a strict and cold existence, of a life requiring exquisite balance. *Like walking the knife edge above spinning worlds in Anderswar.*

Which reminded her of another question. "What about now? Why did you remain in Veraene? Why bargain with us at all?"

"Ah, that." Valara lifted her hand to show the ring. "Because Daya would not allow me. She—he—they told me clearly they wanted deliverance, for themselves and their brothers, sisters. I had not understood before what they meant. I'm still not certain."

More pieces from history and her own memories fitted together to complete the picture. Daya. Lir's emerald. Once joined together with the other two.

Even through the enveloping magic, Ilse could hear the wind thumping against the Mantharah, like a vast fist hammering on a door.

Or like an angry supplicant, demanding satisfaction of its god.

Deliver us all, the voice like bells had cried out.

We are all bound to these jewels, Ilse thought. *Just as they are bound to us.*

A man was created free, the philosophers said. It

was his own choices, however, that bound him in the end. Even the choice to do nothing, to deny responsibility and claim that one was powerless to act, that, too, would bind a soul to the same life, the same questions, again and again.

"So then," Ilse said softly. "I have my answers. Now I give one to you. We do as the jewels ask of us. If we refuse, we are set to this same task in our next lives, and the next, and so on until the end of eternity. If we deliver them to freedom, that in turn sets us free. So. We must recover the other two jewels and join them all together, as they once were."

"I—" Valara broke off and stared at the Agnau's surface. "No, I cannot argue that. But how? Leos Dzavek has Rana—the ruby—locked away in his castle. We cannot hope to attack him in that stronghold. Remember how it was before?"

"I remember."

She did. If Ilse closed her eyes, she could see ghostly images of Zalinenka. The hundreds of guards who stood outside the gates and patrolled the lower halls. Even before Károví divided itself from the empire, the court had its factions who did not always restrict themselves to mere speech to gain their point.

"So we do not attack," she said. "We infiltrate. But not yet. First we need to recover the missing jewel."

"Asha," Valara said. "I hid her, him in Autrevelye."

Three hundred years ago, when Valara Baussay had lived as Imre Benacka. *And I read about you from a book written by a prison official named Karel Simkov. You died before you would admit to Leos Dzavek where you hid those jewels.*

"So search your memories," Ilse told Valara. "Find Asha and bring her back here. I shall stay by the Mantharah and keep Daya safe. Once you return, we can plan our next steps."

Valara's lips curled back in a snarl, as if she were a dog. No, a fox. Then her eyes closed and she touched the ring again. Her lips moved in a silent conversation. A long pause followed before she released a sigh.

"No choice. Or as you said, the only choice left." She stared at the ring upon her finger, and for a moment, her features seemed to shift in the Agnau's strange light, from woman to man and back again. "The only choice," Valara repeated softly. "Would that I had accepted this before." She glanced up, once more the Morennioùen queen, no traces of her former selves apparent. "Let us make our plans then."

THEY SPOKE OF practicalities next. What were the implications of Valara's search? How long would it require? What if Leos Dzavek detected her presence there?

A few hours, no less, Valara insisted.

What if you need more? Ilse asked, equally insistent. *And what about the time difference? A single hour in Anderswar can mean days, years, in this world.*

More arguments followed. Each of them was practiced in evasion, obfuscation, the many other intricate maneuvers one encountered in royal courts. In the end, the knowledge that they had to act for the future—theirs and their kingdoms—decided the argument.

"One day, then," Valara said. "No longer."

"How can you know when you return? Anderswar—"

"—is not invincible. Trust me to know that." Her lips thinned to a sardonic smile. "Though, indeed, you have little reason to trust me. But what I say is true. Once I have the sapphire, I can traverse the void more precisely. I can return before the sun sets."

She took off the ring and laid it between them.

"One day," she repeated. "If I do not return before then, consider me dead, and do what you must."

FOR VALARA BAUSSAY, it was as though she had carried a great weight this past year, one that grew heavier with every moment. Valara pressed both hands over her eyes a moment to regain her equilibrium. She still heard echoes of Daya's bell-like voice within, but softer now. *Soon I will be alone.*

"I must go in the flesh," she said. "I can read the signs more easily that way."

Ilse nodded. Her hand had closed over the ring, but loosely. A cautious woman. Good. She would need to be.

Valara seated herself on the sandy shore. She would do this properly, the way she had read in the old philosophers' textbooks and journals. The oldest ones of all said that forms were irrelevant. That you did not need even word or thought to work magic. For herself, Valara took comfort in the ritual.

Ei rûf ane gôtter. Komen mir de strôm. Komen mir de vleisch unde sêle. Komen mir de Anderswar . . .

Her first journeys to Autrevelye had taken place with wrenching suddenness that left her ill and almost blind. This time, she felt nothing more than a subtle displacement, a momentary dizziness as her body accustomed itself to new surroundings. Then the rest of her senses caught up. Mantharah's keening winds had vanished. The scent of magic was strong here, but nothing so intense as the steam rising from the Agnau. And less tangible, the sense that she was alone.

She released her breath, opened her eyes.

She sat in a darkened room that smelled of old stone and wet earth. Water trickled over the rough-cut walls. Strange how she had missed that sound at first—as if she had to relearn how to listen. The floor itself was smooth, worn to a velvet softness, as though many travelers had visited this chamber before.

Expectations, she reminded herself. Autrevelye read them from her mind to construct itself anew each time.

A plume of musk drifted past her. Shadows rippled away with its passage. The shadows turned upon themselves, revealing a lean dark wolflike creature. It curled around to face her. Its lips drew back from yellowed teeth in an unnatural grin. Rikha. Her first and only guide in this other world for the past five years.

Rikha snuffed at the floor and growled. "You returned."

"I did."

"But without the emerald, without Daya. Did a thief overcome a thief, perhaps?"

She felt a prickle of irritation, suppressed it. "I left Daya in safekeeping. Though that is not your concern."

"No." It laughed softly. "Nothing concerns me, not even your fondest wish."

True enough.

In her early days with magic and Autrevelye, Rikha's presence had terrified her. Then she had attempted to treat the beast as one of her subjects. She had mastered her terror, but Rikha had only laughed when she gave it orders. Slowly, they were learning to deal with each other.

"You want the sapphire," Rikha said.

She nodded. "And for that I need your help in remembering. I know about my brother, about his search and mine for the jewels, but that is not quite . . . enough. Can you help me?"

Rikha tilted its head and regarded her with a clear implacable gaze. "Autrevelye never forgets, lady. Neither does your soul."

Her skin rippled at the tone of his voice. Of course. It was all a part of his nature, and Autrevelye's. They only knew death and rebirth. Life itself was only a brief interlude between the two. Strange, how humans viewed everything in reverse.

"I do not forget," she said. "Please take me to where Leos Dzavek last captured me, when I was Imre Benacka."

"Do you order me?" he asked, his tone soft with menace.

She smiled. "Of course not. I beg a favor of you, Rikha."

"Ah, that is different. Come, lady, and we shall find your past."

She stood and laid her hand on Rikha's shoulder. They paced forward slowly, and with a few steps, the darkness ebbed away, the stone room faded into a bleak desert, then to a jungle of sweet-smelling flowers. In silence they passed through a grove of silver trees and crossed a river, skimming through the air just above the surging current. The sun above had stopped in the sky, and the air itself had turned still. In Autrevelye, in the outside worlds, time might be pouring into the future, but here it was frozen.

They stopped at last at the edge of a barren cliff. Ahead stretched a wasteland, a pale desert of sand and rock. The cliff itself was part of a stony ridge that divided the desert from an even more desolate mountain range. Valara didn't need Rikha's explanation for why he'd brought her to this place. She already knew— she'd come this way untold centuries ago as a different person, almost a different soul. Here, she had once fled, desperate, with Lir's jewels in her hands. Here, Leos Dzavek had captured her, when her name was Imre Benacka.

My brother, my king. The man who captured me,

killed me, or nearly so, and revived me so he could take me prisoner and rip the truth from my throat.

And here, just last summer, she had returned in her quest to rediscover her past.

In that moment, the sun dropped toward the horizon. The golden plains turned dark red in its dying light. Blood touched the cliff face and the rocks behind her. "This is too much," she murmured.

"We've not begun to explore excess," Rikha answered. He snuffed the ground and with his forepaw indicated a depression where dust had collected. "That spot."

Valara touched the soft red dust. She saw no footprints at first, then realized the prints were as red as the ground. *Scarlet for eternity,* she thought. Dzavek's prints, she noted, were the silver gray of twilight. She dug into the dust with her fingers, tasted the salt of old tears and the metallic edge of panic. She heard snatches of voices she recognized—Dzavek and herself arguing loudly. Both called out words of magic. Valara felt a sharp stab and plucked back her hand. Immediately, the voices cut off.

Future and past together. It was almost too unnerving to continue.

Rikha sniffed at the ground. "The tracks lead on."

"Then we do as well."

It was a trail in opposite directions, a looping path across rivers and lakes, over bare hills and thickly forested plains. Two sets of prints—one laid down by Imre Benacka, one by Leos Dzavek. Several times the prints disappeared beneath landslides, or lay submerged where rivers had changed their course. She could see where Dzavek had broken off his search, only to return again and again. Rikha himself, a creature of Autrevelye, had to circle around with his nose in the dirt until he found the trail once more.

Rana's hiding place lay underneath a waterfall, hidden behind a cascade of water and mist. Wind and rain and water had smoothed the dirt; only a shallow pit remained where Dzavek had dug up the ruby. Crossing back and forth over the area, Valara found her tracks leading onward, backward. Handprints covered the branches and higher rocks; footprints dotted those leading across the frothing water.

"You tried to disguise your trail," Rikha said. "You knew someone would follow you."

Memory returned, much stronger. Oh yes, she remembered that day. On the farther bank, she had climbed down the rocks from the next plateau. Valara followed, gripping the same rocks, hearing, as though her own self were just ahead, the uneven gasps as she eased herself down the sheer cliff. Above, the land stretched into a wide and even plain. Here the prints were spaced farther apart, as though she had come in this direction running as fast as possible, leaping ahead of pursuing danger. Valara ran the same path backward, matching leap for leap, each one longer and longer, until . . .

The tracks disappeared.

Valara cried out in shock and fell to her knees. Rikha hurried to her side. His muzzle wrinkled in surprise. "Where next?"

Where indeed? She pressed her palm over the last footprint. Fear and urgency vibrated from its essence. The signs were clear. She'd run headlong over the packed dirt. But from where?

She rocked back on her heels, willing herself to remember that terrifying day. Dzavek in pursuit. The sapphire clutched in her (his) sweat-slick hands. The knowledge that he had to break the trail, except that footprints and handprints in Vnejšek were not so easily hidden. He had to make a true break, to leap from the magical plane into the ordinary world and back, to an entirely different point. Only then could he escape Leos Dzavek.

I remember now. I leapt into nothing. I dared him to follow me. He never could, my brother. He always wanted a sure victory.

It was a gamble she could not refuse, could not resist.

"Follow me," she said to Rikha, "if you can."

Without waiting for his reply, she launched herself into a run, each stride lengthening into the next, each leap coming higher, until she took that last measured stride and, calling aloud to the gods, vaulted into the unknown.

Dimension vanished. Darkness. Nothingness. No direction. Falling. Dying. Living.

A brilliant ribbon of light arced before her. Pale footprints dotted that ribbon, each one an impossible distance from the next. All around the wind hurtled past, the sky was an inky void, and she had nothing to guide her but a thin path and her own footsteps.

Step. Leap. Fly. And live.

The ribbon ended, and she tumbled through the centuries onto a desolate plain, where she lay gasping for breath.

Body. I still have my body. I'm alive.

She tried to scramble to her feet, but her knees gave way, and she collapsed into an aching heap. A dark red streak landed next to her. Rikha rolled onto his feet. "The trail continues," he said. She tried to stand a second time and failed. Rikha merely nudged her with his nose. "Do not bother with walking. Time for you to ride."

With his assistance, she crawled onto his back and clung to his neck. "Go," she croaked.

A clear order. And this time Rikha obeyed.

He galloped forward, her weight as nothing to him. The tracks led them to a narrow valley, where the high gray walls shut out the sun. Here the footsteps circled a bare patch of dirt. Valara could see two deep indentations. She dropped off Rikha's back and dug into the hard ground, not caring how her nails broke or her fingers bled. Rikha pushed her aside and scratched at the packed mound, breaking it apart, while Valara scooped out handfuls. In her hurry, she nearly missed the small dark speck, the size of her thumbnail, which was half-buried in the loose heaps of dirt.

Asha.

Valara carefully extracted the sapphire and cupped it in her hands. Its color was much darker than she had imagined—a blue so deep it looked black, but when she touched it, indigo fire sparked at her fingertips, the lights echoing a complex melody of bright pure notes.

With Asha, I could free my kingdom and hold it safe against the world.

Briefly she saw herself at the head of an army. Her heart leapt up. Just as quickly the image faded and she heard Ilse Zhalina's voice saying, *We must make the right choice this time.*

Valara tore off a strip from her shirt and wrapped Asha securely within it. She would not lose this jewel again, even if Dzavek chased her through all Autrevelye. After tucking the bundle inside her shirt, she climbed onto Rikha's back. "Let us go."

CHAPTER TWENTY-TWO

IN ALL THE old texts, scholars spoke of the *instant* of translation, as if magic transported the body into the magical plane in an eyeblink. Like so much else, the phrase was poetical but not accurate. Ilse plainly saw Valara's body shimmering in the air a long moment before the woman vanished from sight. Even then, whether by some trick of sight or expectation, the ghost of her figure remained, outlined in wreaths of mist and fog.

On impulse, Ilse reached toward the spot where Valara had sat. A wayward puff of air broke the illusion apart. She stopped, exhaled. Suppressed the urge to follow Valara into the void. The other woman was right. Ilse would only prove a burden and distraction. Better that she remain here to safeguard the emerald.

She glanced down at the ring in her hand. Again its weight surprised her and its surface felt unnaturally warm. Daya, Valara called it. A living creature, one who hoped, just as she did. A memory floated up from another life. She had held this jewel, or something like it, in her hands. She had relinquished it to another person. Out of duty? Relief that it would no longer be her responsibility? She couldn't remember precisely, only an old sense of regret that she had done so.

With some trepidation, she slipped the ring onto her finger.

One more day. Less, if she could believe Valara's claims. Ilse herself had no such confidence. She would have to start work now to assure her own survival.

She checked her sword and her daggers. Both were in good condition, though she would need to clean her sword and its sheath. There were grasses on the plains, low trees, and patches of snow. She could wipe down the blade, cut switches to clean out the sheath.

First, however, she decided to make a circuit of the Agnau itself. She did not want any surprises. Any more surprises, she reminded herself. The past five months had been filled with nothing but the unexpected.

The Agnau measured several miles in circumference. Its shores remained low and smooth, covered with the same black sand she found at the entrance. Once a few hundred yards beyond the Mantharah's entrance, however, the cliffs rippled inward then outward, like folds in a cloth, nearly to the edge of the lake, so that she had to edge carefully between them and the seething magical substance of the lake. From time to time, she knelt and sifted through the hot black sands, thinking that she would find more clues to her past, or the world's, but she found nothing. These were as barren as these cliffs stretching upward to the sky. And yet, a millennium or more ago, life had poured out in a season of love and life.

You and your beloved Toc have loved beyond life and death, Tanja Duhr once wrote. *You have loved beyond the imaginable. We poor humans cannot imagine and so must stumble through our lives, more blind than Blind Toc, more alive to grief than Lir herself.*

She needed barely an hour to finish the circuit.

One hour. And you have not returned.

But their agreement was for an entire day.

Ilse wanted to shout, to send her spirit soaring into the void after Valara's. An unprofitable venture, she decided.

After carefully scanning the plains with sight and magic, she ventured down the slopes and scouted the immediate area. The wind had died away, and the afternoon was fair and chill, the sky a hard gray. She found ice and snow packed into crannies and fissures around the base of the cliffs. The snow was old, granular, but clean enough to drink. If she had to, she could strain the water through her shirt. She packed her helmet full. A flicker of movement caught her eye—a hare or other small animal darting through the grass. That reminded her. She could braid the grass into snares, as Galena had taught her on their journey from Osterling.

At the thought of Galena, her eyes stung with tears. She swiped them away, angrily. *I must not mourn her too soon—none of them—or else I won't be able to carry onward.*

Onward. Yes.

She gathered an armful of grasses and returned to the Agnau. She stowed these in a shallow bay with an overhang, a few yards in from the entrance. Sheltered from snow or rain, warmed by the lake, it would make a perfect sleeping spot.

Another expedition yielded a small quantity of pine twigs and peat, cut from the earth with her dagger. She also discovered wild oats growing in a gully. Farther on, a patch of plantain. The leaves were tough, but they would make a drinkable tea. Her two prizes were a hollow stone that could serve as a cook pot, and a block of frozen snow for water.

It took her several trips to carry everything back to

camp. She drank off her water and built a fire. Scrubbed the cook stone clean with snow, and set the plantain leaves to simmer. The oats she spread over a flat stone next to the fire. By the time she finished the sun had reached the midpoint in the sky. Exhausted, she sank to the ground and took up a fistful of grass to scour her sword, but the effort proved too much. She leaned back against the cliff wall and stared upward.

Noon. Valara had crossed into the magical plane at least two hours ago. She should have returned with the sapphire before now. Valara had spoken with absolute certainty of her ability to do just that.

She misjudged the time, Ilse told herself. *But she will return with the jewel. Then we shall make our next plans.*

Without thinking, she rubbed the wooden ring. Magic ran beneath its smooth surface, reminding her that Daya was no man-made thing, but a being created by the gods. Ilse closed her eyes and focused on the point between the ordinary and the magical planes. Yes, she could hear its voice, a silvery stream of minor notes, like the wind keening through the rigging of a swift-moving ship.

You told Leos Dzavek where to find us, she said. *You stopped his brother from running free to Morennioù. Why?*

For several moments she heard nothing but a faint humming, then, *Because he, because she, they lied. They would keep us bound. And she learns too fast this brother-sister-cousin. She remembers her magic. She would know as he does, as the brother does, how to bind me stronger.*

Its voice blurred into music again, as it spoke about the centuries in Anderswar, hidden. Working through plans, though its nature was not given to such. Absorbing magic. Thinking that if it had one chance, it would break from its prison. But not alone. Ilse heard three strong chords, followed by a long, long note that vibrated through her bones.

You must deliver us, Daya said at last.

I know, Ilse whispered. *I promise.*

She rested her head on her hands. The ring felt heavy on her finger. The strong green scent of magic filled the air, the sweet fragrance of wildflowers and new grass, an impossible contradiction to the frozen plains outside the Mantharah's walls.

Death and rebirth. The eternal contradiction of magic.

She thought about a world without the threat of war. Removing the jewels would not accomplish that—she was not so foolish to think so—but it would make the wars much harder to carry through. Would Valara see that? She might tell herself that she only wished to defend Morenniou, but like Armand, like Dzavek, she might soon persuade herself to a different, more murderous course. Was that why she had not yet returned?

If I took the ruby, then I could bargain with her.

She rubbed her aching eyes with her knuckles. The fire had died away. The oats were as roasted as they would be. She chewed a few handfuls, drank the lukewarm tea to wet her throat, and felt the headache recede. The winds were rising again, a thin high keening. Snow hissed against the Mantharah's walls, only to vanish into meltwater.

Running just beneath the windsong, she heard Daya speaking again. *Go in spirit. Go through the world of flesh in spirit with me. We shall take Rana. We shall make the leap into Anderswar and back to here, to the Agnau. Then you shall have two of us, and Valara Baussay has no choice but to follow.*

She remembered now. The oldest mages, the ones

who served the chieftans of Erythandra in the northern plains, before they moved south to conquer and make an empire. It was part of their initiation, to walk in the spirit but remain in the ordinary world. There were no written records, of course, but the old tribes had handed down the stories, priest to priest, until those stories reached the days when scribes set them to parchment. If she left her body here by the Agnau, her spirit could glide the miles to Zalinenka, unseen by guards. She and Daya could take Rana and escape through Anderswar and thence back to Agnau.

Flesh in the spirit. And spirit in the world of flesh.

A sense of vertigo swept over her, recalling her first time in Anderswar and that disembodied sensation, as if she were floating in an ocean of mist.

A return to ordinary chores restored her sense of place. She buried the fire. Laid out her sword and dagger in their sheaths. Then she lay down on the warm sands and clasped her hands over Daya. *"Komen mir, lâzen mir,"* she whispered. "Lir give me courage. Toc give me strength."

The current contracted around her, then blossomed outward. Her spirit rose to standing, her body shifting slightly as the two separated. She breathed deeply, felt the muted sensation of flesh against cloth-in-memory, and glanced around.

The world had turned translucent. Bright fires—other spirits—were moving about. Two circled the opening between the cliffs—winter foxes on the hunt. From the south came a sense of many more. Rastov and Leos Dzavek's castle.

Ilse turned south, and began the journey to Zalinenka.

VALARA RETURNED TO find Ilse lying motionless next to the Mantharah's cliffs. Her eyes were closed, and her lips parted. In the Agnau's extraordinary light, it appeared as though the other woman were speaking. Right away, she noted that Ilse wore the ring on her left hand.

She thought I betrayed her. She went to Zalinenka. Alone.

Valara wasted no time in fury or second thoughts. With the sapphire clasped in one hand, she lay down next to Ilse and spoke the words to release her spirit from her flesh.

ILSE WALKED FOR hours across the plains, through a world painted in grays and black and muddy white. Her passage left a glittering trail, visible to the spirit eye until she wiped its trace clean. In places, a companion set of tracks dented the snow crust. The tracks were slight, a powdery dusting of snow crystals swept over them; nevertheless, she took care to interrupt her trail on rock outcroppings, or by taking detours through an icy, free-running stream. Strange that her spirit communicated physical sensation to her. Habit or clue to some tenuous connection between body and soul?

As she walked, she thought of Valara. She thought of Raul Kosenmark. And Galena, Alesso, all those others from her past. If she did not succeed, she would be dead and beyond helping anyone, yet she continued this internal recitation of those in danger.

Hours passed. The miles slipped away, impossibly fast. The sun arced toward the horizon, then dipped below. More hours passed, as the last of daylight drained from the sky, leaving behind a scarlet thread of light above the southwest horizon. She sensed Rastov's bright constellation of souls and fixed on that direction. Soon she came to a narrow track cut into the ground. It led to a second, larger path, which joined a third to become a road leading south. Gradually the high flat plains began their long descent, dropping from the plateau toward a broad valley with a river winding through it. She saw at once the large city, its buildings a dark mass. On the nearer bank, at the northern edge of the city, stood a castle. Zalinenka.

Daya had remained silent throughout the long journey, but she felt its presence even stronger here, in this point between flesh and pure spirit. Now it spoke. *You remember?*

Ilse nodded. *I lived there once. My name was Milada Ivet Darjalova. My father was a prince of Károví.*

Four hundred years ago, and yet the roads of time had led her back.

She went on, following the road as it looped down from the plains toward the castle. Sentries stood guard at various points; to her, their bodies appeared cloudy, their spirits like concentrated flames within a darker husk. Ilse forced herself to continue. She was spirit and not flesh, she reminded herself. They could not see her. As she passed the first visible perimeter, one soldier did turn, his expression startled, as if he had sensed her presence, but no one spoke or tried to bar her way.

At last she came to a side gate into the castle grounds. The gates were closed, and six guards stood at attention, swathed in voluminous fur capes against the cold. More guards patrolled inside the courtyard.

Ilse cautiously explored the gate, taking care to stay clear of the sentries. She thought of herself as invisible, but that wasn't entirely true. Spirit alone would fly to Anderswar, and so she existed now as a distilled version of her complete self. Walls and closed doors blocked her, and though darkness obscured her footprints, it could not hide her actions completely. She

waited until the old watch left their post, then followed them to another gate, where they gave a pass-
word. As they passed through, Ilse hurried behind
them.

Once inside, she wandered through a maze of halls.
A wide set of stairs led her upward. She climbed them,
and found herself standing in the castle's great hall.
The room stood empty, draped in blue shadows, yet
from this point, she could number every inhabitant of
the castle, from scullions and lackeys, to courtiers and
nobles. The steady pulse of heartbeats sounded in her
ears, and the presence of hundreds crowded against
her skin. Running just below the surface was Rana's
song.

The call drew her upward, and she climbed two
flights up a broad curved stairway to another gallery.
She passed two cavernous rooms, then turned down a
narrow corridor, past antique statues and fluted columns of snowy marble. No more servants appeared.
No sentries or guards stood in attendance. Warnings
nipped at her consciousness, but the ruby's song drew
her onward, as if it were a magnet and she the metal
filings. She came at last to a tall carved door, painted
dark red, like a scarlet drop in Zalinenka's white in-
finity.

She glanced around. The corridor remained silent
and deserted. She tested the latch. Unlocked. Her fingers sank into the metal, but not completely. She pushed
harder, and the door swung open.

It was a large room, with a freshly laid fire. Scrolls
and books filled the many tall shelves. A graceful desk
stood by a window, and several chairs circled the fireplace with tables at their sides. By the largest chair
stood a pedestal carved from a single block of marble.
On it rested a small wooden box, its lid opened wide.

Even before she saw the dark red gleam inside the box, Ilse knew from Rana's rising song that she had found the ruby.

Slowly she approached, hardly daring to breathe. Rana lay in a bed of white silk, its surface alight with magic. Its song beat against her thoughts, a complex pattern of dark and light notes. Her hand had just touched the ruby, when the door closed behind her.

"Andrej. You came back."

Ilse plucked her hand away. Her skin contracted, as if her spirit still inhabited a body. Keeping her movements slow and deliberate, she turned around.

Dzavek stood at the entrance to the room. The outline of his face wavered, and through his eyes, Ilse saw the pale stones of the castle walls. He'd left his body behind, just as she had, and spirits in the realm of flesh could sense more than any guard.

"Milada," he whispered.

His once-brilliant eyes widened. Age had clouded them, but it had not obscured the intelligence behind them. She remembered, from the distance of dreams and almost-forgotten days, how they had argued so passionately about Károví and its people, and whether the connection with the empire could be broken. She had not loved him—theirs was a marriage arranged by their fathers, both high-standing nobles whose families traced their lineage back to the old kingdom, before Erythandra had absorbed Károví into its domains. But she had always admired him.

"Leos."

He smiled. "So you recognize me."

"It took me some time. You expected Valara Baussay."

"Yes. Where is Andrej? He sent you to find Rana, of course."

"Not directly," she said, "but yes."

"He was always persuasive," Dzavek murmured. "Is that why you betrayed me in the end?"

She shook her head. "I never did, Leos."

"Then why did you leave me?"

It was their old argument of loyalty and honor. She wanted to tell Leos that she had intended to serve both him and their kingdom, without betraying her own honor. She checked herself. In his eyes, the king was the kingdom. Her reasons were unimportant. Her personal honor meaningless. She had acted against him, therefore against Károví.

More than once, she reminded herself.

And so she simply said, "I left because I could not do otherwise."

"We must each act according to our purpose," he murmured.

He waved his hand, and ghostlike rings, silver and white, flashed their brilliant gems.

Though she heard no spoken invocation, the air thickened at once. She retreated from the pedestal, uncertain what he meant to do. It was then she heard the footsteps, slow and deliberate. Dzavek pointed toward the wall and a small door that Ilse had not noticed before.

The door swung open to reveal Dzavek's body framed between the ivory posts. Dzavek's spirit glided toward his body. For one moment, there was a doubled image. A heartbeat later, the two merged into one, sending a shock through the magic current. Dzavek blinked and drew a long breath. He passed a hand over his face. He appeared dazed and his skin gleamed with sweat.

Watching him, Ilse was reminded of Raul's first secretary, Berthold Hax, in the days before his death. The face leached of warmth and color, the lines etched with the knife edge of pain, the strange distant gaze, half focused on this world, half on the void and journey to the next life.

He's dying. He knows it. He knows he cannot escape death forever.

Dzavek walked unsteadily past Ilse to the marble pedestal. He gathered up Rana into his hands and closed his eyes. Though he did not move his lips, the current stirred. His face smoothed. The unhealthy gray vanished in the wake of a ruddy flush, and he stood straighter. It was like watching an invisible hand brush away the centuries.

"Leos . . ."

"No," he said. "Do not argue with me, Milada. We have never agreed on these points. I do not wish to harm you, but I shall not let you betray me again." His eyes opened to show them brilliant as before, but too bright, too intent. "I see you have Daya. Show me where you left your body. I ask you now. I will not ask so gently again."

He advanced. Ilse took a step back, thinking swiftly what to do. She heard Daya's faint song, a tremolo of minor notes. Underneath, almost inaudible, Rana's deeper chords. What had been their song before the emperor's mage divided their souls into three?

You know nothing about him, Dzavek had said.

It was then she understood. He had been the priest who entrapped a magical being inside a jewel. He had been the emperor's mage, who divided its soul into three, to prevent any thief from taking the whole.

And he will do more, she thought. *He is that desperate.*

All the while, Leos Dzavek had continued to press forward, driving her into a corner. His flesh could not hold her spirit, but his magic could. She had to escape into Anderswar, lure him far away from the Mantharah, and hope Valara Baussay discovered Lir's third jewel in time. It might mean her soul trapped in the magical plane, but she could not risk his capturing ruby and emerald both.

She was about to murmur the invocation to magic, to make that leap, when a ripple of shadow and light caught her eye. Valara Baussay stepped over the threshold into the study.

"Leos," she said softly. "You forget yourself."

Her spirit shape was little more than a brush of darkness against the ivory walls. Her eyes were bright and fierce. Two dark patches—her tattoos—stood out clearer than in the flesh.

Leos swiveled around to face the intruder. "Andrej."

His voice was like the hiss of metal over stone. His lips thinned to a sharp line. He and Valara stared at each other, their expressions a mirror of like emotion. A wolf and a fox, Ilse thought. Two beautiful, savage animals.

"Give me the ruby, Leos. Give me Rana."

"No. I have need of it—to protect my kingdom."

"So that you might send more ships against mine? I cannot risk that."

Leos smiled faintly. "Ah, yes. You said much the same, that other time, when you tried to persuade me to yield to the emperor. A month later, you led his army against me."

The old challenge and response had grown more bitter over the passing centuries. Ilse circled around to the far end of the room, thinking she might take advantage of the situation while their attention was locked on each other. Dzavek glanced toward her sharply, but when Valara Baussay glided closer, his attention flicked back. His hand tightened around the ruby, which gleamed dark and ruddy, so that its light spilled through his fingers like blood.

Valara paused. Her chin jerked high. She lifted her

right hand in a fist and muttered a phrase. A dark blue fire poured through her translucent skin.

Dzavek's mouth softened into a smile. "You have Asha."

"And you, Rana. We are well matched."

Wolf and fox stared at each other. The bitterness was gone, the only emotion left a cold calculation of the other. Then, so swiftly Ilse did not see the gesture until complete, Valara swept both hands up. Her lips were already moving in the invocation to magic, but Dzavek acted only moments behind.

"Ei rûf ane gôtter. Komen mir de strôm unde kreft. De leben unde tôt."

Magic burst against magic. For one instant, the air burned bright and still, so still, it was as though the world's hourglass had paused in turning. Then, a gout of cold fire rushed outward. It tore through Ilse's spirit essence. Blinded, she fell back against the wall. This was like the moment when flesh translated to spirit, dissolving, caught by the winds of magic. More and she would vanish altogether.

. . . ei rûf ane gôtter. Ei rûf ane Lir unde Toc, ane bruodern unde swestern . . .

All three jewels were shouting, great ringing tones that echoed from the walls. The winds of magic did not lessen. They streamed around and through Ilse, but no longer tearing at her essence. She could see nothing—the fire burned brighter than before, if that were possible—but she heard and tasted and smelled the magic, felt the signature of all three jewels pressed against her ghost form. Daya, the strongest, like a brand upon her finger. Rana, dark and angry. Asha, a river of silver. They spoke a language beyond her comprehension. Older than Erythandra. As old as the world itself, born from the Mantharah when Lir and Toc made love.

. . . komen mir de strôm. Komen mir alle kraft . . .

The words vanished into a crescendo of bright tones. Ilse heard them, saw them, silver shaded with dark and edged with the sharpest of light. Faint, oh so faint, she caught a glimpse of Valara's signature, the fox slipping between, and once of Leos Dzavek's. Then the magic of the jewels overwhelmed her again. As from a distance, she heard a single bell tone, and the word, Now.

Now.

The air cracked, the world divided. Her vision turned black . . .

. . . silence . . . emptiness . . . the faint tattoo of her own heartbeat . . . the green of magic rolling over her skin . . .

Her vision cleared. It took her more moments before she could make sense of what she saw. She crouched on a hard surface. Splinters and other debris covered the floor around her. Smoke filled the air, dense and black. A few crimson sparks floated slowly to the ground. Except for a hissing noise, the study was eerily silent, invisible behind that black veil. Her first instinct was to touch her ring finger. Yes, there was Daya, or at least its essence.

The smoke stirred. A voice—harsh and low—spoke a word, and the darkness lifted.

Valara knelt by the doorway. Her eyes were wide, rimmed with pale circles, her ghostly essence thin and insubstantial. "Ilse?"

The room lay in shambles. Smoke blackened its walls and ceiling; dozens of cracks marred the tiled floor. One bookcase had collapsed, scattering papers and books everywhere, and the floor was littered with the shattered remains of Dzavek's desk.

The sight recalled Ilse to her senses. She scrambled toward the last place she had seen Leos Dzavek. She found him stretched out on the floor, pinned beneath the marble pedestal. She dropped to her knees beside him. "Leos."

"My brother."

He coughed noisily. Ilse tried to lay her hands upon him, but her spirit sank through his body. Cold, cold, cold. He was dying in truth this time.

Dzavek jerked upright, in spite of the pedestal's weight. His eyes were blank, unseeing. But then he sniffed the air, like a dog scenting a fox, and he swiveled around to Valara Baussay. "Andrej. You . . ." He coughed. "You will not—"

He crumpled over. Ilse wrapped her fingers around his wrist. Her touch meant nothing, and yet he stopped and gazed into her face with his blind eyes. They were almost white now, like a winter snowfall.

"You never loved me," he said.

Truth at last.

"No," she said softly. "Because you loved Károví too dearly. You were a king, Leos, even before they set the crown upon your head. And yet, I would have been proud to have been your wife and your queen." Memories of those early days came back to her, of the time before Leos Dzavek and his brother traveled to Duenne and the imperial court, when she and he had been companions, if not lovers. He had returned entirely changed. The jewels. The break with his brother.

"But you doubted me," she said softly. "You believed I wished to betray you. I never did. I left because I loved Károví, too, and I did not wish to watch our people die in war."

"You loved that man."

"I did," she admitted. "Then and now, Leos. But I also love both our kingdoms, as much as you love Károví. I would see them live in peace. Can you understand?"

His lips moved soundlessly. Ilse bent close and kissed her once betrothed, spirit to flesh. Leos must have felt that insubstantial gesture, because he shuddered and laid a hand over his heart. There was blood behind the clouded eyes, and his lips were chilled. "It is time to die?" he said.

"Time and long past, my love."

He closed his eyes. Breathed out a long slow breath, so easily that she did not realize at first what was happening, until his body went limp and fell through her arms to the floor. She reached toward him, as if she could recall him from death. Stopped herself and touched his brow. She felt the difference at once, a stillness that went beyond sleep. "He's gone," she whispered.

The magic current stirred. The air in the study turned thick. It was a tide of magic, greater than any she had ever dared to summon. For one moment, Ilse felt its burning brilliance course through her veins. It was like the first time she crossed into Anderswar, when colors sang and the air tasted of light. She heard the echo of a familiar voice. It spoke in a fluid Erythandran, with an accent of years ago—Leos. A triplet of voices overlaid it—Daya's and Rana's and Asha's. She had the sense of a conversation among elders, one not hers to share. Then the current shuddered, ebbed away.

Before her lay a thin film of ashes. Leos Dzavek's body had vanished.

And so we give the flesh to the earth. The spirit itself lives on.

Abruptly, voices sounded outside the room. The door banged open, and a stocky man appeared in the opening. Ilse froze, then realized he did not see her. She felt a hand on her wrist. Valara. Together they drew back against one wall, taking care not to disturb anything.

More guards appeared behind the first. They looked stunned. Finally, one stepped over the threshold and stared around the room. He called back an order, giving someone's name—Duke Markov.

Ilse held her breath, grateful for the shadows. She waited until the guards withdrew, then glanced toward Valara. The other woman seemed to guess her question. She held up her right hand with Asha still clenched in her fist. So the emerald and sapphire were still theirs. Rana, however . . . Valara shook her head, echoing Ilse's thoughts. There was no time to search. When the crowd dispersed, except for two sentries, they slipped out the door and fled toward the stairs.

CHAPTER TWENTY-THREE

TWILIGHT WAS FALLING by the time Miro Karasek came within view of Rastov. Unconsciously he reined his horse to a stop. The horse blew a rattling breath, as if to argue against further delay, but it offered no other protest. The plains themselves were a blank, black expanse below the sliver of a new moon, but Rastov was a collection of stars, its walls and towers illuminated by thousands of lamps.

He had ridden almost without pause since falling from the magical plane onto the open fields outside Laszny's garrison. A week spent with only a few hours' sleep snatched while the next posting station saddled his new mount. Even before that, he had lost half a month for those few moments in the magical plane. He could only pray to Lir and Toc that he was not too late.

Though for what, he could not yet tell. He had no reason to believe the Morennioùen queen had crossed into Károví. If she had returned to Morennioù, Dzavek would find the second invasion much harder. More men and women would die. It would be another bloody conflict like the first one. But if she chose to come here . . .

If. Maybe. Second doubts could choke a man into inaction.

He gave his horse the signal to walk, then called up a magical beacon to light their path. He wanted to gallop the final distance, but he knew the dangers of headlong riding over the plains at night. And so it took him almost two more hours before he reached the city gates.

There, the sentries called out the expected challenge.

"Duke Miro Karasek," he called back. "On the king's business."

A torch flared, and the gates swung open to admit him. Miro returned the sentries' salute, but his thoughts were on Valara Baussay and his king. The sense of unease had increased, and he spurred his horse to a fast trot, for once using his status as general and noble to force his way through the streets.

He took the most direct route across town, the wide boulevards that the architects for Károví's first kings had laid out a thousand years before. Soon he came to the slopes leading toward the Solvatni River and negotiated his horse down the winding streets toward the bridge to the castle. A breeze grazed his face, carrying a trace of green. He drew rein and concentrated on its signature, but the breeze died away before he could identify it.

Apprehensive, he rode faster, telling himself that he worried for nothing, but the sight in the courtyard only confirmed his fears. Soldiers swarmed in all directions. Officers shouted orders. A runner darted in front of Miro, nearly letting the horse trample him.

"Duke Karasek. You've returned."

A captain appeared breathlessly beside Miro's horse.

"What happened?" Miro said.

"An attack on the king. The last hour. Magic, I heard."

Miro vaulted from the saddle and tossed the reins to the man. "See to my horse." Without waiting for an acknowledgment, he pushed through the mass of soldiers and into the castle.

Turmoil had taken possession of Zalinenka's halls. Pages and guards ran in all directions. Černosek's personal secretary hurried past muttering to himself. The strong scent of magic permeated the entire hall.

Hers.

He recognized Valara Baussay's signature at once. Others, too. A chaos of magical fingerprints. Miro caught hold of a passing runner and learned the attack had taken place in the king's private chambers. He let the boy go and elbowed his way to the main stairs, mounted them two at a time to the next floor. The scent of magic increased with every step, and he raced down the corridor to Dzavek's suite of rooms.

A knot of guards and councillors stood outside. In their midst were the Scholar and Brigand—Černosek and Markov—along with the castle guard's senior commander. "Magic," Šimon Černosek was saying. "It woke me, even before your messenger arrived."

He broke off at Miro's entrance, and his lips thinned. Feliks Markov jerked around. For one moment, his eyes widened, then his face smoothed into an unreadable mask. "Duke Karasek. You show exquisite timing. Coincidence? Or perhaps your well-known forethought."

"Neither. I came with . . . with news concerning my mission."

"Have you found the Morenniouèn queen?" Černosek said. "Your Captain Donlov returned with the ship a few days ago, but his report was . . . incomplete."

Miro glanced at the crowd of guards. The senior commander took his hint and withdrew; the others followed.

"Yes and no," Miro said quietly. "We intercepted her where we expected, but she escaped by crossing into Vnejšek in the flesh."

Černosek's pale lips parted. "And?"

Miro was aware of Markov watching him closely. The man had no magic abilities, but he could read a human face with unnerving skill. He frowned, as if angry and embarrassed. "She crossed the Gulf before I could stop her. I had no wish to lose weeks or months with a chase through Vnejšek. I decided to return at once and warn the king—"

"Did you expect her to come here then?"

Markov spoke mildly, but Miro did not mistake that tone for indifference. "No. I expect she's fled directly to Morennioù. Which means we must prepare for a second invasion. Or rather, that would have been the king's wishes before . . ." He broke off, too shaken by the sudden reversal of everything he expected to keep up his inventions. He ran a hand over his face and managed to recover himself. "Tell me what happened here."

"An attack," Markov said drily. "Magical in nature. The king has vanished."

He continued to speak, something about how the entire castle had reverberated with magic, so that even the most oblivious had noticed, but Miro found it difficult to attend. He could only think that he had made the wrong choice and failed his king.

Weariness from the past week swept over him. He put a hand out to steady himself. Černosek caught his arm. "You are ill."

"No." Miro drew back from Černosek, mistrusting the man's motives. "Not ill. Tired and saddle-sore. I can sleep later. You say the king vanished. What else? Have you examined these rooms yet?"

"A cursory look," Markov said. "Enough to ascertain there was an attack. I wanted Černosek to inspect the magical traces himself."

He took the risk. "Let me do that. I know the Morennioùen queen's signature. I can confirm if she was present, or someone else." He added, "It would not do to assume anything about the identity of those who attacked our king and our kingdom. We do have other enemies."

The Scholar and Brigand exchanged intent looks.

"He's right," Černosek said at last.

Markov appeared less convinced, but he merely shrugged. "We do not have time to argue. Examine the room. Meet with us directly after at my private chambers, so we might discuss how to proceed."

Miro waited until the two had rounded the corner before he pushed the door open.

Light from the corridor showed a chaos of papers and books strewn over the floor nearest to him. Windows at the far end admitted faint illumination from the stars. By their light, he could make out more destruction. Several shelves had collapsed, and the writing desk lay in splintered pieces. He drew an unsteady breath at the sight. The flux and whirl of magic were dying off, but the strong scent nearly overpowered him.

He took a torch from its bracket and walked inside the study, letting the door fall shut behind him.

Destruction. That was his first reaction. A chaos left by unrestrained magic. He closed his eyes and let his senses spiral outward. Definitely her signature. He picked it out from the confusion—the scent and image of a fox, swift and secret, gliding through the rooms. With a shift of focus, he turned to the magical plane to sift through the traces left by other visitors. Dzavek, of course. Several guards. A strange alien presence that had to be the ruby. Valara Baussay and another woman whom he could not identify. That gave him pause. One of the Veraenen company?

From a distance, he heard the guards' voices through the door. They had resumed their conversation about the night's events. Miro listened a moment, heard nothing that he had not already guessed, then turned back to examine the room in more detail.

"*Ei rûf ane gôtter,*" he said softly. "*Komen mir de strôm. Widerkêren mir de zeît. Ougen mir.*"

His vision darkened. Now he saw the room from the past. All the lamps had guttered, the fire burned low in its grate, casting a reddish hue over the tiled floor. On a tall marble pedestal, Miro saw the box where Dzavek kept Rana.

Servants appeared to rebuild the fire. Others took away a tray with its wine cups and flask. A brief interlude of waiting came next, while Miro wondered if he had misjudged his timing. Then, the door swung open. A shadowy figure stood framed in the lamplight from the corridor.

His breath went still. This was not Valara Baussay, but a stranger. A Károvín. No, he saw traces of Veraenen blood in her features, which were translucent in the vision, like the faded ink drawings of centuries past.

I know her. She was there, when we attacked.

Her signature intensified. It was like sunlight glancing through the clouds. He watched as she hurried into the room, making directly for the marble pedestal with its open box. She had just touched the ruby when Dzavek appeared, also in the spirit. He spoke. The woman turned and answered. Their mouths moved in a silent conversation that Miro wished he could hear. He watched the turns in her expression—fearful, controlled, a brief inward look that might be grief or shame.

Events moved more quickly. Dzavek rejoined his body. Unexpectedly Valara Baussay appeared. King and queen spoke at once. Or was it brother to brother? He could not tell. The air shimmered with magic's current, waiting only for a word . . .

A blinding explosion lit the room with fire. The sight was so vivid, so real, that Miro imagined he could feel a hot wind blow through his hair. Before he could react, the bright light vanished, and smoke blanketed the room, making it impossible to see.

No movement. No sign of any presence, flesh or spirit. Miro waited, unable to breathe.

At last a shadow emerged from the haze. A thin arm swept upward, its motion echoed by a trail of gray and black. Gradually the smoke dissipated, revealing the destruction wrought by that explosion.

Valara Baussay crouched at the far end of the room. Miro released his breath. *She lives. She survived.*

Leos Dzavek lay crumpled on the floor. The unknown woman knelt beside him. Dzavek jerked upright. His eyes stared, unseeing, but then he stiffened and his face swiveled toward Valara Baussay. His lips were moving. He meant to summon more magic before he died. And he would die—Miro saw that plainly.

The woman touched his cheek. Dzavek flinched, turned toward her. There was a look on the king's face that Miro had never seen before. An expectant look, as if the dark dreary centuries had dropped away, and the man saw the hope of sunrise. The woman continued to speak, her whole manner tense. He could not make out her words, but Dzavek's gaze was fixed upon her face, as though she were sharing a last and vital clue, one important to them both.

She leaned close. Kissed him upon the lips. Miro could almost hear the king's breath as he exhaled. He thought it was just an ordinary breath, but then the king went limp and collapsed onto the floor. The woman touched his brow. Her lips formed the words *He is gone*.

Around him, the cloud of magic ebbed away, leaving behind a burning smell. His torch, which guttered in his hand. By its flickering light, the room with its wreckage looked even more desolate now. Miro extinguished the torch.

For a while, he could do nothing but stare at the scene, thinking, *The king is dead*.

A deep, breathy note sounded, just below the surface of his thoughts. Rana's song. Here, in the study. Miro dropped to his hands and knees and plunged his hands into the debris covering the floor. *Steady,* he told himself. *Do not lose this chance through panic or carelessness.*

He closed his eyes. In spite of his weariness, he found it easier to draw his thoughts to a single point of focus. *Ei rûf ane strôm. Ei rûf ane juweln.*

The current hissed and whispered.

Then, *Ei bin unde was. Wir sint unde waerest unde werden.*

Rana was babbling a confused chorus of tones. Each syllable merged with the next, rising in pitch until he no longer heard them, and then dropping into deep-throated chords that vibrated in the air.

The fireplace. Its song in his ears, Miro hurried to the grate and knelt. Yes. Beneath the thick ashes he saw a dark red glow. With a set of tongs, he pushed the still-hot coals aside, then drew the ruby toward himself.

The ruby's polished surface flickered with magic. *Daya. Asha. Daya. Mantharah. My sistersbrotherscousinsloversI.*

Miro cradled the ruby in his palm, his thoughts centered on Valara Baussay and all her possible plans. Clearly, the guards had arrived before she could make a search, and so she and her companion had abandoned the ruby. But they would return. And they were not the only ones. Both the Scholar and the Brigand knew about Rana's existence. If Miro did not produce the ruby, they would search the entire castle.

And we would have a greater war than even Leos Dzavek desired.

He took out a handkerchief and wrapped the ruby securely into a knotted bundle, which he tucked inside his shirt. It was no proof against magic probing, but the confusion outside might allow him to pass without facing Černosek or the other mages. A few words to erase all magical signs of the intruders' presence. Černosek would expect that. He wiped away his own recent past—a risky move, because Černosek's skill easily surpassed his own—then laid down a series of ordinary spells used by magical trackers. The spells would not stand against a thorough examination, but they would give him enough time for what came next.

He turned toward the door, thinking he must set off before Černosek decided to return. He had taken no more than a few steps before grief smote him.

My king has died.

It had seemed impossible. How could death take the immortal king?

Because he was never immortal. Dzavek had known that, though he'd never spoken his thoughts aloud. That is why he planned to take Morennioù and its emerald. Yes, it was a matter of revenge. More important, he wanted to provide for his own kingdom's future.

Contradictory reasons, from a contradictory man.

Miro rubbed a hand over his eyes. A dull pain had settled under his ribs, near his heart. Such a sentimental reaction. His father had trained him better.

No. He had not. He, too, grieved for the Leos Dzavek of history.

Miro shook away the present grief. He had to act.

Outside, the guards came to attention at his appearance. "Tell Duke Markov that our intruder died in battle with the king," Miro said. "However, this man had a companion who escaped with the king's ruby. We won't know more until we capture him. I'll track him down at once, while the trail is fresh."

The guard ran to execute his commands. Miro headed directly to the stables. Rumors must have spread even here, because the stable hands had all gathered to trade excited whispers. At Miro's entrance, they all stood.

"Saddle a fresh horse," he told them. "Send a runner for provisions and gear for a week's ride."

He drank a mug of soup while he waited. Sooner than he expected, the stable boy reported the horse saddled and ready. Miro swung onto the horse, felt it twitch and sidle in response to his own nerves. He settled it with a hand on its neck and soothing words. A sturdy beast, the kind he loved best. He took that as a good sign, and his heart beat faster as he passed through the outer gates of the castle. Until this moment, he had felt his future unbounded. He might have done anything, gone anywhere.

This will be the end of my hunt, he thought as he urged his horse toward the northern plains.

CHAPTER TWENTY-FOUR

VALARA'S SPIRIT REJOINED her body with a shock that doubled her over. She gasped, choked out the words to summon the current. Too quickly, the magic overwhelmed her. She lay back, eyes closed, and breathed slowly through her nose until the nausea faded. It was the presence of the Mantharah. Its magic was too strong. It was like walking along Enzeloc's cliffs in a hurricane. She could not judge her balance.

Every bit of her from scalp to toe ached. Her hands felt as though her muscles had locked into fists a hundred years ago. She released a shaky laugh. *Maybe they did.*

She rolled onto her side. Her hand unfolded to reveal the sapphire. *Asha.* Her breath caught in renewed wonder. *So I have not lost you yet. Not again.*

Still cupping the sapphire in one hand, she levered herself to sitting. Overhead, the mid-morning sun shone down upon them.

My brother is dead, came her next thought.

It didn't matter that her body had died a dozen times or more since their plot to steal the jewels and divide an empire. They were brothers in the soul. Now he was dead, he who had defied the void between lives, who had survived four centuries, while an empire had broken into kingdoms, and the wheel had turned for new lives, new souls.

A strange sensation assailed her—one she could not properly identify. It was not precisely grief. Regret?

She glanced toward her companion. Ilse lay motionless on the ground, eyes blank and staring upward. One arm was flung outward toward the Agnau, the other lay over her breasts. She still wore Daya the ring on her finger, just as she had in spirit form. Valara set the sapphire to one side and crawled over to Ilse. Her skin was warm. A strong erratic pulse beat at her throat.

She lives.

Valara had not been certain. Those last few moments in Dzavek's chambers were a blur in her memory. She had tried to kill Dzavek. He had stopped her—easily. His reply was an explosion of magic that ripped through her spirit. She remembered then, the jewels, singing in great booming voices, like waves thundering against a cliff, like the bells of Morennioù castle. For a while after, she was too deaf and numb to understand much. Only when the guards appeared had she roused herself enough to escape with Ilse.

More tentatively, she touched the wooden ring. Its surface was warm and silken, with a strong current of magic rippling under her touch. Much fainter came the whispering of voices.

. . . awake, awake to the flesh, awake to life . . .

Ilse gasped and pitched upright. Valara caught her before she fell against the stone cliff. Ilse fought her blindly. Her skin burned fever-hot. She was choking, a terrible strangled noise deep in her throat. Quickly, Valara summoned the magic current. Again, it was too much. The current rushed in like a flood tide, but then she found the balance. *Soft, soft, softly,* she thought, and the magic obeyed.

Ilse drew a wheezing breath, coughed, and breathed again. Valara continued to murmur in Erythandran until the fever faded and Ilse breathed more easily. Then she lowered Ilse to the ground and searched around for water. She found the shallow cook stone. It was dry, but a handful of snow lay next to it. Valara scooped that up and, holding up Ilse's head, let the melt-water trickle into the woman's mouth.

Ilse coughed up the first mouthful, but swallowed the next. "Leos," she whispered. "Leos, I'm sorry. It wasn't—"

"Hush," Valara said. "You did well."

"I betrayed him," Ilse whispered. "He thought I did. But it wasn't true. I wanted . . . peace. No more war. He didn't understand."

Valara hushed her, ran her hands over the other woman's face with as much gentleness as she could. It wasn't something she had learned from mother or sister. Not in Morennioù. Ilse murmured something incomprehensible. As Valara bent closer, she caught a glimpse of strong memories running like a flood tide through the other woman's thoughts.

. . . *she saw a young woman running through the snow-dusted forests. She wore the rich clothing of a noble, a jewel in her cheek. An equally young man waited in a clearing. He was handsome, his face the pale brown of the empire's southwest provinces. They spoke in Károvín. He was an emissary from the emperor. There was a chance for peace, he said. If she would but promise to persuade the new king to treat with them . . .*

I will, the young woman said.

Before she finished speaking, a shout echoed through the forests, and an army appeared . . .

"He died."

"Yes. It was time."

"I never loved him. We were betrothed by our parents."

Ilse lay quietly, her gaze upward toward the sky, away from Valara. Her eyes were like dark bruises, her face gray with exhaustion. "So. What comes next?"

So many questions hidden inside that one.

"Our plans depend on the jewels," she said slowly. "We must withdraw, certainly. The king is dead, but the king certainly has advisers, councillors, other mages. We cannot remain here in case they track us. But *where* depends on Daya and Asha."

"We won't have long," Ilse murmured. "Nor will they."

Her gaze crossed Valara's. They both smiled faintly.

She was no bad ally, Valara thought. Clever. Stubborn. Subtle. She would do well in Morenniou's Court. Already her thoughts were running back to her kingdom, and how she would present this woman to her councillors.

They helped each other to stand. Valara retrieved the sapphire. It burned like a tiny blue flame in her hands, and its song rose up clear and bright and joyous, each word as distinct as a bell tone. *Rana, my brother. Rana, my sister, my cousin, my love, myself.*

There it was again, a sense of regret. Of things left undone. Awkwardly, Valara ran her fingers over the sapphire, sensed the threads of magic and song, like a fabric woven in several dimensions. *Asha, I'm sorry. We . . . We lost Rana. We had to leave too soon. Before the king's mages discovered us. But we will go back for her. I promise.*

No and no. Turn. Open your eyes and you will see her.

Asha spoke so emphatically that Valara glanced over to Ilse before she realized she had done so. The other woman stood still. Her eyes were wide, her expression astonished. She was staring at Daya.

"Did you hear?" Valara asked.

"I did. And . . . I think I know what Asha means."

Without waiting for Valara to reply, Ilse made for the gap between the cliffs and the ridge overlooking the plains. Valara hurried after her, the sapphire held tightly in one hand. Its song had fallen silent, but the magic remained, its current pulsing in time with her own heartbeat.

"Ah." Ilse exhaled. "I should not be surprised."

Valara shaded her eyes against the sun's glare. She could just make out a dark speck moving against the shimmering expanse of plains. A rider, galloping directly toward them. "It's Duke Karasek," she said. "The man who attacked us. I know his signature."

They could not run. Karasek with his horse could overtake either one of them easily.

"We must go at once to Autrevelye—"

"No." Ilse pulled Daya from her finger and handed her to Valara. "Take Asha and Daya. Give me enough time to distract this Duke Karasek, then attack with all your magic, and all the magic of the jewels. If he does have Rana, you will need their help."

She drew her sword and strode down the ash-strewn mountainside to the plains. Even before she reached the lower slopes, the horse slowed to a canter and then came to a halt. Karasek dismounted and waited patiently. It was that patience that unnerved Valara. Since their first meeting, he had countered every action she took and guessed every change in plans. That he appeared so soon after Dzavek's death said he had guessed again, and arrowed directly from the Jelyndak Islands, to Rastov, to here.

Ilse paused a few steps away from Karasek. Valara murmured an invocation to the magic current. But far quicker than she anticipated, Karasek drew his own sword. Metal flashed against the dull sky.

"No!" Valara shouted.

Winds shrieked across the edge of the cliffs. The Agnau had turned pale, and its molten surface heaved as colossal waves rolled across its breadth. Daya cried out in shrill tones, Asha's voice rose higher, blending with the winds. *Sint unde waerest unde werden unde—*

Valara shut out their voices. She raised her fist with Daya and Asha. *"Ei rûf ane gôtter,"* she cried out. *"Ei rûf ane—"*

A force—like a concentrated wind—swallowed her words. A dazzling light struck her face.

"Wir komen de gôtter."

Valara blinked. An incandescent light illuminated the Mantharah and its heights. From its midst, two vast figures approached, their faces like suns, one with eyes like the stars, the other with great dark voids where eyes should be. First came Lir with Toc behind. The next moment their places changed. First and last, as the legends said. Together and separate—the paradox of magic.

Lir folded her hands around Valara's numb ones. Toc clasped both of theirs within his. Together, sister and brother spoke in a language unlike any Valara knew. Their lips did not move, but their voices filled the air with rippling tones, like raindrops on a canopy of summer green leaves.

Asha thrummed. Daya grew heavy, an impossible weight.

Lir spoke a word. A light blazed. A shrill cry echoed from the Mantharah's cliffs. Asha sang, and Daya's darker voice rose into a glorious chorus of bright notes that tumbled and rolled together, pleading and crying and laughing.

Look, look, look, cried the jewels.

Look, Lir commanded, as she and her brother released Valara's hands.

Valara drew a sharp breath of surprise. The plain wooden ring she had worn for so many weeks had vanished. In its place was an emerald. Lir's emerald. But not as she remembered it. No longer plain or dark, it gleamed like burnished magic.

Lir brushed fingertips against Valara's cheek, her caress like the touch of memory. Toc's blank gaze turned toward her, his gaze as penetrating as if he still possessed eyes.

Lir who quarreled with Toc and then forgave him. Toc who carved the world's foundations with his sword, purely because he could. For all his strength, Toc had died. For all her wisdom, Lir had wept in the darkness, uncomprehending. Each night, she set her glittering tears in the sky, in remembrance of her lover and her brother, until he returned.

A warm breath tickled Valara's face. A sharp green scent, like that of wildflowers and new grass, filled the air. Lir was speaking, but her voice was too much like the wind and thunder, and Valara could not understand what she said. Her vision blurred; the unnatural light dimmed. She blinked again, wiping away the unexpected tears from her eyes.

Lir and Toc had gone.

She knelt beside the Agnau, her hands clenched so tight, they ached. Dazed, she unfolded them. Two jewels lay there, emerald and sapphire, gleaming softly against her hands.

I wasn't dreaming. The gods came.

"Your majesty."

Valara stumbled to her feet. Karasek stood a short distance away. A few steps behind him came Ilse, whole and unharmed. Ilse gave Valara a brief smile.

No humor, but an assurance. Of what? Her attention veered back to Karasek. Dust and sweat streaked his face, and dark bruises circled his eyes. He met her gaze steadily. "I've come to negotiate."

He took a cloth bundle from inside his shirt and unwrapped its folds. When she saw what lay inside, Valara sucked in her breath. *Rana. He brought me Rana.*

"What do you want?" she whispered.

"Peace. Honor, for us both."

The same demand that Raul Kosenmark had made. Again, she had the sense of history pressing in toward her.

"I am not yet the queen," she began.

"And I am no king," Karasek said. "But I think we both have some say in our governments. If we do not speak first, who will?"

He pressed Rana into her palm—a brief contact, no more—then stepped back. Valara closed her fingers around the jewels. She and Karasek looked at each other. "How did you find me so easily?"

"You and your companion left a trail. I've erased it."

So much revealed behind that simple statement. A part of her listed that as an item to remember when they negotiated in truth, with her installed as queen, and him an emissary from abroad. *That would not be honorable,* said a voice she remembered from lives long ago.

Honor. She had once held that above all, but then she had lost her way between lives. She remembered once, centuries ago, a chance with the same soul as this man Karasek. She could not recall exactly what passed between them. Not dishonor, but a misunderstanding.

There were no simple patterns. No single thread that one might pluck away, and thus undo centuries of mistakes.

Dimly, she heard Ilse speaking. "Remember what you promised. The jewels are not mere things. They are thinking creatures like us. We cannot treat them as objects to bargain with."

Honor. A promise kept. Her brother's voice saying, *Yes, it is time to die.*

"Yes," she murmured, half to herself. "And I think I know the way."

Without giving herself time to consider, Valara spun around and rushed to the Agnau's edge. She plunged her hands into the lava. Fire burst into life—magic fire that coursed through her body, stronger than any she'd ever experienced. Her head jerked back and her throat opened in a scream.

From far away, she heard Ilse's voice, calling to her. Then Miro Karasek's. Thereafter, she heard nothing but the jewels. Their voices rose into a single note, so pure that her bones ached and her blood sang. Each gem burned a pinpoint in her palm, searing her flesh. Two pinpoints, then three, then two again, marked her palm, the count wavering with her concentration. She lost track of how many she held. Now they filled her hands, swelling to gigantic size. It was the ending. She had died and her soul taken flight into the void. One moment between, one moment of stillness and expectation, before death lifted her into forgetfulness . . .

The moment ended. A voice rang out. Like the rushing tide, the magical current surged forward, and a brilliant light exploded in her mind.

Three. Became two. Then one.

For a long moment, Valara could not breathe. The magic had released her, but she could not bring herself to open her eyes, to see what the jewels had become.

"Valara?"

Ilse's voice, hardly more than a whisper. Gradually,

Valara became aware of two arms holding her upright. She was kneeling, her hands still submerged in
Agnau's lake. Ilse crouched next to her. Karasek knelt
on her other side, holding her by the shoulders. The
Agnau had smoothed to a glassy calm. Shaking, she
withdrew her hands from the silvery lava, and gave a
cry of shock. In spite of the agony she had suffered,
her hands were unscathed, her skin seemingly untouched by the lava. Still uncertain what had happened, she unfolded her hands.

A single jewel lay in her palm. Glistening droplets
of creation beaded on its polished surface; hints of
ruby, sapphire, and emerald flickered in turn, only to
disappear into flashes of opalescent white.

Ishya, said the jewel. *Daya unde Asha unde Rana.
Waere unde werden.*

A dazzling light, like a miniature sun, filled Valara's
hands. The jewel swelled, its shape lengthening into
the figure of a man, a woman, an alien creature such
as Daya had appeared in the void between worlds.

Ishya stepped onto the Agnau's smooth surface. It
spoke, incomprehensible words like the silvery notes
of a flute. Then it walked toward the center of the
lake. With every step it grew in size and transparency,
until at last it blended with the rising steam.

Valara massaged her palm, which felt warmer than
the rest of her. "And so they are free," she murmured.

She tried to stand, but her legs buckled. Karasek
caught her and lifted her into his arms. He was speaking to Ilse, something about his packs, but Valara was
too exhausted to make sense of what he said. *Words
like rain and thunder and wind,* she thought, recalling
Lir's speech, though she knew Karasek was just a human male.

She tried to tell him so, but her tongue got tangled.
Karasek carried her away from the Agnau to a shaded

nook beneath the cliffs. Ilse tucked blankets around
her. One of them brushed a hand over her forehead.
They murmured the invocation to magic, and she
dropped into sleep.

ILSE WITHDREW HER hand from Valara's forehead.
The woman slept—she could read that swift descent
into slumber, the sudden stillness, which reminded her
of the moment when a soul left the body for Anderswar. Not death, but something like it. She wondered
if sleep were a reminder, sent by the gods, of that void
between lives.

"And what next?" she murmured. "What next, indeed?"

"Water," Karasek said. "Firewood. A hot meal."

At her startled look, he smiled. "It's an old cam-
paign strategy. Solve the practical matters first, and
the hard decisions become . . . not easy, but easier to
address."

He spoke for himself, too, she realized. Dark bruises
under his eyes, the creases etched around his mouth
and eyes, deeper ones between his brows—all those
spoke of grief and weariness. And underneath it all a
palpable air of tension.

*I have seen that look before. I have seen you before,
in lives past.*

Karasek held out a hand, to help her stand. She regarded the hand first—he had removed his gloves to
handle the jewel, she noticed—then lifted her gaze
back to his face. "How many did you kill?" she asked.
"Back there, on Hallau Island?"

He flinched. "I . . . do not know."

So. No assurance that Raul lived. Others had died,
however. She had a vivid recollection of Katje, run
through with a sword and falling limp to the ground,
the strings of life suddenly cut. Another image followed,

of Raul stabbing a Károvín soldier. Her own hands felt sticky with blood, though she had cleaned them long ago. She rubbed them absentmindedly.

Karasek was observing her closely. "You are—you were Milada."

Again he had surprised her. "I was," she said with some difficulty. "And you?"

He made a quick gesture of denial. "Nobody. No, that is a lie. I was a captain in the army. Leos Dzavek sent me to arrest you that night, when you met with the emissary from Veraene."

Something in his voice, the way his hand swept up and outward, recalled another moment in a different life. *A laughing voice, an exaggerated politesse.* It was a memory far removed from this moment and this life, but now Ilse knew when she and the jewels had met this man for the first time. "You were a commander for the emperor before. You sailed—"

To Morennioù. Five hundred years ago. I was there, as was Raul Kosenmark.

Raul. Her last glimpse of him had been a blur of shadow, the golden gleam of his eyes in fire and moonlight as he fought against the Károvín.

All the tears she had refused these past weeks broke through. She wept, a silent flood of grief that she could not restrain. For Raul. For Galena, lost to her family. For Katje and the others who died on Hallau. For herself, bound to an exile that no longer served any purpose.

I want him. I want Raul. Not Lord Kosenmark and heir to Valentain. I want the man I came to love. I want . . . to be Anike, and he Stefan, so we might live our lives in quiet, far away from the affairs of kings.

But however passionately she wished it, her dreams could never come true in this life. Raul had died on that miserable island. She almost wished that Károví's

soldiers might overtake her, so that she would not
have to struggle on alone.

Later I will think what I must do. Not yet. Not yet.

Karasek made no move to comfort her. He stood in
silence, as if he understood she could not bear the
least touch of sympathy. His patience was like the
jewels', waiting for deliverance in Anderswar. It was
the best gift he could bestow her.

At last her grief emptied out. Ilse released a shuddering breath and wiped her eyes with the back of her
hand. "You are right," she said. "I do need sleep. You,
as well."

Her voice sounded harsh to her own ear. She could
not begin to guess what Karasek made of her. They
had been enemies once, in lives past. Of that she was
certain. They had also been friends, but lives and centuries could change anyone. She had just witnessed
that fact made flesh and act.

If he shows any pity, I shall stab him.

To her relief, he had the grace and intelligence to
guess her needs. In a quite ordinary tone, he said, "I'll
take first watch and start a meal cooking." He hesitated, then added, "And afterward, we will talk. All
three of us."

WHEN VALARA WOKE, the sun was directly overhead,
a white disk against the hard gray sky. Someone—
Karasek, no doubt—had erected a length of canvas to
make a screen for her. Above the constant scent of
magic, she smelled rain and lightning. She stretched
underneath her blankets, as memory slowly collected.
The Agnau. Karasek. The three jewels.

A strange, strong emotion flooded her, a sensation
akin to that of magic flooding her body.

*I have done what the jewels and the gods required.
What my soul wished these past four hundred years.*

Her palm ached with the memory. She rubbed it with her thumb. The flesh felt thick and ridged where she'd gripped the jewels, and when she stretched her hand, the skin pulled tight. A scar of magic, she thought, as she examined it. In the center, a knot the color of new milk, bluish-white against her golden skin. Dark pink threads spiraled out between her fingers and around to the back of her hand. On impulse, she summoned the current to change the scars to ordinary flesh.

Ei rûf ane gôtter. Komen mir de strôm . . .

Nothing. She felt nothing, not even the least wisp of current. Frightened, she repeated the invocation, but the words stopped in her throat and even her thoughts stuttered and died away. Nothing. Worse than nothing. She saw magic's current, felt its presence pulsing around her, a vast ocean spilling over from Mantharah, from the imperfect divide between spirit and flesh. But when she reached out to touch it, it receded.

What has happened? Why can't I work magic?

She pressed her hands against her eyes. One felt warm and soft. One burned with an unnatural fever. A mark of magic and the gods, she thought, laughing silently. It was not as she had expected. The laugh caught on a sob. She bit down hard on her tongue. No tears, no. It was not as she had expected, but she should have known better.

It took her several long moments before she could breathe steadily, before her heartbeat slowed from its first panicked rush. Later, she would examine the situation. She would be calm and dispassionate. It was not the end after all. She was still queen of Morennioù, or she would be, once she took the throne. Even if she no longer had magic, she still had her duty. It would have to serve. So she told herself.

Later, I will tell myself all this a second time, a third. Until I can believe it.

She rubbed away the tears. Drew in a long breath. Ran a hand through her knotted and tangled hair. Appearance did not matter, her father had once told her. Only courage did.

Time for courage, she told herself.

She crawled from the half-shelter to find Karasek and Ilse Zhalina speaking together by the edge of Mantharah's lake. They had built a fire, and she could smell the rich scent of black tea brewing. Karasek's horse was tethered nearby. Valara caught the words *patrol, search,* and *perimeter.* She listened closer and gathered that the general confusion at Zalinenka had worked in their favor, but soon that dearly bought time would run out.

I came for honor, he had said. An honor that ran deeper than his oath to Leos Dzavek. What else had he done in honor's name? What had such a decision cost him?

She stood, catching their attention immediately. Karasek broke off his conversation. Sometime during her sleep, he had washed away the dust and sweat.

"We'll eat, then break camp," he said. "I've done what I could to delay pursuit, but unless I return within a few days, my fellow councillors will take additional measures. And I have several tasks I must accomplish before then."

More hints. She ought to insist on precise information, but she was strangely afraid to at this moment. Perhaps later, in private, she could question him more thoroughly.

"What have you told them?" Ilse asked.

"That I was tracking Leos Dzavek's murderer."

"Ah." Ilse glanced toward Valara. "So you were, in a way. What comes next?"

"For you, evasion," he said. "For me, I must return as quickly as possible and report my findings to Duke Markov. I planned to tell him that we were mistaken, and that Morennioù's queen had nothing to do with King Leos's death. She most likely returned home at once, when she escaped my patrol."

"Then who did kill the king?" Valara asked.

He shrugged. "Leos was not without enemies, but most of those belonged to minor factions within the court. Outside of Károví is another matter. Immatra in particular would like to expand its territory. If our kingdom fell into confusion, they would have an opportunity to claim and hold our northern coastline."

It seemed too simple an explanation. Apparently Ilse thought the same because she said, "Would your councillors believe that? And what if they believed you too well? It does Károví no good to avoid war with Morenniòu, only to provoke war with another kingdom."

An excellent question, Valara thought, and one that clearly discomfited Miro Karasek, because he glanced away uneasily. "I think . . . we cannot avoid war. But to answer your question, the most I can do is distract them for a time. I erased your signatures before I followed you. And matters are rather confused in the palace."

She took in the unspoken implications. *He cannot deceive them forever. Which means they will someday discover his part.*

Now it was her turn to be discomfited, but she refused to dwell on that. "What about us?" she said. "What do we do next?"

His mouth quirked into a humorless smile, as if he guessed her thoughts. "First we prepare the ground here, in case Markov sends his trackers north. I shall lay down signs for a second camp farther south, and trails leading east to the coast. You have the simplest task. You go home."

She was vividly aware of two things in that moment—the sudden change in Ilse Zhalina's expression and her own sense of balance utterly overturned. They were of the same root and branch, she thought, struggling to keep her face under control. *We have both lost a great deal. She has lost her Lord Kosenmark. I have lost my magic. Is that too great a sacrifice? The gods do not think so.*

The idea of the gods caring struck her as absurd. She smothered a laugh, caught the startled look from both her companions, and shook her head. "I am sorry. But I cannot trust the roads through Autrevelye. I must find another passage home."

It was the most transparent lie she had ever offered to anyone. She held her breath, expecting Karasek to protest, Ilse to point her sword at Valara's throat and demand the truth. But no. To her astonishment, both seemed to accept this outrageous explanation.

They would, neither of them, last a week in Morenniou's Court.

No, that was not fair. Ilse's gaze had turned inward, as if other problems claimed her attention. And Karasek's eyes narrowed in a different kind of calculation.

"I know what to do," he said after a moment. "You will head west and south. Once I've reported back to my colleagues, I can rejoin you. I can—" He paused, and in a somewhat less natural voice said, "If you agree, I can escort you to Taboresk, where my holdings are. Then to a port city, where ships can be hired for longer voyages."

Her heart beat faster. Home. He was offering her a passage home. Another inexplicable gift. "Are you making atonement?"

"As you did?" he asked.

A pointed observation. Yes, they had each done the other harm. He, by leading an invasion against her kingdom. She had betrayed her brother and her homeland—Karasek's homeland—more than once throughout history. If she examined her life dreams honestly, she suspected she would find more instances of her perfidy.

"We are none of us perfect," she murmured.

"Like children whose tongues stumble before they learn to speak," Ilse said softly. "So we, the children of Lir and Toc, stumble and fall, from life to life, until our minds and hearts and souls learn to speak with wisdom."

An old, old quote from a poetess long dead, one even Valara knew from her early days in the schoolroom. *She has spent too many lives evading her true love. And now, for this life, it is too late.*

Karasek could not know about Raul Kosenmark, but he seemed to have caught the essential meaning. "We were children once. We are no longer. Peace, then," he said. "Between all our kingdoms."

As if his words released them, they all stood and set to work. Karasek had brought ample supplies. He and Ilse had gathered more dried peat while Valara slept, and had cooked a meal of dried fish and oats—plain but hot and filling.

They ate with good speed, then worked together to divide Karasek's gear into two heaps. Most went into a pack he designated for them; the rest went back into his remaining saddlebags. Under his direction, they buried their garbage and covered the campfire with loose dirt, stamped the dirt into smoothness, and scattered more dirt and gravel over that. Karasek paced around, inspecting the site. As he did so, he murmured the words in Erythandran to erase all traces of their presence from the past.

"Will that suffice?" Ilse said.

"If my other plans succeed, it won't have to," he answered. To her questioning look, he said, "I'll fabricate a larger camp farther south, and lay down trails from there to the eastern coast to mislead any trackers, before I circle back to Rastov. You two should head southwest toward the mountains. Here is the route you must take."

He outlined the landmarks they should watch for: the village called Kámenmost, with six houses and a sizable goat pen, where they should turn due south; the stream, almost a ditch, that they should follow; and the stone outcropping that marked the wooded ridge where they should make camp. *He makes a good general,* Valara thought, as she took in these precise and ordered details. *Even of such a small army.*

"The country's wild," he said. "You won't meet up with any cities or towns, and very few farms, but I would caution you not to use any magic, and to keep a constant watch."

I have no magic, Valara thought. Again pain lanced through her. It was as though the gods had scooped out her vital organs, leaving nothing but a void. She drew a long breath to calm her nerves. It was not a subject she wished to discuss with either Karasek or Ilse Zhalina. Not today.

She had no need to just yet, because Ilse had taken over the conversation. "When should we look for you?" she said.

Another interval where he calculated plans and counter plans. "Ten days," he said at last. "Whoever arrives first waits for the other—but no longer than

three days. Longer than that, and you must consider
me lost."

Lost. Almost the same words she had used to Ilse
Zhalina the day before. Valara suppressed a shudder,
not needing further explanation. They had left several
other important subjects untouched. No questions
about Markov's spies, nor what Valara and Ilse might
do if the other councillors doubted Karasek's story.

"So we have another parting," she said.

Karasek gave a brief smile. "We've had several."

He mounted and offered Valara a salute. Valara returned the gesture. *A soldier and a leader. What might
have happened if he had come to Morennioù in peace?*

With a pang, she dismissed that thought. She could
not alter the past, only the future.

"Farewell," she said.

"Until ten days," Karasek replied, then wheeled his
horse around and set off toward the coast. Ilse hoisted
their pack over her shoulder, but Valara lingered, still
watching Karasek.

"Will he make it?" Ilse asked.

"He will."

She spoke more in hope than certainty.

Ilse offered no reply. She turned to go, but Valara
continued to watch, one hand shading her eyes, as
Karasek's figure dwindled in size. He had not looked
back since his departure, but in her mind's eye, she
saw him as he had appeared in Autrevelye, one hand
raised in farewell.

CHAPTER TWENTY-FIVE

THE JOURNEY HOME from the Jelyndak Islands took all the latter weeks in spring and well into summer.

They could not sail directly into Tiralien's harbor, of course. The ship was too well known among the port officials, and after Gerek's escape, Markus Khandarr or his agents would keep a vigilant watch in all the coastal cities.

So they returned in twos and threes, each group taking a different route.

That same day, Gervas sailed with the launch's pilot back to the mainland, taking with him the casks with Detlef's and Katje's ashes. Gervas also had a letter for Theo, addressed via Baron Eckard, to bring him home from the Kranjĕ Islands. The rest spent another day removing their belongings to the ship and erasing all signs of the battle and their presence on Hallau. Gerek worked alongside the others, sweating in silence under the glaring sun of late spring. He disliked the empty city. He found the island itself unsettling, with its rocky ground swept clear by magic of grass and trees. When at last he boarded the launch to return to the ship, he stared east and over the ocean, rather than take one last glimpse of that miserable dark place.

They waited only on the next tide before the ship's

crew raised anchor. Then, with evening shadows falling over the horizon, they set sail for the open seas, taking a great arcing path to the south outside the coastal patrols. For weeks their horizon was of water alone, the great rolling swells and the shimmering sky above. Osterling appeared as a cluster of lights to the north. Gerek knew only because one of the ship's crew told him.

Around the point and northwest. Two guards and Alesso Valturri landed in a remote section of coast on the far side of the peninsula. Three more in Pommersien, where they would hire on with a caravan heading northeast. Gerek Hessler thought the ship might continue onward to Valentain, but after a few days to take in water and new provisions, the ship circled around to the east once more.

Someday, Gerek thought, as he leaned over the railing and watched the waves curling away from the ship's sides. *I shall return on my own. I shall leave my office and my books, and walk through these kingdoms I've only read about.*

Lord Kosenmark had not spoken with Gerek since that first night. He locked himself in his cabin and relayed his orders through Ada Geiss, now the senior guard for the expedition. Late at night he walked the decks, but alone and silent. On those few encounters when his path did cross Gerek's, he was unfailingly polite. But his manner was distracted and remote, the air of a man eternally preoccupied with faraway matters.

She was there, Ada had told him. *Nothing of a break between them. It was all lies, I think, what came before. Politics or whatever they call it.* Zhalina had disappeared in the middle of battle, in a magical cloud, according to Ada, and had chased the Morennioùen queen into the nothing. Neither woman had returned, nor the Károvín officer who had pursued them. If Gerek had not arrived with the ship, Kosenmark would be on that island still, waiting for her.

From his single conversation with Kosenmark, Gerek knew better than to believe the last remark, but he listened in attentive silence as Ada spoke about the battle and the days following. How the Károvín had sent their own healer to tend all the wounded. They had worked alongside the Veraenen to bury or immolate the dead.

They were good to us, like comrades, Ada said. *It would be a shame if we had to fight them in war.*

War. It hovered like thunderclouds on the horizon. Perhaps that was the reason for their long, long journey. Kosenmark did not sail without purpose, as some of the guards believed. No, he sent his people to wander, so they might report what the ordinary folks, in cities, towns, and around the countryside, said about Armand of Angersee and his war, and to confirm the rumors of factions and bickering in Duenne's Court. Sitting alone in his cabin, Gerek could foresee two very different courses for Kosenmark and the kingdom.

They are inextricably entwined, after all.

The thought gave him no comfort.

On a dark, moonless night, off the coast between Fuldah and Konstanzien, their ship met a smaller ship—a cutter that had the air of a smuggler. Signals were exchanged by lantern shine. Satisfied, the ship's master sent word to Lord Kosenmark. Soon Kosenmark, Ada, and Gerek had crossed over to the new ship and climbed aboard.

They reached shore two days later, landing on a lonely spit of land where Gervas waited with four sturdy horses and a string of mules bearing packs. With the proper clothes, they transformed themselves into a company of merchants and started on the final segment of their journey home.

It was late in the evening of a mid-summer's day, two months since Gerek Hessler inadvertently left, when the four arrived at the stables behind Lord Kosenmark's grounds. A storm had just passed, the sky overhead was streaked with clouds, and a thick mist hung in the air, burning bright in the dark red glow of sunset.

Gervas and Ada dismounted first. Gerek stifled a groan as he clambered down from his horse. His body ached from scalp to toe. The horse blew a rattling breath, and swung its head around. Gerek rubbed its nose.

"Shall we wait for nightfall, my lord?" Ada asked.

Kosenmark still sat on his horse. He started, as if recalled from a distant dream. "No," he said. "If we have watchers, they already know we've arrived."

Ada and Gervas collected the gear and headed toward the house. Gerek waited, uncertain. Kosenmark had made no move to dismount. Finally the man glanced down. He smiled, the first Gerek had seen since . . .

. . . since almost never.

"Go," Kosenmark said softly. "And thank you, Gerek."

Wordlessly, Gerek handed over his reins to a stable hand. His muscles cried out with every step, but he trudged between the sheds and low buildings, to the wide swath of green outside the gates. Three guards stood at watch. They admitted him without challenge or greeting, for which he was grateful.

He passed through the gates into the wild lower gardens. A hush lay over the grounds, a sweet soft quiet of twilight. It was like the pause between one breath and the next, Gerek thought. Between the invocation of magic and its presence. He paused in the middle gardens and breathed in the ripe scent of roses and lilies, the crushed grass beneath his feet. From the house came a rill of incense floating through the air.

Inside that house waited his duties, regular and dull. (Though not so dull as he had first expected.)

Somewhere, in the kitchen no doubt, Kathe and her mother supervised the preparations for the evening. He had not allowed himself to think of Kathe since landing on Hallau Island.

I must talk with her later. Tomorrow. She will grant me that much, I think.

He followed the lane down the side of the house, slipped past the kitchens, bright and busy with noise, and entered by another door. This wing of the house proved deserted, but from a distance he heard the echo of conversation and music. Nadine's voice rose in a laughing exclamation, answered by Eduard and another man's voice. Gerek paused and smiled painfully, thinking of his own first encounter with Nadine. A stranger would see only the glittering exterior of the house. They would not perceive the secret corridors, the sudden trips and traps, the shadows underneath.

Was he sorry he came here?

No. He had done good work, if not the work he had expected.

He turned into the stairwell and climbed to the floor where he had his rooms. As he rounded the corner from the landing, he saw a figure standing far off. A woman, whose height and form were familiar to him, even in the shadows. She turned, and the light from a lamp fell across her face.

Kathe.

Gerek's heart gave a painful leap. He took three swift steps toward her before doubt stopped him. But Kathe was already running toward him. She took his hands in a fierce grip. Gerek could not trust himself to speak. He could only take in her presence, the warmth

and strength of her hands, the brightness of her eyes
as she stared back at him with a wondering gaze that
called up all manner of hope.

"You're not in the kitchen," he said at last.

A fluid sentence that made no sense, and yet said
everything he wished. Kathe laughed as if she understood him completely. "No, I'm not in the kitchen.
Why should I be?"

There were tears beneath that laughter. He drew
her closer. "Kathe, what's wrong?"

She shook her head. "Nothing. At least—I hope
nothing. I heard you had come. Ada sent word
throughout the house. And so I came to say—If you
would still like an answer to your question. The one
you asked before. And I can't see why you would. But
I have one." She stopped and met his gaze directly, her
cheeks flushed with embarrassment. She drew a long
breath and said, almost steadily, "If you would still
like an answer to your question, my answer is yes."

Yes. She said yes.

All the weariness and doubts tumbled away from
him. He was grinning, and saw that foolish grin mir-
rored in Kathe's face. For a moment, the briefest sorrow overtook his delight—it was not fair that he
should have such joy when Lord Kosenmark had
none—but just as quickly, he forgot Kosenmark and
the rest of the world in the amazement of his own
great happiness.

"Do you still want that answer?" Kathe whispered.

Gerek lifted a hand to her cheek. "Oh, yes. Yes, I do."

TOR

Award-winning authors
Compelling stories